William Shaw

Memoir of the Rev. William Shaw

Late General Superintendent of the Wesleyan Missions in South-Eastern Africa

William Shaw

Memoir of the Rev. William Shaw
Late General Superintendent of the Wesleyan Missions in South-Eastern Africa

ISBN/EAN: 9783744750851

Printed in Europe, USA, Canada, Australia, Japan

Cover: Foto ©Raphael Reischuk / pixelio.de

More available books at **www.hansebooks.com**

MEMOIR

OF THE

REV. WILLIAM SHAW,

LATE GENERAL SUPERINTENDENT OF THE WESLEYAN

MISSIONS IN SOUTH-EASTERN AFRICA.

EDITED BY

HIS OLDEST SURVIVING FRIEND.

WITH PORTRAIT AND VIEWS.

NEW EDITION.

LONDON:

WILLIAM NICHOLS, 46, HOXTON SQUARE.

1875.

PREFACE TO NEW EDITION.

THE present edition is not a mere abridgment or condensation of the former one; but contains exactly the same matter, with the exception of a few pages of documents, and of the Sermons and Charge, &c., which formed the Appendix.

In the Preface to "The Story of my Mission in South Eastern Africa," (1860,) Mr. Shaw justly remarks, "The following narrative is to some extent an Autobiography, containing an account of my personal labours in this great work." As such, it was not only desirable, but absolutely necessary, to embody much of "The Story" in the present volume,—desirable, because no one could tell the history of Mr. Shaw's life better than himself,—necessary, because scarcely any other material was available for the purpose. From the narrative of sundry journeys in South Africa, and from a few memoranda which have escaped destruction, it has been barely possible to compile a consecutive history of the outward life of my old friend. Of his inner life we know little beyond the fact of his conversion, and his subsequent uniform, consistent walk with God. When all other sources of information were wanting, I have here and there furnished a few lines or pages as connecting links; and as this portion of the volume is in a distinct type, no one need confound Mr. Shaw's own narrative with my supplementary remarks.

The Illustrations are from drawings taken on the spot by the Rev. Thornley Smith.   The Portrait is from a photograph, and is undoubtedly the best likeness of Mr. Shaw extant.   All his portraits are like him, as it was impossible for any artist to miss the peculiar kindly, yet dignified, expression of his features.   It is remarkable how little his countenance changed between youth and age. The face which I saw for the last time on the evening of November 25th, 1872, was much the same, and very little changed, from that which cheered me for the first time on the 10th of February, 1830.

W. B. B.

CONTENTS.

ILLUSTRATIONS.

LIFE OF THE
REV. WILLIAM SHAW.

CHAPTER I.

Early Life, 1798-1819—Voyage to Algoa Bay, 1819-1820.

Of the early life and parentage of William Shaw we have few particulars to record. His father, a man of highly respectable character, held an appointment of trust in the North York Militia, which was for some time stationed at Glasgow. Here the subject of this memoir, the eleventh child of the family, was born December 8th, 1798. Mr. and Mrs. Shaw were members of the Established Church, and brought up their large family in the fear of God, giving their children the best education within their reach, from which their youngest son especially profited. Mr. Shaw, senior, retired from the army in 1812, leaving, however, his young son William under the care of his elder brother. From the education and general ability of his younger son he had some reasonable expectation of being able to procure for him in due time a commission in the regular army. This scheme was frustrated by his conversion, and connexion with the Methodist Society, in November, 1812, at Harwich. Persecution, not favour, was now the order of the day. The regiment was removed to Ireland in 1814. At Newry, the Rev. Samuel Alcorn, the Superintendent of the Circuit, aware of the zeal and competence of the young volunteer, urged him to commence preaching. His letter is worth preserving as a specimen of the style of the Minister of that day. It is dated " Newry, 5th December, 1814."

" MY DEAR BROTHER,

" I RECEIVED your highly esteemed favour, and have only to say, that on the very important subject of preaching, I am fully satisfied *you ought to preach*. Show this to the first preacher who comes to Dundalk, and he will no doubt publish for you ; or show it to any of the Leaders, and they will publish for you. Many of your friends here are sorrowing after you and many of your dear brethren. Read much, study, and pray, and live for God. *He has something for you to do.* My love to Brother Pearson and all the brethren and sisters. Farewell.

" I remain, your affectionate brother,

" SAMUEL ALCORN."

In an unfurnished room in the barracks, Mr. Shaw preached his first sermon from Rev. vi. 17. He had for some time past been in the habit of exhorting in the prayer-meetings, the first attempt having been made in Scotland, when he was " constrained by a great love for souls to speak a few words by way of exhortation to the people." On July 10th, 1815, the regiment was disbanded, and William Shaw returned to Wisbeach, where his parents then resided. Having brought recommendatory letters from Ireland, he was immediately placed on the " Local Preachers' Plan." Lay agency, in the shape of Local Preachers and Class Leaders, is essential to the carrying on of the work of Methodism. Every Minister must first have been accepted as a Local

Preacher, in which office he has the opportunity of employing and cultivating his preaching talents. Fastidious hearers, who affect to think lightly of the services of the local ministry, instead of thankfully endeavouring to benefit from these gratuitous and self-denying labours, are ignorantly doing what they can to destroy Methodism. Men of good taste had rather listen to plain, easy, characteristic speech, though occasionally rude, than to the more verbally correct common-places by which the pulpit is occasionally lowered. Much kindness and Christian love were manifested to him by the Methodist people at Wisbeach. As he had been well trained, and was in every respect competent as a teacher, he was recommended by Mr. Bacon, one of the Ministers of the Circuit, to commence a school at Long Sutton. The school opened in January, 1816, and succeeded beyond all expectations, financially and otherwise. In this village Mr. Shaw became the prop and stay of the small Methodist Society.

At this time Mr. Shaw was powerfully impressed with a desire to engage in the Missionary work, and his views were seconded by the Ministers of the Circuit, Messrs. Millman and Bacon. After passing, according to Methodist usage, through the Quarterly and District Meetings, he was proposed as a candidate for the foreign work to the Conference of 1817. The proposal was, on his part, accompanied by a condition, which at that time could not be complied with. Mr. Shaw, having entered into a matrimonial engagement with Miss Ann Maw, stipulated that if sent abroad he should go as a married man, although willing to conform to the rule which very wisely enjoins a single life on all probationers labouring in

England.　The President, the Rev. J. Gaulter, rather summarily decided against the reception of Mr. Shaw into the Mission work on such conditions.　Supposing that his name had been placed on the list of reserve for the home work, Mr. Shaw decided upon waiting until after Christmas of that year.　The appointed time came.　No call to a Circuit reached Long Sutton, and on inquiry being made of the President, he declared that he had no such name as William Shaw on his list.　Our fathers, with many excellencies, were not all of them exact men of business.　Under these circumstances, preparations were made for the marriage, and all the arrangements completed, when at the last minute a letter arrived from a Minister, calling upon him to supply a vacant position, with the sanction of the President and Missionary Secretary.　This letter had been delayed ten days, by a strange blunder of a village postmaster.　Had it arrived sooner, the marriage would have been deferred, and Mr. Shaw would in all probability have remained in the home work.　But it was now too late: the marriage took place on the 30th of December, 1817.

The rule which defers the marriage of Methodist Ministers until the period of probation is passed, has been the subject of much discussion.　It is pleaded that no other Ministers are similarly restricted.　This is true ; but while Curates in the Establishment and Congregational and Presbyterian Ministers are in this respect free to act as they deem proper, it must be kept in mind that the congregations by which they are supported take upon themselves no responsibility in the matter of the support of a wife and family.　The stipend of the Curate, of the Congregational and Presbyterian Minister, is not of necessity increased in consequence of the marriage of the new preacher. Neither do the congregations enter into any engagement as to the support and education of their Ministers' children. Such being the case, they have no claim to interfere with the domestic position of their Minister, and pecuniarily it is a matter of indifference to them whether he marry or remain single. It is a point which with them is very properly left to his own prudence—or imprudence (in some cases). The Methodist economy is otherwise; it provides, after the period of probation is passed, a home or lodging for a married Minister, with a moderate allowance for each child, and also educational allowance for each child for six years; hence it is financially necessary to regulate the period of the marriage of its Minister. Considering the youth of the majority of probationers for the ministry, the delay of a few years is on the whole a great advantage, not only to our young Ministers in the home work, but to those who are stationed in the Mission field. And, so far as the churches are concerned, they are decidedly benefited by the rule which saves their Ministers generally from the temptation to form hastily unsuitable connections.

Mr. Shaw's early marriage would, in the case of most men, have been an imprudent step; but it must be borne in mind that the bridegroom, though young in years, was never, strictly speaking, *a young man*, and the bride was some years his senior. Both of them were prudent, steady Christians, constitutionally cheerful, yet with minds free from all the illusions of romance, looking forward complacently to a life of labour, supported by the sense of duty, and by the consciousness that whether that life was to be spent in the care of a school or in the more important labours of the Christian ministry, they would be working for Christ. It is unnecessary to state that the union was a very happy one. Mrs. Shaw was, in every respect, fully equal to her position as the wife of a man whom, in after years, colonists and colonial governors delighted to honour. Of Mr. Shaw's religious experience we have little to record. Like many men of deep and eminent piety he was very chary of speaking of himself, though on suitable occasions he never hesitated to testify to the power of Divine grace in his own experience. With him Christianity was a life : he walked with God, and he walked wisely towards them that are without : his uniformly happy, yet serious, deportment left upon all associated with him the impression of a noble God-fearing and God-like character. After an intimacy of forty-four years I can unhesitatingly state, that I never heard him speak a hasty, unadvised word, or give expression to any feeling contrary to the royal law of love.

Mr. Shaw did not remain long in the sphere in which he appeared to have tied himself by his marriage, and consequent inability to enter the home ministry. Meanwhile, he continued his acceptable labours as a Local Preacher, and in the course of his journeys to distant localities he had two narrow escapes from serious accidents. His mother had been dead some years, and after Mr. Shaw's marriage the aged father died. Two children were born to the young teacher, and, humanly speaking, he bade fair to be a fixture at Long Sutton. But events were in progress in reference to a distant part of the world which, in a short time, removed him from his quiet home and narrow sphere, and placed him in the position in which he was, above all men, most qualified "to serve his generation by the will of God." To these events we must now turn our attention.

The termination of the Continental wars in the year 1815, which enabled Great Britain to disband her large military and naval armaments, restoring to other countries a portion of the commerce and carrying trade which she had almost exclusively monopolized during the long-protracted contest, threw out of employment a very large portion of her population, and effected throughout the United Kingdom extensive and almost general distress; for, however triumphant and glorious the close, it was dimmed by intense suffering, which continued with unabated force to the beginning of 1819.

At this juncture, too, political questions of grave importance aggravated the difficulties of the Administration. A loud and deep demand, long pent up, arose for Parliamentary Reform, both from the enlightened and from the less informed classes of society, which the Tory Government of the day resisted. Public meetings began to be held throughout the land, especially in the manufacturing districts, where distress more particularly prevailed, and where designing men, taking advantage of the troubled times, inflamed the minds of the ignorant by exaggerated statements of their sufferings, and of the tyrannical disposition of the Government. Seditious papers and insurrectionary speeches led to covert military training; and an unwise yeomanry interference with a Reform meeting held at Manchester, resulting in death and injury to several of the populace, gave such an impetus to the spirit of disaffection and irreligion, that demagogues such as "Orator" Hunt, of "Radical white hat" notoriety, Dr. Watson, and others, with one R. Carlisle, who opened a shop in the leading thoroughfare of the metropolis, whence he vomited forth reprints of republican and blasphemous tendency such as Paine's "Age of Reason," "Rights of Man," "Toldoth Jeschu," and more modern attacks upon Christianity, found ready and willing votaries to their wild schemes of what they called social regeneration. The ministry unfortunately fanned the destructive flame by its violence towards the friends of the people, who deprecated unconstitutional methods of repression; while the passing of the celebrated "Six Acts" appeared to fill up the vial of popular indignation. A revolutionary crisis, and the break up of all the time-honoured institutions of the country, seemed impending, and everything betokened a dissolution of society, which the near approach of a much dreaded reign rendered more than probable.

It was during the height of the hurricane that "on the 12th of July, 1819, being the last day of the session, Mr. Vansittart, Chancellor of the Exchequer, made that far-famed speech which was the leading cause of the embarkation for the Cape of Good Hope of more than four thousand settlers of various descriptions. Lord Sidmouth, in the House of Lords, harangued to the same purpose, and fanned the deluding flame which had been lighted up in the Commons. Mr. Vansittart is reported to have said, ' The Cape is suited to most of the productions both of temperate and warm climates, to the olive, the mulberry, and the vine, as well as to most sorts of culmiferous and leguminous plants; and the persons emigrating to this settlement would soon find themselves comfortable.' The considerate and grave character of two ministers, so at war heretofore with everything like fancy or fable, caused their statements to be received with full credit and confidence, and they were regarded as a warrant of success. It is strange to relate such to have been the infatuation, that those who disagreed on all other subjects agreed on this alone." On the representation of the minister, the "faithful Commons" at once and unreluctantly voted £50,000, to carry the emigration into effect. The promulgation of the governmental scheme was received with avidity by the public, and the applications for permission to avail themselves of the facilities offered were numerous beyond expectation. The number to be accepted was restricted to four thousand souls, and the disappointment of the unsuccessful candidates, amounting to above ninety thousand, was bitter beyond conception. The utmost care was employed in the selection of the emigrants. The regulations issued from Downing Street required certificates as to character from the Ministers of parishes, or some persons in whom the Government could repose confidence; offered passages to those persons who, possessing the means, would engage to carry out at the least ten able-bodied individuals above eighteen years of age, with or without families; that a deposit should be made of £10 for every family of one man, one woman, and two children; others beyond this number to pay £5 each, &c.; so that, notwithstanding an ungenerous sneer of the " Civil Servant " " that it was the wish of the ministry to get rid of the dangerously disaffected," Government had reserved to itself the right, and exerted it successfully, to prevent the emigration of such useless and ill-assorted characters for its new settlement.*

In the Government proposal provision was made for the supply of the religious wants of the settlers. Parties of not less than one hundred families, uniting to form a settlement, were entitled to take a Minister of whatever denomination they might prefer. To this Minister the Government guaranteed a salary of £100 per annum. A number of Wesleyan families, chiefly connected with Queen Street Circuit, London, and others, not Wesleyans, united for this purpose, and wisely resolved to take out a Wesleyan Minister with them. They advertised for a Minister, and of course found out that no respectable, accredited preacher would be willing to go out, unless duly sent and in connexion with the authorities of the Wesleyan body at home. Mr. Shaw, justly viewing this as a providential opening to a field of labour, missionary in its character, corresponded with Mr. Wynne, the then manager of the affairs of the Queen Street party, and expressed his willingness "to accompany them, provided they would consent to receive him in the capacity of a Wesleyan Missionary, appointed by, and in connexion with, the Missionary Committee and Methodist Conference in England."† The Missionary Committee received the proposal at first with some disfavour. Why, it is difficult to say. Missions to English Colonies had been the rule since the first Missionaries were sent out in 1769 to New York, followed in due time by Missionaries to

---

* See "History of the Cape Colony." By the Hon. John C. Chase, M.L.C. 8vo. Cape Town, 1869. A valuable and fair narrative, which it is much to be regretted has not been reprinted in England.

† "Story of my Mission." By William Shaw. 12mo. 1869.

what is now called Eastern British America. To these Missions, and to the West Indian Colonies, Dr. Coke's labours had been mainly confined. After due consideration, however, the Committee adopted the Mission, and accepted Mr. Shaw as their Missionary, influenced in a great measure by the advice of the Rev. George Morley, Superintendent of the Queen Street Circuit, who was interested in many of the emigrants, and especially solicitous for their spiritual welfare.

Mr. Shaw's own narrative will now furnish the most succinct and interesting record of this critical period of his history; a period identified with the beginning of a new colony, which introduced into Southern Africa a spiritual, intellectual, and commercial life, of which we see, partially, the results in our day.

Having returned from London after my examination and appointment, I began to prepare for the departure of myself and family. But a letter from the late Rev. Joseph Taylor, Resident Secretary at the Mission House, Hatton Garden, hurried us away. He stated that it was requisite we should immediately go to London, as the vessel in which we were to sail would be ready in a few days. On Sunday, November 21st, 1819, I preached a parting sermon, to a crowded congregation, in the old Methodist chapel, at Long Sutton, Lincolnshire; and our numerous friends gave us many tokens of their regard and good wishes. It would not interest the general reader to detail particulars of our most affecting parting with our near relatives and friends. Many tears were shed, and many kind words of sincere love and gratitude were interchanged. Our greatest trouble, however, was, that the only condition on which the aged Mrs. Maw would consent to part with her daughter was, that we should leave our first-born child, then an infant, with her and his aunt; so that if we "perished in the sea, or in the deserts of Africa," they might at least have this relic of a lost family remaining, to whom they might show kindness and love for our sake. We were induced, from various considerations, but mainly from deep sympathy for our aged mother's feelings, to comply with her request, although this formed the most painful portion of all our parting experience.*

We finally took leave of my aged father, and other friends, at Wisbeach, on the evening of November 24th; and, after travelling safely all night in the stage-coach, arrived in London next morning, when we proceeded at once to the house of the Rev. George Morley, from whom, and his kind-hearted and excellent wife, we received the most affectionate and considerate attentions during our residence in London.

I had only arrived in time for my Ordination, which had been fixed to be held that very evening, November 25th, 1819, in St. George's Chapel in the East, together with that of the Rev. Titus Close, a Missionary, just about to proceed to Madras. This Ordination Service had an unusual interest attached to it, as a considerable number of the intended settlers, with their friends, from various parts of London, attended to witness my dedication to the office of the Ministry for their future benefit. The Ministers engaged in the service were, the Rev. Messrs. Charles Atmore, Samuel Taylor, George Morley, Joseph Taylor, and Richard Watson. The Rev. G. Morley addressed the people, specially referring to those about to emigrate; and the Rev. R. Watson delivered the charge to the two young Ministers. It was a solemn service. I had never witnessed a Wesleyan Ordination, and scarcely knew what was expected from me on the occasion. When called upon, however, I spake in

---

* This child is now the Rev. William Maw Shaw, M.A., Vicar of Yealand-Conyers; who has recently published a sermon on "New Testament Absolution," which is worthy of the name he bears.

the simplicity of my heart, reciting an outline of the circumstances connected with my early conversion to God, and the reasons which induced me to believe that I was moved by the Holy Ghost "to take upon me the office, duties, and responsibilities of a Christian Missionary."

The Government functionaries who had the management of the embarcation of the settlers, made an unexpected alteration in the arrangements, and the party to which I was attached was not to sail in the vessel originally designed. This occasioned some delay, and meantime a severe frost set in, by which the Thames was frozen over, and we were consequently detained in London till February, 1820. Although this was very trying to many of the people, and a serious injury to all those whose finances were limited; yet to me it afforded considerable advantage, inasmuch as it gave me an opportunity of becoming personally acquainted with some of the leading Methodist Ministers at that time in London, and of hearing sermons preached by the Rev. Joseph Benson, Dr. Adam Clarke, the Rev. Jabez Bunting, the Rev. R. Watson, and others. At that period, alas! there was no Theological Institution, in which Candidates for our Ministry and Missionary work could secure a preparatory training; and, consequently, I did not enjoy the inestimable benefit which, by the wiser arrangement of subsequent date, has been conferred on the gifted rising race of our Ministers. It was, however, some compensation for this disadvantage, that for a season I had opportunities of studying some of the best pulpit models among the Wesleyan body of that period, and of receiving many private advices, as to my reading and general deportment, from men who were not only competent to afford me this assistance, but generously took the trouble to do so.

The last time I was privileged to hear the Rev. Joseph Benson preach, was on a Sunday in the month of January, 1820. He had taken an appointment for the forenoon and evening of that day at the Lambeth Chapel: being, however, in very advanced age and rapidly declining health, he had requested the Rev. Joseph Taylor, the Resident Secretary at the Mission House, to send one of the young preachers connected with the Mission department to assist him, should he find it requisite to avail himself of such help. I was fixed upon for this duty, and under Mr. Taylor's directions proceeded to the Lambeth Chapel, where I arrived some time before the service was to begin, in order to be at Mr. Benson's disposal. After this venerable man of God entered the vestry, he said to me, "Are you the young man sent from the Mission House to help me?" "Yes, Sir; but I trust you feel yourself able to preach. I would much rather sit and hear you, than stand before the congregation of this chapel to preach for you." He smiled, and said, "Well, I mean to preach this morning; and before I leave the pulpit I shall decide whether it will be necessary for you to preach for me in the evening or not." Very much relieved in my mind as to the forenoon service, I entered the chapel, and, after the usual devotional services, Mr. Benson announced for his text Romans xv. 4. After a clear exposition of the passage, such as might have been expected from this able commentator on the Holy Scriptures, he gradually warmed with his theme, and dwelt on the authority, fulness, and sufficiency of the Word of God, together with its hope-inspiring and soul-comforting truths, in such a manner as to rivet the attention of a large congregation for nearly an hour. I can never forget the earnestness and energy of his manner: his words flowed fluently, and yet it seemed to me that he felt language to be inadequate to utter all his great conceptions, and to express all his intense anxiety that every hearer might receive the benefit. In fact, this noble pulpit effort quite exhausted his feeble frame, and he announced that he would not be able to preach in the evening; but with a view of lessening in some degree the disappointment to the congregation, and at the same time most kindly striving to secure for me an attendance at the evening service, he informed them that "Mr. Shaw, who was going out as Missionary to the English settlers about to embark for South Africa, would occupy the pulpit in his place." In his concluding prayer he offered most fervent supplications for me and the settlers, that God would have us in His holy keeping, and bless us, and make us a blessing. The responses of some in the congregation, with other unmistakeable symptoms, showed that the sympathies of the people were drawn forth by the petitions of the Minister. To me it was a season of deep solemnity. I called it to remembrance to my great comfort on many occasions afterwards, especially in times of unusual difficulty. I ever regarded it as a great privilege to have had the blended prayers of such a man and such a congregation specially offered to God on my behalf, and on behalf of the great work to which I had been already "set apart by the laying on of the hands of the Presbytery." Surely the "effectual fervent prayer of a righteous man availeth much."

To the eminently wise and godly counsels of the Rev. George Morley and Rev. J. Bunting, (afterwards the venerable Dr. Bunting,) I am especially indebted. The remembrance of their advices in subsequent years often enabled me to steer a steady course, when I should otherwise, in all probability, have missed my way without a pilot, in an unknown ocean, abounding with dangers seen and unseen. No doubt, on the review, my first grateful homage and gratitude are due to Him "whose I am, and whom I serve," and "from whom all holy desires, all good counsels, and just works, do proceed;" yet I cannot overlook, in this recital, my deep obligations to those who were the instruments in His hand of rendering me (and may I not say the Mission through me?) such invaluable service.

Among the pleasing reminiscences of my sojourn in London is my introduction to the late Joseph Butterworth, Esq., M.P.

He was at that time one of the General Treasurers of the Wesleyan Missionary Society; and, being in the habit of attending the Great Queen Street Chapel, he knew several of the settlers who were going out with me, and was much interested in their welfare. Besides showing me much personal kindness, he also gave me some most valuable advices, which I found of great service when in subsequent years I was obliged by circumstances to enter into frequent correspondence with Government officials. At a Missionary Meeting held in Great Queen Street Chapel on the 27th of January, 1820, Mr. Butterworth occupied the chair, and on that occasion he introduced me to Lieutenant Vicars, father of the late Captain Hedley Vicars, whose most interesting and edifying Memoir has recently been so extensively read. This gentleman was at that time on a visit to Mr. Butterworth, in London. He had been aroused to earnestness and decision in religion under the ministry of one of our Missionaries in Newfoundland; and I well remember the effect produced by his simple but truly Christian address in favour of Methodist Missions.

Most of the settlers with whom I was connected embarked early in January, at Deptford, on board the ships "Aurora and "Brilliant," which were to convey the party to Algoa Bay: and I made frequent visits to preach to them on board. It was gratifying to see the kind pastoral feeling which was displayed towards them by some of the London Ministers. The Rev. George Morley, Rev. Joseph Sutcliffe, and other Wesleyan Ministers, visited them and preached to them, offering them both advice and consolation suited to their circumstances; and as several of the Baptist families belonged to the Eagle Street Chapel, the late Rev. W. Ivimey, the well-known Minister of that place of worship, also took an affectionate leave of them, preaching a most appropriate discourse on the occasion. The text selected by the Rev. Joseph Sutcliffe, when he preached on the deck of the "Aurora," with a numerous company of the settlers before him, was, "Now the Lord had said unto Abram, Get thee out of thy country, and from thy kindred, and from thy father's house, unto a land that I will show thee: and I will make of thee a great nation, and I will bless thee, and make thy name great; and thou shalt be a blessing." (Gen. xii. 1, 2.) The short discourse, delivered in his inimitably quiet and placid manner, by this saintly Minister, produced a deep impression. Much of this was no doubt due to the strikingly appropriate text, and the easy style in which it was made to furnish lessons suited to the circumstances of the people; but he was a Minister greatly beloved, and there was ever much unction in his discourses. Even then he was venerable in appearance, although he did not enter into the heavenly rest till thirty-seven years afterwards, having died on the 14th of May, 1856, at the patriarchal age of ninety-four years.

Early in February, my wife and I embarked with our infant child, and took possession of the small berth that was allotted to us. In those days the best modes of fitting up emigrant ships had not been devised; and although much attention had been given by the Government officials at Deptford to make all things as convenient as possible, yet we were, perhaps unavoidably, much crowded. The Missionary Committee would have made a private arrangement with the master of the vessel, to provide for us on the passage; but we declined this, on the principle that, as we were going with the settlers, we would prefer, during the voyage, to fare just as they would have to do. Although his resolution cost us some severe privations while on the voyage,—seeing that settlers in emigrant ships were not at that period so well provided for as in these days,—yet we never regretted that we had adopted it, as it showed the people that we meant to identify ourselves with them; and by this means also the whole passage-money, which the Society would otherwise have had to pay, was saved. Having embarked, and endeavoured to make our berth as comfortable as possible, we then awaited the day when the anchor was to be heaved, and we should proceed to our far distant destination.

On Sunday forenoon, the 6th of February, 1820, I had read prayers and preached on the deck of the "Aurora." The settlers who were going out in this vessel and the "Brilliant"—which was lying alongside of her at Deptford—had all been some time embarked. There was therefore a full and rather large attendance at public worship. As soon as service was concluded, the pilot announced that, all being now ready, and wind and tide favourable, we should set sail immediately after dinner. Accordingly, about two o'clock, the anchor was weighed, and the "Aurora" moved off, and we soon began to float down the river. The day was clear and fine; and I well remember the people stood around me on deck, while I gave out Dr. Watts's cheerful and encouraging hymn from the seventeenth page of the Wesleyan Hymn Book. As we were passing the Royal Hospital of Greenwich, although tears were streaming down many cheeks at the time, they were singing in full chorus,—while many of the veteran tars of old England were looking at us with evident surprise and interest,—

> " The God that rules on high,
>   That all the earth surveys,
>   That rides upon the stormy sky,
>   And calms the roaring seas;
>   This awful God is ours,
>   Our Father and our Love;
>   He will send down His heavenly powers,
>   To carry us above."

It would be difficult to describe the various and conflicting emotions which were passing through the minds of the large group of men, women, and children, that crowded the deck of the "Aurora" at this time.   Many wept to think that they were leaving dear old England and the much-loved friends from whom they had just parted, without any prospect of returning to their native country.   They were going to a land of which none of them had any knowledge whatever; but all rejoiced in a cheerful hope that at length, after many wearisome delays, they were on their way to a region in which, under the blessing of Divine Providence, they would be enable to found new and happy homes for themselves and their children.

We came to an anchor in the evening, a little below Gravesend, where we were detained more than a week, waiting a favourable change in the wind; during which I went ashore, and had an opportunity of preaching in our chapel.   We heaved anchor again on the 15th of February; and, after passing down the Channel, finally lost sight of our native shores.

The occurrences on board of ship during a passage of ten weeks from the Downs to the Cape, need not be recited in detail. We had a remarkably fine passage.   The weather was generally most agreeable, with occasional variations of squalls and stiff breezes, producing the usual discomforts of a rolling vessel, which, in the case of a crowded emigrant ship, invariably occasions adventures both ludicrous and dangerous.   Several children were born, and some died, on the passage.   But of the adults only one was numbered among the dead,—a fine young married woman, who had embarked in bad health.   She was a truly pious and devoted person, and had been connected with the Society at the Hinde Street Chapel, London.   While I read the funeral service, and her remains were lowered in the usual manner over the gangway into the ocean, all felt that it was in "sure and certain hope of resurrection to eternal life," at that period when "the greedy sea shall its dead restore."

At the commencement, I established regular worship as follows:—on the Lord's day forenoon, we assembled on the deck

of the vessel; the capstan was rigged out with flags, and constituted the pulpit, from whence I read the Liturgy, and preached;
the people joining in singing the hymns in an edifying manner.
In the evening I usually preached between decks. We had also
domestic worship regularly, on the morning and evening of each
day, reading the Scriptures, singing a hymn, and prayer, both
in the cabin and also between decks, where the greater part
of the settlers were accommodated. I attended each place
alternately; and, in my absence from either, proper persons
were appointed to conduct the worship. It was very rarely
indeed these arrangements were interfered with; and they
proved a great source of comfort to the people, and I have no
doubt were the chief means of preserving the general good
feeling and harmony which prevailed, with very slight exceptions, to the end of the passage. No fatal accidents occurred:
but on two occasions a sailor fell overboard. In the first
instance, the man happened to have a rope in his hand, to which
he clung with amazing tenacity till relieved from his perilous
situation, affording me a good illustration for a text, on which
I subsequently preached: " Seeing then that we have a High
Priest that is passed into the heavens, Jesus the Son of God,
let us *hold fast* our *profession*." If Christians would always
"hold fast" their principles with as firm a grasp in every time
of spiritual danger, as the poor sailor held on by the rope for
his life, they might constantly sing,

"As far from danger as from fear,
While Love, Almighty Love, is near."

In the course of our passage we called at Madeira, but only
remained a few hours there. We also saw the Peak of Teneriffe;
and on the south of the Line, on the opposite side of the
Atlantic, we passed near the Martin Vaz Rocks. We sighted
the Cape of Good Hope on Monday, the first of May, and during
the whole of that day were employed in approaching and beating

into False Bay: during the night we anchored in Simon's Bay. I did not fail to remember that on this day the Wesleyan Missionary Meeting was being held in London, and hoped that the prayers of thousands then ascending on behalf of Missionaries would be answered on us just entering our field of labour,—as also on all others,—in " showers of blessings." I landed on the jetty at Simon's Town, on Tuesday morning, the second of May, and on the next day proceeded to Cape Town.

On my arrival at the Cape, I met the Rev. E. Edwards, who had just commenced preaching in this place, having, with the aid of some pious soldiers and others, fitted up a wine store as a temporary place of worship. I had the pleasure of commencing my public ministry in South Africa by preaching in this building on Thursday evening, the fourth of May, to a small congregation of civilians and soldiers, on Acts xi. 23 : " Who, when he came, and had seen the grace of God, was glad, and exhorted them all, that with purpose of heart they would cleave unto the Lord."

While in Cape Town,—the acting Governor, Sir Rufane Shawe Donkin, being away on the frontier,—I called on the Colonial Secretary, and requested information as to the channel through which I was to derive the promised means of support from the Government, after my arrival in the new settlement. But the Secretary—who I afterwards learned was a Roman Catholic gentleman, and held this high office before the Relief Bill was passed—either knew nothing, or affected to know nothing, of my claim on the Government. He said, " All that can have been promised to you is *toleration.* You will be *permitted* to exercise your ministeral functions;" and that he represented as rather a concession to the peculiar circumstances under which the British settlers had come to the country. This induced me to show Colonel B. a letter written by Mr. Goulburn, at that time Under Secretary of State for the Colonies, in which the obligation of the Cape Government to "provide for" my "decent maintenance" was distinctly stated. The Secretary's tone towards me was now suddenly changed; and at length he pleasantly bowed me out, saying that, on my arrival at my destination, I could address the Government on the subject.

When the Cape Colony capitulated to the British troops in the year 1806, it was stipulated that the Dutch Reformed Church should retain its pre-eminence and peculiar privileges; and as, by long standing regulations, no Ministers were permitted to exercise their functions in the Colony, among the white or so called Christian inhabitants, excepting those who were duly authorized by the authorities of the Dutch Church,—the English Governors of the Colony, with a strong desire to conciliate the Dutch inhabitants, interpreted the terms of capitulation so rigidly as to refuse permission to other Ministers to exercise their functions,—excepting as Missionaries among the black and coloured races. The Lutherans had, indeed, by special permission long before, established their form of worship in Cape Town; but this was probably only because many officers and soldiers of the army which had formerly served under the Dutch Government were Germans, and several influential resident families were also members of the Lutheran Church. The military and naval Chaplains of the English Church, with the Chaplain for the Governor and other English gentlemen of the civil service, could not be decently objected to; and as part of the British army consisted of some Scottish regiments, a Missionary of the London Missionary Society was tolerated in the capacity of the Scotch Presbyterian Minister.

When, however, the Rev. J. M'Kenny was appointed by the Methodist Conference to Cape Town in the year 1813, he was not permitted to discharge his ministerial duties, although he had been sent out at the earnest solicitation of a large number of the soldiers connected with the British army then serving at the Cape. It was intended by the Missionary Committee that while he should preach to the soldiers, and such of the white inhabitants, English or Dutch, as might be willing to attend his ministry, he was also especially to turn his attention to the large slave population, who at that time greatly needed religious instruction, and were being rapidly proselyted by the resident native Mohammedan priests. But it seems that the civil and ecclesiastical authorities thought that the slaves had better become believers in the false Prophet, than that the prejudices of some of the adherents of the dominant Dutch Church should be shocked! Mr. M'Kenny, finding that he was not likely to obtain permission to preach, requested to be removed to Ceylon. This request was complied with ; but the Methodist soldiers at the Cape reiterated their request for the services of a Pastor, and the Wesleyan Missionary Committee, not at any time easily intimidated by opposition, appointed the Rev. Barnabas Shaw his successor.

On his arrival the same objection to grant him leave to preach was urged by the Governor ; but Mr. Shaw nevertheless very properly commenced religious services in a private house, which were attended by some of the soldiers; and when, under the promptings of a sense of duty, he afterwards proceeded on a Mission among the Namaquas in the interior, Mr. Edwards, who had been sent from England to aid him in the Mission, was subsequently induced, under Mr. Shaw's direction, in 1820, to take the step of fitting up a temporary place of worship, having previously ascertained, through some private friends, that, while he must expect no formal permission by authority, yet his doing so would be winked at, as the preaching in a private room had already been for some time past.

The coming of the British settlers, however, caused a great

change. It is due to the Tory Government of Lord Liverpool to say, that without proclaiming any order in council, or in any other formal manner announcing that the freedom of religious worship was to be, henceforth, the right of all the inhabitants of the Colony, the liberal arrangement of Earl Bathurst, then Secretary of State for the Colonies, whereby aid was offered towards the support of a Minister for each party of one hundred settlers, without respect of religious denomination, showed that, *practically*, the question of religious toleration in the Colony of the Cape was settled. As I had long before received and put faith in the dictum of an eminent English lawyer, that " the Toleration Act travels with the British flag," I resolved to regard the matter in this point of view; and hence I never applied for any licence or permission from any functionary whatever, but at once proceeded to discharge all public duties wherever I met with any class of people willing to receive me in the capacity of a Minister. I preached, and celebrated the services for marriages, baptisms, and funerals, never allowing it to be supposed that I considered any man in a British Colony had any right to interfere with my religious liberty as a free-born Englishman.

On one occasion a gentleman high in office asked me by what "authority" I did these things; and I simply showed him my certificate of ordination, and of the usual oaths required by the Act of Toleration, which I had taken before the Lord Mayor of London. At another time the acting Colonial Secretary intimated that the Government conceived I should confine my labours to the locality where the settlers resided for whom I was the recognised Minister; but as I had no mind that the Government should assume the authority to direct my ministerial conduct, I quietly proceeded in my own way, without taking the slightest notice of this intimation; and I heard no more about it.

On the 5th of May, Mr. Edwards, from whom I had received the most affectionate attentions, rode with me on horseback from Cape Town to Simon's Town, and going on board preached to the people in the evening. On Sunday, the 7th, after conducting Divine worship on deck as usual, and trying to instruct and encourage the people by preaching on the words, " A good hope," I went ashore, and preached in a private dwelling-house, where a few soldiers were in the habit of assembling for prayer. A small congregation of about thirty persons were present, and appeared to enjoy the opportunity. A message was subsequently sent to me on board the " Aurora," by the resident Clergyman, stating that I had no right to hold religious services in Simon's Town ; and if I presumed to do so again, it was hinted that certain disagreeable consequences to myself would inevitably follow. Had we been detained longer in the Bay, there is little doubt but that I should have braved this petty threat, and again preached to the poor people, who were anxious to hear the Gospel. On the 10th, however, we weighed anchor once more, and proceeded in company with the " Brilliant," which had the remainder of our party on board, besides some Scottish families under Mr. Pringle. This amiable and Christian gentleman afterwards became Secretary of the Anti-Slavery Society in England, and is well known as a lyrical poet of first-rate gifts, whose poetical compositions have served to render familiar to English readers many of the localities and frequently recurring scenes of Southern Africa.

The Coast was not at that time very well known to our skippers ; but the various vessels, under the protection of Divine Providence, all arrived safely, and we anchored in Algoa Bay on Monday, the 15th of May, being exactly three months from the day on which we left Gravesend. It was night when we reached the anchorage ; and our first engagement, after the noise and confusion consequent on casting anchor, and making

the ship snug and trim, was to assemble between the decks,
and hold a meeting to offer solemn thanksgiving to Almighty
God for all the mercies of our passage out, and to implore His
blessing on our entrance into the country now before us.

Next morning, as soon as the day dawned, most of the people
came on deck to view the land of their future residence. As
the sun rose over the wide expanse of ocean towards the east,
and gilded with his light the hills and shores of the Bay towards
the west and north, a gloom gradually spread itself over the
countenances of the people. As far as the eye could sweep,
from the south-west to the north-east, the margin of the sea
appeared to be one continued range of low white sand hills :
wherever any breach in these hills afforded a peep into the
country immediately behind this fringe of sand, the ground
seemed sterile, and the bushes stunted. Immediately above
the landing-place, the land rose abruptly into hills of considerable elevation, which had a craggy and stony appearance, and
were relieved by very little verdure. Two or three whitewashed
and thatched cottages, and Fort Frederick, a small fortification
crowning the height, and by its few cannon commanding the
anchorage, were all that arrested the eye in the first view of
Algoa Bay; with the exception of the tents of the British
settlers, many of whom had already disembarked, and formed
a camp half a mile to the right of the landing-place. The
scene was at once dull and disappointing. It produced a very
discouraging effect on the minds of the people, not a few of
whom began to contrast this waste wilderness with the beautiful
shores of Old England, and to express fears that they had
foolishly allowed themselves to be lured away by false representations, to a country which seemed to offer no promise of
reward to its cultivators. However, the needful preparations
for landing, and the anxiety to be relieved from the discomforts
and monotony of their long confinement on board of ship,

changed the current of their thoughts, and thereby afforded some relief to their gloomy forebodings.

The landing was not unaccompanied by difficulty or danger : but the Government had considerately sent round from the Cape one of His Majesty's frigates, and its commander took charge of the debarcation of the settlers. A very heavy surf generally breaks on the shore of this bay; hence boats of the ordinary description can rarely land their passengers, but flat-bottomed boats, of a peculiar construction, and worked by warps, receive the passengers on the outside of the surf, who are thus conveyed safely *over*, or as sometimes happens *through*, the successive surf rollers. When the boat is warped as far as the depth of the water will allow, the passengers, watching the opportunity of a receding wave, jump out, or are carried out on the shoulders of men, to the sandy beach beyond the reach of the sea. I believe this is a different method to that pursued in a similar case at Madras ; but it is, probably, less dangerous. At all events, under the blessing of Divine Providence, such was the care of the English sailors and Scottish soldiers who aided in the working of the boats, that no serious accident occurred, in the landing of the whole body of the settlers, with their wives and children, and large amount of goods of various. descriptions. It is surprising that, although there has been a good deal of improvement in the construction of these surf boats, and the manner of working them, yet the above continued to be the mode in which passengers and goods were usually landed, up to the time of my departure from the country in 1856.

As several vessels had arrived before us, we had to await our turn ; and, consequently, the whole party were not landed till some days had elapsed. In the interval I went on shore ; and after rambling with others some hours in a most unsatisfactory inspection of the neighbourhood, I was unable to get on board again in the evening, and was obliged to take up my quarters in a miserable place used as a canteen or liquor shop. Fearing to lie down on the earthen floor, I crept into the space between two large barrels, the broader parts of which were in juxta-position, and thus afforded me a rude sort of couch, on which I essayed to take my first night's rest in this part of Africa,—obtaining as much sleep as my uncomfortable bedstead, and the noisy carousals of a drinking party at the other end of the wretched building, would allow.

By the 25th of May, the whole of our party were safely landed, and encamped with the other settlers, awaiting the arrival of waggons, which were to convey them to the district of Albany, where the settlements were to be established, at a distance from Algoa Bay of from eighty to one hundred and twenty miles. While here, having obtained a Hottentot guide, I went on a visit to Bethelsdorp, and received a most kind and Christianlike welcome from the Rev. George Barker. This Station was founded by the Rev. Dr. Vanderkemp, one of the first Missionaries of the London Missionary Society in Southern Africa.

On Sunday, the 28th of May, I preached my first sermon in what is now called the Eastern Province of the colony. I took my stand close to some pyramidical stones which in a singular manner rose above the surface of the ground to a considerable height, and stood close to the road within a short distance of the settlers' camp. It is remarkable that the Wesleyan Chapel now stands in the main street of Port Elizabeth, very near the spot, which is well remembered, although the stones have long since been removed. With reference to God's goodness to us thus far, I preached from "Ebenezer," the Stone of Help: "Hitherto hath the Lord helped us." (1 Sam. vii. 12.) In the afternoon I preached again on the same spot, endeavouring to improve the melancholy event of the death of one of the settlers who came out in the "Brilliant." He had been a Local Preacher in London, and died after his arrival in port; and I was thus called upon immediately to perform the sad office of reading the funeral service over one of my charge. He was interred in the burial-ground, which had already been selected for the interment of certain sailors, soldiers, and others, who had been drowned, or had died at this place. It has become the principal burial-ground of the town. A considerable number of the settlers attended these services. I preached twice during the week; and on the following Sunday a part of the commissariat store was prepared for Divine service, and I conducted Divine worship therein. There was a considerable congregation of settlers and soldiers. Many of the latter told me they had not heard a sermon for three or four years previously to my arrival in the Bay. During this Lord's day I also celebrated the sacrament of the Lord's Supper, and was joined therein by a goodly company of serious communicants.

When the Government issued proposals in England for this emigration, one of the regulations was, that each head of a family, or other settler, who was to be entitled to one hundred acres of land, should deposit ten pounds, to be repaid through the head of the party after arrival in the Colony. Some of the parties consisted of individuals whose head .or leader advanced the whole deposit-money for himself and ten or fifteen other settlers, who were articled under various kinds of agreement to the head of the party, to reside with and to assist him, —he being entitled to the whole of the land allotted for each of the settlers who accompanied him. But the greater number, including the whole of the party with which I was connected, paid their own deposit-money, and each man had a claim for land in his own right; while the head of the party (Mr. Sephton) was simply elected by themselves as their representative, for convenient transaction of business with the

Government functionaries, in all affairs involving the public interests of the whole.

The Home Government had sent out to Algoa Bay a good supply of agricultural implements, and other useful utensils, which the settlers were allowed to purchase, if they thought fit, on account of a portion of their deposit-money. And as it was impossible that they could provide themselves with the means of transit to the district of Albany, the colonial authorities, with great consideration, caused the Dutch farmers from various parts of the Colony to come with their waggons and convey them thither, in the same manner, and for the same rates of remuneration, as had been usual in the transport of troops. The Commissariat was also employed to provide rations for the settlers on a fixed scale, until it would be practicable for them to raise crops. Towards payment of the expenses incurred hereby, one-third of the deposit-money was ultimately detained by the Government, who had from necessity disbursed a much larger amount than that proportion of the money originally deposited would refund. Mistakes and blunders were, of course, committed by the authorities; but no candid persons among the settlers will, on the review, hesitate to speak with gratitude of the kind and considerate arrangements made by the Government on their behalf.

Having awaited our turn, at length, on Monday, the 5th of June, I loaded the two wagons assigned me; and, in company with many other settlers, we started on our journey up the country. The cavalcade, as it wound along the so-called road, and ascended the heights which intersected tho path at various parts of our course, had a very picturesque appearance. The African wagons, covered with white sail-cloth tilts, each drawn by twelve or fourteen oxen, urged on by stalwart Dutch Colonists in rather primitive attire, or by tawny Hottentots with hardly any attire at all,—the noise occasioned by the incessant cracking of their huge whips, and the unintelligible jargon of the leaders and drivers, when urging the oxen, or while talking with each other,—all combined to produce in our unsophisticated English minds wonder and amusement. In some parts, however, the roads were rough and rocky; and from our inexperience in the African mode of packing a wagon, so as to make it comfortable, we were dreadfully jolted, and in general the men preferred walking; but the women and children suffered a good deal from knocks and contusions on head and shoulders, and other parts of the body.

In some places it was highly dangerous to remain in the wagon, as the road was often uneven and precipitous, and the wagons were not unfrequently overturned. On one occasion I was sitting in the wagon with my wife and child, as we approached the bank of the Bushman's River, at which there was at that time a deep and almost precipitous descent towards the drift or ford. Being seated in the back part of the wagon, which was rather an English than a colonial arrangement, we could not see anything in front. The Dutch driver, finding we did not descend, came behind the wagon, and tried to make us understand that it was desirable to do so. He had learned a few words of English from the British soldiers, and, putting his hands to each side of his face, and giving a very expressive twist of his head, he exclaimed, "*Break neck.*" This was sufficiently explicit to cause our immediate descent from the wagon, which forthwith went off with such a noise and run, as made us tremble for our goods, and thankful that we were no longer in the vehicle ourselves.

We were first taken to Reed Fontein, near the western banks of the Kowie River, where it was understood the party was to be located; but after a short time it was ascertained that we had been placed on lands designed for another body of settlers! This was felt to be very vexatious, but there was no remedy;

and wagons were sent to remove us to another location,
some twenty-five miles distant, and which we had already
passed on our journey up the country. We arrived at our
final destination on the 18th of July, 1820. Here we were
immediately joined by the bulk of our party from Algoa Bay.
It is not easy to describe our feelings at the moment when we
arrived. Our Dutch wagon-driver intimating that we had at
length reached our proper location, we took our boxes out of
the wagon, and placed them on the ground; he bade us
goeden dag, or farewell, cracked his long whip, and drove away,
leaving us to our reflections. My wife sat down on one box,
and I on another. The beautiful blue sky was above us, and
the green grass beneath our feet. We looked at each other for
a few moments, indulged in some reflections, and, perhaps,
exchanged a few sentences; but it was no time for sentiment,
and hence we were soon engaged in pitching our tent; and
when that was accomplished, we removed into it our trunks,
bedding, &c. All the other settlers who had arrived with us
were similarly occupied, and, in a comparatively short time, the
somewhat extensive valley of that part of the Assagaay Bosch
River, which was to be the site of our future village, presented
a lively and picturesque appearance.

Mr. Shaw's admirable narrative has conducted us to the
final settlement of the QUEEN STREET party, afterwards
generally known as the SALEM party. He will soon tell
us of their trials and difficulties, and how bravely they
were borne and overcome.

To young people, or to those in the prime of life, blessed
with vigorous bodies and sanguine dispositions, and unen-
cumbered by family cares, I can imagine nothing more
delightful than to engage in the noble enterprise of founding

a new colony, especially in such climates as South Africa, Australia, and New Zealand. The undertaking makes and educates the men and women engaged in it. The first settlers in Albany (the Eastern Province) were, to begin with, a fair specimen of the average worth of the middle and lower classes of English society. Those of them who lived to see the completion of their great undertaking felt themselves, and were acknowledged by others, to be a class altogether different from men whose faculties had not been tried and drawn out by similar experiences. A more thoroughly practical, sensible, manly, and in all respects respectable population than that which formed the nucleus of the British colony in South Eastern Africa I never heard or read of, though no doubt the Puritan settlers in New England, more than two hundred years ago, and the population of New Plymouth, (Taranaki,) New Zealand, in 1853, may have been somewhat equal to them.

It may not be amiss, before we begin with the history of the settlement, to give another picture of the landing and location of a distinct body of settlers, as related by the Hon. J. C. Chase, M.L.C., in his excellent History of the Colony of the Cape, 1869.

" The first two vessels with the adventurers (the 'Chapman' and 'Nautilus,' transports) left Gravesend on the 3rd of December, 1819, lost sight of the white cliffs of Albion on the 9th, arrived in Table Bay on the 17th of March following, on the 9th of April anchored in Algoa Bay, and safely debarked on the following morning at its little fishing village, with anxious, beating hearts, made still more uneasy by the forbidding and wild aspect of the shore. This, however, was quickly relieved by the hearty welcome of the few officers of the little garrison and others, whose kindness and solicitude were beyond all praise. Alas! as this is penned, hardly one of these now survives to receive the acknowledgments of gratitude, and but few of the pioneers by these vessels live to make these acknowledgments.

"Upon landing the settlers were disappointed to find their locations distant full one hundred miles from the port, although one party had solicited to be set down near the mouth of the Great Fish River, where some of the most sanguine had already planted in imagination 'sufferance wharves,' and dreamt of innumerable vessels to be anchored in that estuary. Wagons were, however, provided by Government in sufficient number, at the cost of the immigrants,—a debt which was afterwards most considerately remitted, as was the charge also of rations issued for several months; in fact, the British Government of that day behaved with the greatest liberality to the young plantation. On the 18th of April, the first, or 'Chapman party,' commenced their inland progress, in ninety-six wagons, from Algoa Bay, afterwards named Port Elizabeth, which at that time numbered thirty-five souls, (including its small garrison,) inhabiting two houses, stone-built, and a few huts. A more desolate and unpromising place indeed can hardly be conceived.

"The journey was propitious; splendid rains had fallen a few months before, the rivers were running, the ponds (vleys) overflowing, the pasturage luxuriantly rich, astonishing the travellers, who had pictured Africa as arid, waterless, and sterile. Game, too, was abundant,— the hartebeest, springbok, quagga, ostrich,—but the country

devoid of inhabitants and cattle; while the blackened
gables of the farmhouses recently burnt by the Kaffir
savages furnished proof how terrible the invasion of 1819
had been. On the 26th the party, with great ease, crossed
in their wagons the Kowie River mouth, where now vessels
of more than three hundred tons lie at anchor; and on the
evening of the 28th arrived at a deserted farm, called 'Korn
Place,' (a promising, but delusive, augury,) under the mud
walls of a house not long consumed by the enemy. Here the
immigrants decided to sit down permanently, and call the
embryo village 'Cuylerville,' in compliment to Colonel
Cuyler, whose attentions and kindly manners during the
time he accompanied them on their long and fatiguing
journey were unremitting. On the following day a few of
the party, with some military officers and Colonel Cuyler,
proceeded to inspect the mouth of the Great Fish River,
which raised high expectations of its future navigability;
and on the 3rd of May Colonel Cuyler took his leave, with
this ominous caution, 'Gentlemen, when you go out to
plough, never leave your guns at home.'"

CHAPTER II.

Progress of the Albany Settlement, 1820–1823.

BEFORE giving the experience of the first settlers of 1820 in Albany, we must explain the position of the district in which they were located. What is called the district of Albany was the *Zuurveld*, which had for forty-five years previous been the battle-field of the Hottentot inhabitants, the Dutch colonists, and the Kaffirs. We must quote the "History of the Colony of the Cape" again. "It will be obvious that the Colonial Government, when it located the new comers in this, which was deemed a most desirable tract of country, regarded them as a portion of the frontier defence, and as forming an impregnable barrier to Kaffir aggression. Had this honourable but dangerous position been understood beforehand by the emigrants, and had they come prepared to bear the responsibilities of such a position, no one could have objected to the arrangement. There was no intended deception. The most experienced colonist *at that time* never dreamt that the Kaffirs could prove to be such powerful and dangerous neighbours. This was not fully understood until the first Kaffir war of 1834–5. All the arrangements of the new settlement kept in view the formation of a comparatively dense population. The grants of one hundred acres of land, to which the farms were limited, and which appeared satisfactory to English notions, were absurd for the purposes of grazing, and generally not adapted to cultivation. It was most unjust to place, say, a party of one hundred families, upon an extent of land not larger than an ordinary Dutch farmer grant, which varied from six thousand to ten thousand acres. Nothing but the wish of the authorities to form a dense, concentrated population could explain the unfair policy of confining an English family to a farm of one hundred acres, while six thousand were scarcely deemed sufficient for a Dutch boer. The consequences were such as might have been foreseen. In a few years most of the one-hundred-acre farms were deserted, and the active, energetic emigrants scattered themselves over the eastern districts, creating new industries, and giving an impulse to the progress and prosperity of the colony, which has been continued by the second generation, and which, we trust, will long continue. These results, though not anticipated by the planners of the colony, have been the most important of all.

"From the year 1775, the Great Fish River had been deemed the eastern boundary of the Colony, and was finally declared to be such by Lord Macartney in 1798; but the Kaffirs had, nevertheless, continually encroached upon the Dutch settlers on the west of that river, and so persistent and destructive were these intrusions, that in 1811 the Government was obliged to drive them out by force. In 1816, and following year, their daring outrages and depredations recommenced, when the Governor, Lord Charles Somerset, was called to the frontier, where, on the 2nd of April, 1817, he had a conference with the chief Gaika, who pledged himself most unequivocally and un- reservedly to aid Government in procuring retribution for any depredations, and to punish depredators with death.

This, the first or 'Reprisal System,' was inaugurated with the consent of the chief, the following being the terms agreed upon :—The chief to restrain Kaffirs from plundering ; restore such cattle as should be found among the Kaffir herds ; permit the Colonial Government to enforce restitution of plundered cattle from any kraal to which such should be traced, or permit the party following them to seize an equal proportion, should restitution or compensation be resisted.

"In 1819, troubles again broke out. The Kaffirs—more than five thousand—invaded the Colony, attempted to carry the military cantonment of Graham's Town (then garrisoned by three hundred and fifty Europeans and a small party of Hottentots) by storm, but were repulsed. They then laid waste the whole of the Zuurveld ; after which a commando was raised, under the command of Colonel Willshire, (afterwards Sir Thomas, the hero of Khelat.) The barbarians were once more ejected, several chiefs surrendered, and the arch-instigator of the inroad, the prophet Lynx, or Makanna, was taken and deported to Robbin Island, and the Zuurveld in this its desolate state was destined to be the abode of the British Settler.

" On the cessation of hostilities, the Governor, Lord C. Somerset, had another interview with Gaika at the Gwanga, on the 14th of October, and in the spirit of the report made to the Government in 1809, and the recommendation of the elder Stockenstrom in 1810, then chief Magistrate of Graaff Reinet, Colonel Brereton and Colonel Cuyler represented to Gaika that it appeared impracticable to secure the repose of the frontier as long as the Kaffirs had ready access to the Great Fish River jungles ; that therefore, in order to protect the Colony from depredations, and Kaffirland from the visits of the Colonial troops to punish aggression, the Fish River ought no longer to be the boundary, but the Chumi River and Keiskamma. Gaika, his son Macomo, the chiefs Eno, Botman, Congo, Habana, and Garetta, with their interpreters, the Governor and his staff, his interpreter being Captain Stockenstrom, (afterwards Sir Andries,) being present, agreed to the proposal, and engaged at once to move beyond the new limits; that the troops should destroy every vestige of a kraal within them, and that military posts should be erected between the two rivers, to prevent the future occupation of the ceded territory by any petty chief.

"This territory, often interchangeably named 'ceded' or 'neutral,' intervened between the new immigrants and the Kaffirs, a breadth of about thirty miles by fifty,—a country, in fact, not originally belonging to them, but to the Gonnah Hottentots, and known as 'Gonaqualand.' It was only taken possession of by the Kaffirs after the year 1752, when an Ensign Beuteler found them to the east of the Kei River, which river they crossed somewhere about 1760, under Khakhabe, the grandfather of Gaika."*

A few words on the condition of the Cape Colony in the year 1820, taken from the same excellent authority. Its population numbered 110,380, of which 47,988 were white, (Europeans and Dutch colonists,) 28,835 Hottentots, and 33,557 slaves. In addition to Cape Town, there were nine villages called towns. Very few churches or Ministers in the Eastern Division of the Colony. There was a chaplain in Graham's Town for the troops; but it was remarked at

* "History of the Colony of the Cape." By Hon. J. C. Chase. 8vo. 1869.

the time that the Sabbath had halted at the Sundays River, and found it difficult to get across. The currency was a depreciated paper issue; the rix dollar, originally worth 4s., having fallen to 1s. 6d. and 2s. The Government was a very capricious fatherly despotism, in which the good intentions of the Governor were commonly neutralized by the opposition of his subordinates. There was no free press and no public opinion; and no trade or export from the Eastern Division of the Colony, beyond a few articles of little value, such as salt, soap, and skins. The only event which held out hopes of the much needed changes in the administration being in due time effected, was the advent of the English settlement. It is estimated that by the emigrant ships and by other arrivals, before the end of 1820, five thousand souls were settled in the " Zuurveld," a belt of land extending eastwardly from the Sundays to the Great Fish River, an area of three thousand square miles; but as only that part of the district which lies near the sea was to be occupied by the settlers, the area appropriated to them at first was about one thousand five hundred square miles, or less than a million of acres.

We now return to Mr. Shaw's journal, which gives the experiences of the Salem and other parties on entering into the possession of their " broad lands," the hundred-acre allotments. The original settlers were apt to expatiate on their castles in the air, the erection of which cheered them amid the hardships and tedium of the long passage from England. Unfortunately most of these day dreams have not been recorded. On one occasion, an emigrant, boasting to a sailor of his claim to a grant of a hundred acres, was confounded by his reply: " Why, man, what's that ? In Africa it requires a thousand acres to graze a goose."

The general appearance of the district is picturesque and pleasing. Excepting during very severe droughts, the country is covered by a coarse grass, and usually has a verdant aspect. The Mimosa studs the plains and slopes of the hills. In many parts a thick shrubbery grows in patches, as if planted for ornament, and gives the country a park-like appearance; while in other places, favoured by shelter from the high winds, trees of a much larger growth shoot up to a considerable height; among which are most conspicuous the straight and tall Euphorbia, with their naked and melancholy-looking branches, relieved, however, by the *Erythrina Caffra*, or *Coral-lodendrum*, known among the Dutch farmers and English colonists as the *Kafferboom*. This often grows into a large and umbrageous tree, and is sometimes met with standing apart. In the spring season it is covered with innumerable blossoms, of a brilliant scarlet colour, giving it a very gorgeous appearance.

The location assigned us extended on both sides of the Assagaay Bosch River for about six miles in length. It consisted of a series of valleys and bottoms of light alluvial soil. These valleys were of various and unequal width, and followed the winding course of the river, which had its source in the Zuurbergen, a range of mountains not far distant to the north. It was rather a great drain to the high lands than a river; for, although at the time of our arrival it was flowing, yet we afterwards found that for several months of the year it does not flow; but, like many periodical streams called rivers in Southern Africa, it consisted chiefly of long reaches of comparatively deep water, but with occasional intervals of from ten to thirty yards in width, called "drifts," or fords; where, excepting after heavy rains, it was generally possible to cross the bed of the stream dry-shod. In many parts the water was brackish ; but it afforded an abundant supply for all ordinary purposes, and for the large amount of live stock accumulated at a subsequent period by the settlers ; while at various points there are valuable and never-failing springs of water of the best quality for drinking and culinary purposes.

The hills bounding the succession of long, low valleys on both sides the river, wind gently down from the extensive flats or plains which extend for many miles on the common level of the country. These plains, as well as the connecting slopes, are covered with grass, affording in most seasons an abundant supply for cattle. The sides of the hills descending to the valleys are in many parts variegated with patches of wood, of several varieties, affording abundance of fuel, and of poles, &c., for building and other purposes. The bottoms by the river side were in most places nearly destitute of trees, and presented a great extent of land ready to receive the plough ; and when the white tents of the settlers were pitched and dotted up and down on their several homesteads, the scene presented to the eye was at once romantic and pleasing. It was not like a soldiers' encampment, but rather suggested the idea of a large number of persons who had recently gone forth from some crowded city to enjoy the pure air, and bask under a beautiful sky, in picnic parties of pleasure. There were not wanting among the settlers those who admired the beauties of nature, and who often expressed to others of similar tastes their admiration of many lovely nooks and corners where the hand of man had as yet done nothing ; but all were soon awakened to the necessity of dealing with the stern realities of life. The tents were very hot during the day, and cold at night. They were not always a protection from the occasional heavy showers of rain, and in the frequent high winds they were anything rather than safe and secure dwellings. Hence every one was soon busily occupied in cutting poles, and conveying them to the respective homesteads, or handling the hatchet, the adze, the hammer and nails, and other implements and materials required for building operations.

After a while a great variety of fragile and grotesque-looking huts or cottages began to arise. These were generally built in the style called by the settlers " wattle and daub." A space of ground was marked out, according to the views of the future occupant of the structure, large enough for one or two rooms. The best generally were designed for two rooms of about ten by twelve feet each, forming a building of ten by twenty-four feet. Strong upright posts were planted all round the building about two feet apart; these were firmly fixed in holes dug in the ground to the depth of eighteen or twenty inches to receive them; they rose to the height of about six feet above the ground; thinner poles were planted between the stout posts, and then a quantity of smaller wood, slender branches of trees or shrubs, was cut, and used for the purpose of wattling all round the building. When this was completed, it had the appearance of a great wicker vessel or huge basket. A wall-plate, being generally a large pole squared by the adze, was nailed on the tops of the upright posts on each side and end of the building. A roof, consisting of as many rafters as were necessary, all of poles, was securely nailed to the wall-plates. On the rafters were nailed, or sometimes tied, laths at proper distances, to which the thatch of rushes or reeds, cut from the bank of the river, was fastened by means of cord made from the rushes. When the whole was covered, the walls were usually plastered over, inside and out, with clay mixed and prepared with water, and tempered by treading with the feet in the same manner as brickmakers prepared clay for bricks before pugmills were invented. At first there was no plank for doors, or glass for windows: hence a mat or rug was usually hung up in the void doorway, to do duty for the one; and a piece of white calico, nailed to a small frame of wood, and fastened into two or three holes left in the walls for the purpose, admitted light into the dwelling during the day, when the wind rendered it inconvenient to keep these spaces open. The floors of these dwellings were usually made of clay. Ant-hills, which had been deserted by the ants, were used for this purpose; and, when properly laid, they made hard and level floors, which were kept in order by being often smeared over with a mixture of fresh cow-dung and water,—a mode of securing clean and comfortable *earthen* floors, which, however strange to English ideas, all natives and colonists of Africa know to be indispensable. After awhile those who aspired to neatness and comfort found pipe-clay, and at length limestone, from which they obtained lime, and thus they were enabled to whitewash their tenements, which gave them a more cheerful and greatly improved appearance. I have described the better class of structures erected by the settlers at the beginning; but there were many whose first attempts were miserable failures, and hardly served to protect them from the weather. Some, taking advantage of particular spots favourable to their purpose, thought they saved themselves labour by digging out holes, and burrowing in the ground, placing a slight covering over their excavations; while others, again, filled up interstices between perpendicular rocks, and thus obtained very substantial, but rather cold and uncomfortable, quarters.

There was a ruinous wattled and reed building, which had been erected by a Dutch farmer during his temporary sojourn on these lands. It stood in a central situation; and it was resolved that it should be public property, and be used for general purposes of utility. It was about fifty or sixty feet long, ten or twelve feet broad; and the walls from the earthen floor were about five feet high, with an open roof thatched with reeds. This building was for some time used as our temporary place of worship. It was likewise the "town hall;" for here all public meetings of the settlers, on matters of general concern, were holden. Here were also kept the commissariat supplies, where the rations of meat and flour were distributed. Part of the building, being separated from the rest by a temporary screen, was also, on occasion, used as a "lying-in hospital;" and here was born a child of one of the settlers, who afterwards grew up to manhood; and whom, on the 25th of November, 1848, I had the gratification, in conjunction with other Presbyters of the Wesleyan Church, to ordain to the office of the Christian ministry.

All these contrivances for dwellings and public buildings have long since passed away; and the settlers now generally occupy good and substantial stone or brick houses, which, as they gradually surmounted their early difficulties, were erected on their homesteads and farms; and not a few of them have taken care to provide their families with every convenience and appliance requisite in that country for domestic comfort. But I have thought the English reader might wish to know how they managed to obtain shelter for themselves at first; and, should any of the surviving British settlers of 1820 read these pages, they will not regret this reference to their early difficulties, over which, by the "good hand of God" upon their enduring industry, they have long ago so nobly triumphed.

On the arrival of the settlers they were immediately placed in all parts of this district. The first parties being set down near the Great Fish River, and, consequently, furthest in advance; the next arrivals were located on the nearest available spot to the westward; and so on with each fresh batch, till all the most promising spots for location were occupied, from the mouth of the Fish River in the east to the Bushman's River

on the western extremity of the district. A small party of
Scottish settlers, under Mr. Pringle, were settled in the Cradock
District, on the Baviaans River, about one hundred miles to
the north of Albany, and in the midst of a number of Dutch
farmers, who, at that period, occupied that part of the country.
There was considerable diversity in the soil of Albany. In
some places it consisted of a stiff red loam; in others, a rich
black earth prevailed; while, in parts near the sea, the ground
was almost entirely loose sand, only held together by the crop
of long coarse grass which was growing upon it; but, in general,
the settlers who were best acquainted with agricultural pursuits, deemed the country likely to render a rich return for
such labour as might be bestowed upon it, if the land were
judiciously treated, as the various qualities of the soil seemed
to require. Some parts of the district were intersected by
masses of loose stones and stratified rocks, lying near or on the
surface; and, in some instances, the first division of the lands
made amongst the settlers in the several locations, caused an
undue proportion of these plots, unfit for cultivation, to be
included in the allotments of individuals.

I must bear my testimony to the determined industry with
which these first settlers, with some exceptions, set to work.
The Government had engaged to supply them with rations, to be
paid for from the deposit money paid by them into the Colonial
Office in England, till they could raise crops of food for themselves; and all but a few drunken and "ne'er-do-weel" sort of
persons commenced digging and planting with the greatest
industry. But it was labour under difficulties. Many had
never been accustomed to handle the spade, and were much
better acquainted with the works and ways of large towns and
cities, than with the occupations and modes of life which most
prevail in our agricultural villages and districts. There were
ploughs; but they had been sent from England, and were not

adapted to breaking up the rough African lands; and happy was the settler who could command the means for purchasing some trained oxen, and obtain the assistance of any stray Hottentot or impoverished Mulatto who understood the use of the strong and rudely contrived ploughs, by which the Dutch boers of the country generally broke up the virgin earth. The management of the oxen, and the guidance of the plough, with such bullocks, unaccustomed to the yoke, and by drivers who knew not how to control them by the use of the unwieldy African whip—to say nothing of the intense heat of the sun, which sometimes, notwithstanding it was the winter season, shone out with overpowering lustre—rendered these field occupations toilsome and unsatisfactory.

It was, however, surprising to see the extent of land which had been broken up by the spade and plough, during the first two seasons. From the gardens were raised, in many places, various esculents in abundance, which afforded promise that horticulture would prove a profitable employment; but the wheat, of which considerable quantities had perhaps been inconsiderately sown at first, proved an entire failure, in consequence of a fatal blight which became general. It was called "the rust," from its covering blade, stem, and ear of the plant with reddish-looking spots, which, if rubbed when in the early stage of the disease, left rusty stains on the hand; and in a few days it completely destroyed the tissue of the plants, as rust will in time corrode iron. Nothing could be more promising than were the crops of wheat in all the early stages of their growth; but just as the stems began to shoot into ear, and in some cases even after the grain was formed in the ear, this blight attacked it, and the whole crop became worthless. The disappointment was great the first season; but it was supposed that the disease might arise from some cause connected with the first cultivation of the ground and sowing it with wheat,

and that it would perhaps not appear again. But after repeat-
ing their attempts for two or three seasons with the same result,
the settlers were quite discouraged, and gave up all hope of
being enabled to raise bread for themselves and their families
from the ground. Other kinds of grain, indeed, they soon
found, could be easily grown: rye, barley, oats, and Indian corn,
were raised in large quantities; and, by various ingenious contrivances, these kinds of produce supplied the want of flour and
bread made from wheat.

The first three or four years were spent in great suffering
and privation. The general distress, however, would have been
much greater, but the settlers were enabled, by purchase or
barter with the older Dutch colonists, to obtain a supply of
horned cattle. These cattle grazed and increased on the common pastures, and the cows afforded a considerable supply of
milk, which, with pork and the various kinds of grain already
enumerated, and pumpkins, potatoes, and other garden produce,
enabled them to feed their families. Many also made butter
and cheese, and, by carrying these articles regularly to the
Military Stations for sale, they obtained the means to purchase
a few groceries. The latter were not, however, always to be
had in the scantily supplied stores, and the settlers soon
discovered that a plant which grows throughout the district
could be used in the form of decoction as a refreshing beverage,
only not *quite* so good as tea; while roasted barley, when
ground into a fine powder, formed a substitute for coffee. Now
and then wild honey from the rocks or woods furnished the
means of sweetening those beverages. Happily, as the older
Dutch colonists possessed large herds of cattle and sheep, flesh-
meat could generally be obtained at small cost: hence there
was never a period of actual starvation. But if the climate
had not been of the most healthful kind, it is likely that the
extremely low and coarse diet to which numbers were unavoid-

ably limited, with exposure to rain and damp, and the rapid alternations of heat and cold, would have induced extensive disease and premature death. But this was not the case. The people were generally in the highest health, perhaps from being much in the open air; and some medical men who had accompanied the settlers from England left the district in disgust, as being not likely to afford them any opportunity for the practice of their valuable profession.

The non-issue of rations by the Government, after the settlers had been nearly two years on the ground, became the signal for a considerable number of the people to abandon their allotted lands. At first it was intended that the capital of the district should be at a spot called Bathurst, chosen for its great beauty of situation, and its proximity to the mouth of the Kowie River, which was regarded from the first as likely to become the future port of the settlement, whenever suitable works could be constructed for removing or deepening the bar at its mouth. On the return from England of Lord Charles Somerset, however, Graham's Town—already the head quarters of the troops—was constituted the capital of the district. This measure was very unpopular for a time; but events have shown that it was a better arrangement than that first meditated.

In consequence of the proclamation fixing Graham's Town as the capital, there arose a great demand for mechanics and labourers of all kinds, for the purpose of erecting houses and barracks. Hence most persons who were qualified to enter upon these branches of industry, gradually withdrew from their locations, and obtained employment at high wages, or became masters on their own account. As the town increased rapidly, an opening for trade was presented, and stores and shops soon began to rise up for the supply of the troops and population of various classes. Thus Graham's Town, from being, at the time when the settlers arrived, a mere military cantonment, with some ten or fifteen small and chiefly temporary dwellings erected by married officers and non-commissioned officers, and a few camp followers,—soon began to assume the appearance of a bustling and rising town.

In October, 1823, when the settlers had been about three years and a half in the country, a fearful storm occurred, during which the rains fell and the winds blew in a most terrific manner. The dwellings of the people, including some that had been deemed very substantial, were in numerous instances blown down: others were washed away by torrents of water. The rivers, rising much higher than had been conceived possible, overflowed their banks and carried off the standing crops; while in some instances individuals were swept away with the strong current, and drowned. The distress which followed this catastrophe was very severe, and many very worthy persons were reduced by it to great straits. Besides a limited amount of pecuniary aid, promptly offered to the distressed by Government, it must be recorded to their lasting honour, that various benevolent persons, in Cape Town and India, on hearing of this calamity, contributed considerable sums for the relief of the distressed. The late Rev. Dr. Philip, whose acquaintance I had previously made, on occasion of his visiting the frontier, and H. E. Rutherfoord, Esq., took a leading part in this generous movement. Mr. Rutherfoord undertook the laborious office of Secretary to the Committee in Cape Town, on whom was devolved the work of distributing the funds contributed for this object. This gentleman corresponded with me very frequently on this matter; and his letters, still in my possession, show the anxiety felt to relieve the most pressing cases as promptly as possible. The duty of distributing the earliest remittances among the greatest sufferers, was committed to me. As I was already known to the whole body of the settlers, and, in consequence of my frequently visiting the various locations in my

ministerial capacity, I was perhaps as well, or better, acquainted
with the circumstances of the people than any other person,—
I could not decline to render aid in the distribution of this
relief, although I found it required much time, and was a duty
of great delicacy and difficulty. But, while engaged in this
labour of love, my removal to Kaffraria became necessary;
and, before I left the Settlement, a local committee of Ministers
and gentlemen was formed, who acted in concert with the
committee in Cape Town, and on this committee ultimately
devolved the difficult work of distributing the large funds which
had been contributed in India and elsewhere for this truly
benevolent purpose.

This was the crisis of the Settlement. Many who remained
on the lands were in great difficulties. The clothes which they
had brought with them from England were now worn and thread-
bare; there were but very limited means of purchasing, at the
enormous prices then charged, the needful materials for
replenishing their wardrobes; and not a few were glad to attire
themselves in the costume that had prevailed among the Dutch
farmers, and others, in South Africa, before the arrival of the
settlers. At this period I was myself obliged to ride about the
Settlement dressed in a sheep-skin jacket and trowsers, with
a broad-brimmed hat, made from the leaves of the *Palmiet*,
which grew in some of the streams. My dress was in fact
similar to that worn by a large number of persons; and it was
well adapted for "roughing it" on the road and in the jungle;
but not exactly such a dress as an Englishman prefers when
circumstances pecuniary and otherwise will allow of an alternative. Even the females had to exhibit their characteristic
ingenuity in devising dresses from the coarse kinds of cotton
stuffs which at that time were brought to the Cape from India,
and sold at high prices. In some instances the well-dressed
sheep-skin was formed into a skirt or frock; and hats and

bonnets, made also from the same material as those worn by the men, were in very general use. It is a pity that all this occurred before the days of photography, or many very respectable families in Albany, and other portions of the Cape Colony, might now possess some portraits of their fathers and mothers, the "founders" of the Albany Settlement, exhibiting very grotesque costumes of a highly historic character.

It was complained at the time, and it has occasionally since been rather sneeringly said of the first English settlers in Albany, that they were generally unfit to form the population of a new country. It was affirmed that they were a race of Cockneys; and that persons with such unpromising antecedents as weavers, pen-makers, pin-cutters, &c., were found in considerable numbers among them. I need hardly say that this was a gross exaggeration, founded upon a few exceptional cases. That in such a large body of people there were some who had probably mistaken their providential call when they resolved to emigrate to South Africa, is not unlikely; but, after a long and intimate acquaintance with the settlers, I have been led to regard them, on the whole, as a very suitable class of persons for founding a new colony. About one half had emigrated from London, and other large towns and cities in Britain, and the remainder came from various agricultural villages and districts. Observation and experience have led me to the conclusion that these proportions in the classes of emigrants to an entirely new country, are better than a body of people selected *wholly* from agricultural districts. Those from the towns and cities comprised a large number of artificers and mechanics, possessing skill of a kind most valuable in a new community; while others from the towns had a perfect knowledge of the principles of trade and commerce, and a general intelligence far exceeding the average of that displayed by the class of agricultural labourers in England. There was also a fair proportion of half-pay officers, and other educated persons of gentlemanly tastes and feelings, who, from various causes, had been led to emigrate from Great Britain at this period. Hence the settlers of Albany really had amongst them men adapted to every want of society as it exists in a newly forming community.

The advantage of this diversity in the capacities and qualifications of the settlers became very evident when the people were reduced to their lowest state. Nearly the whole body of the mechanics soon found very profitable employment in the town; and when that seemed to be overstocked, many of them removed to Algoa Bay, Uitenhage, Somerset, Graaff Reinett, and other towns or villages in the eastern districts of the Colony. Those who did not possess mechanical skill, but who, having come from the cities and towns of England, understood trade, obtained small supplies of goods, and travelled, at first as hawkers, among the Dutch farmers, selling goods at rates that were held to be mutually advantageous. Notwithstanding very stringent laws to prevent all traffic with the native tribes, a smuggling trade was also commenced by some of the settlers. It is among my earliest pleasant reminiscences that I availed myself of an opportunity to write a long communication to the Government to show how much better it would be to legalize this trade, and to appoint fairs at which the settlers and Kaffirs might meet for the purpose of barter. In 1823, the first attempt of this kind was made by authority of the Government; and it afterwards grew into a system which continued for some years, till at length the trade was released from all restrictions, and greatly extended. Into these openings for trade, both among the Dutch farmers and the native tribes, many of the settlers entered with much skill and energy; and thus not a few individuals who hardly seemed likely to succeed as cultivators of the ground, commenced trafficking with the investment of only a few pounds sterling, or, in some cases, with goods obtained entirely on credit, in reliance on their known good character: and this was the foundation of a long course of successful trade, which has in almost every case supplied them with ample means of support for their families in comfort and respectability, and, in some instances, led to the realization of very handsome fortunes. As a further evidence that a full proportion of well educated and intelligent persons were included in the number of the emigrants of 1820, I may mention that, in the course of years, the Colonial Government was glad to avail itself of the services of some of them, who have been engaged in the civil service of the Colony as Civil Commissioners, Magistrates, Justices of the Peace, or in other prominent and responsible offices; while, as will soon appear, others became teachers in academies, and Ministers of religion.

Thus many of the very individuals whom some would have thought unsuitable to people a new country proved most valuable members of the community, and by their skill and general intelligence have developed the resources of the colony; while, by drawing off from their locations, they left more scope for the class of agriculturists, for whom by their mercantile energy they provided markets which have gradually stimulated and rewarded their industry in the cultivation of the soil and the care of cattle and sheep. The one hundred acres granted at first to each settler did not allow sufficient extent for grazing their stock, and the settlers were in the beginning rather inconveniently crowded on their locations; but as more than one half ultimately abandoned their lands, which were afterwards granted to the actual residents, or otherwise became their property by purchase from the original owners, this evil was remedied, and, so far from being overcrowded, the locations and farms in Albany are at present much too thinly populated.

Now that there is a great and steady demand for agricultural produce, the coast part of that district might on a good system

reccive five times its present European population as agriculturists, with great advantage both to occupiers and owners.
One reason why the rural population of Albany has of late
years been so much reduced, is the disturbance and losses the
people were called to endure, in consequence of the Kaffir wars;
but the chief cause has been the numerous openings in the
districts more inland, by the migration of the Dutch Boers
beyond the boundaries of the colony, and by the more recent
founding of new districts, by the Government, on the frontier.
Some of these new districts are better adapted to the purposes
of sheep-walks than Lower Albany, which is chiefly fitted for
agricultural occupations. The growth of wool has been found
to be a most profitable pursuit; and this proved a sufficient
inducement to a large portion of the settlers, and their
descendants, to migrate from Albany to the other districts of
the Eastern Province.

CHAPTER III.

Religious Progress of the Albany Settlement, 1820–1823.

HAPPILY the history of the pastorate at Salem and its out-parishes, as well as the Missionary labours of Mr. Shaw in the Settlement, can be given in his own words. From occasional memoranda found among his papers, we find that he has underrated his labours, and has left unnoticed the details of the hardships of his early ministry. One cause of this was, no doubt, his own inherent modesty and unwillingness to say what might appear to glorify himself. Another was the feeling in him, singularly ever present, and to him most sustaining, that he was working for Christ, and felt it a pleasure to be permitted to suffer for Christ's sake. "In labours more abundant," (2 Cor. xi. 23,) might have been his motto. Frequently, after walking long distances, or riding on tired horses, he preached four times in one day. The Sabbath was his most laborious day, and other days did not much differ from the Sabbath day. At the time mainly referred to in this chapter, 1820–1823, it must be remembered that Mr. Shaw was a very young man, (from twenty-two to twenty-five,) a period of life in which most young men, however favoured by early advantages and mental gifts, are seldom called upon to exercise the self-restraint which is essential to the success of a Minister placed in the most trying position in which a Minister, be he young or old, can be placed,—that is, the pastorate of a large body of settlers,

SALEM IN 1848.

who, though mainly Methodists, were not so altogether.
A large number of them were his fellow-passengers ; and
we all know that no circumstances are more unfavourable
to the exhibition of human nature, or are better adapted to
draw out the weak points in character and the defects in
temper to which we are all more or less prone.   Through
this ordeal Mr. Shaw passed scathless.   Those who saw
him daily in the exercise of his ministry on shipboard
were those who felt the impress of his character
in succeeding years.   To them especially he was a
hero.   What struck the author of these sketches most on
his arrival in the Albany District in 1830, was the reverential tone in which all who knew Mr. Shaw spoke of him.
It was not enough for them to praise his dignified bearing
as *the* Minister, combined as it was with the deep sympathy which he evidenced on all occasions for their trials
and difficulties, or his meekness of wisdom at all times, or
his indomitable and methodical zeal in his pastoral
labours.   These qualities other men might surpass in
varied degrees ; but to them their chief pastor, William
Shaw, was a being to whom none could be compared,—
their ideal of *the* perfect man and Minister.   His married
life was no hindrance to his pastoral or Missionary labours
in distant localities ; for Mrs. Shaw was as zealous as her
husband, and had as deep a sense of the obligations and
responsibilities of the Christian Ministry.   In her husband's absences she was able to exercise an influence for
good upon the Salem society. Her pleasant, lively manner,
her open countenance beaming with kindness, and her
frank, loving conversation, made her at once popular and
useful.   To the churches she was as a mother in Israel,

competent from her intelligent piety, and her deep Christian experience, to exercise discreetly a wise and happy influence on all around her.

My first care, on our arrival at Salem, was to establish religious ordinances for the benefit of the settlers who were under my special pastoral oversight. The rude structure originally erected by a Dutch farmer, who had removed to another farm granted to him by the Government, was used, as already stated, for various purposes for the common benefit of the people, and it served very well as a temporary chapel. For lack of a pulpit, I was accustomed to stand on a small box; and a writing desk, placed on the top of an American flour barrel, behind which I stood, formed the resting-place for the Bible and other books used in public worship. The people soon provided themselves with stools or benches; and, in the course of a few weeks, the congregation had been regularly formed.

The place of worship constituted as great a contrast as could be well conceived to Great Queen Street Chapel, and other chapels in London, where most of the people had been accustomed to attend Divine service. Its earthen floor and unceiled roof, thatched with reeds, and open at the ridge-poles,—its reed and mud-plastered walls, through which several holes were opened to let in light and air,—and its dimensions, say sixty feet by twelve or thirteen feet, brought painfully to the minds of the people the greatly altered circumstances under which they now offered their prayers and praises to the God of heaven. There was another source of discomfort, and indeed of some danger, connected with this temporary place of worship. The mice and rats had found a home in and around it, and this proved an attraction to snakes and other reptiles. On one occasion I was standing in a Class Meeting, giving the quarterly tickets; and while I was speaking to one of the members, another jumped up, and said in alarm, " O, Sir, there is a *puff adder* between your feet !"   Looking down I saw that the creature—one of the most deadly of the South African snakes—was indeed lying on the ground close to my feet. I quietly stepped aside, while some of the people with a stick attacked and destroyed the dangerous reptile, and we resumed our meeting, which was not concluded without praise offered to our heavenly Father, by whose gracious providence I had been preserved from the " serpent's bite."

Notwithstanding the discomforts of the place, a considerable portion of the people speedily began to attend morning and evening service on the Lord's day, and many of them likewise attended the week-night services which were also commenced for Prayer-meetings and preaching the word. The more private means of grace established among the Methodists for the promotion of personal piety and religious communion were also soon commenced. Several individuals of consistent piety, and possessing intelligent minds, were appointed as Class Leaders ; the Sacraments of Baptism and the Lord's Supper were duly and regularly celebrated; and all the usual means and appliances, enjoyed by the members of the Methodist Society in England for their spiritnal benefit, were thus provided for the people of my charge. A few families were Baptists, and they established religious services for themselves, which were efficiently conducted by Mr. W. Miller, one of their own number, who, although not having enjoyed the advantage of early education, was nevertheless a person of strong sense and a ready speaker. He was a good man, and for many years was the centre of union and the chief religious instructor of the Baptist denomination in the Colony. A portion of the people were Episcopalians, and they were pleased to find that at the forenoon service on Sundays I regularly read the liturgical service of the Church of England, as abridged under the direction of the Rev. John Wesley.

In my public ministrations, I avoided as much as possible all religious controversy,—feeling that, as many attended who had not been trained in Methodistic views, it would for various reasons be best, without compromising my own principles, to confine my sermons chiefly to a range of topics at once experimental and practical,—in a word, to the great and, by all evangelical Christians, admitted essentials of religious truth. It was soon apparent that this was the right course; for many who had been early trained in connexion with other religious bodies in England, whether as Churchmen or Dissenters, thus found nothing repulsive in my ministry, and therefore became my regular hearers. I always considered that Wesleyan Methodism, when rightly understood and properly administered, is "anti-sectarian and of a catholic spirit;" hence I readily admitted to the communion of the Lord's table such persons of other denominations as exhibited suitable moral and religious qualities; and a portion of these, in the absence of Ministers of their own denominations, used to avail themselves of the privilege of our "open," although not indiscriminate, communion.

Having thus established Christian ordinances at Salem, I soon became very desirous of visiting the other parties of settlers scattered in various localities of the district, for the purpose of ascertaining their religious state and condition. In those days this was an undertaking of no small difficulty. There was, at the time, no map of the district showing the relative positions of the various settlements; and, excepting the principal line of road by which the settlers had reached the country from Algoa Bay, there were no roads leading to their several locations. I could only obtain very vague information from some Hottentots, who told me to travel in the direction of certain distant hills, and that I should find settlers' tents to the right or left, as the case happened to be. On these early journeys, of course, I frequently missed my way, and was at times benighted in the woods, which at that period were infested with various kinds of ferocious animals. I could not always obtain a horse, and hence I had frequently to walk over considerable distances through rugged districts, upon unformed paths, and not seldom having to wade through the unbridged streams that intersect the district.   Indeed, several years subsequently to this period, my Missionary colleagues, before they became familiar with the country, often missed their way ; and occasionally it happened that a Missionary had to solace himself at night in the midst of a bush, by seeking such security and repose as could be obtained from climbing a tree and seating himself in its branches, to await the return of day.

At the commencement I frequently slept on the ground in the tents of the settlers, or, on subsequent visits, in their unfinished huts ; where, as I wrapped myself in such bedding as could be procured for the night, there were neither doors to bar out burglars, nor windows to keep out the cold air ; nor, indeed, in many cases, so much of a covered roof as prevented an extensive view directly over head of a large portion of the sky, tempting one to scan such constellations of the beautiful stars,—and the stars do shine out beautifully in that clear atmosphere,—as passed the field of vision. The reader, however, must not suppose that I made any considerable progress in astronomical studies under these (favourable ?) circumstances ; the truth is, I was generally so fatigued with my journeys, and the duties which I had to perform, that, regardless of comfort or discomfort, a deep sleep soon closed all meditations ; but it re-invigorated me for the work of the following day. During this period of my missionary career, I often realized, in more respects than one, the exceeding truth of the maxim, "The rest of a labouring man is sweet, whether he eat little or much." I soon began, however, to reap a good reward for these toilsome journeys. I visited in rotation nearly all the principal settlements; and preached to as many as I could assemble at the various places which presented the most likely points for forming congregations. Everywhere I was received by the English settlers with great kindness, and even gratitude. They felt thankful to the man, previously wholly unknown to them, who had come to them in their rude and hardly-formed homes in the wilderness, to preach among them the " glorious Gospel of the blessed God."

In some of the locations I found several who had been Methodists in England, and a few of whom had wisely brought with them their proper credentials as such. These individuals, among whom there were two or three Local Preachers, became valuable assistants, and greatly aided me in establishing regular opportunities for public worship in the more central portions of the locations. One of these zealous Local Preachers was the late Mr. Pike. He came with what was called the "Nottingham party." The arrangements with Government, for sending out this party of about fifty families, were conducted by an agent appointed under the auspices of the Duke of Newcastle, who had generously aided some of them in emigrating to the Cape, with the view of improving their circumstances. At a meeting of these settlers before they left England, a clergyman very properly recommended to the head of the party that on Sundays prayers, and occasionally a sermon, should be read for the benefit of the people. But a service conducted by an irreligious person was not likely to be conducive to much edification. A young man imbued with religious feeling, therefore, ventured to inquire whether he might be permitted to conduct religious services with such as were disposed to unite with him. The mere inquiry was sufficient to arouse the spirit of bigotry.

On close examination, he was induced honestly to avow, that
he was a " Methodist;" and he was at once informed he could
not be permitted to proceed with the settlers to South Africa.
However, there were others whose names had been included in
the list of accepted persons, who had been accustomed to attend
the Methodist preaching; but they kept their counsel as to their
religious predilections.   Among these was Mr. Pike, who, being
a devout man, and having occasionally preached or exhorted
in the villages near his residence, felt constrained, soon after
the vessel sailed from England, "to speak and to teach,"
among his fellow emigrants, "the things concerning the kingdom
of God."   The appointed "head" of the party, and others like-
minded, persecuted this good man for his attempts to promote
a spirit of piety among the settlers; and perhaps the more
bitterly, because the great pains taken to shut out Methodists
from any connexion with this body of settlers had thus been
rendered utterly futile.   In the course of events, the nominal
head of the party died at Algoa Bay, and thus never reached
the place of location, which the people, from a becoming feeling
of gratitude to the Duke of Newcastle, called " Clumber."   The
other persecutors of Mr. Pike were successively removed by
death in a very remarkable manner; and as there was no longer
any "let or hindrance," he commenced regular religious services
in a wood close to his tent.   After he had erected his first rude
dwelling, he opened it for worship.   His simple piety and
manifest godly sincerity won for him the love of his fellow
settlers; and they actually elected him as the nominal head of
the party, and he became the friend and counsellor of the people.
By the aid of his influence, and the co-operation of the comparatively large congregation which speedily grew up at this
place, we were enabled to erect a suitable chapel, which stands
on a beautiful natural mount, in a most picturesque valley,
and, being centrally situated, has long been one of our best

attended places of worship. This excellent man died many years ago; and his remains lie interred in the burial ground attached to the chapel, to the erection of which his piety and zeal contributed so greatly.

On my earliest visits to the various locations, we worshipped God under the shade of the spreading trees, or shelter of the rocks, whenever the company was too large to find room in the settler's tent or hut. Gradually the people built more or less commodious dwellings for themselves, as described in a previous chapter; and in several places they erected buildings of similar materials for the purposes of public worship. There was very little money among them in those days; hence the original chapels, which served their purpose very well for a time, were generally erected by the joint labour of their own hands. As the settlers rose to circumstances of greater comfort, and built more substantial dwellings for themselves, they began to feel that it was not seemly for them "to dwell in ceiled houses," while "God's house" was comparatively a "waste;" hence they provided means, "and went up to the mountain, and brought wood to build the house;" for they believed that which is written to be applicable to *every* house of prayer where God's word is truly preached, and His holy sacraments are rightly and duly administered: "I will take pleasure in it, and I will be glorified, saith the Lord." The result was, that in course of years the Methodist settlers, and those who wished to worship with them, erected, at considerable cost and labour, a number of substantial chapels in various parts of the settlement; which, being in localities distant from the towns, formed the only places of worship to which the scattered people could resort for the public service of God. They were generally well placed in elevated and picturesque spots; and many of the settlers learned to say, with feelings of true devotion, concerning these humble temples of God's grace,—

> " O happy souls that pray
>   Where God delights to hear !
> O happy men that pay
>   Their constant service there !
> They praise Thee still ; and happy they
> Who love the way to Sion's hill ! "

Chapels of this class were erected by the settlers at Clumber, (Nottingham party,) Green Fountain, Ebenezer, (James party,) Traape's Valley, Bathurst, Port Frances, Reed Fountain, Collingham, Manley's Flat, Seven Fountains.   All these places of worship, situated in various parts of the district of Lower Albany, were well attended during the earlier period of the Settlement ; but the gradual migration of the population to other portions of the Eastern Province has rendered some of them, for the present, unnecessary ; and public worship is now only continued in those chapels that are in the most central localities with reference to the existing diminished population of that part of Albany.

It soon became apparent to me, that unless the Methodist Mission could be made to bear upon the European population, consisting of the military in Graham's Town and the out-posts, and the great body of the English settlers, they were likely to remain almost entirely without the means of religious instruction and consolation, in the wild and desolate region in which, by the providence of God, their lot was cast.   There was only one clergyman, the Rev. Mr. Boardman, connected with any of the parties of settlers ; and he did not feel himself called upon to itinerate, so as to provide for the regular religious instruction of those who were not included amongst the people (Wilson's party) whom he regarded as his special charge.   The troops, consisting of English and natives, had no Chaplain. The London Missionary Society, indeed, had a few years before established a Missionary Station (Theopolis) in the district ;

but this was for the exclusive benefit of its Hottentot residents;
and as that Society, pursuing what I must ever regard as a
very mistaken course of action for any Missionary Society
having Missions in our colonies, did not allow its Missionaries
to devote any systematic labours for the benefit of European
colonists, the Missionaries at Theopolis did not consider
themselves to be at liberty to attempt the formation of congregations among the settlers. Hence it became evident, that
unless I made great efforts to extend the benefits of the Wesleyan Mission to the white population,—at that time the most
neglected people in the colony,—there was no hope that their
case would receive speedy attention from any other quarter.
I therefore worked hard, and I was constantly either in the
saddle, or walking on foot, to visit the various parts of my
extended sphere of labour.

In order to give greater solidity and effect to the labours of
the Methodists, after I had personally visited all I could find, I
arranged for a general meeting to be held at Salem, so as to
bring the people into acquaintance with each other, and to
produce among them a sympathy of feeling, and unity of action;
hoping that, by a proper organization, their efforts in various
ways, and in all parts of the settlement, might, under the
Divine blessing, tell with greater and more permanent effect,
than could otherwise be expected. The church arrangements
of the Methodist system afford peculiar advantages for missionary
action, especially among the scattered population of the colonies;
and although the obstacles were neither few nor small in bringing
this system into full operation, yet I hoped, by introducing the
most earnest of the people to each other, to unite them as one
faithful band of "witnesses" for God, each acting, in his own
neighbourhood, for the spiritual welfare of those living within
reach. The following extract from my Journal shows the
nature and extent of my labours at this period. The entry

under date January 2nd, 1821, was made when we had been about six months in the country, and shows that the plan adopted for bringing the most active and intelligent of the people together was productive of resolves which led, in due season, to important practical results.

"Christmas Day, 1820.—Held a Prayer-meeting at five o'clock this morning. The power of God was present. Preached at ten: after dinner, rode to Graham's Town, completely wet on the way by a heavy rain: preached in the evening at Mr. Lucas's, to about twenty persons, in English; and immediately after, at their own request, to about the same number of Hottentots, in Dutch. One of them prayed after my sermon, and it affected me to my very soul to hear him cry out with peculiar earnestness, '*O Heere, zend leeraar voor ons arme Heidenen!*' 'O Lord, send a teacher for us poor Heathen!' meaning one who should reside among them, and give them instruction regularly. I am told that the number of Hottentots in the army stationed here, including their wives and children, and those who live as servants in the town, is scarcely less than *one thousand souls!* These are all as sheep without a shepherd, and most of them have come from some of the various Missionary establishments; but alas! in Graham's Town there is *no Minister*, not even for the Europeans; and both classes, generally speaking, (what marvel?) are sunk very low in drunkenness, lewdness, and many other deadly sins.

"January 2nd, 1821.—According to appointment, a wagon-load of our friends arrived from various settlements, and this evening we held a meeting for the purpose of forming a Sunday School Society, for promoting the establishment of Sunday Schools throughout the whole District of Albany. Many judicious and pious remarks were made on the subject by various friends; and so strong a feeling was excited in favour of those institutions, as will, I doubt not, issue in an extensive establishment of a system of education most admirably adapted to the circumstances of the rising generation in an infant colony. It appeared from the reports, that three schools already exist: one at Salem, one at Green Fountain, and one at Somerset Place, which contain, in all, one hundred and thirty-six scholars; of whom six are Dutch, ten Hottentots, and the rest children of the English settlers.

"3rd.—This day being appointed for our Quarterly Meeting, I preached at nine; immediately after which we held a Love-feast: a more interesting and affecting detail of Christian experience I never heard given on any occasion. After dinner, the temporal business of the Circuit was transacted by the Leaders, Stewards, &c. It appeared that there was a small increase in the Society, which now amounts to one hundred and fifteen members. It was determined to build a small chapel at New Bristol immediately, and also at Graham's Town and Green Fountain, as soon as the way appears open. I met the Local Preachers, of whom there are ten, including those admitted on trial. They are full of zeal; and for sense and piety are not, I am persuaded, inferior to those of the greater part of our country Circuits in England. It was intended for three of them to have addressed us in the evening; but Mr. Barker, of Bethelsdorp, arriving at tea-time, on his return from Theopolis, where he had been to see Mr. Ullbright, who is at the point of death, I engaged him to preach; and he delivered a sensible and useful sermon before the largest congregation of Europeans ever seen before in the District of Albany. After sermon, I renewed the covenant, and administered the sacrament to upwards of eighty persons, who remained together for that purpose. Through the whole of these meetings, an extraordinary degree of seriousness, spirituality, and fervour was evident; and all agreed in opinion, that these were presages of good days to come. Even so, LORD JESUS!

"I ride every other week upwards of one hundred and thirty miles, and must in future regularly preach eight times during my round, independent of my Sabbath labours at home, and occasional labours in other places; but, after all, I cannot go to many who are saying, 'Come and help us.' I should desire occasionally to go to the frontier, the Keiskamma, where there are upwards of a thousand British soldiers without any Chaplain; and also to visit Bruintjes Hootge, the inland boundary of the district, where there is a considerable population of Dutch and Hottentots without a Minister. I am anxious to visit Somerset, where I hear a number of people are collected together, and to preach regularly on the Sabbath at Graham's Town, and some other places; but I can only be at one place at a time. Allow me then to entreat you, if you have not yet done it, to send a zealous, lively Missionary to my assistance: there is work for more than another Missionary in the District, and I hope we should be able to help considerably in supporting him."

My earliest visit to Graham's Town, destined to be the future metropolis of the Eastern Province, was made in the month of August, 1820. I have already described its aspect at this time. It was chiefly a military station, and head-quarters of the troops, which the Kaffirs had boldly attacked in the previous year, and—by a clever surprise, conducted by overwhelming numbers, with great bravery, storming the *cannon* hastily run out against them—very nearly secured a triumph over the small detachment of troops that were on the spot at the moment to resist them. The arrival of the British settlers soon gave an impetus to the place, and, as already stated, its population began to increase. Several mechanics and others from Salem, and various parts of the settlement, sought and found employment in this place; and, being added to the military, formed an aggregate population that greatly needed religious ordinances, while, as stated in the above extract from my Journal. there was neither church nor chapel, nor a resident Minister of any denomination. I therefore at once resolved to put Graham's Town on my Circuit Plan as a place to be visited by myself and the Local Preachers as frequently as possible.

A reference is made, in the above extract from my Journal,* to my having preached at the house of Mr. Lucas on Christmas day, 1820. I had already preached in his house several times before.   He was a Sergeant-Major in the Cape Corps Cavalry; and, together with a comrade, Sergeant-Major Price, of the same regiment, received me on all my earliest visits to Graham's Town with the heartiest welcome and greatest kindness. There is reason to believe that some officers and soldiers of the celebrated Roman legion which held possession of Great Britain for so long a period during the first centuries of the Christian era, were greatly instrumental in the introduction of Christianity among the ancient Britons, long before the time when Augustine reached these shores as a Missionary from Rome to the Saxon race, then settled in Kent. It is surprising how frequently evidence may be traced in ecclesiastical history of the devotion and zeal of Christian soldiers. There have been at all times, in a profession not usually regarded as favourable to piety, "Centurions" who have feared God and worked righteousness; and "devout soldiers," who have gladly attended upon Ministers to receive religious instruction and consolation, and to aid in the propagation of the truth.

It has already been shown in a previous chapter, that it was owing to the representations of a considerable number of Methodist soldiers in the army, serving at the Cape, that the first Methodist Missionary was sent to Southern Africa; and the two excellent men, whose names I have recorded above, were themselves of that religious Society when stationed near Cape Town. They were both converted, and became decidedly

* Page 67.

religious men, under the preaching of Sergeant Kendrick, of the Twenty-first Light Dragoons, to whom reference has already been made. When removed to the frontier on military service, they often mourned their entire separation from all the public means; but they maintained their character as good men and smart soldiers. On my first visiting them at the East Barracks, they were overjoyed to receive a Methodist Missionary. Arrangements were immediately made for establishing preaching in one of their rooms in the barracks; and as Sergeant-Major Lucas, being a married man, was already building himself a house outside the walls of the garrison, he took care to have one large room, in which a considerable number of persons could assemble to hear the Gospel preached. These first services were soon attended by as many as could find accommodation; and it was known that certain commissioned officers, being either ashamed to enter a Methodist Meeting, or, perhaps, afraid lest sitting in a Sergeant-Major's quarters, amongst a mixed concourse of private soldiers and civilians, might be deemed altogether incompatible with military regulations, used to indulge their curiosity, or seek religious edification, by listening to the preacher while standing outside near the door or windows. Thus was Methodism, and through its means " earnest Christianity," indebted for its introduction into Graham's Town, under hopeful circumstances, to the piety and zeal of these religious soldiers. In how many other places, both at home and abroad, have the character and efforts of the same class of men contributed greatly to advance the interests of religion! I therefore rejoice in the deep interest which has latterly been awakened amongst the Methodist public in England on behalf of the religious interests of the army. As a professedly Christian people, we have done no more than our duty in the erection of the handsome church at Aldershot, and the appointment of a resident Chaplain at that place. These arrangements, it is hoped, will be followed by more systematic efforts on the part of Wesleyan Ministers, in all the garrisons of the empire, for the promotion of the moral and spiritual benefit of the army. We owe this as a debt for the many benefits conferred on Methodism and its Missions by pious officers and soldiers in all parts of the world, from the days of John Haime, who, with other Methodist soldiers, was present at the memorable battles of Dettingen and Fontenoy, and was afterwards, for many years, a man of mark among the early Methodist Preachers ;—of Captain Webb, who, when in active service, was one of the earliest and most conspicuous instruments in the introduction of Methodism into what were at that time the British Provinces of America, which has issued in the formation of the METHODIST EPISCOPAL CHURCH OF THE UNITED STATES, the largest "voluntary" and united Church that the world has yet seen ;—and of many others, who might be named, down to the present times. There exist abundant materials for a most interesting and instructive volume, which might be written under the title of "Methodism in the Army;" and I hope that some competent hand may be induced to undertake this labour of love. But I must leave this topic,—not, however, without offering my humble prayer that these renewed and extended efforts for the spiritual welfare of our brave soldiers may be greatly honoured and prospered by the blessing of the Divine Master!

In the course of a few months it was found that the room in Mr. Lucas's house was too small to admit the increasing numbers who wished to attend the services ; and the East Barracks being a mile distant from the town, the locality was inconvenient for the storekeepers, tradespeople, and their families, who wished to attend. I therefore hired a large room in the High Street, which had been used as a mess-room by the officers of the Royal African Corps, now about to be disbanded. Here we continued to worship with overflowing congregations for some months longer. The building was at length sold, and the congregation could then only obtain accommodation for a time in a carpenter's shop, belonging to one of our people on Settlers' Hill. This was, however, so small and inconvenient, that we were glad, after a time, to obtain the use, for Sunday services, of a good-sized building which had been erected to accommodate a so-called Odd Fellows' Lodge. Meantime, I had felt constrained to take measures for the erection of a chapel. I memorialized the Government for the grant of a piece of ground on which to build a place of worship ; but although my application had the approval of the deputy Landdrost or Magistrate of the district, so many delays and difficulties were raised by the chief functionaries at Cape Town, that I resolved to cut the matter short, by purchasing a plot of ground for the purpose, in the best place which at the time I could find for sale ; for there were not then many willing to sell who were able to give a legal title to their property.

The following extract from my Journal, dated exactly one year after our arrival at Algoa Bay, explains my views and feelings at this period concerning the erection of our first chapel in Graham's Town. The first portion of the extract, in reviewing the state of affairs in the Settlement, contains both light and shade, and expresses my joys and griefs, my hopes and fears, as a Minister of the Gospel.

" This is the anniversary of our landing at Algoa Bay. The review fills me with astonishment. Within one year desert and solitary places have been peopled by a multitude of men ; to make room for whom, even the beasts of the field have very evidently retreated from their ancient haunts ; houses have arisen, and villages sprung into existence, as if by magic ; hundreds of acres of land, which had hitherto lain untilled, have been disturbed by the plough, and the clods torn to pieces by the harrow; but what is better than all, many of those hills and dales, which echoed with no other music than the dreary screams of the jackal, the harsh croaking of the frog, or the dissonant notes of the raven, now resound with the praises of the Saviour. But while I view these things with satisfaction and delight, I must confess those feelings are mingled with regret and sorrow, that so little actual spiritual good has been done. The leaven of preaching, Prayer-meetings, and Sunday Schools has been introduced among a considerable number of the settlers; but the trials, cares, and vicissitudes which always attend the first adventurers in a new Colony, have hitherto counteracted its influence, and too generally produced worldly-mindedness, violation of the Sabbath, and an awful disrelish for the solemnities of religion. While, however, these circumstances tend to humble me in the dust, as having been so far unsuccessful, they are at the same time loud calls upon me for increased diligence; and I trust I can say, I am resolved to spend, and be spent, in the service of my God, and in promoting the spiritual benefit of all to whom I can obtain access.

"A strong sense of duty has urged me to visit other settlements, and Graham's Town, over and above what are considered as the demands of regular performance of duty at my proper Station. I am aware that if a chapel is built, service must be held on the Lord's day; but I am living in hopes of seeing another Missionary shortly, by whose assistance this may be effected. Indeed, such is the desire of the people for a chapel and a Missionary, that I have, as it were, been compelled to open a subscription for that purpose, which already amounts to a handsome sum for an African village; and I have no doubt of raising at least one half, if not three fourths, of the money necessary to build a convenient and decent place of worship; the rest, I have reason to believe, may be borrowed. Should we succeed, (and why should we not?) in forming a chain of

Mission Stations among the numerous heathen nations who inhabit the eastern coast of this continent, then the importance of a good Mission establishment in this District will be fully acknowledged.

"I trust, if you have not yet sent me help, you will consider these circumstances, as well as that we are about shortly to build a chapel in Graham's Town, the largest town in the district, a place where there is *no* place of worship and *no* Minister; and that there are several thousands of souls who, as far as I can see at present, must live without the means of grace, unless you send them one of those many soldiers of the cross, who are only waiting their destination from you."

The erection of our first Chapel in Graham's Town, although a plain call of duty, involved me in no small perplexity. In a country where there are many "well-wishers," but few having means to render much aid in such a work, he who commences chapel-building must needs take considerable responsibility upon himself. As the chapel was to be for the use of an English congregation, I knew the Missionary Society would not be likely, if requested, to grant any sum in aid of the undertaking. Nothing remained but that I must beg from all who were willing to give. A considerable number of persons subscribed small sums, as much, indeed, as generally they were at that time able to contribute; for money was scarce, and the country was then very poor. The building and land cost about £500, and first and last, with continuous effort, I was enabled to raise about one half the money; and, with no small difficulty, the remainder was borrowed at interest, till the income from pew-rents and collections should in time pay off the debt. When I laid the foundation-stone, with prayers and tears, in the midst of some fifty or sixty persons, I had but half-a-crown in my pocket, and only a number of promises of support, which were yet to be realized. But it was God's cause, and was committed to His gracious Providence, in humble trust that the zealous efforts we intended to make in raising the requisite means, would be crowned with success. While the building progressed, I was often in great straits to find money to meet the just demands of the builders. I frequently had to pay the cost of materials out of my own small allowances, and thus deprive myself and family, for a time, of many of what are called the necessaries of life. And here I rejoice to have an opportunity of recording, with grateful remembrance, the temporary assistance I occasionally received in the extremity of my difficulties from the late Adjutant Macdonald and his wife; for when I could do no more, they lent or procured for me temporary loans of small sums, which helped me over these first difficulties. Messrs. Lucas, Price, and Macdonald, all belonged to the army: the last-named, with his wife, had received spiritual benefit from our ministrations, and joined our church in Graham's Town. They were all liberal contributors to this first chapel. All of them have departed this life, and I trust have long ago discovered that the Saviour's promise, while it is generally fulfilled even in the present time, is realized in its utmost extent in that happy world to which, through His merits, they have been introduced: "Whosoever shall give you a cup of water to drink in My name, because ye belong to Christ, verily I say unto you, he shall not lose his reward."

I trust that this record of my early difficulties in chapel-building will not be cited by any as a justification of rash speculations of that kind. The case was peculiar. In the *same* circumstances I know not that I should another time pursue a different course; but if any will plead this case as a precedent to warrant rash and inconsiderate plunging into pecuniary embarrassments in the erection of chapels, where the call is less clear, and the ultimate prospect of success is much more doubtful, I would remind such persons that the result proved that

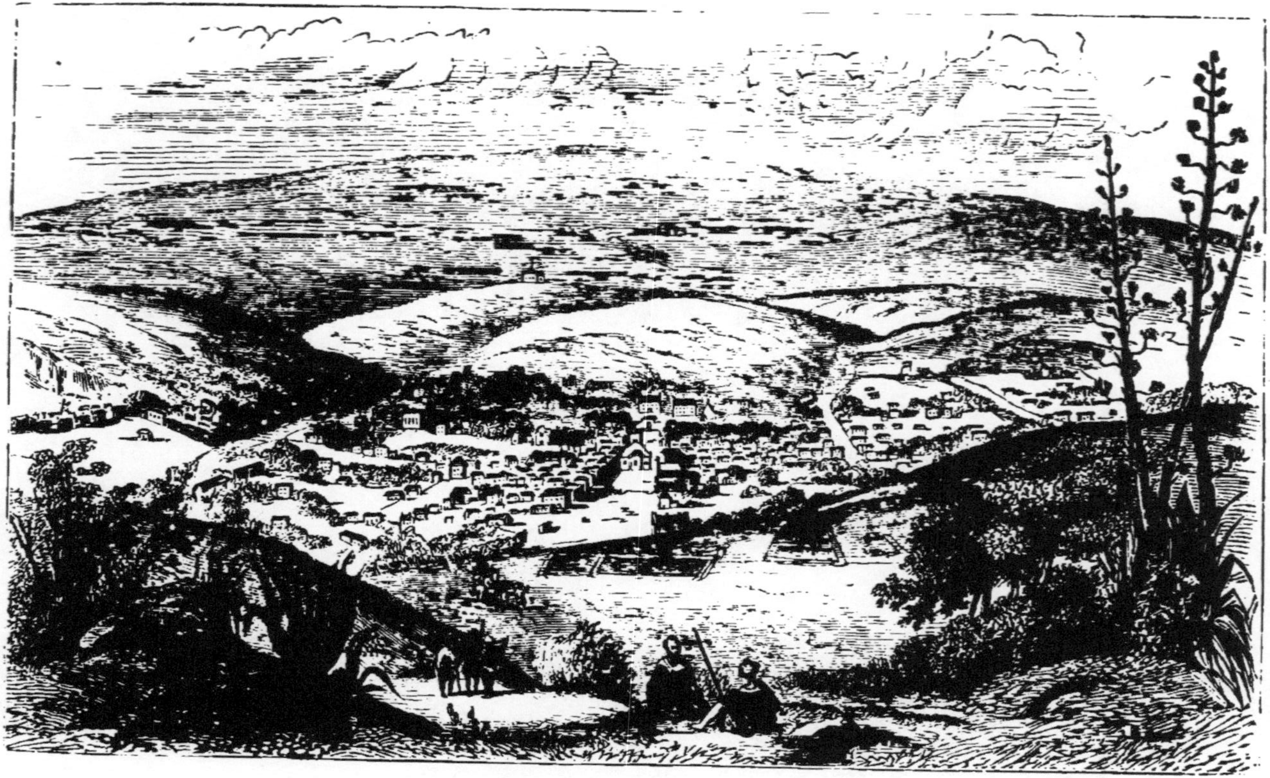

GRAHAM'S TOWN IN 1842.

all was right in this instance. No permanent embarrassment
was the result. We have always met our engagements ; and
although we subsequently built some much larger and more
costly chapels, for which, at times, we had to borrow thousands
of pounds, yet we were enabled to obtain these large loans with
far greater ease and facility than sums of ten or twenty pounds
were at first borrowed. It is to me a great satisfaction to reflect
that in all our chapel affairs connected with that country, no one
has ever lost any money ; nor has any person ever been compelled to pay any deficiency to meet obligations on account of
our chapels, beyond such sums as have been from time to
time voluntarily and cheerfully contributed by a liberal
people.

The foundation stone of the first Wesleyan chapel in Graham's
Town, referred to above, was laid on December 5th, 1821.   The
following entries in my Journal will best state my feelings and
views at that time concerning this event.

"October 16th, 1821.— At length I have succeeded in purchasing an eligible plot of ground, for the erection of a chapel
at Graham's Town. It has brought upon my mind a burden
which I would gladly have avoided ; but the step has not been
taken without much prayer and due respect to the advice of the
town clerk of Ephesus, 'Do nothing rashly.'

"December 5th.—This morning I had the satisfaction of
laying the foundation-stone of the new chapel at Graham's
Town. Prayer was offered to God for His blessing. Although
Graham's Town has had a considerable population, English,
Dutch, and Hottentot, for some time, yet I found on my arrival
no place of worship in it whatever, nor any public recognition
of the being of God. Of course morals were at a standard
extremely low. Some alteration for the better has at length
taken place. We have now a regular and decent congregation ;
and I trust, if God enable us to lay on the top-stone of the new

chapel, much more good will be done ; and especially when a Missionary shall arrive to take up his abode in the town."

On New Year's Day, 1822, I laid the foundation-stone of a chapel at Salem. The congregation continued to worship in the old reed and pole house. But now we set about erecting a more substantial and commodious building. The people cut down some fine yellow-wood trees, that were growing in a part of their location ; where, also, they procured a sufficient supply of rushes for thatching : and thus, with great labour, a portion of the materials was collected. As very little money was at that time in the possession of the friends of this undertaking, and the mechanics were all employed in Graham's Town, it was resolved to erect the building in such a manner, that nearly all could aid by the work of their hands. The ground being suitable for the purpose, the walls, which were about two feet thick and very solid, were constructed of pounded earth, slightly sprinkled with water : the prepared clay, being shovelled, to the depth of a few inches, into a moveable wooden frame, which was about six feet long, and one foot in depth, was then beaten or rammed by an instrument like one of those used by paviours. When the frame was filled, and the clay had remained a short time therein, it acquired consistency, being bound together by a constant sprinkling of water, during the beating or ramming part of the process ; the frame was then removed further on the wall, to repeat the operation. The result was that the walls were built in great blocks of earth, instead of large blocks of stone. After a layer of earth had thus been carried all round the building, a day or two was suffered to pass before another was placed thereupon, and in that bright climate the action of the sun was sufficiently powerful to dry and harden the material. This building stood for about ten years ; and when it was necessary to remove it, for the purpose of erecting a more suitable chapel, the clay walls were found to be so strong, that they occasioned much more labour to take down, than would have been required had the walls been made of brick or stone.

Many settlers and Missionaries built houses, during the early period of the Settlement, on a plan somewhat similar to what is called "Devonshire cob," of which many cottages in the south-western parts of England are erected. The process of building is, however, somewhat different to that just described : as, on this plan, the clay is well saturated with water, just as if bricks were intended to be formed thereof; and it is then mixed with chopped straw or grass, and laid on in layers about six inches in depth all round the building, leaving it for some days, till all is thoroughly dried by the sun, and ready to receive another layer, when the operation is repeated till the walls are raised to the required height. I have entered thus into detail because it is possible that this book may be read by some future Missionary or settler, who may be placed in similar circumstances ; and when a *substantial* building is required, where no masons or bricklayers are to be had, or where their wages would exceed the available means, I can recommend walls, built on either of the above principles, as likely to meet the necessities of the case ; since they require no mechanical skill, beyond taking care to keep the walls upright, while in process of erection.

Having commenced building the chapels at Graham's Town and Salem, and being still engaged in my regular itinerating visits to various parts of the Settlement, I was very fully occupied. I was, however, at that time a very young man ; and my abundant horse exercise, and other out-door employments, probably tended to give vigour to my constitution, which was originally not very strong. I had very little time or opportunity for reading or study ; and in a land where there were no booksellers, the opportunities of adding to my stock of books, at this period, were few and far between. It may be, however, that this necessity drove me to study more closely than I otherwise might have done, the small collection of standard works on theology and history which I possessed. Most of my sermons were studied on horseback, and, however defective in both matter and style, yet as they were generally adapted to the religious and varied circumstances of the people, in the absence of a better furnished and more competent Ministry, they were usually well received. All classes of the community were accustomed to attend the services, and I had reason to feel grateful that the great Head of the Church was pleased to use me as an instrument for the conversion of sinners and the confirmation of the souls of His saints. But it was not possible that I could give sufficient attention to the various places which required pastoral care.

The Local Preachers whose names I had introduced into the *first* Circuit Plan, were resident in various parts of the Settlement; viz., at Salem, Messrs. Oates and Roberts; at Smith's party, near the mouth of the Kowie River, Mr. Richard Walker; at Wilson's party, Mr. J. Ayliff; at New Bristol location, Mr. Shepstone; and at Clumber, the Nottingham party, Mr. W. Pike. I only mention the names of such as still continue, or of those who were accredited Preachers at the time of their decease. Some of those who were admitted on the first Plan, had been accredited Local Preachers before they left England; others had only occasionally conducted Prayer-meetings, and delivered exhortations in workhouses, hospitals, and cottages; but in the moral destitution of the Settlement, I found them all work to do, in promoting the religious welfare of the people; and our small Societies and congregations were greatly indebted to the zealous and laborious efforts of these brethren, who helped me much in the Lord. At a subsequent period two of them, Messrs. Ayliff and Shepstone, were introduced into our regular Ministry, and have proved themselves eminently faithful and useful Missionaries among the heathen tribes of Southern Africa;

while another of their number, Mr. Richard Walker, as a Catechist or Assistant Missionary, has rendered very valuable service for many years past on more than one of our Stations among the native tribes.   From a variety of causes the original number of Local Preachers whose services could be rendered available was diminished at a very early period : hence I wrote with earnestness and frequency to the Missionary Committee, to send at least one Missionary to aid me in my work.

I was, however, grievously disappointed about this time.   The Rev. Joseph Taylor had informed me by letter, that a Missionary had been directed to proceed from Cape Town to assist me in Albany ; but very soon after I had been cheered with this intelligence, I learned by a letter from Cape Town, that, previously to the arrival of these instructions, Mr. K., the Missionary referred to, had been sent off to the Bechuana Country, in company with Mr. Melville, a gentleman who was going to that region in the capacity of a government agent, and who had resigned a highly respectable and lucrative office in Cape Town, that he might go to the far interior, hoping thereby to promote the great work of Missions beyond the Orange River ; and although the Rev. T. L. Hodgson had just arrived from England, yet I was informed that he had come out with a special appointment for Cape Town, and I must therefore wait some other favourable opportunity before I could obtain help in Albany. This was very trying, but Divine Providence soon relieved me from my difficulties, and sent me helpers for the work wherein I was engaged.   The Missionary Committee, finding that I had been thus disappointed, promptly sent out for Albany the Rev. William Threlfall, a young man of deep piety and ardent missionary zeal, who reached Salem in May, 1822.

I had previously paid a visit to Somerset and Graaff Reinett; the former being about ninety, and the latter one hundred and seventy, miles north of Salem.   I visited Somerset at the

special invitation of R. Hart, Esq., who had been an officer in
the Cape Regiment, but was now the superintendent of an
extensive farming establishment conducted for the Colonial
Government, with a view to raise supplies of grain and cattle
for the troops on the frontier. After a few years the British
settlers were in a position to contract for these supplies, and
consequently this establishment was superseded, and the place
became a town, the head of a district, and residence of its Local
Magistrate and Civil Commissioner. On this my first visit I
was received with great kindness and hospitality by Mr. and
Mrs. Hart, and was happy in the opportunity of preaching the
Gospel to many who had long been deprived of the means of
grace, including a considerable number of what were called
" Prize Negroes,"—persons who had been found in the Portu-
guese slave vessels when captured by our cruisers on the coast.
When this Government farm was broken up, these people were
free to go where they pleased. Many of them ultimately settled
in Graham's Town, where they subsequently formed an interesting part of one of our native congregations.

We—W. Shaw, Broadbent, Kay, and Threlfall—all took part
in the opening services of the first chapel at Graham's Town,
which was dedicated to the service of God on Sunday, November 10th, 1822; and also at Salem, where the chapel was
opened for worship, December 31st, 1822. A letter which I
wrote about three months afterwards, will explain my views
and feelings on the general affairs of the Mission at this
period.

" Salem, *March* 29*th*, 1823.—We are making some small
progress on this Circuit, chiefly in matters preparatory, and in
securing a foundation for permanent work in Albany. The
Graham's Town chapel, which is a neat and substantial stone
building, was opened on the 10th of November last. I preached
in the morning; Mr. Kay in the afternoon, in Dutch; and Mr.

Threlfall in the evening. Mr. Barker, the London Society's Missionary, assisted in the services, and preached on the next evening, (Monday,) on which day we held a Love-feast in the chapel, and had a good season.   One thing that contributed to make it more than ordinarily interesting was, the presence of several of our Hottentot Society, who spoke with considerable propriety and feeling of the work of God in their souls. Mr. Barker, who favoured us with his presence on this occasion also, was requested to interpret, for the benefit of the English persons present, what was said by the Hottentots in Dutch. All, of every class, were much gratified and, I trust, edified on the occasion.   For my own part I cannot describe what I felt while sitting in the pulpit, and beholding before me Europeans and Africans in a mixed group, formerly so rare a sight in this colony,—hearing them tell, each in his own tongue, the wonderful dealings of God towards them; and this in a chapel which had cost me no common pains and perplexity in erecting, owing to a variety of circumstances, which I could neither foresee nor control.   When I considered how God had blessed, in the short space of about two years, our small and obscure beginning in Graham's Town, I indeed 'thanked God, and took courage.'   It was mentioned at the opening, as a motive for those present to give something more than on any common occasion, that this chapel is the first substantial building ever erected for the worship of God in the whole of the important and rising District of Albany.   I feel the more sincere gratitude to those friends who, by affording their pecuniary aid, enabled us to effect this important and new thing in Graham's Town.   A few individuals, whose names I would mention, but that they love to do good in private, rendered us the most praiseworthy assistance.   The chapel has been well attended ever since it was opened : all the pews are let, and more are being erected, to give additional accommodation to the persons not yet provided with seats. I hope much good will be done in that chapel to those who attend.

"We commenced a Sunday-school in Graham's Town immediately after the chapel was opened, in which there are about sixty scholars. We need very much a building for a school-house and chapel, for the Hottentots of Graham's Town, to be erected near the barracks. A great and good work might be done among them, if this were effected; but we cannot expect much without we have such a place. About five hundred rix-dollars have been subscribed, principally by the Hottentots themselves, towards this object: but we cannot enter upon it until we receive your reply to our request in the annual Minutes sent home two months ago, for a grant of fifty pounds to aid us in carrying into execution our plan.

"The Salem chapel was opened on the 81st of December, when brother Threlfall preached, and we held a Watch-night. On the 1st of January, Mr. Barker, of Theopolis, preached, and Mr. K. in the evening. Every one was affected with the consideration that a Christian congregation was now assembled, in a commodious and substantial place of worship, where, less than three years ago, the silence of the desert was undisturbed by the exercise of Divine worship. I hope this chapel will prove a blessing to future generations. It has cost me a great deal of trouble, as I had personally to superintend the building in its progress; but the poor people have helped as far as their peculiar circumstances and poverty would allow. At one end of the building a school-room is partitioned off: we have fitted it up with desks, &c., in a convenient manner: and, through the medium of H. Rivers, Esq., our Landdrost, I have prevailed on the Governor to appoint Mr. Matthews (mentioned in a former letter) to be schoolmaster to the settlers at Salem and its neighbourhood, with a salary from the Colonial Government, the only instance of the kind as yet in Albany. Thus our people will have the benefit of a free day-school, as well as Sunday-school, for their children.

"The settlers are still in general greatly depressed, in consequence of the failure of their successive crops: only one kind of wheat, called Bengal, has as yet succeeded; but that does very well, as do rye, barley, and oats. I have procured a quantity of the Bengal wheat for seed for our people, and I hope they will have better success this year. They are just beginning to plough. There has been, in many peculiar cases, very great distress among them; but when I think upon the accounts from Ireland, the distress among the settlers appears comparatively nothing. I speak generally; for I know, as hinted above, there have occurred some very distressing cases among the settlers. I have myself distributed aid to a considerable amount in a variety of such cases; which have arisen most frequently from accidental causes, and things more immediately connected with an infant state of society."

The Mission in Albany now assumed a regular and settled form. The congregations steadily increased, and our prospects of usefulness were very pleasing. We felt, however, that although there was full-work for two men, we were hardly justified in retaining three on the ground at that time, since very little could be expected from the people, to aid in defraying the cost of such a staff of Missionaries. I had been some time desirous of visiting Kaffraria, to see whether there was any opening for the establishment of a Mission among that numerous but heathen and barbarous race of people. I will narrate, in another part of this work, the steps that were taken, and which ultimately led to the commencement of a Wesleyan Mission in that country, at the end of the year 1823. As, however, there were difficulties which it took some time to remove, before we could commence the Kaffir Mission, my junior colleague, Mr. Threlfall, became somewhat impatient at the delay. He was dissatisfied with having to spend his time and strength almost exclusively in preaching to European settlers, since he had volunteered for the foreign department of ministerial labour, with a view to preaching the Gospel among the Heathen. I laboured to convince him that he was wrong in the view he took of our work in Albany, which, in my opinion, could not fail to be a great means of enabling us, at no distant date, to enter upon the difficult enterprise in Kaffraria, with much greater facilities and prospects of ultimate success, from our having a considerable body of European Christians so near, who would be likely to sympathize with us, and in various ways to aid our labours. We did not entirely agree in opinion on these points, but on all other subjects we were as one heart and soul. He was truly a holy and zealous young Minister; and notwithstanding his disappointed feelings in being obliged to labour amongst European colonists, instead of preaching the Gospel to the Heathen, which he strongly desired, I must bear my testimony here, as I have done in other publications, to the earnestness with which he strove to win souls. His labours among the settlers were brief, but "he was a burning and shining light." He was greatly loved and respected by them; and not a few attributed chiefly to his pulpit and pastoral efforts their being aroused to a sense of the importance and value of real religion.

Mr. Threlfall's views regarding the call of a Missionary in Africa, as being rather to labour among the Heathen than amongst professed Christians, had the entire sympathy, at that time, of the Rev. B. Shaw, who acted very much thereon in reference to the work at Cape Town, where the opportunities of gathering a considerable and influential English congregation were to some extent postponed in favour of efforts to collect a congregation of black and coloured people, to whom the Missionaries preached in the Dutch language. Perhaps, if I had not gone to South Africa as a Chaplain or Minister of a party of settlers, I might have adopted similar views; but, however this may be, I am fully satisfied by our past experience, that wherever there is a British Colony in juxtaposition with heathen tribes or natives, it will be our wisdom to provide for the spiritual wants of the Colonists, while at the same time we ought not to neglect taking earnest measures for the conversion of the Heathen.

As the Rev. B. Shaw favoured Mr. Threlfall's views, at a time when the prospect of an early commencement of the proposed Kaffir Mission was somewhat clouded, I consented that he should leave Albany, and proceed to Cape Town. On his arrival in May, 1823, he was at once introduced to Captain Owen of the Royal Navy, who had command of a surveying squadron employed on the Eastern Coast of Africa, and who offered to take him in H.M. frigate the "Leven," and put him ashore at Delagoa Bay, where Captain Owen represented that there was a most promising opening for a Mission. Mr. Threlfall without hesitation consented to go, and was eventually put on shore at the place indicated. There he remained about a year, living in the greatest discomfort in a very unhealthy climate, and was finally brought away, in what was considered to be a dying state, by the Captain of a whaling vessel. After he reached Cape Town, his health somewhat improved. He was then sent, at his own request, to our Station at Khamies Berg, Namaqualand, which being an elevated and salubrious region, the climate in a short time greatly renovated his health. After a time he started on a long and toilsome journey towards the country of the Great Namaquas and Damaras, on the Western Coast, among whom he hoped to preach the Gospel. He was accompanied by Jacob Links, an excellent native (Namaqua) Missionary. They were both attacked at night, while sleeping under a bush, and barbarously murdered by some miserable natives, for the purpose of plundering them of the few articles of food and other necessaries which they had in their possession. Thus did the excellent Threlfall offer up his life in the service of the Gospel.

Before I removed from Albany to commence the Kaffir Mission, in the latter part of 1823, the chapel in Graham's Town, which had only been dedicated for worship about a year previously, had become much too small; and as the congregation had greatly increased, we found it much easier to obtain means for enlarging the building than for its original erection. We therefore resolved to add to the length of the chapel one half of its existing dimensions, and to introduce a gallery at one end. By these means it was rendered capable of holding twice the original number of worshippers. While this work was in progress, it was necessary for me to proceed beyond the borders of the Colony on my projected Mission: hence Mr. K. was unavoidably left alone for a few months, till the arrival of the Rev. Samuel Young, who was speedily sent out by the Missionary Committee, to occupy the vacant Station at Salem, and whose steady and judicious labours and conduct proved of the greatest service to the Mission in Albany. I remained in Kaffraria for six years, when I was removed at the request of my brethren, and by the appointment of the Missionary Committee and the Conference, to Graham's Town, where it was thought I might best serve the cause as the resident Minister and Chairman of the District, which at this time was becoming very much extended in its geographical limits. During the six years of my residence in Kaffraria, we were enabled, under the guidance and blessing of Divine Providence, to establish four important Missions among the Kaffirs, and other parts of the country were opening to our labours.

The Missionary Committee nobly sustained us at this period, by reinforcing our numbers from time to time. In the early part of the year 1830, the Rev. Messrs. Palmer, Boyce, and Cameron arrived.   Mr. Palmer laboured diligently in Albany, and was very useful for about three years : he then proceeded to take charge of a Station in Kaffraria, where he prosecuted his work with most exemplary zeal and fidelity; and, after enduring much hardship, and encountering some serious dangers during two Kaffir wars, died suddenly while engaged in a noble and generous effort to secure the safe removal of the Missionaries and people of two Stations from a place where they were believed to be exposed to imminent peril of attack from exasperated foes.   Messrs. Cameron and Boyce happily still survive; but although that circumstance restrains my pen, yet I cannot refrain from saying that Mr. Cameron, who is at present stationed in Cape Town, has fully developed the great ability and devoted piety of which he gave very early promise. He has laboured in the vineyard, both within the Colony and in the far interior; and beyond many is an able workman, rightly dividing the word of truth.   The Rev. W. B. Boyce, after spending about thirteen years in Southern Africa, constrained by family reasons, returned to England; from whence, after two years, he proceeded, at the call of the Missionary Committee, to New South Wales, in the capacity of General Superintendent of Wesleyan Missions.   After a lengthened residence in that Colony, he took a distinguished part in preparing the way for the formation of the Australasian Conference, of which he was nominated the first President.   Mr. Boyce is now in England. A warm and mutual friendship, which dates from our first acquaintance, renders it needful for me to speak of his personal qualities under restraint; but the great and valuable services which he was enabled to render to our South African Mission, must, without regard to any feeling of private friendship, be made to appear in another part of this work, when I refer to the early history of the Wesleyan Missions in Kaffraria. Messrs.

John Edwards and W. J. Davis were the next Missionaries sent to reinforce our number.　Both of them have laboured long and most successfully in very remote parts of the interior; and I trust the great Head of the Church will yet spare them to be the instruments of turning many to righteousness.

The work in Albany had steadily progressed under the care of the Missionaries, during the period of my residence in Kaffraria.　It continued to do so after my appointment to Graham's Town.　In the year 1831, there was a remarkable revival of religion among the young people of the congregation. Several respectable families, who had for some time been attendants at our chapel, also participated in the religious quickening which was now vouchsafed by the Lord the Spirit.　Many were truly converted, and from that time commenced a course of consistent piety, which continues to this time; while others, after some years of Christian devotedness, died happy in the faith of our Lord Jesus Christ, leaving the most pleasing reminiscences to their surviving friends, of the beauty and excellence of their religious character, and their devoted zeal in the cause of their Redeemer.

The enlarged chapel now became much too small, notwithstanding that many families who had been originally Independents, Presbyterians, or Episcopalians, had transferred their attendance to the St. George's Episcopal church, or to the Independent chapel, which had been recently erected in the town.　The growth of the congregation rendered it once more necessary to take steps for the erection of a larger Methodist chapel; which it was resolved should also possess a much improved architectural character, and stand on a better site than that occupied by the old building.　The people contributed liberally; and a chapel, which cost in all about three thousand pounds, was erected.　It afforded comfortable accommodation for a congregation of seven or eight hundred persons.　It was opened for public worship on Sunday, the 16th of December, 1832.   I preached in the forenoon; the Rev. Mr. Monroe (Independent) in the afternoon; and the Rev. W. J. Shrewsbury in the evening.   The Rev. Mr. Davis, Baptist Minister, preached on the following Monday evening.   The collections at these opening services amounted to more than one hundred pounds: showing the growing means and the increasing interest of the people; for at the opening of the first chapel the collection scarcely exceeded twenty pounds.   Most of the pews were speedily let; and the large additional accommodation soon began to be occupied by an increasing and serious congregation. The old chapel was retained as a school-house and place of worship for the use of a native congregation; consisting, at this time, chiefly of prize Negroes of various African nations, and Hottentots, for whose benefit Divine worship had been some time conducted in the Dutch language.

Having for family reasons obtained leave from the Missionary Committee to visit England, I left the Colony, for that purpose, in the month of March, 1833.   I was succeeded at Graham's Town by the Rev. W. J. Shrewsbury, who had been several years in South Africa, and had commenced the important Mission among the tribe of Kaffirs belonging to the great Chief Hintsa.   His reputation, as a faithful Minister of Christ, had preceded his arrival in Southern Africa; for the events connected with the destruction of the chapel in which he had preached in the Island of Barbadoes, and his providential escape from the hands of a mob excited to fury against him by the most groundless reports and extravagant misrepresentations, had given him an undesired, but honourable, notoriety among all who wished well to the black and coloured races in our Colonies, and who felt interested in the progress of Christianity among them. The very able and truly evangelical character of Mr. Shrewsbury's ministry, together with his zealous pastoral efforts, was of the greatest service, and many were thereby attracted to the new chapel. A most painful domestic bereavement obliged him to leave South Africa and return to England, after a comparatively short sojourn in Graham's Town; but he left behind him an undying reputation for piety, ministerial ability, and fidelity. On my departure for England the Mission had not been quite thirteen years established, and the state of the work in Albany at this time is correctly represented in the following extract from a report which I wrote for the use of the General Secretaries of the Missionary Society in London.

"A second chapel has been built in Graham's Town by the Wesleyan Society. It was opened on the 16th of December last, and is a very handsome and substantial building, capable of accommodating about eight hundred hearers. The original chapel, which affords room for upwards of four hundred persons, is now used as a school-house, and also as a place of worship for the black and coloured population, for whose benefit it is requisite to hold separate services, as they do not generally understand the English language.

"Within a period of thirteen years, no less than thirteen substantial chapels have been erected in various parts of the settlement by the voluntary contributions of the inhabitants. In several parts of the District, were it not for these chapels, the settlers would have no facilities whatever for regularly attending public worship. Sunday schools have been established in connexion with these places of worship; and, in the Wesleyan schools alone, about eight hundred children and adults, including white and black, bond and free, are taught to read the word of God, and instructed in the principles and morals of the Christian religion.

"By these means not only has the English population been preserved from moral degeneracy, but the tone of moral and religious feeling now existing amongst them would not suffer by

WESLEY CHAPEL, SCHOOL, AND MISSION HOUSE, GRAHAM'S TOWN.

a comparison with the high standard which prevails in the most enlightened districts of Great Britain. At the same time the aborigines have not been neglected ; many of those who reside within the British settlement have been brought under the influence of Christianity; a very encouraging number have received baptism, and are now consistent members of the Christian Church."

CHAPTER IV.

The Kaffir Mission, 1823–1830.

WITH Mr. Shaw, the English settlement at Salem had always been regarded as a stepping-stone to a Kaffir Mission. He remarks:—

FROM the time when I received my appointment to Southern Africa, as Chaplain or Minister to a party of British settlers, my mind was filled with the idea that Divine Providence designed, after I had accomplished some preparatory work among the settlers who were located on the border of Kaffraria, that I should proceed beyond the colonial boundaries, and establish a Wesleyan Mission among the Kaffirs. Hence I resolved not to be disobedient to the heavenly call; but while steadily pursuing the work of the day, my eye was constantly fixed on Kaffraria, as a great field for future Missions. I thought about it, talked about it, read every scrap of intelligence I could obtain concerning it, and often prayed and engaged others to pray with me, that "a wide and effectual door" might in due season "be opened" before us into these "regions beyond." My views and feelings on this subject were expressed in a letter to the Missionary Committee, written at Salem in the year 1820, only a few months after my arrival at that place.

"This Station will be the key to Kaffirland, a country abounding with heathen inhabitants. Certainly the present is not tho time for penetrating that country; but I hope the present turbulent spirit of that people will soon begin to subside, and then I should wish to see a Wesleyan Missionary ready to take advantage of the opportunity to enter and proclaim upon their mountains 'good tidings, and to publish peace and salvation.' The time might soon follow, when you would see on your lists Stations among the Tambookies, the Mambookies, and the various tribes of people between us and Delagoa Bay.

"I hope the Committee will never forget that, with the exception of Latakoo, which is far in the interior, *there is not a single Missionary Station* between the place *of my residence*, and *the northern extremity* of the *Red Sea ;* nor any people professedly Christian, with the exception of those of Abyssinia. Here, then, is a wide field,—the *whole eastern coast of the continent of Africa!* If ever the words of the Saviour were applicable to any part of the world at any time, surely they apply to Eastern Africa at the present time : ' *The harvest is great, but the labourers are few.*' How should Christian men pray that the 'Lord of the harvest would send forth labourers into His harvest !'"

I was now in correspondence with the Governor, through the Landdrost of the District, for the purpose of obtaining permission to establish a Mission in Kaffraria. The Government was was at first, however, very much opposed to my project. The non-intercourse policy was deemed the only safe system for preserving the peace of the border : consequently, although a letter which I had written as to the desirableness of establishing fairs or markets within the Colony, under the sanction and surveillance of the Government, to which the Kaffirs might resort for barter and trade, had been well received, and secured for me the respect of the high officials of the Colony, yet it was deemed very undesirable that any Missionary Society should be permitted to commence a Mission in Kaffraria. The Governor was not inclined to allow any attempt of that kind to be made, beyond the establishment which had recently been commenced at Chumie ; this Station being a species of combined political and religious Mission, sustained at the cost and charge of the Colo-

nial Treasury, and consequently under the immediate instructions and control of the Government.

The Amaxosa or Border nation was at this period, and till a
very recent date, politically divided into two nearly equal
parties; the tribes living furthest from the sea being called by
the Colonists the Gaika tribes, and those inhabiting the coast
country being designated the Dhlambi tribes,—from the names
of the two most powerful Chiefs then living near the Colony.
The coast tribes, however, included the tribe of Hintsa,
(Amagcaleka,) the most powerful of all the Chiefs, who, indeed,
was regarded by them as the hereditary paramount Chief of the
whole nation.

This Station, (Chumie,) a semi-official Mission of the
Colonial Government, aided by Missionaries of the Scotch
and London Societies, which had succeeded to the original
Mission commenced by Dr. Vanderkemp and Williams, of
the London Missionary Society, 1799–1818, was at that
time the only Mission in Kaffirland. Mr. Shaw wisely considered that by these brethren the Gospel call had been
presented to the Gaika tribes, and that his plain course
was to begin with the Amagonakwabi tribes near the
coast.

I resolved, "God being my helper," steadily to pursue the
openings of Divine Providence in this direction; and, if aided
by the Society at home with the requisite means, to use my
utmost efforts to establish "a chain of Wesleyan Mission
Stations," beginning near the border of the Colony, and
extending along the coast country of Kaffraria to Natal and
Delagoa Bay.

He had made himself acquainted with the ethnological
and political relationships of the Kaffir tribes.

The Gaika tribes at this period, besides that of the Amangqaika, comprised the Amanbalu under Enno, the Imidanke under Botuman, and the Amantinde under Tshatshu, with some smaller dependent clans. The coast tribes consisted of the Amagcaleka under Hintsa, the Amandhlambi under Dhlambi, and the Amagonakwaybi under Pato, often at this period called the Congo tribe, from a colonial corruption of the name of Pato's father and predecessor Kungwa. To these were also attached a number of petty clans, who were more or less under the control of the respective Chiefs. The whole nation was thus divided into two nearly equal portions; and efforts were made from time to time by Kaffir politicians to preserve "the balance of power." The circumstances of the border, however, together with those ever-recurring causes of irritation and dispute, which, with more complete knowledge of the native African races, we are now aware always existed, had produced very great alienation and strife among them. The coast Kaffirs, living in a separate part of the country, and being placed under an entirely distinct jurisdiction, owing no fealty to the Gaika Chiefs, and having at the head of their confederation the great Chief Hintsa, were impatient of all interference in their affairs by Gaika, from whose tribes they had latterly been entirely dissociated by the course of political events.

Mr. Shaw paid a visit to Chumie, August 22nd–September 12th, 1822, and again, in company with Mr. Shepstone, and John Tzatzoe as interpreter, in July, 1823, on his way to visit Congo, Pato, and Kama, the Chiefs of the Gunukwabi tribe, among whom he hoped to establish his Mission. Having obtained the consent of the Chief, they at once returned to the Colony, to make preparations for the removal of their families, and for the commencement of their great undertaking.

My visit to the country of Pato having cleared away the last difficulty, nothing was now required but that we should as soon as practicable remove into Kaffraria, and take up our residence near that Chief.   Accordingly, on September 10th, 1823, I removed my family from Salem to Graham's Town, preparatory to our departure for Kaffraria.   It will not surprise the reader that a happy connexion with the settlers of Salem, which had lasted for nearly four years,—reckoning from my first introduction to them as their Pastor in London, before we migrated to Southern Africa,—could not be dissevered without mutual pain and regret.   But I was satisfied as to the path of duty; and the people who were thus to be deprived for a season of the residence of a Minister in the midst of them, believing that it was better they should submit to this temporary disadvantage, rather than the opportunity for establishing a Mission should be lost, kindly acquiesced in the arrangement, and sent us away with many tears, offering, at the same time, many prayers for our safety and success.   Thus the little Society at Salem became a mother Church not only to the other Methodist Churches within the Colony, but likewise attained the honour of standing in that relation to many native Churches which have since been formed "in the regions beyond."

At this time the Rev. B. Shaw, of Cape Town, wrote, in reply to a letter from the Rev. W. Shaw, the following remarks : "Were I in your situation, I should go into Kaffirland, and leave your colleague and the Local Brethren to do their best.   Considering the wants of this land, they (the Colonists) would still have their portion, and especially as they have got a Minister, and are going to erect a chapel at Graham's Town.   It is impossible for me to say whether or not you ought to take a carpenter and mason with you, as I am unacquainted with the local circumstances of the country altogether, nor do I consider myself as having anything to do in an official way in your part of Africa." This letter was dated July 10th, 1823. It is strange that no Biography of this the first of our South African Missionaries, the man whose journals, written in the purest idiomatic English, helped to raise and perpetuate the Missionary feeling in England, has yet appeared. A selection from his journals, preceded by a brief notice of his previous history, and a continuation of the same to the end of his life, would be a valuable addition to our Missionary literature. The Rev. Barnabas Shaw had no showy qualities, and he never had a Missionary sphere commensurate with his abilities; but he was one of our worthies to be held in everlasting remembrance.

We now return to Mr. Shaw's own statement :—

We were detained at Graham's Town by imperative family circumstances; meantime, a terrific storm occurred, and continued ten or twelve days, during the month of October, which not only did great damage, but filled all the rivers to overflowing, so that the Great Fish River, at that time the colonial boundary, could not be crossed for several weeks. Our time was, however, fully occupied in making many needful preparations for our arduous undertaking. Two wagons were purchased, each to be drawn by twelve oxen; we also provided the needful outfit of horses and saddlery, bedding, and other articles required in the wagons, which for a time were to form our only sleeping accommodation. Cooking utensils, camp stools, and tables, with a supply of meal, and groceries, which we calculated might last us some months, it was needful to take,—there being no stores or shops in the land whither we were going. The only food which we should be able to purchase from the natives, would be cattle for slaughter, milk, and Kaffir corn, with, possibly, pumpkins, and some other vegetable productions.

At length, all things seemed to be ready; my wife had recovered from her recent accouchement, the wagons were already partially loaded, and our departure was near at hand, when suddenly there was an alarming rumour of a Kaffir inroad. Parties of the natives had, within a few days, carried off many cattle from some frontier farms, and murdered two or more herdsmen; going off with the cattle with such rapidity to their fastnesses in the mountains, that the small body of troops in the neighbourhood had no chance of overtaking them, or recovering the plundered property. This report naturally produced much excitement in the country; and some of our kind-hearted friends who had often expostulated with me on the folly of going to live among these native tribes, now resolved to offer a final remonstrance on the subject. They represented to me, that the Mission was as yet too hazardous; that time and the course of events, bringing the Kaffirs more into intercourse with the English, would be likely to smooth, if not entirely remove, many existing difficulties; that it was doubtful whether I ought to leave the various congregations which had been gathered in Albany to the care of one Missionary, even for a few months, supposing that the Missionary Committee should send another Missionary within a year, which they regarded as doubtful: and, above all, it was urged that recent events showed the untamed and ferocious character of the Kaffirs, and that nothing could be expected to result from this rash procedure, but that myself, and wife, and children, with all who accompanied us, would be robbed and murdered, since even the Government regarded the Dhlambi and Congo or Coast tribes as the most audacious of the whole Kaffir nation, they having actually stormed and nearly captured Graham's Town only five years before that time!

I cannot say that these suggestions and remonstrances produced no effect on me. I felt my mind burdened and oppressed with a load of care and anxiety. But happy is the Missionary who has a good and faithful wife, that sympathizes in his objects and aims, and who, in addition to an affectionate heart that affords solace in sorrow, likewise possesses a sound judgment, qualifying her to offer counsel in time of difficulty. Many Missionaries have been so favoured, and can understand my feelings, while I acknowledge how much benefit I derived from the self-sacrificing spirit and noble bearing of my wife at this trying crisis. When I repeated to her what our friends had urged upon me, and asked what she thought we ought to do; entering into the whole case with calmness and clearness, she gave utterance to several pertinent remarks, saying in substance, and nearly in the following words, "You have long sought and prayed for this opening; Divine Providence has now evidently set the door open before us; expenses have been incurred in the purchase of outfit; you stand pledged to the Chiefs; and the character and conduct of the Kaffirs only show how much they need the Gospel. We shall be under Divine protection;" closing all with these emphatic words, "*Let us go in the name of the Lord.*" With a full heart and streaming eyes, I answered, "That reply has settled the matter, and we will start as soon as I hear that the Great Fish River is likely to be practicable for the wagons to pass." I now felt that I could almost have addressed our kind friends in the words which Paul spake to the disciples at more than one place, when going on a mission which portended danger: "What mean ye to weep and to break my heart?" "None of these things move me, neither count I my life dear unto myself, so that I might finish my course with joy, and the ministry which I have received of the Lord Jesus, to testify the

Gospel of the grace of God."　But when our friends heard my final resolve, they "ceased" from further importunity, and said, "The will of the Lord be done."

On the 13th day of November we left Graham's Town, and commenced our journey to Kaffraria.　The party consisted of (1.) Myself and Mr. Shepstone.　We rode on horseback.　(2.) My wife and Mrs. Shepstone, with their respective children, my wife's youngest being a babe about six weeks old: these were all placed together in one wagon, and were most uncomfortably crowded.　The other wagon contained many heavy articles, with spades, pickaxes, and implements of various kinds.　(3.) In the second wagon, three or four native women with children, being domestics, or wives of our two wagon-drivers and interpreter. The drivers were Hottentots; and the interpreter was a young Kaffir, who had married a Hottentot wife.　Having resided some time at the London Society's Station of Theopolis, he had obtained a very limited acquaintance with the frontier patois, or native Dutch; and it was through him that we hoped to communicate with the Kaffir Chiefs and people, on our arrival and settlement in their country.

At that period, Dundas Bridge, which now spans a deep gully at the lower or northern end of High Street, in Graham's Town, and through which the Kowie stream or river flows, had not been erected; and it was not very easy to cross it with loaded wagons: hence an accident occurred to the *riem chain*, or wheel-lock, of one of the wagons, while running down the rocky bank to the stream, by which two or more spokes of one of the wheels were broken.　"A bad omen," said one, "at the very starting; you had better even now give it up and stay with us."　Some slight repair was soon completed; and we continued our course, until we had arrived at a spot about six or seven miles from town.　At this place it was requisite to *uitspan* or unyoke the oxen, and make preparations to stay during the night; and here about a dozen of our friends, who had accompanied us on horseback, took an affectionate leave of us; not, however, till we had all knelt down on the green grass, and two or three of their number had poured forth earnest prayers to the God of heaven, that He would have us in His holy keeping, and give us a safe journey and a prosperous entrance among the Heathen. To many who reside on the frontier and in Kaffraria, it will seem strange that what is at present regarded as an every-day occurrence, and a journey which now excites no more apprehension among the Colonists than a trip from London to Paris usually does in England, should have been regarded as so serious an undertaking. But at the period to which I am referring, (1823,) for Europeans to go with their wives and children among the Dhlambi tribes or coast country Kaffirs, was considered to be an almost certain course to destruction. The amazing difference which time and the changes produced by missionary labour, commercial intercourse, and political events, now present in this respect, is only a part of the manifold evidence which is patent to all men, proving the steady progress and improvement which has taken place in that country.

I cannot more accurately narrate the principal circumstances connected with our removal into Kaffraria, and reception by the Chiefs, than by quoting a few passages from a communication which I wrote at the time, and which, whatever attention it may have arrested at that period by its publication in a missionary periodical, will, I am assured, be entirely new to the great majority of those who are likely to read this volume. It was requisite that we should enter Kaffraria by way of the Chumie, and pass through the country of Gaika; and, consequently, our journey being very circuitous, we had to travel upwards of one hundred and sixty miles, while the distance by a more direct road, which I afterwards marked out and opened on my first visit to the Colony, was found to be about eighty miles. In travelling to Fort Beaufort, on our way to Chumie, we were also obliged to pursue a route much more circuitous than that which the troops subsequently opened up in a more direct line. Just about the time we started, I learned that a strong commando of troops and Dutch farmers was about to enter the north-western portion of Kaffraria, to make reprisals for the large number of cattle recently stolen by the Kaffirs; and that another military force would simultaneously go on the same errand among the coast Kaffirs. As these operations were to be commenced at opposite ends of the Kaffir frontier, our travelling in the country, while the Kaffirs were under the excitement produced by the entrance of the troops among them, did not seem a favourable conjuncture of affairs. It will be seen that there is some reference to these events in the extract below.

After our friends took leave of us, as narrated above, the night became very rainy. Our canvas tent attached to the wagon, not having been properly made, proved but a poor shelter; and as the water dripped through upon us, we were obliged to spread a large umbrella. My wife and children huddled together for shelter under it, as best they could; and Mrs. Shepstone and her children occupied the wagon; so that at the commencement we did not enjoy any very luxurious accommodation.

"The next day we arrived at Kooster's Drift, or Ford, over the Great Fish River: all the fords had been rendered impassable for wagons during several weeks, by the very heavy rains that had fallen: the river was still deep and rapid. There is a perpendicular fall at this place, from the top of the south bank to the water, of between twenty and thirty feet: the river had, however, during the rains, far overflowed its channel. Some soldiers had been at work, cutting a road to the river through the bank; and it was with great difficulty, though promptly aided by them, that we succeeded, after about three hours' toil, in getting both the wagons and everything else safely to the opposite side of the water; but it was very dangerous work. One of our men was nearly drowned; but we had reason to be thankful to God that all ended well. Ours were the first wagons that had crossed that ford since the rains.

"We proceeded on our journey from the Fish River on the 15th, and in the afternoon crossed the Gonappe, which was also done with great difficulty. On the following Monday, the 17th, we crossed the Kat River, and arrived at Fort Beaufort, a new fort, building with a view to check the incursions of the enterprising Kaffirs in that direction. The country around this place is extremely beautiful.

"On Wednesday, the 19th, we proceeded on our journey through an unoccupied and trackless country, until the next morning, when we entered Kaffirland, and arrived at Chumie, the Station of the Government Missionaries. Messrs. Thomson and Bennie and Mrs. Thomson received us in the most friendly manner; and circumstances rendering it necessary for us to remain with them ten days, we received from them such marked hospitality and kindness as leave us much their debtors. Mr. Brownlee had not returned from Cape Town, but was on his way, accompanied by a Missionary of the Glasgow Society, who on his arrival will, in conjunction with Mr. Bennie, commence a Station, under the direction of that Society.

"A commando had entered the coast part of Kaffirland, while we were on the road, and had proceeded to Pato's country, to make reprisals for the cattle recently stolen, and which had been traced in that direction. I therefore deemed it proper to send a messenger to Pato, to know if he were still friendly, and still desired us to take up our residence with him. In a few days the messenger returned with Pato's earnest entreaty, that we would proceed to them immediately: he sent, at the same time, *seven men* to protect and assist us, in our journey through Kaffirland to his residence. Everything being therefore more full of promise than we had anticipated, we commenced our journey from Chumie on the 1st of December, and on the 5th arrived in safety at the place selected for the Station when I was here the last time.

' "We had to make a road for the wagons from Chumie to this place, in doing which many a tree fell before the hatchets of the Kaffirs who accompanied us, and who, including several that had followed us from Chumie, amounted to between twenty and thirty in number. The road was intersected by a great number of streams, that run from the mountains in the north into the Keiskamma; fords over these had to be discovered, rendered passable, &c.,—in all which we found the Kaffirs very useful: the only remuneration they expected or received was presents of beads.

"Although surrounded in many places by multitudes of people, the men sent by Pato were so attentive, that we lost nothing during the journey; notwithstanding that the Kaffirs, like all other barbarous nations, are notorious for thieving.

"We crossed parts of the districts under the authority of the Chiefs Gaika, Enno, Botuman, and Dhlambi, before we entered the district under Pato, which is a long narrow slip along the coast. Gaika and his son Makomo we saw at Chumie; Botuman we saw at a place where we unyoked our oxen, near his residence; he would have been very glad to have received us into his district, if we had not been under a promise to Pato.

"We were received on our arrival here by Pato and his brothers, Kobi (Congo) and Kama, with a great number of their people,

as though we had been making a triumphal entry: all was
bustle; and, as is usual where many wild, untutored people are
assembled together, all was noise and clamour; everything
about us was wonderful, and excited the greatest astonishment;
our wagons, our wives, our children, all were examined with
attention, and appeared to make the spectators wonderfully
loquacious.   Our wagons were drawn up under the shade of
one of the beautiful yellow-wood trees that grow along the
side of the river; here we outspanned (unyoked) the oxen, pitched
our tent, and praised God for having brought us in safety to the
place where we would be.

"The next day Pato and his brothers, with a number of their
Council and inferior Captains, assembled: a variety of subjects
were discussed, connected with my intentions, and purposed
mode of procedure, &c.; and all appeared well pleased.   They
said some flattering things, in the true Indian style, which I
should not repeat here, only that it may help to give you an
idea of some parts of their character.   Among other things the
Chiefs said, From henceforth I should be their *father*, and they
would make of me, as the interpreter rendered it, a '*bescherm
bosch*,'—*i. e.*, a bush of defence from wind and rain; meaning,
I should be their defence in an evil day.   These expressions, beyond doubt, resulted from sincere and honest feelings;
but they could not avoid tinging them with the flattery and
adulation usually employed when addressing a Chief or
Headman."

Having thus established ourselves on the River Twecu, close
to the residence of the three brother Chiefs, Pato, Kobi, and
Kama, we immediately commenced building operations.   Until
a house could be erected, we lived under the umbrageous
branches of some noble yellow-wood trees growing by the side
of the stream; the wagon and its attached tent affording, when
it did not rain, tolerable sleeping accommodation at night.

We used to perform our very scant toilet in the morning in a sheltered nook of the river. Our wives and the domestics managed the cooking, and we usually ate our meals and performed our daily domestic worship in the open air, often with scores of the natives, especially women and children, looking on with undisguised surprise and amusement. Indeed, from about ten o'clock till a short time before sunset, we were frequently beset by crowds, who remained around us the whole day. Their curiosity at first, and afterwards their pilfering, became so troublesome, that I was obliged to ask the Chief to appoint one of his men as a sort of sentry or police-officer, in order to protect our wives from much annoyance, particularly during the absence of myself and Mr. Shepstone from the wagons. This was readily granted, and an old umpagate undertook the duty with great good-will. He carried the usual Kaffir *intonga*, or fencing stick : and when boys or men ventured to make themselves, as he considered, too intrusive, a few hard strokes and raps falling on those who were unlucky enough to be at the moment within reach of attack, soon dispersed the crowd. I mention this principally to show that when it was known that the Chiefs had really issued an order, and armed this man (Kalaku) with their authority, no one dared to resist. In fact, his *intonga* was as effective a protection as the staff of a policeman could be in London. But, after all, the crowds of gazers and idlers, who kept up an incessant gabble all day long, and many of whom were intent on seizing any favourable moment for stealing such articles as happened to be unavoidably left lying about on the ground, frequently occasioned much annoyance. Sometimes, indeed, our food was stolen out of the cooking-pots, when the servant's attention happened for a short time to be diverted to some needful occupation. It required patience and temper to endure these petty annoyances, which were especially trying to our wives. But we soon learned to look for the approach of sunset, when we should enjoy some degree of quiet; for we observed that as that time approached, the natives invariably began to leave us, those who had come far going first, until at length, by the time the sun had disappeared, scarcely an individual remained.

These crowds of natives assembled around us daily for several weeks after our arrival in the country. Many came to offer us articles of food for barter. We required a constant supply, as I had regularly to provide for more than twenty persons, including children and the natives, servants, &c.; and as we speedily hired a number of men to assist us in our building operations, food was likewise required for them. I agreed, however, to pay them wages, and therefore left them to purchase their own food, only supplying them occasionally as the nature of their employment rendered necessary. The reason the natives always dispersed at sunset, we soon discovered to be, that it was then necessary for the men and boys to go to the common fields and look up their cattle, and drive them to their folds for the night, after which followed the process of milking the cows, while the women were also busy in preparing food. The supper, at seven or eight o'clock in the evening, being the principal meal for all Kaffirs, no one likes to be absent from his place in the mess circle at that hour. The men, the women, and the children used to eat in separate groups; but woe to the wight that was missing at supper time! No food would be saved or put away for the use of the late comer, who, when arriving after time, could never hope to make up his loss, but must go supperless to his couch (mat), and learn to be a more careful observer of punctuality for the future.

I have mentioned that we carried on a sort of barter with the Kaffirs for food, and paid wages to the men who assisted in our work. The question will naturally arise in the mind of the reflecting reader, what constituted the medium of barter and of payment of wages among these people in this low state of barbarism. I will endeavour to explain this, and at the same time remove an absurd prejudice which has fastened itself on many ingenuous minds who have never been placed in circumstances favourable to the practical consideration of this subject. It involves, of course, a question of morals. It would be unjust to take anything from natives which is not in their country a fair equivalent for that which they give. I admit this, or rather I would strenuously contend for it, as a matter of mere justice between man and man. And yet I felt no scruple in dealing with the natives for such articles as we required for our personal use, and giving them in barter beads, buttons, brass wire, cotton handkerchiefs, and pieces of iron ; for these were in fact the principal articles which we used in exchange, and in which we paid the wages of our work people. Many Missionaries in other uncivilized countries have felt obliged to act in a similar manner. We had, indeed, at this time no option in the matter. The natives knew nothing of the value of money. A few of them who had been in the Colony had some very vague idea concerning it; but the Dutch farmers had never accustomed them to the use of it. In fact, at that period, they had very little else but paper rix-dollars themselves. Hence we could purchase nothing from the natives with money. I have more than once, as a mere experiment, knowing, however, pretty well how it was likely to end, offered gold or silver in one hand, and a brass button or two in the other, for the purchase of a " basket " of milk, or other article of food ; but the buttons were invariably preferred. Indeed, at that time no real Kaffir residing in that part of the country would have parted with anything that he valued in exchange for money in any form.

The intrinsic worth of the articles necessarily given by us in exchange (like bank notes) was indeed small ; but their relative value at the time and for many years afterwards was very great. We paid the daily wages of a Kaffir in beads, buttons, or brass wire, giving him the choice of these articles on an adjusted scale as to quantity and value. But he felt himself to be liberally rewarded for his labour, because, after providing himself with food, his wages would leave him a surplus by which he could in one month purchase from his countrymen an ox; or in two months he could easily save from his wages sufficient to purchase two or three cows, or three or four young heifers. Indeed, although at this time the cost to us for the labour of a Kaffir,—such as it was,—certainly did not exceed threepence a day, yet we could have had any number of Kaffir labourers, as soon as they discovered that it was a ready road to wealth. Many a native, after continuing some time in our employment, managed, on leaving us, to purchase as many cows and heifers with the proceeds of his labour as placed him in the condition of a Kaffir gentleman; and, as they all possessed a common right to the grass lands for the use of their cattle, he speedily retired from business with what he deemed a competence! Certainly our circulating medium at this time was more convenient than the cowrie shells used by the natives of Western Africa among themselves. The beads, buttons, and brass wire maintained their value in the country for years, because they were required and considered essential as an ornamental part of the dress of the people, more especially that of the females; and no marriage could be celebrated in the country without the interchange of large quantities of these commodities.

While busily occupied in various pursuits connected with the erection of our buildings, in all which I found the assistance and experience of Mr. Shepstone to be invaluable, I availed myself of frequent opportunities to exercise my great commission as a preacher of the Gospel to this people. Watching favourable opportunities, I used to assemble a group of them,

and desire them to sit down on the grass, while I told them the
"good news" which I had brought to them. It was at first
very difficult to induce them to listen with patience. They
were fond of argument and disputation. I was constantly
interrupted on these occasions by questions; and often found
myself in the position of a person to be catechized, rather than
in that of the teacher. Gradually, however, these visitors and
strangers began to listen with more attention. On one occasion,
while engaged with a party of this kind, I wished to introduce
something like an act of worship, in addition to my familiar
talk with them concerning the Gospel; but as they had never
been accustomed to any kind of religious worship,—for the
Kaffirs are not even worshippers of idols,—they did not readily
comprehend my intentions. I, however, desired the interpreter
to explain that I wished them all "to kneel on the grass as
they would see me do. I was about to speak to God, and ask
Him to do us good; and, as He is great and holy, we must
prostrate ourselves before Him." After some difficulty they all
imitated me, and knelt down in a circle; but there was one
droll fellow among them who, on looking around and noticing
the new and strange attitude which they had assumed, could
not restrain his risible faculties; he began to laugh immode-
rately; a fit of cachinnation spread itself around the circle,
and, for the time, worship was rendered impracticable. This
sort of difficulty often occurred afterwards in various places,
when we itinerated among the people. But let the Missionary
cultivate the grace of patience; for patience and firmness will,
in time, by the Divine blessing, remove any obstacle of this
kind. The people soon become orderly and attentive; and when
individuals who have not been accustomed to worship prove
noisy and ill-behaved, they are immediately taken to task, and
subdued into quietness, by their better instructed or better
informed countrymen. I have not unfrequently, at subsequent

periods, seen a plebeian Kaffir reprove a Chief for disorderly conduct during public worship. The argument adduced by them in such cases is, that even if they do not believe the Gospel, yet civility and good manners towards the teacher, who does believe, require that he should not be disturbed or affronted while engaged in the worship of God.

A very short time after my arrival in the country, I requested the Chiefs to assemble their petty Captains and principal Counsellors, that I might confer with them on some matters of great importance to their welfare. When they were consequently assembled, I endeavoured in an address of some length to explain to them, that now that they had received a Missionary, it was requisite they should put a stop to all stealing from the Colony; that I had recently received intelligence from the English Commandant that some cattle had been stolen and traced into their country; that unless they would put an end to these marauding expeditions of the people, it would be of little benefit for me to dwell among them; and that peace which they professed to desire with the English could not be maintained. The Chiefs expressed many thanks for the trouble I had taken; and said that it was an evident proof to them that I meant to be their friend; but that it was not easy to restrain so many thousands of their people. "There were always some men with bad hearts, however good the intentions of the Chief might be," &c., &c. I told them that I was well aware of all that, but I knew the Chiefs had great power; and that, although they could not always prevent bad men from robbing, yet they could afterwards punish them for it when detected. After much discussion, they told me that very strenuous orders would be immediately sent through the tribe; and certain principal men, whose names were given to me, were appointed "watch and ward" of certain drifts or fords along the Keiskamma River, through which any cattle stolen from the Colony must be driven; and that these persons should receive strict orders to capture not only all stolen cattle passing through these fords, but the robbers also, if practicable. I have the best reason to believe that, from this time, and for a series of years afterwards, no robberies were perpetrated by the Amagonakwaybi tribe upon the Colonists. No stolen cattle were traced during all those years among them; nor during that time did a single patrol of military, or party of burghers, come after any cattle into the country of these Chiefs. Occasionally, a batch of stolen cattle were captured from robbers belonging to other tribes, who attempted to bring them through their country; but they were promptly and invariably brought to me, that I might furnish a passport to the Kaffirs whom the Chiefs sent in charge of them to the nearest military post, that they might be restored to their lawful owners.

At a very early period, also, after our settlement with Pato, I received a communication from Major (now Lieutenant-General Sir Henry) Somerset, at that time Commandant of Kaffraria, stating that the Government was desirous of bringing about a good understanding with the Dhlambi or coast tribes. As already stated, these tribes had for some years been treated by the Colonial Government as enemies, and rebels against their lawful Chief or King, Gaika. But the authorities now began to discover that the policy which had recognised Gaika as the supreme or paramount Chief of Kaffraria was a mistake, fraught with consequences detrimental to the peace and quiet of the border. Major Somerset therefore wished me to induce not only Pato and his brother Chiefs, but through them their powerful neighbours and allied Chieftains of the Amakhakabi tribe, including old Dhlambi himself, with his sons Dushani and Kye, to meet him in a friendly conference. I communicated his message to the Amagonakwaybi Chiefs; and, after some hesitation, they sent messengers to inform the Dhlambi

Chiefs. Before the latter would decide on the course to be pursued, Dushani and one or two of his brothers, including Umhala, were sent to see and converse with me on the subject. Dushani expressed great astonishment on finding us in the country with our wives and children. He had scarcely had any previous intercourse with white men. He said, indeed, that he had heard of our arrival; but could not believe that any Englishman would venture to live among them, until he came and saw us actually settled in the country, and without any armed force to protect us. However, he remarked, "It is well that you have come; we want peace; and you must be our mouth to give our words to the white Chiefs." After some discussion, all the principal Chiefs agreed to meet Major Somerset at the place he had indicated, being one of the fords over the Keiskamma; but they consented only on the condition that I accompanied them, and remained present at the interview. Not wishing to be mixed up with the political arrangements of the country, I strove to avoid this; but it was in vain that I sought to be excused. If I refused to go, then they would not meet the Commandant as requested. As, however, it was highly desirable that the meeting should take place, so that a better understanding might be established between them and the colonial authorities, I at length reluctantly consented, and informed Major Somerset of the circumstances; reminding him, at the same time, that the personal safety of myself and all our Missionary party would be jeopardized, if any untoward event, leading to a collision, occurred at the meeting.

At the appointed time, (January, 1824,) I started with the Chiefs from our home, accompanied by parties of their warriors. On the road, a messenger met us, and stated that Dhlambi was afraid of treachery at the interview, and would not trust his person near the troops. He had often been pursued by patrols during the previous wars, and more than once had

narrowly escaped being taken prisoner. He knew, also, that
a price or reward had been offered for his capture. It was
soon, however, evident that the messenger was sent to ascertain
whether I was really with the Amagonakwaybi Chiefs; hence,
very shortly after we reached the spot where we were to bivouac
for the night, Dhlambi, Dushani, Umkai, and a large body of
their people, made their appearance. After some formal in-
terchanges of messengers and greetings had taken place
between the respective Chiefs, and I had shaken hands with
old Dhlambi, for many years past the terror of the frontier, the
Chiefs and people divided into distinct parties, to make their
preparations for supper and a night's lodging.

I can never forget that night. We were to sleep in a deep
glen, surrounded by a very wild and broken tract of country.
They selected an extensive bush to serve at once for shelter,
and as their garrison for the night. It supplied them with
sufficient fire-wood, and water was not very distant. Several
oxen which had been brought for the purpose were killed;
the butchers and their numerous assistants broiling and eating
various parts of the internal viscera of the animals, while
engaged in their occupation of skinning and cutting them up.
These men were all entirely naked, and seemed wonderfully to
enjoy their occupation, and the titbits which they were eating;
for, at intervals, they sang and danced after their barbarous
fashion, and in a manner anything but agreeable to European
notions. At length, the animals being cut up, the beef was
distributed to the various Chiefs and vassals. Great care was
taken to observe the proper gradations of rank in this distribution. The breast portions of the animals, cut up after their
peculiar method, were regarded as the prime parts, and these
were reserved specially for the great or principal Chiefs.

I afterwards noticed that the Chiefs were attended by their
servants with some form and ceremony. Their cooks broiled

their beef on the burning embers with particular care; and, when the steaks were ready, took branches from the bushes, which they intertwined, and thus formed a kind of mat or receptacle on which the meat could be placed. The flesh was cut into long strips, from three to twelve or more inches in length, and about an inch broad. The attendants likewise produced large milk sacks, which had been brought on pack-oxen; from these they poured the sour and curdled milk into vessels made of rushes or grass platted together, and then placed them at the feet of the principal person in the group. A sort of ladle was provided, made from a calabash or small gourd. The attendant, or master of the milk sack, who enjoys certain privileges, dipping this ladle into the milk, drank a portion of it, to show that there was no poison or dangerous ingredient mixed therein. The Chief then used the same instrument, and partook of the milk, passing it round the circle. In like manner, it was curious to see how they managed to eat without knives, forks, plates, or dishes. The headman of the circle, taking up one of the long slips of flesh described above, and putting part of it with his left hand into his mouth, cut off, with a javelin which he held in his right hand, as large a morsel as was agreeable to himself, or at least convenient for him to masticate. He then passed the remainder of it to the person next him; who, having performed the same pleasant operation, passed it on in turn to his neighbour, and so on round the circle. It evidently required some tact, and was regarded as a species of polite etiquette in this style of feeding, so to adjust the morsels, as that there might be sufficient for each one in the party to receive a piece. If the headman sees that the strip of beef is too short to go all round, he sometimes sends another piece round the opposite side of the circle.

A bountiful supply of beef from the parts most esteemed

was duly forwarded to me by the Chief for myself and the natives attached to my party. The latter had brought my small tea-kettle, which, being filled with water, and boiled for my use, with some admixture of tea and sugar, and a few biscuits, together with a steak broiled before the wood fire, supplied me with an abundant meal, for which I had a sufficient appetite, having eaten nothing since an early breakfast. Having partaken of my supper, I had time to look round me, and I visited various parts of the bush, which seemed like a large sylvan city. There were between two and three thousand Kaffirs assembled, all well armed with their full complement of spears or javelins, fencing sticks, and knobbed sticks, or clubs. They were distributed into parties of from twenty to fifty men. Each party had its separate fire for warmth and broiling their beef ; and the blaze of so many fires, in all parts of the wood, with the naked Kaffirs flitting to and fro, the incessant noise and chatter of most of the people, contrasted with the gravity of some of the Chiefs and counsellors, who sat conferring together, combined to produce a strange scene.

I felt no fear, but I was not sure there was no possibility of danger ; for I could not forget that I was the only European present, an unarmed individual, amidst this great gathering of some of the wildest men, including the most notorious robbers, of Kaffraria. When some of the Chiefs came to my fire to have some talk with me as to the best course for them to pursue, I felt it my duty to advise them to take from the thieves and restore to Major Somerset certain cattle which had been recently stolen by a bad set of people, who had for some time detached themselves from their proper tribes, and were living as a sort of lawless banditti on the border of their lands. After the Kaffirs had finished their suppers, leaving marvellously small remnants of the cattle that had been so recently slaughtered, the noise began to subside ; and, having prayed with the few people who were attached to me, I adjusted my saddle for my pillow, rolled myself on my sheep-skin kaross, and, placing myself with my feet towards the fire, I was soon asleep on the rough ground. In truth, notwithstanding the wild character of my companions, I was so wearied that I slept till sun-rise as soundly as I could have done on any curtained bed of down.

Early in the morning, certain spies sent out by the Chiefs returned to our bivouac, and reported that they had seen a colonial force which had reached the western side of the Keiskamma River, near the ford that the Commandant had appointed (the Line Drift). I observed that these spies were very closely questioned as to what the "commando" consisted of; and from my interpreter I learned the particulars of the report, which I afterwards found to be remarkably accurate as to the proximate numbers of the force, and its relative proportions of troops and burghers. The whole body was mounted, and consisted chiefly of a portion of the Cape Corps Cavalry and a small party of Dutch farmers; the entire force comprising about three or four hundred men. They had encamped during the previous night in a beautiful vale, near the banks of the river. After the Chiefs had held some consultation, they asked me to go with them to the heights, which commanded a view of the camp; and having reached this spot, they very carefully scanned it. I desired them to show themselves on the heights, and we soon noticed that they were observed by the troops below. I now recommended them to send two of their men as messengers to the Commandant, to report that they were arrived according to his request. One of these men was provided with a white rag, obtained from one of my attendants, and this was tied on the top of a stick as a flag of truce: thus equipped, the two emissaries went off quickly down the very long and steep descent, and the Chiefs watched them till they saw they had safely arrived within the camp.

The Chiefs now retired to join the body of their people, and shortly afterwards their messengers returned from the camp accompanied by the Commandant's interpreter, a South African Dutchman, named Bezuidenhout, who was instructed to inform me and them, that the Major would march up the heights before midday, and to request that the Chiefs would meet him on the High Ridge, where he proposed the conference to be held. Much private consultation was held among them as to the principal points which they were to urge in the discussion with the Commandant. It was agreed that they should request to be recognised by the Government as independent Chiefs over their respective tribes, without any interference from Gaika, and that all communications should hereafter be made direct through the Missionary to them, without being sent through him, whom they acknowledged to be a great and powerful Chief, but denied that he had control over their affairs. Dhlambi and Dushani were to urge that they and their people might be permitted to re-occupy the country lying between the Keiskamma and the Buffalo rivers, from which they were driven during the previous war, and which, like the " Neutral Territory " between the Fish River and the Keiskamma, had been left uninhabited ever since. If these requests were granted, the concession was to be taken as a proof of the good will of the Government, and they would then comply with its wishes as to the restoration of stolen cattle ; depredations in the Colony should be severely punished ; and Hottentot or other native deserters from the Cape Corps should be delivered up to the colonial authorities.

At the appointed time, Major Somerset and his force rode up the hill. On the first intimation by the scouts that they were in motion, the Chiefs assembled their warriors : they formed in clans under their several petty Chiefs and headmen, and then combined in larger divisions, according to the hereditary branch

of the Chief's houses or families to which they respectively
belonged. It was curious to see how every man at once
recognised his own clan, and how the stronger clans exhibited
pride in their relative numbers. At length the whole body,
comprising between two and three thousand fine athletic and
active men, but forming only a small portion of the force of
their respective tribes, moved to the middle of the High Ridge,
and took up a position just at a spot where two deep ravines,
one on either side of the height, caused the space on the top to
be so narrow that their line completely occupied it, having
bushy precipices on either flank. As soon as the Major reached
a part of the ridge which was within a few hundred yards of
their position, he saw at once how skilfully it had been chosen
in case of any untoward event leading to a collision. Their
flanks could not be turned, and, if they wished, the whole
of them could easily escape to the right and left, and in a few
moments disappear in the woods. He therefore sent his interpreter with the request that they would move a little higher up
the hill, as he wanted to bring his force further up. But this
they resolutely refused to do. Meantime I went to the Commandant, and told him that the Chiefs were all in good temper,
and had come in good faith. On receiving this assurance,
the Major very fairly proposed, that the interview should be
held half-way between the respective forces, now facing each
other; the two lines being about three hundred yards apart.
This proposal strengthened their confidence, and, after a short
delay, the principal Chiefs, with myself and a private interpreter of their own, advanced to meet the Commandant and his
principal officers.

There was a lengthened discussion, the particulars of which
I need not recite. Suffice it to say, that the Major promised
that the several points which they had urged should be conceded,
and the Chiefs on their part engaged that certain deserters

should be given up, and a considerable number of cattle which
had been stolen should be restored,   At the request of the
Commandant they fixed a time, (three days,) within which
period they would capture and restore the cattle. He desired
that one of the Chiefs would accompany him to his camp as a
hostage, until this was done.   None of the Chiefs would
volunteer, till at length I persuaded Kobi (Congo) to go. He
consented, on condition that I would go and stay with him in
the camp. Accordingly, I agreed to do so. We accompanied
the force back to their camp, and the Kaffirs broke up and
returned home well pleased with the result. On the forenoon
of the third day, we saw the promised cattle driven down the
hill by a party of Kaffirs, who, on reaching the camp, delivered
them over, as directed by Dhlambi and Dushani, to the Commandant; and thus terminated this interview, which had been
managed with very great tact and discretion on the part of
Major Somerset. Kobi (Congo) and I returned to our home
among the Kaffirs, and we soon found that the result of the
meeting had afforded abundant satisfaction. The Dhlambi
Chiefs expressed themselves in extravagant terms of delight,
that they could now re-occupy the vacant lands, and "sleep in
peace," and I was hailed everywhere by the Kaffirs as the friend
of Dhlambi and Pato.

I have detailed the circumstances of this Conference between
the Commandant of the frontier and the Chiefs at some length,
because it introduced a great change in the system of intercourse
between the Government and them, and was followed by a
period of almost unexampled peace and tranquillity on the lower
part of the Kaffir border, which lasted without the slightest
interruption for about ten years. And the reader will perceive,
that if the narration of this episode has occupied considerable
space, it has enabled me at the same time to present a description
from actual observation of Kaffir habits when the men are

assembled for war, or other purposes, in any considerable bodies. The same system of bivouac, and of feeding themselves when in the field, is adopted by all the tribes of Southern Africa.

In a remarkably short time, we completed a "wattle and daub" house, thatched with rushes, and divided into four rooms, in which both families obtained accommodation, until a second and similar dwelling was erected. We now began to feel ourselves tolerably settled, although we had very few appliances indeed for ministering either to our convenience or comfort. But those who have resided in the open air for a few weeks will be prepared to regard a dwelling of any kind, however rude and humble, as a great improvement in their position. It was resolved, that the next building should be a school-chapel; but mean time we cleared away the underwood from a spot which was sheltered and shaded by large trees on the bank of the river: and here we established our regular religious services. Several families now came, and requested permission to reside on the Station; and these persons formed the materials of our regular congregation, to which were continually added many strangers, who, from time to time, used to come into the neighbourhood to visit the Chiefs, or for traffic, and other purposes.

As the place was likely to grow into a village, I resolved to give it a name; and what name could rise to my mind as suitable to designate the first Methodist Mission in Kaffraria, but the name of the venerable Wesley? Hence from this period it was called "Wesleyville." As we subsequently gave names to all our regular Mission Stations, I will here assign the reasons why we did so. Some persons have censured Missionaries and Colonists for giving European names to their settlements. It is said we ought to retain the native names, which are represented as being much more euphonious and expressive than the names which are often applied to places by Missionaries and others. In answer to these observations, so far as Kaffraria is concerned, I may state, that in that country there are no towns, and no native names of their kraals or villages. The Kaffirs only give names to their rivers, and the more remarkable ranges and peaks of the mountains in their country. If a particular spot has a name, it will on inquiry be found to be derived from some headman, who lives, or recently lived there: e.g., Kwangubene, the native name of one of our Mission Stations in Natalia, was retained. Now, Kwangubene simply means, "in or at the place of Ngubu;" a man of some note of that name having formerly lived there. This name happened to be easy to pronounce, and therefore it was accepted as being sufficiently distinctive, since the neighbourhood had, during the last generation, been so called. But while the Kaffirs usually distinguish a tract of land with the name of the nearest river, that name is a common indicator to any spot for many miles near, and on either of its banks, and is therefore far from being definite. The greatest difficulty, however, is, that the names of most of the rivers in the parts of Kaffraria near the Colony are unpronounceable by Europeans, in consequence of the occurrence of clicks and other peculiar sounds in the words. I have met with persons who contended for the importance of retaining the native names of places, and have been much amused to hear them, while arguing in favour of their views, pronouncing these names in such a manner that no native in all the land would recognise them, but would at once suppose them to be some foreign words. The native name of Wesley-ville, as given by a Kaffir, would be, when translated, "the Missionary's place at Twecu,"—Etwecu being the name of the small river tributary to the Tyelomnqa; on which the village was erected. But no European who has not mastered the language would ever pronounce these names properly, and they are far from being unusually difficult. King William's Town, situate on what the Colonists denominate the Buffalo River, is called by the Kaffirs Eqonce, from the name of the beautiful stream which flows past the town. The name, as used, signifies to be " at the place on the river Qonce;" the q and the c representing clicks quite unpronounceable by Europeans who have never learned the language. Hence, if Europeans are to read, write, and speak of these Settlements, missionary or otherwise, as a general rule, it is absolutely necessary that they should be designated by some pronounceable name; and what persons. have a greater right to give names to villages or towns than those who found or build them ?

We steadily pursued the work of our Mission, and before the end of June, 1824, the two wattled cottages for our residence had been completed : other cottages were in progress for the dwellings of our native servants, storehouses, &c.; and at a subsequent period the framework of a larger building was put. up; and although a longer delay occurred before we could fix the roof upon it, yet the wattled framework served as a screen from the wind, and we now usually held our worship therein. A regular congregation had been collected, the brother Chiefs,. Pato, Kobi, and Kama, with their respective retinues, generally attended Divine service on Sundays; and to some extent, even at this early period, the Heathen began to pay outward reverence to the Lord's day. They saw that all our works were regularly suspended on that day, and that it was devoted to the duties of public worship; and, under our instruction and advice, many of them began to observe it; and thus was the Christian Sabbath gradually established in this part of the land.

As soon as practicable, I endeavoured to form a School for. the children of the natives who lived near us. This was, however, a work of great difficulty; but on Sunday, the 80th: of January, 1825, there were upwards of sixty Kaffir children.

present at the Sunday School. This was less than fourteen months from the commencement of the Mission; and my journal, in stating the number, adds concerning them, "They are making progress, and behave very well; but I am grieved to see so many children—many of them Chiefs by birth—in a state of nudity. What must be done to raise this degraded race? So much is to be done, that it is difficult to determine at what point, or in what way, to commence the labour of love." Long after this period, benevolent and truly Christian persons in London, and other great cities of Britain, observing the neglected condition of large numbers of poor children in the crowded lanes and courts, established what were called "Ragged Schools," for the amelioration and improvement of their condition, which have been followed by immense benefits: but our Kaffir boys and girls did not possess even "rags" to cover them; a very few had small pieces of calf skins and skins of other animals thrown over their shoulders, but the vast majority were entirely naked; so that ours might have been called "Nude Schools."

We observed, after a time, several tokens in the congregation of an increasing interest in the truths which were imparted to them in our addresses and sermons; and on one Sabbath forenoon, when discoursing on the Saviour's love, I observed the big tears coursing down the cheeks of two or three men whose countenances were far from prepossessing, and whose previous habits of life scarcely encouraged the hope that the Gospel would subdue them into penitence and prayer. But the grace of God possesses a wondrously transforming influence wherever it is not "received in vain." These persons and others were followed into secret places and spoken with plainly and pointedly concerning their souls' welfare. At length several of the people being under the influence of the Spirit of grace, I resolved to form them into a Class, and to meet them apart from others, that I might speak with them individually once a week concerning their spiritual state; for whenever a Heathen says in effect to a Missionary, " Sir, I would see Jesus," it behoves him to strive to bring the inquirer to the Saviour, that, believing in Him, he may " obtain forgiveness of sins, and an inheritance among them that are sanctified." On the 22nd day of March, 1825, I held the first Methodist Class-Meeting in Kaffraria, at which six of the natives were present. My memorandum on the occasion states : " We were exceedingly gratified with the truly earnest manner in which they expressed their desire to save their souls. How pleasing to hear a Kaffir say, ' I am always glad when I hear the bell ring to call us to church! I could not be at rest to live where I could not hear the great word.' A Kaffir woman said that all her sorrow and distress of mind arose from a consciousness that she was a great sinner. Something that was said on that text, ' Ye ought to take the more earnest heed to the things which ye have heard,' &c., appears to have been strongly impressed upon her mind, and she is truly taking ' earnest heed ' that Divine truths run not out of her heart. May this form the beginning of good days ! " After the Class-Meeting held on the following week, I made this entry in my journal: " It was a pleasing and profitable occasion. We have good reason to hope well of all who were present; but they are very weak in the faith, and very ignorant, and must be treated with much tenderness and forbearance. We shall consider them on trial for an indefinite period, and when it is deemed expedient they will be baptized."

In this manner we pursued our quiet course of duty, keeping up regular religious services at Wesleyville, and making frequent visits on a regular plan to various Kaffir kraals, which were a few miles distant, for the purpose of preaching the Gospel among them. This led subsequently to a settled system of extensive itinerancy. Twice in each quarter of a year I used to ride to some remote district occupied by the tribe, and remain from home four or five days, holding numerous religious services at the Kaffir kraals, and conversing with the people concerning the things of the kingdom of God. As I used to sleep in their huts during these journeys, I was thereby brought into close contact with all classes of the natives. I found by this means that their confidence in me was constantly increasing, while I was thus also becoming more and more familiar with their social state, and their habits and modes of thought. Of course it was not, in some respects, a very agreeable kind of life. The native huts were without chair, stool, couch, or bed of any kind. The habits of the people, although somewhat ceremonious, were not in accordance with European notions of cleanliness or propriety; and I used to return home weary, hungry, and far from clean and tidy. For, after sleeping for a week in my clothes on the ground or a mat, and being often by unavoidable contact with the people smeared with the grease and red ochre with which the Kaffirs cover their persons and skin clothing, a bath or complete ablution, with entire change of garments, was rendered indispensable. I am, however, persuaded that all Missionaries whose health will allow of it, should pursue this course, and thus frequently mix with the natives in their ordinary and every-day places of abode. Nothing will so certainly, under the Divine blessing, give them personal influence over the people; nor can any other plan but that of an extensive and regular itinerancy around the centre of each Mission Station, awaken an interest in the great objects and aims of a Christian Missionary among the natives living in kraals scattered all over the country.

In the early part of February, 1824, I found it necessary to leave my wife and family at Wesleyville, and visit the Colony, for the purpose of obtaining various needful articles which could not be brought with us, but which were wanted to enable us to carry on our building operations with facility; and supplies of various kinds had also become requisite, as, like all persons unaccustomed to provide prospectively for the consumption of large families for a length of time, we had miscalculated in various essential articles the quantities which would probably be required. On this journey I resolved to cut and open a direct road to Graham's Town. With great difficulty we opened access for the wagon to the Keiskamma, and removed large stones and other obstructions from the ford across the river, so as to render it practicable for wagons. In many parts numerous trees had to be cut down to open our way, and banks were at various points on the line cut through by means of the spades and pickaxes taken with me for the purpose. I took with me certain natives, who were very serviceable in this laborious undertaking. At length we completed a tolerable wagon way across the then uninhabited "neutral" territory, and struck into a very rugged path which had been formerly cut through the Fish River bush by the Boers and troops during the previous Kaffir war; and, following this route, we crossed the Trompetter's Ford, and proceeded to Graham's Town over the heights of the Governor's Kop. This road through the Fish River bush had, however, not been traversed by wagons for several years; and, besides being originally a very difficult and rocky path, we had much to do in clearing it from various obstructions which had accumulated since the road had ceased to be used. From this time it became the chief line of main road for entering the coast parts of the country.

The whole district, from Wesleyville to within a few miles of Graham's Town, over which we travelled, being uninhabited, we found therein a great variety of wild animals, roaming at large. The spring-bok, bush-bok, hartebeest, and qwagga, were frequently met with in troops and flocks in the grassy country of the neutral territory. ' Wolves and jackals were numerous; hippopotami, or, as the Colonists call them, " sea-cows," were at that time frequently met with in the Keiskamma and Fish Rivers; but elephants, at this period, literally swarmed in the great bush on both sides of the last-named river. The numerous quiet and sequestered nooks and corners, sheltered by rocky precipices covered with bush, affording large supplies of the kind of trees and herbage which constituted their chief food, rendered this neighbourhood a favourite resort of those huge animals. The African species is much larger than the Indian. I was obliged frequently to traverse this road; and, for several years, I scarcely remember any instance of my passing along this route without falling in with herds of elephants, roaming through the bush in quest of food. I have seen them in numbers from two or three to more than one hundred. Ten or twenty in a single group were very frequently met with. Occasionally, when travelling on horseback, I have been startled by coming suddenly on a number of these animals, and being brought into a very unpleasant proximity with them. When accompanying a wagon, this rarely happened, as the noise occasioned by the loud cracking of the whip used by the wagon-driver generally startled any elephants near at hand, and caused them to stride away in another direction; but the com-paratively noiseless travelling on horseback gave no such warning, and it was needful to keep a sharp look out, lest an encounter with one of these monsters, alike undesired on either side, should accidentally occur. On one of my journeys to the Colony, I was accompanied on horseback by my faithful Kaffir servant, Kotongo. On our being about to return, he was very uneasy that we had no gun. The country through which we were to pass being much infested with elephants, and also by banditti of plundering Kaffirs, Kotongo urged the propriety of my borrowing a musket for him to carry. On my saying the Kaffirs knew me to be a *Fundis*, (Teacher,) and why should a Minister carry arms? he said, somewhat sarcastically, That might be; but he was not certain that, if we fell in with any elephants, they would recognise me as a *Fundis!*

On my first visit to the Colony, at the date mentioned above, I took with me the young Kaffir Chief Kama and two or three of his attendants. It was a good proof of his confidence that he was willing to go with me; and his people consented with reluctance; but they were ashamed to express their apprehensions, since I was leaving my wife and children among them. No Kaffir Chief, had, however, visited the Colony for many years; and in no instance had a Chief visited it since the arrival of the British settlers. Hence the event created considerable interest on both sides of the frontier. Kama was received by the British in Graham's Town, both civil and military, with great kindness. Many presents of clothing and other articles were given to the Chief by various friends; and, besides some clothes, the Commandant sent to Kobi, (Congo,) by Kama, a present of a horse. The young Chief attended Divine worship in the English chapels at Graham's Town and Salem; and he witnessed, on these occasions, the administration of the Sacraments of Baptism and the Lord's Supper. At one of these services, although not understanding our language, he had been seized with an apparently irresistible emotion, and shed "floods of tears." After our return to Wesleyville, and on attending public worship a day or two afterwards in our sylvan chapel, when Divine service was concluded, he narrated the various circumstances connected with his visit to the Colony; speaking in high terms of the kindness and hospitality of the English, and describing the seriousness and solemnity which he had observed in their religious assemblies, showing that they considered God's worship to be a work of great importance. His statements excited no small interest. A visit to the Colony by the Chief Kobi, or Congo, as he was then generally called, two months afterwards, produced equally gratifying results. On being shown the chapel at Graham's Town, at that time the largest and best building he had ever entered,—the resident Missionary, after explaining the purpose for which it was erected, stating that it was God's house, in which His people worshipped Him, and heard His word preached,—the Chief replied, with his hand upon his mouth, and his eyes fixed on the ground, "I am astonished; and therefore cannot express myself. The place is a wonder to me, and therefore I am dumb!" After he had attended the Sunday services, both in Salem and Graham's Town chapels, the Missionary reminded him of the congregations which he had seen assembled during the day, and endeavoured to impress him with an idea of the importance of the Gospel, which was now sent to him and his people. "Yes," said he, "I now see a great day, great things, and a great people; and I wish we had seen them sooner."

These visits of the Chiefs of the Colony were at once an evidence and an effect of the good understanding and the feeling of mutual confidence which had recently arisen on both sides of the border; and there is no doubt but that the favourable impression made on the minds of the Chiefs, and which they did not fail to communicate to others, had great influence in producing that unusually long period of comparative repose and freedom from war and Kaffir marauding which the British settlers of Albany were now privileged to enjoy during some ten successive years.

At Wesleyville we lived in great peace and safety. For a long time we retired to rest at night without any particular precautions for securing the door or window fastenings. Although the Kaffirs were great pilferers by day, yet we found that burglary was rarely or ever committed. As their huts had no fastenings, their wattled doors being merely tied with "riems," or slips of bullock hide, and indeed frequently with nothing but green withs, twisted together, it had become a maxim of Kaffir law that " every man's house or hut is his castle ;" and for a stranger to intrude into it when the owner was absent, or at night when he was asleep, was regarded as a very high crime and misdemeanour. · The culprit was considered to be similar to a prowling wolf, and might be killed when caught in the act ; and, at any rate, when convicted of the crime, he was punished by the very heaviest fines. How strangely contradictory are the notions of men regarding morality and relative justice, when not guided by the light of the Divine word ! The same men who affected such great indignation at the idea of committing a burglarious act, considered that to enter your cattle or sheep fold during the darkness of the night, and carry off a portion of your live stock from thence, was in no respect disgraceful conduct : only, if you caught and convicted the culprit, he must pay the fine, that is all ; but he did not lose his character or standing in social life, in consequence of such dishonest proceedings. Cattle and, subsequently, sheep were frequently stolen from our folds. Our people often pursued the robbers ; but, as they generally came from other tribes, we did not allow them to proceed to extremities, lest fighting and bloodshed should result, which often happens when the Kaffirs plunder each other's cattle-folds. However, as soon as an opportunity presented itself, I did not fail to bring a case against a certain robber before the Chief. The proof of his guilt was perfectly complete in the view of the court, and he was heavily fined ; the stolen cattle were returned, and I distributed the cattle paid as penalty among the people of the Station, who at some risk, and with great trouble, had traced out the robbers. For a long time after this we were not nearly so much troubled and annoyed by the cattle-lifting propensities of the people.

During the first year of our residence at Wesleyville, we had a season of alarm for a few days. In consequence of recent events, a neighbouring clan avowed their purpose of attacking Kama and his people; and as some of the latter were daily on our premises, there was reason to fear that we might be mixed up in the quarrel. One day, while Kama and some of his men were lying on the ground and chattering together, near where I was standing, a man shouted the war cry from a neighbouring hill, and instantly the whole party, with many others on the place at the time, seized their weapons, and rushed off at a very high speed. Presently, on the heights opposite the Station, we saw a strong party of the hostile clan approaching with shields, spears, and warlike head-dresses. Kama and his men rapidly obtained from his kraal similar appliances, and set off to meet their enemy. In a very short time they confronted each other. Kama inquired what was the meaning of an armed force like that coming into his country. He was answered by an assagay or javelin, hurled at him by the Chief of the opposite party. Instantly the whole were engaged. The conflict, however, did not last long. They had no fire-arms, but fought exclusively with their assagays. The attacking party soon found that they had undertaken more than they could accomplish. Kama's people were also rapidly increasing, numbers coming to his help from all sides. The enemy, finding himself likely to be surrounded, scattered and fled into the nearest bush and deep ravines, and thus escaped total destruction; leaving, however, three men killed on the spot. A considerable number were wounded also on both sides. As soon as we could obtain our horses, I and Mr. Shepstone rode to the scene of conflict, hoping to be useful, if not in preventing bloodshed, at least in assisting any who might need our help; but every wounded man who could possibly crawl away or who could be removed by the aid of his comrades, had already disappeared; and after a careful search amidst the long grass, we only found one man alive, who was very dangerously wounded in the abdomen, from whence his bowels were protruding. After giving him some water, we directed our people, who had followed us, to assist in burying the three men who were killed. With much reluctance they complied, protesting that their bodies ought to be left to the wild beasts! The wounded man we set on a horse, and, supporting him thereon, with great difficulty removed him to our residence.

Every attention was paid to his case that common humanity dictated, or our circumstances allowed. Mr. Shepstone was most assiduous in his care of this poor fellow. He attended to his wants, replaced the protruding bowels, and otherwise secured the healing of his dangerous wound, by such operations and bandages as a practical turn for surgery, aided by our medical books, suggested. The man somewhat rapidly recovered under this treatment; but we had much to do to prevent the people from abusing him, and depriving him of the food which we sent for his daily use. At length, both he and they were made to understand that we had nothing to do with the native quarrels; but, when any of them were sick or wounded, we should always strive to do them good, and save their lives, without considering whether they were friends or foes, or making any distinction as to the respective tribes and clans, to which they might belong. At the time, some of Kama's people seemed displeased at our care for this man; but the abiding impression made upon the mass of the people by this incident, as we eventually discovered, was, that "the Missionaries are the servants of God, and therefore the friends of all."

At length, when this man seemed to be nearly well, and after he had frequently expressed his thanks for the kindness shown to him, one night he suddenly disappeared, and in the morning was not to be found. Some of our people, however, traced his "spoor," or foot marks, for a considerable distance, till it became evident that he had proceeded directly to his own home in the clan from whence he came. It appeared to us, at the time, strange and ungrateful, that he should not have taken leave in a more becoming manner; but, some time after, we learned that this was one of the singular customs of the country. It is not unusual for a man who has been under the care of a native doctor, and recovers, to make his escape, lest a heavy demand should be made upon him in the shape of cattle for medical fees. No doubt, after all, this poor man thought that we should expect remuneration for the attendance and food supplied to him; and hence he ran off in this singular manner, to avoid being detained, till what he doubtless supposed would be a very heavy claim could be satisfied.

The first decided result of our religious instruction of the natives at Wesleyville appeared about one year after the commencement of the Mission. Hobo, a native of mixed race,— being a descendant of the famous Gonaqua Hottentot Chief, Ruyter, by a Kaffir wife,—was the victim of severe pulmonary disease, and, coming to us for medicine, he was led to take up his abode on the Station. While afflicted, he received the Gospel testimony, and, on his evidently sincere and earnest profession of faith in Christ, I baptized him with water, in the name of the Holy Trinity, in the hut where he lay sick: shortly after which, he died in great peace, and in joyful hope of a glorious immortality. This event occurred in December, 1824. But the first public baptismal service at Wesleyville was held on the 19th of August, 1825, the centenary of the day on which Wesley was ordained to the office of a Preacher of God's holy word. On this occasion, three of the native converts were baptized in the presence of a large assembly of the people. The event was a source of much encouragement to us; for we viewed these persons as the first-fruits of a great harvest, which will, in time, be gathered from among the various Kaffir nations. Nor has this hope deceived us. A system of quarterly administration of the baptismal rite has been introduced on all our Stations, and I believe that no quarter of a year has ever passed, since that date, in which some of the adult natives have not been, in this manner, received as fully accredited members of Christ's visible Church, on one or other of our Stations. The aggregate of these quarterly baptisms has been steadily and largely on the increase for some years past.

Amongst the natives whom I baptized at Wesleyville, were the Chief Kama and his wife. The latter is a daughter of the great Chief Gaika, and sister of Makomo, the noted leader in the late Kaffir wars. Kama and his wife, amidst many temptations and serious difficulties, designedly put in their way by the heathen Chiefs, to seduce them from their steadfastness, are still members of the Church, and regular in their attendance on its ordinances. But I must not pursue the details of our proceedings at Wesleyville any further in this place. Various occurrences will, however, be narrated in subsequent portions of this volume, illustrative of the state and condition of the people, with the progress of our Mission among them. It shall therefore suffice in closing this chapter to say, that religious ordinances were regularly maintained ; the number of inquirers and converts steadily increased. The Sabbath was fully recognised by the people at Wesleyville and in all the surrounding neighbourhood. The School was in active operation. The plough had been introduced. A store, placed under the care of Mr. R. Walker, was established, for supplying clothing and useful articles to the natives, in return for the raw produce of the country. A very pretty village had arisen, which consisted, besides our own dwelling and the school-chapel, of a number of cottages erected by the natives, each containing two rooms, forming an immense improvement on the native huts. Many of the people, however, who had not yet accomplished this feat, still dwelt in their huts near the cattle-folds. Some of the converted natives had already died peacefully in the faith of Christ; and a general knowledge of the facts, with some idea of the leading principles, of Christianity, had been communicated to large numbers of Kaffirs who had only been occasional visitors at the Station, or who lived at or near the kraals in the remoter districts where we preached on our itinerating journeys. Such was the state of things resulting from this Mission during the six years of my residence. Early in the year 1830, I was removed to Graham's Town; and I left to my successor a comfortable and substantial mission-house, a commodious school-chapel, and materials for the completion of a large new chapel, already commenced, and which was now much required for a considerable congregation. There were in the native Church, or Society, about forty accredited members or communicants, and a native population of about three hundred souls, who had voluntarily taken up their residence at Wesleyville, all of whom were under the daily instruction and control of the Missionary.

My successor, the Rev. Samuel Young, carried on my plans most faithfully, and greatly extended the work, till he in turn was succeeded by the Rev. William Shepstone, who was prosecuting a most prosperous course of missionary labour, when all was interrupted, and for a season apparently destroyed, by the sad events of the Kaffir war of 1834. The great influence which the Mission at this period exercised over Pato's tribe, kept them from joining their countrymen in that war; but as they had nearly all removed to the neutral territory by the permission of the Colonial Government, Wesleyville was left much exposed; and the Missionary and people, surrounded by daily dangers and alarms from the hostile Kaffirs, were constrained to abandon the place, which was soon afterwards burned down.

An attempt was made to re-establish Wesleyville after peace was restored ; but as it was no longer in the centre of Pato's tribe,— which continued to dwell in the neutral territory,—the village never regained its former importance ; and as it was again burned down during the war of 1848, no further attempt was made to recommence that Station. The lands, however, had been granted by the Chiefs to the Society, and confirmed by the Government ; and certainly they must in all equity be regarded as fairly its property, unless, indeed, the Government, in re-suming possession of these lands, grant a reasonable sum as compensation to the Society, which has expended so much money thereon. One of my own children, and other members of the various Mission families, with not a few of the Chris-tianized natives and their families, lie interred in the village burial-ground, waiting the morning of the resurrection.

While, however, Wesleyville as a settlement was destroyed by these Kaffir wars, there had been seed sown which war cannot destroy. The religious results of that Mission may be exten-sively traced, not only in the early history of the Stations which were subsequently established further up the coast, but also in the lives of the various converts, some of whom are deceased, while a considerable number still survive. The native Christians of the Amagonakwaybi or Pato's tribe are now nume-rous, and may be met with in various parts of the Colony, but more especially in British Kaffraria, at the residence of the residence of the Christianized Chief Kama, and in the neighbour-hood of the Station called " Annshaw," which we formed at the special request of the late Sir George Cathcart, on lands granted by him for that purpose, soon after the close of the last Kaffir war.

CHAPTER V.

Albany before 1834—Causes of the Kaffir War.

In the preceding chapters Mr. Shaw has given his own account of his early life and his labours in South Africa up to 1833, when he left for England. Before his departure the inhabitants of Graham's Town presented him with an address and a *silver salver*, as a mark of their regard. At that time the Albany District, of which he was the Chairman, comprised the Colonial Circuits of Graham's Town, Salem, Bathurst, and Somerset, and the Kaffir Missions, Wesleyville, Mount Coke, Butterworth, Clarkebury, Morley, and Buntingville. The prospects of the Colony and of the Missions were most cheering. All parties were happily ignorant of the series of trials through which Colonists and Missionaries would have to pass, before Kaffirs and Englishmen would be permitted to live together in peace, under the rule of British law.

Meanwhile, we may indulge in a few reminiscences of the singularly happy, contented, and, on the whole, well-to-do population of Albany before the war of 1834. GRAHAM'S TOWN contained, including the military and natives, about three thousand people. SALEM was kept up as a village by the valuable Academy of W. H. Matthews, Esq., one of Mr. Shaw's most useful creations. BATHURST, THE KOWI, CLUMBER, and other of the original locations were mere scattered settlements. The whole country between Graham's Town and the sea was mainly inhabited by settlers, whose farms seldom exceeded a few hundred acres. Among them, however, were some larger landholders. Except a few merchants in Graham's Town, there were none who had accumulated capital, or who might be considered rich. The majority were content to live moderately, earning the means of living as storekeepers, or in the exercise of useful trades, or by Kaffir trading. Commercial life at Graham's Town began with the morning market, to which produce from either Kaffirland or from the Dutch farmers was brought for sale, open to the competition of the various storekeepers. The principal customers to the storekeepers were the Dutch and English farmers and the Kaffir traders. When "the market" had been more than usually filled by Dutch wagons, the stores were proportionately busy. We have heard of the most surprising feats of energetic continuous labour on the part of the wife of one of the storekeepers, who stood behind her counter all day, supplying her customers; and though repeatedly fainting from fatigue, yet returned to her labours like a giant refreshed, not with new wine, but with "*schnaps;*" but this working matron was not of the English settler class. Wagons from the Bay, (Port Elizabeth,) with European goods and other imports, were comparatively few and far between. The Commissariat supplied the troops on the frontier, through contractors, sometimes at the ridiculously low price of one penny halfpenny per ration of beef, bread, candles, &c.: so cheap were the mere necessaries of life in those days from 1829 to 1834. At that time the town was a pretty village, well laid out, with large capabilities of improvement, which in due time, being wisely used, have made the Graham's Town of our day the prettiest town in South Africa. But *then*, the streets were very much just as nature had left them,—unlevel, dusty in dry weather, and almost impassable after heavy rains. A journey down the main street at night was a feat which required (as the writer can testify from personal experience) no small local knowledge and judgment. The roads of the Settlement were mainly made by the wagons which used them : there were very few houses of accommodation, and travellers lodged for the night by the side of their wagons or horses,—a custom pleasant enough in fine dry weather, but which had its disagreeables in the event of rain. So much for outward circumstances. As to the people, I have already stated that in my opinion a more truly respectable and worthy community than these first settlers in Albany never existed. There was a marked originality about almost every individual colonist. Each one had been the architect of his own fortune, and had his own peculiar development. Nobody imitated anybody; for every man was, as a settler, as good as another (or a little better) in his own opinion,—an opinion, however, which was never offensively put forth; for the original settlers were practically in feeling *gentle* and unobtrusive. The circumstances in which they had been placed in England, and as emigrants shovelled into a wilderness, and left to make their own way, had made these patriarchs of Albany a peculiar people. Their successors, however favoured by education and comparative wealth, cannot be expected to equal them in all those high qualities which distinguished the original self-made man from the more polished specimen of humanity which is the product of our complex civilization.

A more friendly, affectionate, and hospitable people I never knew. Show and style were things unknown; there was no pretence as to appearances. Every one lived as it were in a glass house, and in such a way as suited his circumstances, careless about what any "Mrs. Grundy" sort of neighbour thought of him. Business claims were not by any means absorbing. Then, we were not too busy to be happy: we could spare time occasionally for rest and recreation. The storekeepers and tradesmen would shut up for a day to go to a chapel opening, an Anniversary, or Missionary Meeting, or picnic. This was not idleness, but the result of the easy position, in which, with no artificial wants and a rough plenty, the majority were almost without cares. I am now speaking of *the settlers*, properly so called,—the commonalty. Of course, the richer classes, —few in number,—though highly respectable and, for the most part, very worthy, formed an order by themselves. Keeping within their own circle, too anxious for the maintenance of their position to be quite at ease, they could not afford to be as careless and happy as the majority around them. With the exception of a few families, (such as the Bowkers, a family with a lineage, literary and historical, of which they may well be proud,) who wisely adapted themselves to their circumstances, and have consequently maintained their position, this class of the original settlers has disappeared: their estates are in the hands of the children of those "cockney shoemakers and tailors," as the humbler colonists were mendaciously styled by certain unfriendly critics. Religiously and morally, the settlers were for the most part a "*godly seed*." Whether Churchmen, or Methodists, or Independents, or Baptists, they lived in peace. No angry controversy on religious topics arose among them. I cannot but look back to this period as the golden age of the Albany Colony.

I am obliged, however, to confess that we Methodists were on the whole a plebeian set. Except an editor and printer, and a few wholesale storekeepers, who by general consent were termed "merchants," as importing their goods direct from Europe, and a few persons connected with the army or commissariat, the rest of us were retail store-keepers and artizans. Kaffir traders, and wagon pro-prietors engaged in the carriage of goods within the Colony, were, next to the merchants, our enterprising class, com-manding no small degree of respect. In the country we were small farmers and graziers. In those days we made no pretensions to the gentility which is supposed to be connected with freedom from labour, for we all had to work for our living. None of us were ashamed of this, or of our useful occupations, however lowly they might be. Our successors and descendants need not to blush for us,—*for we made the Colony what it is!* I fear this age of simplicity is now past, and that some of the young "Africanders," forgetting their high origin, are as idle and profitless as if they had been born of *genteel* parents in England. But as I recall the names of these fathers of the Colony, small and great, I feel that their memory is blessed. I dare but mention the names of William Cock, of the Kowi River; Robert Godlonton, for many years the Editor of the Graham's Town Journal; Captain M'Donald, George Wood, Richard and Joseph Walker, Carey Hobson, James Powell, Charles Penney, William Wright, J. C. Wright, Robert Lee, B. Booth, Daniel

Roberts, sen., and jun., James Howse, J. Kidd, C. White, J. Jubber, J. Weeks, Charles Slater, Thomas Cockroft, W. A. Fletcher, with the Cawoods, Cyruses, Webbs, Lucases, Prices, Hartleys, Daniels, Oateses, Trollopes, Bonnins, Temletts, Ushers, and Hooles. Others have escaped my memory. Most of them have gone to their reward. Those who yet remain cannot, in the order of nature, long survive. Their descendants may point to and be proud of an honourable ancestry, not of "Pilgrim" fathers, but of "settler" fathers. Other names, not identified with Methodism, deserve to be respected by all Methodists for their work's sake :—old Dr. Campbell and Dr. Atherstone, Mr. Driver, (the elephant hunter,) Mr. Hart, of Somerset, and Mr. Gilfillan, of Cradock, and J. O. Smith, of Algoa Bay, though mentioned last, not least in the loving respect of the writer of these reminiscences. Taking our Albany friends all in all, I never expect to see their like again.

Our District Meeting consisted of a small number of Preachers. Besides the Chairman, there were SAMUEL YOUNG, a plain, simple-minded, loving pastor and preacher, remarkable for having never missed an appointment: neither rain nor rivers ever stopped him. JOHN AYLIFF and WILLIAM SHEPSTONE, (originally settlers,) eminent Missionaries, in labours most abundant. SAMUEL PALMER, in person almost as handsome as the late Dr. Newton, a laborious and valuable Minister. WILLIAM J. SHREWSBURY, our best preacher, an able divine, and most respectable scholar, as familiar with the Scriptures in their original languages as with the English version. With the exception of Samuel Young all these have gone to their reward. RICHARD HADDY, an able man and a scholar, remarkable for his great perseverance, under which most obstacles gave way to him. WILLIAM J. DAVIS, a most laborious and efficient Missionary, who has since distinguished himself by his two Editions of Boyce's Grammar, and by his *practical* Kaffir Grammar and Dictionary, the last edition of which was printed in 1872, and which has been the first to be honoured by the approval and patronage of the Colonial Government, and by a grant of £100 to Mr. Davis, in tardy acknowledgment of his literary labours;—and some others. We were a happy and united body of Christian Ministers, a real brotherhood, very free and open in our discussions; but the sun never set on our wrath. Our Chairman had impressed his loving spirit upon us all. Mr. Shrewsbury, though the senior of the Chairman, held him in the highest reverence. I may say that I loved him from the first quarter of an hour after our meeting; and though Mr. Shaw was from his nature less impulsive, and did not permit his affections to flow so rapidly, I have reason to believe that very soon our regard was mutual. Our Albany friends did not compare us to Damon and Pythias, as that story was not so familiar as the narrative of the friendship of David and Jonathan, to whom we were generally compared.

In so small a town as Graham's Town then was, our annual District Meeting, with the Missionary services, and the nightly and early morning preaching, created much interest. Hospitalities were freely dispensed, sometimes on too grand a scale to our *then* puritanic tastes. Mr. Shaw discouraged all expense for mere luxurious indulgence, and in due time introduced an almost Spartan simplicity into our friends' banquets. It was our custom, too, on a set day to call formally in a body upon the Civil Commissioner, the Head Magistrate, in fact, the Lieutenant-Governor, of the district. I remember being much amused on the first occasion with our sober procession, two and two, our polite reception by the worthy Mr. Campbell, the polite nothings which were said on both sides, and the evident relief which both parties felt when the ceremony was over. Yet it was not a useless observance for either party, but beneficial in many ways. As Missionaries we were always well disposed to put the best construction on the doings of the Colonial Authorities, and were saved from a sort of professional Colonial Radicalism which few could escape whose lot it was to live under a Colonial Government forty years ago. The times are changed, our Colonies have self-government, and their Parliaments sometimes do extraordinary things, playing legislative tricks which, if done under the old system, would have provoked a revolution, or something like it, but which now is quietly passed over, because done "by ourselves." This is no small benefit arising from the new régime, that the discontent of the Colonists is no longer with the Home Government, but with their own domestic administration. Meanwhile they are learning the art of government, and on the whole are managing their own affairs with average wisdom and discretion.

During Mr. Shaw's residence in England he was stationed from the Conference of 1833 to 1836 at Leeds; three full years, from August, 1833, to August, 1836. The Warrenite controversy and agitation, which resulted in a large secession from the Wesleyan body, was rife in the years 1835 and 1836, the attacks of the agitators being directed not only against the home finances, but also against the funds of the Missionary Society. In these troublous times Mr. Shaw was a firm, uncompromising, but also a wise and judicious, supporter of the Conference. On the news of the Kaffir outbreak reaching England, accompanied by lavish and unjust reflections upon the British Colonists as having brought the evil upon themselves by their rapacious and unjust aggressions on the Kaffir tribes, Mr. Shaw, in a long statement in the "Watchman," and in a letter to the Earl of Aberdeen, vindicated the British Colonists from the wild and wholesale attacks made upon them. Into this controversy it is our privilege not to enter. Those curious in South African history may generations hence find in the British Museum, "A Defence of the Wesleyan Missions in South Africa, by William Shaw, 1839," and "Notes on South African Affairs, by W. B. Boyce, 1839." Our opponents, Mr. Fairbairn, the chief editor of the "South African Courier," and Dr. Philip, the General Superintendent of the London Society's Missionaries, with such of the Missionaries of that Society as agreed with them, honestly believed what they asserted, advocating, however, the most philanthropic principles of action, in which we were one with them; but they blamed the wrong parties,—the Colonists,—instead of the vacillating policy of the Colonial Government. *Now*, there is no difference of opinion as to the injustice done in the excitement of the moment, and in the blindness of party zeal, to the British Colonists. But we must allow Mr. Shaw to speak for himself. His narrative supplements the history of the transactions between the Kaffirs and the Colonial Government, which is to be found in another part of this volume.

As stated above, a peace was concluded with the principal Kaffir Chief by the Governor of the Colony in 1819, in which the boundary between the Colony and Kaffraria was distinctly defined. The British settlers arrived in 1820, and had, of course, nothing whatever to do with that transaction. This treaty was succeeded by a peace between the colonists and Kaffirs, which endured for fourteen years; the general harmony being only disturbed by occasional robberies and murders, perpetrated within the Colony by small marauding parties. A tract of country, intervening between the Great Fish River and the Keiskamma, had been reserved by the treaty of 1819, as a sort of neutral territory, to prevent the too close proximity of the Kaffirs and colonists; and thus to render the danger of disputes and collisions between them less imminent. The Kaffir Chiefs, however, seemed so much disposed to cultivate terms of amity with the English, that Makomo, the son of Gaika, was allowed to re-occupy the Kat River, which, by the treaty, had been included within the limits of the Colony; but which Gaika and his sons chose to say that they had not understood to be ceded as part of the neutral territory. No doubt this concession, for the time, was very pleasing to the Gaika Chiefs and their tribes; and as they were told that they were to hold these lands pending good behaviour, it is likely that they were hereby restrained from many depredations which they might otherwise have committed.

The Dhlambi Chiefs, including the tribe of Pato, with which I lived from 1824 to 1830 inclusive, felt aggrieved by the treaty of 1819, as it had deprived them of their share of the neutral territory, over which they denied that Gaika ever had any right or control, and, therefore, he had no power to cede it away. I represented their views and feelings to the Government of the day; and, at a public interview held between the Commandant of Kaffraria and the Chiefs, in the presence of a

considerable military force and a large assemblage of the Kaffirs,
I rendered important assistance in bringing about a good
understanding between the Government and the powerful Chief
Dhlambi ; whose tribe now moved to their old country, between
the Buffaloe and Keiskamma Rivers, from whence they had
been driven during the war of 1818–19. I afterwards urged
Pato's request, for permission to re-occupy his portion of the
neutral ground on the coast westward of the Keiskamma.
The Government, after much correspondence and discussion,
at length acceded to his wishes, and allowed this tribe (the
Amagunukwaybi) first to occupy a part of it, and then, on their
good behaviour for a number of years, the whole, as far as
the Great Fish River ; and, for some eighteen years, they
remained in peaceful re-occupation of the country that had been
ceded in 1849.

In the year 1828, Makomo thought proper, with his clan, to
attack a small Abatembu tribe, living behind the Kat Bergen,
in doing which he pursued them into the colonial territory ;
and, while the Government was at peace with the nation of
Abatembu, his warriors killed or wounded many of them, and
carried off at the same time a large number of their cattle. For
this outrage it was resolved to expel this Chief from the territory which he had been suffered to occupy, as a special act of
favour, contrary to the treaty of 1819. The repeated robberies
and murders committed by his people, during several previous
years, on the farms of the adjoining Dutch colonists, and this
crowning act of aggression on the Tembookie tribe, were considered to be sufficient evidence that they were unworthy to
enjoy this privilege any longer ; since they seemed disposed to
make the favourable position which they occupied in the valleys surrounded by the Kat Berg, a sort of garrison, whence
they could at their pleasure sally forth and commit acts of
aggression on their neighbours, both white and black. Makomo

and his people were, therefore, expelled by the British and colonial forces, happily without bloodshed, from the Kat River; and obliged once more to take up their abode within the limits assigned to the Gaika tribe by the treaty of 1819.

I have no doubt that this proceeding greatly exasperated Makomo and his people, who could not understand how our Government, acting upon a principle of justice, should inflict this forfeiture on them for an aggression on a neighbouring native tribe. The subsequent war of 1834–5 was, consequently, headed and directed chiefly by Makomo, who despaired of recovering possession of this much coveted tract of land, when he saw that shortly after his expulsion it was peopled by the authority of the Colonial Government. But when the question is raised, What had the British settlers to do with this transaction? the only reply that can be given is, Absolutely nothing! They neither called for the expulsion of Makomo, nor did they aid in any way to effect it. "But did they not get possession of the Kat River lands?" Not an acre of them. The Government resolved to form a large settlement in that locality, consisting of Hottentots and other Africans, born or naturalized in the Colony. These classes of people were invited to take possession: and as they arrived from various parts of the Colony, these lands were subdivided among them. Several villages were formed; and at length a population of this description, without any admixture of European race, saving a Minister of the Dutch Reformed Church, (the Rev. W. R. Thomson,) and the Rev. Messrs. Reed of the London Missionary Society, who undertook the pastoral charge of the people,—was settled in the district from whence Makomo had been driven.

It is quite beside my present purpose to discuss the policy of this measure of the Colonial Government, for which Sir Andries Stockenstrom, at that time Commissioner-General for frontier affairs, is chiefly responsible. I entirely concurred at the time, and do so now, in the opinion that the Hottentot race, having been very improperly deprived by the old Dutch Government of all right in the soil of the Colony, once belonging to their forefathers, it was fair and reasonable that some steps should have been taken to provide those among them who had the means of rendering the land available for their own support, with suitable locations, to be held in their own name and right.

I am decidedly hostile, on grounds both of justice and good policy, to any plan of colonization which deprives the natives of all right in the soil. There should be ample reserves of lands of average value made for them in all parts of a territory, which is governed by our colonial rulers, and generally occupied by our colonists. For a time these lands should be legally vested in trustees, selected from a class of persons who, by their inclination or position, must be naturally careful for their interests; or, perhaps, still better, they might remain under the responsible management of the Governor for the time being, without, however, giving him power to alienate such lands for other purposes; excepting under special authority of the Secretary of State for the Colonies, granted on the concurrent recommendation of the local Parliament. In whatever manner the lands are secured *pro tempore*, there should, however, be a proviso, that, as soon as any of the natives erect appropriate dwellings, and are presumably acquainted with the rights and privileges arising from the ownership of real property, they should receive legal titles, vesting their own lands in their own names in the usual manner; and then they may be safely allowed, like all other classes of the community, " to do what they will with their own." The result in the course of time would be, that the idle and worthless would dispose of their landed property, and be compelled, by their own want of character and thrift, to join the classes who must seek employment from others, to secure for themselves the means of subsistence; while the more industrious and sober would be found, as a class, to rise in character, and support themselves in comfort on their own homesteads and allotments. His Majesty's Commissioners of Inquiry long ago expressed an opinion decidedly favourable to the granting of land to the natives; although it appears from their report to the Secretary of State for the Colonies, printed in 1830, that they considered it "desirable that the Hottentots should not be congregated in one spot; and that, in restoring to them a portion of that territory which was once their own, and in admitting them to the enjoyment of privileges in common with the rest of His Majesty's subjects in South Africa, any measures should be avoided which might tend to impress them with an opinion that they are destined to form a distinct class of the population."*

After the above expression of my views, the reader will perceive that I do not wish to represent the settlement of the Hottentots on the vacant lands of the Kat River as *per se* an evil proceeding. On the contrary, I think Sir Andries Stockenstrom, acting in his capacity as Commissioner-General, deserves all honour for recommending and carrying out this honest and bold measure; which he designed to be at once an act of justice to the coloured people, and a means of defence for an exposed part of the Colony, against the incursions of the border Kaffirs. But it was an experiment; and, however well and honestly intended, it led to some very disastrous results, both as it regards the colonists and the natives. I do not mean that experience shows that it was wrong to grant to the natives the possession of a part of the lands which had belonged to their forefathers. Experience never shows an act of justice to be wrong. But the result in this case has shown that although it was fair and reasonable to grant these people a

---

* Commissioner Bigge's Report on the Hottentot Population, p. 22.

right in the soil, yet the time and *mode* of doing it, in this instance, entailed certain evil consequences.

FIRST, it greatly exasperated the Chief Makomo and his people, and rendered them very dangerous neighbours. SECONDLY, it brought together from all parts of the Colony a great body of natives, exceeding four thousand in number; having among them painful remembrances of grievous wrongs, suffered by some of them from certain Dutch farmers before the establishment of regular government and courts of justice in the border districts; and with yet more painful traditions, some true, and others exaggerated, or wholly false, of injuries sustained from the same class of colonists, at a still remoter period. This concourse of people, including about one thousand able-bodied men, all armed, and well knowing how to use their fire-arms, were thus entirely separated from the rest of the colonial community, whom they were unhappily induced, by a variety of events, to regard as hostile to them and their interests. In consequence of this arrangement, they gradually lost all sympathy with the white inhabitants; and as many of the latter no doubt disliked seeing numbers of people collected together, as they conceived, without means of honest subsistence, and who might be fully and more usefully employed as labourers on their farms, which could not be properly managed for lack of such labour,—estranged and even hostile feelings were gradually produced between the two classes. THIRDLY, this large body of the Hottentots and other races were placed close to the Kaffirs, that they might act as a frontier guard for that part of the Colony; but it was not foreseen that this proximity afforded opportunity for intercourse between the two races, which might lead to serious consequences affecting the peace of the country. In point of fact, there is now no doubt that at a rather early period a friendly intercourse, but, from the circumstances of the time, of dangerous tendency, was opened between the natives located on the Kat River, and their Kaffir neighbours. Many of the former, indeed, could speak the Kaffir language; and not a few were connected in various ties of relationship with the neighbouring Kaffirs, in consequence of that intermingling of tribes and families which always occurs in border districts. Hence there is evidence sufficient to show that treasonable intercourse took place between certain Hottentots and the Kaffirs, a short time before the war of 1834; and although during the war, and the subsequent one of 1846, the great body of the Kat River people rendered valuable service in the defence of the country, yet, at the very commencement of the last war, (1850,) there arose a fierce rebellion among the natives of that settlement, which speedily involved a large proportion of its population, who became most dangerous enemies of the Colony; and, by their alliance with the Kaffirs, for a time placed the colonial border, with its scattered population of British settlers, in the most extreme peril and danger. Indeed, it is undeniable that the greatest atrocities committed during that period were perpetrated by these people and other natives, with whom they were unhappily induced to connect themselves.

During my residence in England I was twice examined, at considerable length, before the " Aborigines Committee " of the House of Commons, which, in consequence of the Kaffir war of 1834-5, had been appointed, on the urgent representations of that most indefatigable and honest friend of Africa and the African race, the late Sir Fowell Buxton, Bart. On the arrival of the mail bringing news of this sudden outburst of the Kaffir tribes on the border districts of the Colony, I also addressed a long letter to the Earl of Aberdeen, at that time Secretary of State for the Colonies, on the subject. This communication was acknowledged with thanks, and was printed, without abridgment, among the evidence collected by the Aborigines Committee. It was also published in a separate form as a pamphlet, and was somewhat extensively circulated.   If any one feels sufficiently interested in the matter to examine that letter and my evidence before the Parliamentary Committee, he will find that the opinions I have expressed in this chapter on the cause of the Kaffir war of that period are substantially the same as those which I then put forth.   During a subsequent residence of more than twenty years, with many opportunities for observing what was going forward, having trustworthy correspondents among the various tribes, being on very friendly terms with most of the principal Chiefs, and having had the honour to be consulted on several important occasions by the successive Governors of the Colony, and other high officials, on matters connected with native affairs and the peace of the border; I may surely claim to be even better acquainted with the whole bearing of the subject than I was in 1835.   I have, however, found no reason to alter, but much to justify the general statement in which I summed up my remarks in one part of my letter to Lord Aberdeen, and which I will here repeat: " Thus your Lordship will perceive that I attribute the present disturbed state of the Kaffir border, not to any cruelties perpetrated by the British settlers upon the Kaffirs; not to any want of humanity in the British officers in their treatment of the native tribes, or of zeal and activity in the protection of British lives and property; but to the moral state and predatory habits of the Kaffirs, the evil tendencies of which have been aggravated by the exceedingly mischievous character of our border policy."

The views entertained by the General Secretaries of the Wesleyan Missionary Society regarding the outbreak of the Kaffir war, are thus clearly set forth in their announcement to the friends of our Missions, as published in the " Missionary Notices " for May, 1835 :—

"Long before this number of our 'Notices' can be circulated, our readers, generally, will have learned, from the public journals, the deeply afflictive intelligence which has arrived from South Africa during the last few weeks. We refer to the fearful calamity which, in the month of December, overtook the settlers in the Albany District, and other portions of the Eastern borders of the British Colony, by an irruption of the pagan Kaffirs, who passed the frontier line at various points, and in very numerous bodies, and have pursued a course of plunder, devastation, and murder, the description of which is too horrible for minute recital in our pages. At the date, however, of the latest accounts hitherto received, (January 30th,) there was reason to hope that the progress of the invaders had been arrested; and that general security and tranquillity would, in some tolerable degree, be speedily restored : but the loss of life, as well as of property, has, we fear, been very considerable; and the distress entailed by the visitation will be both intense and enduring. Amidst these scenes of alarm and peril, we are happy to state, there is reason to believe that the lives of all our beloved Missionaries, and their families, have been graciously preserved. For this signal mercy, we unite with them and their numerous English friends in offering devout thanksgivings to Divine Providence. Their circumstances, however, and those of our Societies in South Africa, are still such as to call for the tenderest sympathy, and entitle them to a very special interest in the prayers of all who have the cause of Christ at heart. When more ample intelligence shall have arrived *from themselves,* we shall endeavour to satisfy the intense anxiety of our readers by publishing the particulars. In the mean time we rejoice to add, that the influence of Christianity, where its truths and institutions had previously been brought into even partial operation, appears to have been considerably pacific and salutary on those Chiefs and tribes who had made any explicit acknowledgment of its authority; and that the mischief has thus been, in some degree, *checked and mitigated*. Had the Gospel been more extensively propagated, and the moral feelings and habits of the natives at large brought under its mild and ameliorating control, by means of a more adequate supply of Missionaries and Schoolmasters than has hitherto been afforded to Kaffraria, even by the united efforts of all the Societies, who can tell how much of the calamity might have been altogether *prevented?* Large and powerful masses of *unchristianized* and uncivilized men can never long be safe neighbours to a Christian colony. We must give them our religion, if we would reckon with certainty on securing their cordial confidence and friendship."

The painful subject is again referred to in a subsequent number of the " Missionary Notices " for the same year, in the following passage; which displays an acquaintance with the subject most creditable to the writer. Much evil would have been prevented, if all popular English writers who at this period hastily undertook to enlighten the world concerning the causes of the Kaffir war, had taken similar care, first, to become thoroughly familiar with the facts, and, afterwards, to apply a sound philosophy in accounting for them.

" It is not our province to dwell at large upon the causes of the Kaffir war. Those who are aware of the irritating effect produced upon the mind of Makomo, by a succession of such measures as that to which the Rev. William Shaw has referred, in his ' Letter to the Earl of Aberdeen,' lately published, (a pamphlet which we strongly recommend to those who desire thoroughly to understand the subject,) will not be at a loss to account for the origin of the recent calamity. But of whatever Makomo and his brother Tyalie might have to complain, in respect to the policy pursued by the Colonial Government, Hintza had no personal grievance to be redressed. His territories were too remote to suffer from any incursions from the Colony. On one occasion, when threatened with invasion from other tribes, he had been defended by the colonial forces; and he had always the means at command for protecting his people against the wrong-doings of any English traders who might visit or reside among them. It would not really serve the cause of humanity to deny, that his native cupidity had no small share in prompting him to cherish and promote the war. It would be a mistaken philanthropy, and a palpable contradiction of St. Paul's description of the Gentile world, to represent mere heathen men as combining in their character all that is noble and excellent. It is not their virtue which entitles them to our sympathy, but their bondage to demoralizing and cruel superstitions, and their need of that Gospel which alone can save fallen man; and the fearful energy even of their vices tends only to strengthen the appeal in their behalf."

CHAPTER VI.

The Kaffir Wars and their Results.

THE brief sketch of the policy of the British Government, and the injurious consequences to the Kaffirs and the Colonists, given in Mr. Shaw's " Story of my Mission," is necessary to explain the position in which the Mission was placed after the first Kaffir war, and in those which unhappily followed.

On my arrival at Graham's Town in March, 1837, I found the people just recovering from the sad results of the previous war. Many of the settlers had been killed, and numerous farm-houses which, before I left the country, had been erected in various parts of the district, had been burnt down. These white-washed farm-buildings added greatly to the picturesque variety and liveliness of the scene, as I used to traverse it on my pastoral and preaching journeys; but they now only appeared as desolated ruins, with blackened walls, and having tales of horror connected with their recent history, which were recited to me by the owners, whom I now found once more living in tents or huts, on property where I had previously seen them occupying very comfortable dwellings, erected at considerable cost, and no small amount of personal labour. It is beside my purpose to enter into the painful details either of this war, or of the two subsequent wars which occurred while I was a resident in the country. Indeed, I cannot more briefly or forcibly state the distress and misery occasioned by the Kaffir inroad of 1834-5, than by quoting the following passage contained in a report transmitted by Colonel (now Lieutenant-General) Sir Harry Smith, G.C.B., to the Governor at Cape Town, in January, 1835 :—

"Already are seven thousand persons dependent upon the Government for the necessaries of life. The land is filled with the lamentations of the widow and the fatherless. The indelible impressions already made upon myself, by the horrors of an irruption of savages upon a scattered population, almost exclusively engaged in the peaceful occupation of husbandry, are such as to make me look on those I have witnessed in a service of thirty years,—ten of which in the most eventful period of the war,—as trifles to what I have now witnessed; and compel me to bring under consideration, as forcibly as I am able, the heart-rending position in which a very large portion of the inhabitants of this frontier are at present placed, as well as their intense anxiety respecting their future condition."

The actual extent of damage sustained by the settlers of Albany, including the losses of the Dutch settlers in the northern border districts, was carefully inquired into, and officially reported by the Government to amount to the estimated value of £288,625. 4s. 9d.

It is hardly necessary to say, that these heavy losses, inflicted on people who were not conscious of having committed—and in fact were entirely innocent of—any act of aggression on the Kaffir tribes, produced very much exasperation. Under such circumstances, it can scarcely be expected that the mass of the people would regard the Kaffirs with very complacent feelings. Indeed, I soon became painfully sensible of a great revulsion in the sentiments of the British settlers in reference to the Kaffir race. Up to the period of my departure, the prevailing feeling was undoubtedly that of kindness and goodwill towards these people. Hearty wishes for the success of the Missions among them, and the progress and improvement of the Kaffir Chiefs and people, were often expressed by all classes of the settlers, many of whom, on the visits of the Chiefs, (which, after I brought the first of them to the Colony, became rather frequent,) received them into their houses, and treated them with much generous hospitality. But the painful events of the war greatly diminished those feelings of kindness on the part of the British settlers. In some minds, indeed, strong sentiments of dislike were produced; and even among professors of religion it was at times requisite, in mild but decisive terms, to speak of the great Christian duty, to forgive our enemies, and to pray for those who despitefully use us. Those who have never been placed in such painful circumstances may think this strange; but candid persons who are acquainted with the history of border tribes in all lands, and embraced in every period of historic narrative, will feel no amazement at such a result.

Unhappily these feelings were, for a time, rendered much more intense than probably they would have been, in consequence of the course pursued by some among the professed friends of the native tribes, who, either from defective information, or so strong a sympathy with the natives as rendered them blind to the just rights and claims of the settlers, were certainly led into a course of action which greatly increased the prevailing exasperation. It was believed that, owing to the interference and one-sided representations of some of these well-meaning but indiscreet gentlemen, the arrangements which Sir B. D'Urban had made at the conclusion of the war, for the pacification and future protection and safety of the country, had been inconsiderately overruled and set aside by the Secretary of State for the Colonies; and in proportion to the confidence which the British settlers had reposed in the judgment and honest intentions of that excellent Governor, were the disgust and vexation universally felt by them, when they learned that his plans for the future government of the border were all to be set aside, and the Kaffirs were to be restored at once to the occupation of a large portion of the territory which they had ceded in 1819; consequently, that the Chiefs, instead of suffering any penalty for causing so much loss and misery by an unprovoked war, regarded themselves as rewarded for their efforts by a considerable accession of territory, that once more placed them in the impenetrable neighbourhood of the Fish River bush, which had, in former years, been the great stronghold from whence their hordes issued to rob and murder.

The opinion which I was led to form upon the case of the settlers, was fully expressed in a letter which I addressed to a friend in England, shortly after my return to the Colony. The following is an extract from that communication :—

" I have already seen enough to be fully convinced of the ruinous consequences, to great numbers of the settlers and country people, by the late Kaffir irruption. I am aware that well-informed persons in England never doubted this; and it could not require any corroborative testimony, if it were not that interested persons have sought to mislead the public mind on this subject. I can assure you that the effects of this fearful disaster will be felt for years to come, both as it respects the *temporal* and *spiritual* interests of the settlers; and I hope you will not hesitate to publish it as my most decided opinion, that if *adequate compensation* be not granted to the sufferers, it will be a most flagrant breach of faith on the part of the British Government, *who sent the settlers to the lands which they now occupy ;* and it will always be justly quoted as a lamentable instance of neglect of British interests, by those who should have fostered and protected them, at the same time that they practically cared for the native tribes. I find that many

of the ruined people are despairing of help ; but I have endeavoured to console them with the belief that the Government
will not abandon them ; and I never will believe (unless compelled by facts) that any administration will refuse to recognise
their just claims to compensation. You know my views on this
subject generally, and they have undergone no change. The
border policy of this Colony, for years previously to the irruption of the Kaffirs, had been very bad, and therefore was very
injurious both to Colonists and Kaffirs ; but for this the settlers
were not to blame : they complained several times of the border
system, and very earnestly entreated for the substitution of
some other plan. They now very naturally think, that it is a
great hardship that any class of persons in England should
hold them responsible for the *effects of a system* which
they *always deprecated;* and that to exhibit charges, which
have not been and *never can be proved,* against an innocent and
well-meaning people, because the system of which *they were
not the contrivers,* but the *victims,* has produced bad consequences, is only to offer *insult* instead of *commiseration* to the
sufferers.

"My utmost efforts shall be used in every way consistent
with my office and character as a Minister of the Gospel, to
calm the tumult of our people's minds. In common with the
rest of the community, they have been *greatly* and *injuriously
excited* by recent events, and, considering the ungenerous treatment which they and their Ministers have received from a party
who affect to be friends of the Kaffirs, but who, *in fact,
have as yet done next to nothing for that people,* I cannot wonder
at the indignation which is everywhere manifest, although
I am bound, by a thousand motives, to exhort them ' to forgive
their enemies,' and to ' pray for them who have despitefully
used them.'"

The British settlers, strong in the conviction of their inno-

'cence of the charges that had been made against them,—
especially the allegation that they had gone on many Com-
mandoes into the Kaffir territory, to make forcible reprisals,
and thereby brought the Kaffir invasion upon themselves,
which was wholly untrue,—resolved to place their denial of
these accusations before the highest branches of the British
Government. They successively addressed His Majesty
(William IV.) in Council, June 17th, 1835 ; the Right Honourable the Secretary of State for the Colonies, (Lord Glenelg,)
January 23rd, 1836 ; and finally transmitted a petition to the
"Honourable the Commons of the United Kingdom of Great
Britain and Ireland, in Parliament assembled." The sole
satisfaction obtained was, that Lord Glenelg was at length, by
the force of facts, compelled to make the British settlers a sort
of *amende honorable*, which was conveyed to them through the
Local Government in the following terms :—

"Deeply regretting, as he does, the promulgation of any
statements which have given so much pain *to these loyal and
meritorious subjects of His Majesty,—the inhabitants of the Eastern
Province,*—Lord Glenelg has expressed his desire that the
memorialists should be informed that *His Majesty's Government
disclaim all participation in the sentiments which have dictated the
reproaches cast on the character of the colonists.* He appreciates,
and cannot but applaud, the solicitude of the memorialists to
relieve themselves from the effects of the statements in question ;
but he has felt it, however, impossible to concur in the ex-
pediency of appointing a Commission of Inquiry. Such a
measure would not, in his Lordship's judgment, answer any
useful purpose, inasmuch as the report of a Commission, and
the evidence resulting from an inquiry, would be too voluminous
for general circulation ; nor does Lord Glenelg regard the proposed Commission as a proper mode of repelling imputations
on a whole people. He conceives there are other and much more

convenient channels through which the memorialists, without
incurring the delay, the expense, and the prejudice which would
attend an inquiry by Commission, might effectually promulgate
their defence against accusation; and to those methods of
vindication the parties concerned will probably, he imagines,
think it expedient to resort."

I returned to the Colony just as the final movements were
being made to restore the neutral country to the Kaffirs, and
consequently when the excitement from this cause was at its
height. The Wesleyan Missionaries had been openly assailed,
and that frequently, by a portion of the press, and also from
the platform, in England, as being hostile to the interests of
the Kaffirs, and pro-colonial in their views and aims. The
basest motives, wholly alien to those which ought to influence
Missionaries in their intercourse with the native tribes, were
attributed to them. One of their number, who had returned to
England in consequence of domestic bereavement, was singled
out for special attack, on account of a paper which, at a time
of great anxiety, he had hastily written at the request of the
Governor, the object and aim of which were probably misunderstood, but certainly misrepresented by the parties referred
o. The whole of these proceedings were evidently got up to
damage the Wesleyan Missionaries as witnesses before the
British public; for it was known that while as anxious as any
class of persons to secure the real interests and welfare of the
Kaffir tribes, yet their views of the cause and origin of the
recent war were not in exact accordance with the representations that had been made by those whom the colonists regarded
as their enemies.

The result of all this was, that for a time a painful controversy
arose between several of the Missionaries of different Societies.
I was reluctantly drawn into it. While I was in England, I
published a long letter, which occupied an entire page of the

" Watchman " newspaper, under the signature of " A Returned Missionary."   The object of this letter was to remove, if possible, the effect of certain misrepresentations which had been made about that time by various influential agencies. And after my return to the Colony, circumstances compelled me to publish a lengthy pamphlet in defence of the views entertained by the Wesleyan Missionaries, and the course of action we had pursued.   It was remarkable that at the very time this was going forward, the Wesleyan and the Scottish Missionaries —most of whom sympathized in our views—were engaged in more extensive and energetic efforts than any others for the promotion of the temporal and spiritual welfare of the Kaffirs. It should also be stated that it was by means of three Wesleyan Missionaries,—the Rev. Messrs. Shepstone, Boyce, and Palmer, who adventured their lives in the effort,—that peace was obtained for the Kaffirs on advantageous terms, when the colonial force was in a condition and ready to inflict very severe chastisement upon them.   Both the Governor and the colonists knew that the Wesleyan Missionaries only advocated just and reasonable arrangements : hence they often obtained a hearing, and thereby became the instruments in either averting impending evil from the Kaffirs, or otherwise inducing the Government to grant concessions, and make such modifications in the varied details of measures as were calculated to secure their interests and welfare.

During the greater part of this period one Governor held the reins ; and made it his boast, when leaving the country, that he had strictly observed the instructions received from Lord Glenelg when he was appointed; and that the troops had never fired a shot against the Kaffirs while he had ruled the country. This was almost literally true ; but every one who resided on the border during that period, knew that this course of winking at Kaffir depredations was no real kindness to the Kaffir people.

It rapidly weakened among them the influence of those motives of self-interest, which might have gone far to restrain them from indulging their predatory habits on the border settlers. They saw that the most troublesome and restless among them —the Chiefs and people who most frequently committed depre‑ dations on the colonists, and enriched themselves thereby— were petted by the Government, which appeared afraid to check them; while the Chiefs and others who showed a disposition to behave peaceably, and gave little or no trouble, seemed to be neglected, if not despised.

This period of licence at length produced the result that was long foreseen as inevitable; being followed by the war which was forced upon General Sir P. Maitland in 1846; and which, in cost and sacrifice of life and property, on both sides of the boundary, far exceeded that of 1834. The Kaffirs had become apt scholars in the art of war; and were better provided with the means of carrying it on. The value of the property taken or destroyed along the line of frontier, during the war of 1846-8, was carefully investigated, and ascertained to be about half a million pounds sterling! Sir P. Maitland was at once a devout Christian and a distinguished soldier. He was so greatly influenced by humane and benevolent feelings, that no man who knew him can doubt but that he would have avoided this war, if he had seen any possibility of doing so. Never was a veteran General less amenable to the charge of a wanton wish to plunge a country into needless war and bloodshed. He tried, by negotiation and the most reasonable proposals, to induce the Chiefs concerned to come to terms, and avoid the alternative of war. In this he utterly failed; simply because the Kaffirs had been long prepared for the contest, and had formed a strong opinion that the English were afraid of them; and that, as they had during the last ten years provided them‑ selves with horses and fire-arms, they would now be a match for the troops and colonial forces; while their vast superiority of numbers would enable them to "drive the white people into the sea."

The result of this war was that, after Sir P. Maitland and Sir H. Pottinger had successively been removed from the government during the progress of hostilities, Sir Harry Smith arrived, and concluded the war on the submission of the belligerent Chiefs; releasing the Chiefs Sandilli and Makomo, who had been some time a sort of state prisoners. It is a singular fact, and shows the evils arising from changing Governors and Commanders at critical periods, that Sir P. Maitland was just on the point of making peace with the Chiefs in January, 1847, on almost the same terms as those which Sir H. Smith dictated on the 23rd of December of the same year, amidst two thousand Kaffirs and a portion of the British troops, all the Chiefs of Kaffraria west of the Kei River being present; but then Sir H. Pottinger had been the intermediate Governor. Having been selected by the Home Government for his reputed great abilities, he was sent to bring the war to a close, and to settle the affairs of the country on a satisfactory and permanent basis. On his arrival, however, he re-commenced the war, which he found languishing and ready to terminate; and, after expending more than half a million sterling, handed over the control of affairs to Sir H. Smith; who, as stated above, thereupon made peace, on much the same terms as had been proposed, and were ready to be accepted by the Kaffirs, when the negotiations were suspended by the arrival of his predecessor.

By the arrangement made at this time by Sir H. Smith, the border Kaffir district, now called " British Kaffraria," was once more placed under the control of British functionaries; and the system which had been in force during the period that Sir B. D'Urban was the Governor, was, in its main principles, again restored. It was singular that, as Colonel on the Staff, Sir Harry Smith had been the Chief Commissioner for Kaffraria under Sir B. D'Urban ; and having subsequently distinguished himself highly in India, as the "Hero of Aliwal," he had now come back in the capacity of Governor and Commander-in-Chief, and once more established the system of which he had been the highest executive functionary in 1835.

For nearly three years after peace was made by Sir H. Smith, the border continued quiet and undisturbed. The frontier settlers were contented and happy; and all their affairs were once more beginning to show signs of renewed prosperity, while the Kaffirs seemed to have learned that the old Chief Pato had spoken truly as well as figuratively, when, being asked by messengers sent by other Chiefs to assist them in a war to drive the English out of the country, he replied, after due consultation with his advisers, " The rock is fast, it cannot be moved." How well it would have been for the Kaffirs, and for numerous border colonists, if this had, by the force of events, become the abiding sentiment of the nation !

But, unhappily, the old error was again committed. The troops were once more reduced to a most inadequate number ; and, as in each previous instance, the Kaffirs soon saw the weakness of the force in front of them. Under these circumstances it was not difficult for certain Chiefs to use their accustomed " dodge," and induce an enthusiast or a knave to pretend to have received communications from the spirits of departed Chiefs; and thus, by vague announcements and special orders of an absurd character, founded upon the national superstitions which the Chiefs easily enforced, to prepare the people for war. For this, when quite ready, they speedily found an occasion, at a time when a body of troops had been ordered to go in support of the native police, who had tried in vain to obtain a fine and restitution for some stolen cattle. Thus arose the war of 1851–2, in the commencement of which Sir H. Smith had a very narrow escape from being seized by the Kaffirs, and the troops at first suffered very severely. Sir Harry had done his utmost to prevent this war. His reputation was at stake; and he had every motive to avoid war, if possible. But although he tried every expedient that could be supposed likely to avert an event dreaded alike by the well disposed among the Kaffirs, by the border colonists, and by the chief officers of Government, yet all proved unavailing; and thus a contest, involving still greater sacrifice of life and property than on any former occasion, was the result.

It is really distressing to look back on these events, and see how much mischief resulted from an unwise economy, which led to the two previous wars, by denuding the frontier of adequate means of defence; resulting not merely in great loss of life and property, but involving the British treasury in such an amount, (millions of pounds,) for extraordinary war charges, as would have been sufficient to sustain an ample force for a whole generation. The Home Government had once more repeated its previous errors, and weakly succumbed to the incessant calls made by certain badly informed, or " penny wise and pound foolish," Members of Parliament, for the reduction of the number of troops kept on the Kaffir border; and had thereby afforded opportunity for this third Kaffir war. But, as on former occasions, it hastily sent out, at great expense, strong reinforcements; including the gallant First Battalion of the Rifle Brigade, which had not long returned to England after being employed against the Kaffirs in the previous war.

Both the country and the Government, however, at length became very impatient of the protracted character and enormous cost of the fruitless contest which was being carried on; and hence Sir George Cathcart was eventually sent (in 1852) to supersede Sir H. Smith, and arrived just as the latter, by a series of concentric military movements, had brought the war to its crisis, and left his successor the easy task and the glory of speedily terminating it. Sir George Cathcart had, however, the more difficult duty to discharge of making arrangements for the future settlement of the affairs of the country. He retained British Kaffraria as before, but compelled the Gaika tribes to evacuate the extensive valleys at the bottom and up the slopes of the Amatola Mountains; which had been their favourite residence, and their supposed impregnable garrison, for several generations; ever since, indeed, their forefathers, intruding from the north-east, had arrived in that part of Southern Africa, and had driven out its original inhabitants of the Hottentot race.

The country thus evacuated the new Governor partially filled up with Fingoes, and the more open districts along the left bank of the Keiskamma by the Kaffir tribes of Kama, Sewane, and Pato, which were to a considerable extent under the influence of the Missionaries, and had taken no active part in the late war, but in various ways had assisted the British forces, and were believed by Sir George Cathcart to be more peaceably disposed than the other Chiefs and tribes. No doubt the Gaika tribes felt these to be most humiliating terms. But there was still a sufficient extent of land assigned for their residence within the limits of British Kaffraria; and, by the arrangements which the Governor made, there was really no ground for the complaint which they urged, that they were crowded into too narrow a space. In reality, they were now to occupy a very fine tract of well-watered and grassy country, quite as extensive as that from which they had been expelled, but not so well situated for enabling them to carry on predatory or other warlike proceedings.

A tribe of Tembookies (Abatembu), living further to the north than the Amaxosa or border Kaffir tribes, having joined the confederacy of Kaffir Chiefs against the Colony, and become dangerous enemies on the north-eastern part of the border, Sir George Cathcart now compelled them to occupy a district of that country which he assigned to them, and which, besides being a very fine country, is sufficiently large for all the purposes of peaceful life; and the lands vacated by them he formed into a new division of the Colony, (Queen's Town Division,) wherein he established a large body of Fingoes and other friendly natives, including the Tembookies of the Wesleyan Mission Settlement of Lesseyton. To these were added a considerable body of European settlers, who, being invited from the other border districts, were placed on farms of more limited extent than had been usual in the other parts of the Colony, so as to concentrate the population; and it was hoped by the Governor that, as that part of the country is open and comparatively destitute of any bushy ravines, which could afford cover for a Kaffir enemy, the united force of Europeans and natives, thus located in the new district, would be able to defend themselves in any future emergency.

It is, however, a great satisfaction to myself and other Wesleyan Missionaries, that we have lived long enough to witness a great change in the opinions of some of the Missionaries referred to, and of many other persons, both at home and in the Colony. And thus we feel that the progress of events has made our justification to stand complete. Judging from recent proceedings and publications, I am happy to believe that controversy on this subject may cease. I would gladly have avoided all reference to it, but that in a book reciting the chief occurrences of my missionary career, it was impossible to avoid alluding to this matter without appearing tacitly to admit the truth of many grievous but groundless allegations against myself, and brethren, and friends, which still stand recorded in various books, written by popular and, in the main, deservedly influential authors.

CHAPTER VII.

The Interval of Peace, 1837–1843.

On Mr. Shaw's return to the Colony, early in 1837, he found the Colonists suffering from the losses sustained during the years 1835–1836, and smarting under the undeserved censure of the prejudiced public opinion at home. Where they, in the consciousness of their innocence, looked for sympathy, they found nothing but reproach. Sir Benjamin D'Urban was recalled in May, 1837, his system set aside, the Kaffir tribes replaced in the strong positions from which they had been driven, and freed from all the restraints imposed upon them by the vigorous administration of Colonel Smith, (afterwards Sir Harry Smith). Add to this, the Lieutenant-Governor appointed to carry out what was called (after the Colonial Secretary) the Glenelg system, was personally unpopular. As Andries Stockenstrom he had been a general favourite as High Commissioner. As identified with the unpopular policy of the Colonial Office, and honoured by a baronetcy, Sir Andries Stockenstrom was universally disliked. A feeling of deep discontent, not an occasional outbreak of feeling, but a chronic displacency with all Government measures, embittered all classes of society. An immediate result of this want of confidence in the Government was the emigration of the Dutch Boers by thousands beyond the northern frontier, which resulted eventually in the formation of the Orange River Sovereignty, and the Trans

Vaal River Republics. The loss of so many stalwart
Boers from the defensive power of the Colony, the gradual
reduction of the military forces, the evident fear of enforc-
ing such stipulations in the treaties as tended to repress
Kaffir aggression on the farmers; and the fact that the
local authorities, anxious to please their superiors, were
more ready to minify and excuse the offenders, than
punish and redress the offence, tended to create a feeling
among the Colonists, most painful to mere lookers on, (if
it were possible to be indifferent at such a time). The
whole body of Wesleyan Missionaries, though not personally interested, felt ashamed of the English Government,
and of the English name. All our prepossessions had
been conservative and loyal in the extreme. We looked
upon the Colonies as an integral portion of the empire, and
the Colonists as samples of the best and most enterprising
of the English population. To read the unjust charges
brought against them, and received as true by liberal and
excellent men and bodies of men, and to find the Executive so far influenced by *ex-parte* statements, as to dis-
allow the only policy which in our judgment (confirmed
by subsequent experience, and admitted, too, by the English and Colonial Governments) was equal to the difficult
task of maintaining law and order on the Colonial frontier
and in Kaffirland,—these things "make wise men mad."
Politics in England are mostly an affair of ins and outs,
in which no doubt great principles and results are involved,
but the immediate issues do not affect private comfort and
social life. In South Africa on the frontier the policy of
the Government touched the question of the security not
only of property, but of *life*, to the settlers. The Mission-

aries believed that the settlers' view of Sir B. D'Urban's policy was, that it was far more favourable to the natives than to the Colonists.

Our Missionaries knew the Colonists, and deeply sympathized with them. I dare say they felt as I did, though I only speak for myself. Government, like property, has its duties as well as its rights. The Cape Government of that day lent itself to vilify the character of the best and most enterprising of the Colonists, deprived them of all protection from the marauding pastoral tribes on their borders, brought upon them two more Kaffir wars, each more injurious than its predecessor (the last of which was concluded by the peace of February, 1853). It was done ignorantly, and from a pressure from without which the Government of that day could not withstand. It is well that our Colonial system has been thoroughly reformed. Most of our Colonies are favoured with self-government, without which *an English* population cannot breathe freely: but our Colonial Secretaries would do well to study the details of our Colonial policy in America before 1776, in the Cape and in New Zealand in more recent times, in order to avoid the mistakes of their predecessors. No Government in the world desires to act more justly than our own, whichever party may be in office ; but parliamentary administrators are compelled to look at the necessities of party, and to succumb to pressing influences which are frequently injurious to the rights of the absent uninfluential Colonists. It is well that under the new arrangements the occasions for interference on the part of the home authorities are reduced so as practically to preclude all possible collision. We have now some chance for maintaining a friendly union with our Colonial brethren in South Africa, America, and Australasia. Under the old system, a Colonial Governor was a respectable gentleman, representing a bundle of equally respectable prejudices, entirely at the mercy of the clique around him, whose policy it was to keep him ignorant of the Colony he was sent to govern, and to make him a mere partizan. The main object of such a Governor seemed to be to turn all loyal British Colonists into Radicals and rebels. The " good old times" were not better than the days in which we now live. May we be thankful, and try, by improvement of our opportunities, to leave the world better for our children than we found it in our young days!

In this excited state of the Colonial community, Mr. Shaw walked most wisely; throwing, as far as possible, oil on the troubled waters; putting in a word here and there to check those unreasonable extreme views, in which men justly irritated are apt to indulge. The case of the Colonists was so clear, that, in his opinion, exaggeration could only weaken the effect of its representation. Every Colonial Governor arrived in that Colony prejudiced against the British settlers, viewing the Kaffirs as an injured people, and in due time became convinced that the converse was the case. At last, after nearly twenty years of actual or *chronic* war, (the intervals of peace being as injurious to the Colonists as the periods of war,) the system of Sir Benjamin D'Urban was re-established substantially, and on the whole with more strictness, and the Kaffir tribes were deprived of a large portion of their territory, which was given to English, Dutch, and Fingoe settlers. We, who advocated the charitable and benevolent policy of Sir B.

D'Urban, may take credit, not for any special forethought, but for a fair share of common sense in foreseeing the issue of the change of that policy in 1836. After millions of English money have been spent, and thousands of lives, European, Colonial, and Native, have been thrown away in the conflict, the system of Sir B. D'Urban of 1835 has been re-established, and for twenty years the frontier has enjoyed comparative peace. The Hon. R. Godlonton, the editor and proprietor of the Graham's Town Journal, and author of several works on South African politics, was from the first to the last the constant, uncompromising opposer of the Glenelg system of compromise; and the ability and fairness with which he conducted this controversy tended mainly to bring it to a happy conclusion.

Previous to Mr. Shaw's arrival the strength of the District had been increased by the transference of the REV. J. CAMERON from Cape Town, and of the REV. W. H. GARNER from England. Mr. Shaw brought with him the REV. G. H. GREEN (and another young man, who afterwards left our work). JAMES CAMERON was one of those extraordinary self-taught men, who, in spite of every disadvantage, achieve a maturity of mind and of preaching power from the very beginning of their career. His examination before the Committee in 1829, and a sermon preached in Lambeth from the text, "*And the disciples were called Christians first in Antioch,*" (Acts xi. 26,) produced such an effect on the minds of some of the leading friends, that the question of his appointment to Africa was re-considered. It was thought that such preaching power would have no proper sphere among the Kaffirs, to which Mission his name was appended. Had there been no

European Colonial population, the objection was very reasonable. He has been a power in Cape Town, in the Eastern Province, and in Natal. In my day, as a preacher and as a theologian he was unequalled in South Africa; and I do not think that he was second in these respects to any of his brethren in England. G. H. GREEN was a loving brother, and, as an excellent preacher, was a valuable addition to our number. W. H. GARNER was a man of ready wit, good sense, and energy, and did good service in the native work. He died in 1864. In 1838 the REVS. JOHN RICHARDS and WILLIAM IMPEY joined the District. MR. RICHARDS was, I think, the first of the students from the Theological Institution at Hoxton whose services were given to South Africa. His studious habits, which were not suffered to interfere with the systematic discharge of pastoral duties, and his excellent preaching, did much to allay a prejudice which some good people entertained against a scholastic training for our ministry. WILLIAM IMPEY, a respectable, educated young man, had not gone through this ordeal; but was from the first an acceptable preacher, and soon stood high in the opinion of his brethren and of the colonial public. The fact that he was eventually the successor of Mr. Shaw in the Chairmanship of the Districts, is sufficient testimony to his worth and general ability. In 1840 the Brethren F. TAYLOR, GLADWIN, HORATIO PEARSE, J. S. THOMAS, W. C. HOLDEN, J. W. APPLEYARD, JOHN SMITH, and THORNLEY SMITH, were sent out. Of these the Brethren TAYLOR, GLADWIN, and the saintly PEARSE are gone to their reward. MR. J. S. THOMAS was killed unintentionally by the Kaffirs in a raid made upon the cattle fold of the people of the Station he then

occupied.   MESSRS. HOLDEN, J. SMITH, and APPLEYARD are
yet in Stations in South Africa.   MR. HOLDEN has gathered
together much valuable matter respecting South Africa in
his works, "*History of Natal*," 1855, and "*The Past and
Future of the Kaffir Race*," 1866, and has proved himself
to be a hard-working Missionary to the natives.   JOHN
SMITH, a loving and diligent preacher and pastor, lives in
the esteem of his brethren.   J. W. APPLEYARD has found a
sphere for his scholarly talents in the revision of the
translations of the Holy Scriptures, and in the composition
of a new and enlarged Kaffir Grammar, respecting which
we quote the Resolution of the District Meeting of the
Albany and Kaffraria District, held at Mount Coke,
December 6th, 1849. (See "Notices," May, 1850, p. 79.)

"*Resolved*,—That we have seen with great satisfaction the
completion and issue of Mr. Appleyard's New Grammar of the
Kaffir Language ;—a publication highly creditable to the learning and research of the author, and which must become the
standard Grammar of the language.   We thus express ourselves
without forgetting the high merits of the Rev. W. B. Boyce's
Grammar of the language, which was the first publication that
supplied the key to the intricacies thereof, by its development
of the principles of what its discoverer appropriately called the
'Euphonic Concord.'   We confidently recommend Mr. Appleyard's Grammar as, in the main, a correct and philosophical
exhibition of the principles and rules which govern this ancient
and interesting African language, so extensively spoken upon
the continent. The manner in which the work has been printed
and bound, at our printing office, cannot fail to reflect credit
upon that establishment ; and the work itself is calculated to
serve the Mission, not only as forming a valuable help to Mis-

sionaries studying the language, but also as suggesting useful
hints to those on whom the duty and honour devolves of completing translations of the Holy Scriptures into the Kaffir
tongue."

MR. THORNLEY SMITH remained for some years in the
Colonial work in South Africa. He was from the first an
excellent and popular preacher. His writings, "Moses,"
"Joshua," &c., are among the best of their kind, and
deserve to be in every family library in which the intellectual gratification and advancement of the young are
duly considered. His little work on South Africa is very
valuable. With subsequent additions to the Missionary
Ministers in South Africa I have but a slender acquaintance. But the men who were my colleagues up to 1843 I
can never forget. No men bear knowing better than
Methodist Missionaries. Of the comparatively young
men taken out and sent into the Mission since 1840 I
have only come in contact with W. SARGEANT and J. R.
SAWTELL; and if these are fair average specimens of our
Missionaries in South-Eastern Africa, the Methodist
Church may thank God and take courage.

Mr. Shaw's first business was the re-establishment of
the Stations ruined by the Kaffir war of 1835–6. Many of
the chapels in the Colony had been destroyed. In Kaffirland, Wesleyville, Mount Coke, and Butterworth had been
burnt down. Clarkebury, Morley, and Buntingville had
remained untouched, protected by the chiefs of the tribes
to which they were attached. By the time their restoration had been effected, the second Kaffir war arose, and
the destruction of property was on a yet larger scale
(1846–8). Again, after what was called "peace," the work

of reconstruction re-commenced, to be interrupted by the war of 1851–3. Since then no open outbreak has desolated the Mission field. Mr. Shaw's labours and responsibilities were increased in 1838 by the annexation of the BECHUANA District, (as a section to the Albany District,) and again in 1841, by the extension of the Methodist Missions to the Colony of NATAL. The superintending this large field of Missionary labour was no easy task. Mr. Shaw's visits were looked forward to with pleasure, claimed by the brethren as a *right*, and in fact *exacted* almost mercilessly, considering the necessity, equally great, for his presence at head quarters. Soon after his return to the Colony he, in May, 1837, visited the distant Stations of Clarkebury, Morley, and Buntingville; and on his return to Graham's Town soon left to hold a District Meeting in the Bechuana Country, August to October. In 1838–9 I saved him the journey to the Bechuana Country, by presiding as Acting Chairman over the District Meeting in January, 1839. The same year, 13th and 20th of August, the Centenary Sermons in Graham's Town were preached: in the morning by Mr. Shaw, from John i. 6: "*There was a man sent from God, whose name was John.*" I preached in the evening. The Meetings which followed were highly successful in a financial point of view.

In October, 1841, Mr. Shaw preached by request a sermon on the death of Miss Somerset, the daughter of Colonel Somerset, which was soon after published. It is the only sermon which Mr. Shaw furnished for the press, which, considering the frequent requests made to him to publish particular discourses, during his more than thirty years of pulpit popularity in the Colony, is no small proof of his sagacity and good sense. A printed sermon, quietly read, is altogether a different thing from the same sermon delivered *vivâ voce* from the heart, with energy and feeling, and preceded and followed by singing and prayer, in the great congregation. This published sermon is no fair specimen of Mr. Shaw's preaching: the matter of the subject did not admit of that continuous exposition and application of the truth which was characteristic of his ordinary ministry. It is, however, neither better nor worse than the average of funeral discourses. Whoever heard Mr. Shaw preach recognised the influence which the study of the thirty volumes of the "Christian Library" had left upon his mind. That invaluable collection of the old English Episcopalian and Puritan divinity is too much neglected in our day. Many object to it, because the various treatises are found in an abridged form, though the abridgments have been made by the hand of a master. In its place the bookshelves of many a study are crowded by the voluminous series of Nichol's Puritan Divines, which no Minister in full work can possibly find time to read, and which are only valuable for occasional reference. So, refusing to avail themselves of the treasures contained in the "Christian Library," many grow up with but a slender acquaintance with the great theologians of the seventeenth century. In some cases, the places of these "giant" minds are occupied by sensational and sentimental divines of what Sir Fowell Buxton terms the "Bible-and-water school." The effect of such twaddle on the Ministry of the future may be imagined. Mr. Shaw, as a genuine Methodist Preacher of the old school, was an extemporaneous preacher. If anything can add to the intolerable annoyance of a read sermon to a Methodist congregation, it is the generally inferior character of the matter of such deliverances. If the Methodist Conference has in any way been unfaithful to the trust committed to it by its founder, it is in permitting any of its members, small or great, to substitute reading for preaching in any of its pulpits. If we are not able to look our congregation in the face, and set before them (without book) the plan of salvation, why should we call ourselves Methodist Preachers? However decorous and becoming may be all our arrangements in the order of public worship, yet neither these, nor instrumental music, nor the voices of singing men and singing women, will make up for the want of a Minister in the pulpit who can preach from his heart, not from his book, to the hearts of the people.

In 1842, in the months of February and March, I accompanied Mr. Shaw in a journey through Cradock up to Shiloh and the Tambookie Country, to arrange respecting the new Mission to the Abatembu tribes. This was our last Missionary-business journey. About this time, as Mr. Shaw and I were standing on one of the hills from which Graham's Town can be fully seen, Mr. Shaw remarked, " It is a great comfort to me that there is not a house in that town in which I have not had the opportunity of offering prayer." What Richard Baxter was to Kidderminster Mr. Shaw was to Graham's Town. In 1843, having received permission to return to England, I removed with my family from Graham's Town to Algoa Bay, by way of Salem, January 30th. Mr. Shaw kindly accompanied us, and remained with us during our detention of fourteen days, awaiting the arrival of the steamer:

our home being the mansion of our old friend, John Owen Smith, Esq., who, though abroad, had placed his establishment at our disposal. We sailed February 14th, not expecting to meet again for many years. I cannot deny myself the gratification of quoting a sentence from Mr. Shaw's letter to me, which I received at Cape Town. "As soon as I reached the shore, I set off homeward, and relieved my mind by a good cry." We kept up a brisk correspondence during my stay in England, (1843–5,) and my residence in Sydney, (1846–56,) but we did not meet until August, 1856, at the Bristol Conference, a few days after my return from Australia, Mr. Shaw having arrived in England a few weeks previously.

I may now be permitted to give a few of my own reminiscences of my dear friend, referring to the period of our co-African career, 1830–43.

Before I left England I heard from the Rev. George Morley and his able and excellent wife the highest commendation of Mr. Shaw. One dingy back room in that dingy Mission House, 77, Hatton Garden, is in my mind associated with Mr. Morley's earnest praises of "*the Chairman of the District*," for such was Mr. Shaw's position. The impression left on my mind was not particularly agreeable. I fancied I should find Mr. Shaw to be a respectable, methodical, high and dry martinet,—an official with qualities suited to his responsibilities, but not of a sort likely to attract a young man just commencing his probation. At Cape Town, and on the road from Algoa Bay to Graham's Town, all I heard from Mr. Shaw's eulogists confirmed the impressions made in Hatton Garden. I was some days in Graham's Town before Mr. Shaw arrived from Wesleyville, he and his party having been detained by the Fish River. On Wednesday, the 10th of February, 1830, I went up to the Mission house, a low thatched cottage of four rooms and a kitchen, large enough for a small family, but generally occupied by two families, *i.e.*, the resident, and the family of a brother in transit to or from Kaffirland. I was ushered into the sitting-room, and heard voices in the adjoining bed-room, the door being ajar. I was told that Mr. Shaw and Mr. Shepstone were there. I could not help hearing their conversation respecting their families in Kaffirland, and the possibility of their being anxious respecting their safety. The tones had nothing official : all was as natural as if the man had not been entirely lost in the Chairman. This was some comfort. When Mr. Shaw appeared, instead of an old man, I saw one apparently not much older than myself, grave and serious in his deportment, but courteous and considerate beyond all I had ever experienced before from a stranger. I was at once at home with him. The African tribes, the Missions, the language, were our leading topics, to both of us, in fact, absorbing ones. He led me down the steps into the yard, towards a sort of thatched hut, called "the den," in which he had placed a tusk of ivory which had been sent from Dingaan, the Great Chief of the Zulus. It was an annoyance to me then, (and ever after,) when some one claimed Mr. Shaw's attention ; but I left, satisfied that I could be happy with the friendship of such a man. Before the District Meeting was over, we were fast friends. I cannot forbear mentioning a curious mistake made by a good man in speaking of me at this time to Mr. Shaw : "It is very singular that the young Minister's library should contain so large a number of *Operas.*" Some of my boxes of books had been unpacked, and spread out in a large room in Mr. Cock's store. Among them were a set of Tauchnitz's Greek and Latin Classics; each volume had the word "*Opera,*" followed by the name of the author; and this occasioned deep searchings of heart to the good brother, until the mystery was explained. This is the only occasion on which I have been suspected of possessing a taste for music.

Soon after the District Meeting I went to Wesleyville, and was introduced to Mrs. Shaw, a noble-looking woman, the fit wife for such a man as Mr. Shaw. She was truly a helpmate. Though naturally timid, and anxious about her husband's safety, yet she never tried to prevent his long and necessary absences, even when left on a Mission Station in the midst of Kaffirs. Mr. Shaw had no doubt made a favourable representation of me to her, and we were soon friends. Ever after I used to call her *Ma,* and Mr. Shaw *Pa,* to the great amusement of strangers. We used to quarrel over Mr. Shaw's library, which I tried to re-modify, not by subtraction but by addition. It consisted mainly of a few classical and mathematical works, the standards of Methodist theology, and "The Christian Library," thirty volumes, 8vo, with the standard divinity of the Church of England and of the Nonconformist Churches. "*The Christian Library*" *had been thoroughly marked; read* and re-read. Here was "*the secret place of thunder.*" Mr. Shaw's preaching was explanatory, experimental, and practical. Sensible people always liked his last sermon the best.

During my residence in Africa, Mr. Shaw exercised an

influence amounting to fascination over me. The more intimately I knew him the more thoroughly I respected him. He had no weaknesses to mar the general effect of his character : there was nothing behind, which, if known, would have diminished his influence. To me he seemed to be an incarnation of conscience and judgment,—a man acting altogether wisely, and from the highest and most noble principles. Under circumstances the most trying he never lost his temper or his self-possession. No man was more enterprising, and yet no man more cautious. Like "Bailie Nicol Jarvie," in Scott's novel, "he never would put forth his hand unless he was sure he could pull it back again." Some people cheaply earn a character for prudence and caution by doing nothing and running no risks. Mr. Shaw's plans for our Mission in Kaffirland were from the first perfect, and needed no subsequent modification. His object was to plant a series of Missions with the great chiefs and ruling tribes as far as Delagoa Bay, and to a great extent he succeeded. Before he left Africa in 1856 our Missions extended from Algoa Bay to the Tugela River, which separates the Natal Colony from Zululand.

From the Rev. Henry H. Dugmore I have received the following contribution to this part of my narrative. The complimentary allusions to myself I cannot leave out, as they are so dovetailed with the rest of the composition ; but when the reader knows that this excellent Minister is by marriage a near relation, he will be able to discount the expressions which apply to me.

"I knew Mr. Shaw by sight and name as early as 1823, when I used to attend the Wesleyan Sunday School in

Graham's Town, and I of course often saw him at the public services on District and Missionary Meeting occasions. But my *personal* acquaintance with him did not begin till I had become a member of Society. In the never-forgotten 'Revival' of 1831, I found peace with God, and under the impulse of a new life was ready for active exertion in the service of my Saviour. Mr. Shaw appointed me Leader of a Class of natives, called upon me occasionally to pray in the prayer-meetings, and made use of my musical tendencies in the Sunday School Anniversaries.

"About the same time he formed a class of youths, to whom he gave weekly instruction in English Grammar, Geography, and History. The class met at sunrise in the Wesleyan Library. It was a precious privilege, in those days of educational destitution, to have such an opportunity. Amongst the other means of self-improvement Mr. Shaw encouraged the members of the class to try their powers in composition by writing short essays on religious subjects. These meetings, although, in consequence of Mr. Shaw's departure for England, they did not last very long, proved to me and, I believe to others also, a turning point in life. They suggested, I think, to Mr. Shaw's mind, my possible call to the ministry; and I soon discovered in different ways, that he was taking a special interest in my mental improvement. It was by him that I was recommended to the notice of Mr. Boyce, who had not long arrived in the country, and whose interest in the young was marked by all his characteristic ardency. To my introduction to Mr. Boyce I owe, in my mental and in my domestic life, blessings the value of which I will not attempt to estimate, but which, probably, I should never have enjoyed, had it not been for Mr. Shaw's kindness in the first instance.

" Of the youths belonging to the class I have spoken of, two became Missionaries, and two Local Preachers. Jeremiah Hartley died in the work in the Bechuana Country from brain fever, brought on by exposure to the sun during the excitements caused by one of the intertribal wars then so rife in that region. James Thackwray, a most loveable character, had his health ruined by the ordinary fever of the country while in Missionary employment in the same District, and returned to Graham's Town only to linger awhile and die. Brooke Attwell still lives, the head of a patriarchal tribe of descendants, a Local Preacher and Class Leader of nearly forty years' standing, esteemed in his old age for a life of usefulness, specially in relation to the army, for which he possessed unusual qualifications.

" The late Dr. Atherstone, who attended Mr. Shaw during a dangerous illness he had in Graham's Town, expressed his astonishment at the calm and peaceful state of his mind ; and on one occasion in particular said that though so serene and collected, he was at the same time in a fever which would have thrown most men into a state of delirium."

CHAPTER VIII.

Jubilee of the Colony—The Second Kaffir War—Missionary Journey—1844-1848.

THE year 1844 was the Jubilee year of the Albany Settlement, and was observed on the 10th of April, in Graham's Town, Port Elizabeth, and other localities, with great rejoicings. Morning services were held in the various places of worship, followed by discharge of cannon and musketry, and evening banquets. At Graham's Town, the general desire was for the Jubilee Sermon to be preached in the Episcopal church, and for the preacher, contrary to all Church of England usage, to be the Rev. William Shaw, the Bishop (*i.e.*, General Superintendent) of the Methodist Church. To this wish the Rev. J. Heavyside, the Colonial Episcopal Chaplain, in spite of the opposition of a few rigid Churchmen, acceded, and Mr. Shaw accordingly officiated. This, however, was but an ushering in of the Jubilee year. The completion of the year was celebrated by the Methodists of Graham's Town after their own fashion. The foundation was laid of the " COMMEMORATION CHAPEL," on the 10th of April, 1845, by Mrs. Shaw, with the usual formalities. The erection and completion of this chapel was retarded by the outbreak of the SECOND KAFFIR WAR, which, after looming in the distance for some months, commenced March 31st, 1846, and continued until January 17th, 1848. Territorially, the results were an extension of the boundaries of the Colony, which had its north-eastern frontier wisely placed beyond certain debateable lands. All the country between the Keiskamma and the Kei Rivers was formed into a dependent province called British Kaffraria, the Kaffir chiefs and people being permitted to hold their lands from and under the British Government. The return of peace enabled Mr. Shaw to undertake what he had long before proposed, a journey northwards into the Bechuana Country; and thence he hastened across the Quathlamba Mountains* to Natal, returning to the Colony through Pondoland and Kaffirland. This extensive and interesting journey commenced March 20th, and continued till August 18th, 1848. Mr. Shaw's journal explains the object of this journey, and gives a fair notice of the country through which he passed. The time had now come for a large extension of the Missions in South-East Africa, and for their consolidation. After a quarter of a century, Mr. Shaw had realized in a great measure the vision of Missionary progress which had filled his imagination in his earlier years. With all its hardship and annoyance, necessarily connected with South African travelling, this must have been to him a happy journey, the particulars of which are given in a letter to the Committee, dated May 8th, 1848.

I left Graham's Town about the 20th of March, on the journey to Natal; the necessity for taking which at this period I have already explained to you in former letters. As it was essential to make some arrangements relative to the resumption of our Border Stations, in what is now called British Kaffraria, I proceeded thither in the first instance, that the work might not be delayed by my long absence. Having arrived at Mount Coke, I had the pleasure to meet Mr. Gladwin, who, with the Government Commissioner of Butterworth, had come down from the country beyond the Bashee, where they had been shut up during the late war.

* Called by the Dutch, "the *Drachenberg*."

Leaving British Kaffraria, we travelled round the north-east side of the Amatela Mountains, by way of the Moravian Institution of Shiloh, to Haslope Hills, where I also made some needful arrangements for the future prosecution of this Mission,—the settlement of the Chief Kama in its neighbourhood,—and other matters connected with our Stations at the western extremity of the Tembookie country.

Mr. Shepstone joined us at Kamastone on the journey to Natal. After considerable detention, we reached Thaba Unchu on the 2nd instant, where we found Mr. Cameron and his family, all well. Thaba Unchu is the chief settlement of the Baralong tribe, with which Messrs. Hodgson, Broadbent, and Archbell established our first Bechuana Mission. This is now by far the largest native town in British South Africa; there cannot be less than from eight thousand to ten thousand inhabitants. The town has a very picturesque, but wild-African, appearance. I was much pleased with the very extensive improvements made by the people in the erection of stone walls around various parts of the town, forming excellent court-yards to their conical-shaped dwellings, most of which are kept very neat and clean. Mr. Cameron's labours are efficient here. There is a considerable church of native converts, a day and Sunday school, and all the elements of usefulness in full operation.

We left Thaba Unchu on the 4th, in the evening, and arrived at Plaatberg at noon on the 5th instant. Here Mr. Giddy resides, and continues to labour diligently to promote the welfare of the people.

You are aware that Sir H. Smith lately proclaimed the whole of the immense territory lying between the Orange River and the Vaal River to be placed under the protection of Her Majesty the Queen : this was done with the full consent of Moshesh and Moroko, the principal native Chiefs, whose rights and interests will by this measure be secured. The Dutch farmers settled in most parts of this country also assented to the arrangement with apparent cordiality. However, these last-named people, ever dissatisfied with the rule of the British, are now stirring up a rebellion, and talk of resisting the authority of the Magistrates appointed by the Governor. We were told, as we were on the road, that the Boers would turn us back again, as they are generally very hostile to Missionaries. However, so far, though we have mixed a good deal with them, I must do them the justice to say, they have treated us with civility, and at two or three places I had opportunities of preaching to them.

In a subsequent letter, dated September 8th, 1848, Mr. Shaw gives a general account of the Mission visited by him in this four months' journey.

Instead of occupying much time in writing a lengthened journal, detailing the minute events connected with my journey, I think it will be more acceptable to you that I should make some general observations as to the state and circumstances of the three groups of Mission Stations, which I visited during my long journey:—

1. *The Bechuana Missions.* I wrote to you at some length respecting these Missions, before I left that part of the country. It is, therefore, only necessary to say, that I was much pleased with the evident signs of improvement on nearly all the Stations, since my last visit. The Thab'Nchu Station has especially improved. The native town has been extended; the people have erected many stone walls and enclosures, and houses of a superior description. The number of Christians recognised as members of our church is steadily increasing; the Chief continues very friendly, and is a regular attendant upon public worship; some of the leading men are members of our society, and in this town of seven or eight thousand Bechuanas, there is no other hinderance to progress in the Mission, but what arises from the natural wickedness of the human heart. A very much larger chapel is, however, greatly wanted. Mr. Cameron is desirous of supplying this defect, but, from various causes, the cost will be so heavy, after the natives have done all they can to assist, that I fear the object cannot at present be accomplished, since the present grant for the District does not afford the means of paying for the timber, &c., which must be purchased and brought from a great distance. I conversed at large with the Chiefs Moroko, Sikonyele, and Karolus Baatze, and found them well disposed towards the Missions. They were all under considerable apprehensions, as to the result of the political movements of the Dutch emigrant farmers, who, while I was in the country, were preparing for a rebellion against the authority of the Queen of England, which, by consent of the several Chiefs, the Governor had proclaimed as paramount in that country. The Chiefs

prefer that the country should be under the authority of the British Government, as the only means of securing them in the possession of their lands, of which the Dutch farmers seem disposed to deprive them. I believe nothing but the severe weather prevented the outbreak of this rebellion while I was there; and, as I wrote you at the time, many predicted that they would make me and my companions prisoners; but out of this danger God's good providence delivered us, and we received nothing but civility from the Dutch with whom we met. Since we passed through the country, the rebellion has broken out; the British troops are gone to repress it, under Sir Harry Smith; and a collision has happened during the last week, at a place beyond the Orange River. I grieve to say, that many lives have been sacrificed on both sides, and there are many wounded; but as the Boers appear to have suffered severely, I think they will now, in all probability, disperse. Mr. Cameron had arrived safely at Thab'Nchu from Natal, where I parted with him. Up to a very recent date the Boers had not disturbed any of the Stations. All the brethren and their people were safe and well; and as the troops were, last week, at a place not more than fifty miles from Thab'Nchu, I hope no serious evil will befall the Stations, which all lie in a cluster around that native town.

On the whole, the friends of our Missionary Society have much reason to be satisfied with the results of our Bechuana Mission. There are many very considerable congregations and societies. The great mass of the people living around the Stations are all feeling more or less of the beneficial influence, even in cases where they have not embraced the truth, but still pursue many of their heathen practices. The numerous Native Christians are, however, daily "witnessing a good confession;" and if the means of the Society were sufficient to enable us to reinforce the numbers of the Missionaries in this District, I believe great and glorious results would speedily follow: meantime, the lack of European Missionaries must be in part supplied by Native Teachers and Preachers. I wish we could afford an Institution, as long since proposed for this District, for training and educating those from among the Natives, whom the Lord may call to preach the Gospel to their countrymen.

2. *Natal.* I entered this Colony, on descending from the Dragen's-Berg, with peculiar feelings. In the year 1829, nearly twenty years

ago, I wrote to you as follows:—" If the British Government sanction the proposed establishment of a Colony at Port Natal, it would be highly desirable to send two Missionaries there immediately, with a view to the introduction of Christianity amongst the Amazulu, or Zoolas, lately under the Chief Chaka." A year afterwards, I had made arrangements for a journey to Natal; but, when just ready to start, I was seized with a dangerous illness, that brought me to the margin of the grave. After having been raised from that bed of sickness, I believe in answer to the prayers of our good people, I received a letter from the General Secretaries, in 1831, requesting me to postpone that journey, as the Society would not be able at that time to authorize a mission at Natal. The British Government did not approve of the formation of a Colony there, till the course of events compelled them. When this event took place, I was so anxious that we should occupy what I knew would prove a very extensive and important field for our Missions, that I sent first Mr. Archbell, and subsequently other brethren there, withdrawing some of our Missionary force from the Colony and Kaffraria, so as to occupy Natal. In traversing the country from the Dragen's Berg to Pieter Maritz Berg, we crossed an extensive region of fine country, nearly the whole of which had formerly been occupied by the race now called Fingoes in this Colony, and who were driven out in the wars with the neighbouring nation of the Zoolas, under Chaka and other Chiefs. Many of the Fingoes are now converted, and members of our church at Graham's Town, and Fort Peddie, &c. Very few have any particular desire to return to Natal. The country is but thinly inhabited by Boers and English settlers: it is, however, a fine Colony, and is, no doubt, destined to become a very important dependency of the British crown. The natives are all Kaffirs, of the Zoola and other nations, and all speak the Kaffir language, with slight variation in their dialects from the language spoken by the Kaffirs on the border of the Cape Colony. The Natal Kaffirs are estimated at one hundred thousand, by the Government and the Missionaries. A large portion of them are settled in various locations, under the direction of the Local Government, which, under His Honour M. West, Esq., the Lieutenant-Governor, has evinced a praiseworthy desire to afford facilities for the establishment of Missions among them.

At *Pietermaritzberg*, besides a highly respectable English congregation, Mr. Richards has collected a congregation of coloured people, who speak the Dutch language; and there is a congregation of Kaffirs, which is already much too large for the small building in which they meet, and consequently they have to be met at two separate services. If the arrangements which I proposed while there can be carried out, the Kaffir congregation may be expected very soon to become very large and very important. It will consist of the Kaffirs who come to reside as domestics and otherwise, with the various European inhabitants of the town; and an efficient Mission amongst them will operate just as our Kaffir Mission in Graham's Town has done; that is, it will prove a centre of influence among all the surrounding Kaffir tribes. I fear, however, that the want of money will oblige me at present to countermand the permission granted for the erection of a suitable chapel for the Kaffir congregation; and, unless that can be obtained, the work must be greatly retarded.

Mr. Davis has made a promising commencement on the *Zwartkops*, or *Kwangubene*, Station. There are about six thousand natives connected with this Station. The Government reserve for this location is in extent, as is supposed, about sixty thousand acres. It is a very suitable tract for the Kaffirs,—a mountainous district, well watered, has plenty of fine timber, and is within fifteen miles of the capital, Pietermaritzberg. The natives have a good market for their labour and produce, which is sure to prove a stimulus to their industry, and consequently will tend to accelerate their general improvement. Mr. Davis has nearly finished his dwelling-house, and the chapel is in progress. A congregation has been collected, and everything is progressing very promisingly among these Heathens, who are only just beginning to learn the very first principles of revealed truth. I had the pleasure, at the request of Mr. Davis, to baptize two of them, as the first-fruits of this large settlement.

The *Indalene Station* is about thirty miles distant from Pietermaritzberg, in a south-westerly direction. It is situated on the Elofu River, and not far from the large river called Umkomanzi. The Station is near the main track, which will in time become a road, between Pietermaritzberg and the Cape Colony. Here Mr. Allison has established himself with the native Teachers whom he took from Imparane, when he went on the Amaswasi Mission. A considerable number of converts also accompanied them, when, in consequence of native wars, and great opposition to the Gospel, they were obliged to leave the Amaswasi (or Baraputsi). The native Teachers and converts under Mr. Allison's care have built themselves very neat and comfortable cottages, so that the Station already presents the appearance of a very pretty village. The temporary dwelling-house of the Missionary, and a chapel, which, however, has suffered from recent unprecedented rains, stand at the top of the avenues formed by the rows of the native cottages; and altogether the work accomplished, considering the comparatively short time in which it has been performed, is highly creditable to Mr. Allison's zeal and taste, and is likewise a striking proof of the industry of the native Christians. The village must be regarded, however, as occupied by natives who are strangers in the land, and this Mission has hardly as yet begun to tell upon the population of the country. The surrounding native population is very large, one of the government reserves being on the adjoining lands. The station is well situated for extensive Missionary operations among the Kaffirs by means of the native Teachers.

After the District Meeting was over, we proceeded from Pietermaritzberg to *D'Urban*, which is the town situated at Port Natal; Pietermaritzberg, the capital of the Colony, being more centrally situated, about sixty miles from the coast. The country at and around D'Urban is extremely beautiful, being better wooded, and altogether much more picturesque, than the more interior portions of the Natal territory. It is in this district that the Cotton Plantations are situated. The people are only at present commencing this branch of industry; but from the high degree of success which has already attended their efforts, and the evident peculiar adaptation of the soil and climate to the production of cotton, I doubt not but Liverpool and Manchester will in time look to Port Natal for no inconsiderable supplies of that article. Hence the population is likely to become large, both of Europeans and natives; and from the nature of their occupation, they will live in more compact bodies or settlements than it is possible for the grazing farmers to do. I consider therefore that our Mission at D'Urban is likely to become of great importance and influence. The Mission premises, erected on ground granted by the Government, are exceedingly convenient. They are situated in a very central part of the rising town. The chapel, erected by Mr. Archbell, when stationed here, has hitherto answered all the purposes required. Mr. Holden, who is at present stationed at D'Urban, is very active and useful. Here is a respectable English congregation; indeed, at present, there is no other place of worship in D'Urban; there is also a very promising congregation of Kaffirs. Mr. Impey preached to them on the Sunday we spent at this place. There were about two hundred present, very wild, and almost entirely naked; but they were attentive, and as soon as a chapel can be provided for them, I doubt not a great improvement will be visible amongst them, as in all other places where regular services are introduced. I met the principal persons connected with the English congregation, and they resolved to erect a chapel for that congregation better adapted to the improved and improving state of the town. When they have carried this resolution into effect,—and they seemed disposed to make liberal donations, and a spirited effort to accomplish their purpose,— the present chapel will become the place of worship for the Kaffir congregation, and it will, for some time to come, be well adapted for the accommodation of that people.

I cannot doubt but our Mission at Natal, now comprising four principal stations, with four Missionaries, assisted by a number of native teachers, has been established in accordance with the design and will of Divine Providence. Its establishment has, of course, involved heavy expenses in removals from Albany and other parts of Kaffraria, buildings, furniture, &c.; all of which have tended to swell the excess of our expenditure during the last two years beyond the sum allotted to us. The expenses were of too miscellaneous a character to render it possible for us to form accurate estimates thereof; but all extraordinary charges will now cease, excepting for buildings, and nothing further of this kind will now be attempted without the previous sanction of the Committee, as there is at present sufficient accommodation for carrying forward the first operations of the Mission; and as the work enlarges, and absolutely requires more erections of chapels, &c., no doubt we shall obtain some enlargement of local ways and means; and it is to be hoped that the friends of the good cause at home will, by the favour of Divine Providence, be enabled to sustain the Society's funds; so that the Committee may feel authorized to meet any reasonable and urgent demand for help to this infant Mission, which future circumstances may render necessary. You will see by the accompanying returns, that there are already in the Natal territory, 3 chapels, 11 other preaching-places, 116 accredited members of Society, chiefly converted natives, with 32 on trial; 9 Sunday-schools, 3 day-schools, with an aggregate of 560 scholars attending them.

3. *Kaffraria.—Eastern Section.* On leaving D'Urban, we proceeded *via* Indalene through all the western portion of the Natal territory, which is occupied chiefly by various native tribes. The distance from Pietermaritzberg to Palmerton on the Izalo in Faku's country, is about two hundred and twenty miles. At the Umzimkulu River Dushani, the successor of the late Chief Capai, came to meet me, and earnestly requested that a Mission might be commenced near that noble stream, for the benefit of his people. It would be highly desirable on many accounts; but the state of the Society's funds renders it impossible to entertain any proposals for the commencement of any new Mission whatever. Arrived at *Palmerton,* being my first visit to this Station, I was highly delighted with its progress under the care of the Missionary, Mr. Jenkins. The place has been well selected: it possesses great advantages of wood and water, and is likely to form a prosperous settlement. A good beginning has been made in the spiritual objects of this Mission, and the gentleman who contributed towards the passage-money of a Missionary from England, so as to enable us to take up this Mission, will be gratified to hear, that I was called upon by Mr. Jenkins to administer the rite of Christian baptism to more than twenty well-instructed native converts, all of whom are truly in earnest for the salvation of their souls. The Mission house and premises are extremely compact, and substantially built. Mr. Jenkins laboured much at them with his own hands, besides the labour of the Catechist. Mr. Jenkins's expenses in erecting this building paid by him, amounted to about £100, which, having inherited some small property, he and Mrs. Jenkins cheerfully gave to the Society in con-

sideration of the state of your funds, so that no charge will be made for this really substantial and commodious Mission house. I saw and conversed with the Chief Faku at Palmerton: he is still friendly to the Mission; and as an expression of our gratitude for his fidelity and kindness during the late Kaffir war, towards the Missionaries and all the people of these Stations, namely, Butterworth, Beechamwood, and Clarkebury, who were obliged to take refuge in his country, and to whom he behaved with great kindness,—taking no advantage of their necessities, but protecting them from the cupidity and lawlessness of many of the natives,—I promised to send him a present of some cattle belonging to the Society. This I believe to be fully due to him; and it will operate beneficially on the minds of others, in case of any future troubles arising in the land. In proceeding from Palmerton to Buntingville, I crossed the Zimvubu river, and found a small vessel named the "British Settler" lying in the river, ready to take away a cargo of produce purchased by the traders from the natives. If a regular trade can be established and kept up with this place by the traders from the Colony, it will prove a great advantage both to the natives and our Missions in these parts. The country on both sides of the Zimvubu, or St. John's River, is quite as well adapted to the growth of cotton as the district around Port Natal,* and it would be a great benefit to the natives, if they can be induced to grow cotton for sale to the traders.

At *Buntingville*, I found an immense population, the refugees from Beechamwood and Butterworth being still here. We were glad to meet Mr. and Mrs. Gladwin in good health, and actively engaged in the work of the Mission. My meeting with Mrs. Palmer was very painful; this Mission sustained a great loss in the death of her husband. Mrs. Palmer proposes to accede to Mr. Gladwin's request, to reside for a time at Butterworth, and take charge of a superior school to be formed there for native young women. I think it likely to be a

---

* It is an interesting fact, and worth recording, that the *first* cotton grown at Natal, from which some vast results will in time be likely to arise, was from seed obtained from a cotton-tree growing in the Mission-garden at our Station of Morley, and which was taken to Natal by a person who went to reside there.

valuable institution, and no one can be better qualified to take charge
of it than Mrs. Palmer, as she speaks the Kaffir language fluently,
and is greatly beloved by the people. Her friends at home, however, naturally desire her return to England, and I fear she will not
remain very long at Butterworth. The brethren Garner, Thomas,
and Jenkins came from their respective Stations, and, while I was at
Buntingville, we held a special District Meeting of the Eastern
Section of the Kaffraria District. I also met the refugees from the
abandoned Stations, and it was resolved to resume the Stations,
Butterworth, Beechamwood, and *Clarkebury,* as soon as practicable:
the return of the people cannot be delayed longer because the planting season is just at hand. The buildings at Clarkebury are injured,
but will not require any very heavy outlay to put them in repair.
Our most serious loss in this part of Kaffirland has been at Butterworth. I could not visit Shawbury or Clarkebury, but called at
Morley on my way to Butterworth. In crossing the Bashie River,
we sustained a perilous accident: the river was swollen with recent
heavy rains, and we attempted to cross it before it had sufficiently
subsided: the wagon upset in the midst of the stream, Mr. Impey
and I were obliged to jump into the water, and get out of the river
as best we could: the stream was so strong that I should hardly have
been able to bear up against it, if I had not been assisted by a Kaffir
accustomed to it. Our wagon was all night in the river, all our
clothes, books, bedding, &c., completely saturated. I had to walk
about naked till I could dry some clothes so as to be able to clothe
myself: it occupied us two days to get our wagon out of the river,
and dry the various articles contained therein. We did not lose much,
but many things were completely spoiled by the water. The Kaffirs
who live here were very friendly, and rendered us all possible assistance; and although the accident might have been very disastrous,
yet we had reason to praise God that none of our party were drowned,
nor was the wagon very materially injured. I have several times
sustained accidents of this sort in the course of my Missionary
career: few people but those who have to travel long journeys in the
parts of Africa not occupied by Europeans, know the difficulties and
dangers which often occur to travellers in crossing rivers and traversing mountainous regions, where there are neither bridges nor roads.

We remained several days at *Butterworth*, and were kindly entertained by the Government Commissioner, W. M. D. Fynn, Esq., who has already re-established himself at this place. It was painful to see the destruction which had been committed on the Mission premises and village during the late war. Previously to that calamitous event I had visited this place, and was delighted with the appearance of the village and its busy hum of industry, as well as the large Christian congregation, schools, &c. Now the walls of the chapels and houses presented one scene of desolation. The Chief Krielie arrived while I was here, having come sixty miles to meet me. At our interview he said he was quite ashamed to meet me. He knew that the Missionaries were his best friends. We had given no reason why our village and chapel should have been destroyed. He had never intended it, and had never given any orders that it should be done; but the mischief had been perpetrated by certain wild and ungovernable fellows of his tribe. However, he would never rest till he had made compensation for our loss, and he hoped I would allow the Missionary to return, and the Mission to be recommenced. I made a suitable reply, and told him I thanked him for his kind words, &c.; but I waited to see his deeds, and that he certainly owed it to us to make at least some compensation, as he had already promised to do. He had sent one hundred head of cattle to the Chief Commissioner on this account; but this was very far from being sufficient.

Leaving Butterworth we pursued our way towards the Colony. The Kei River, however, was impassable for the wagon, and likely to be so for several days. We therefore hired some Kaffir swimmers, who have frequently taken me through this stream on former occasions. By their assistance we got safely through; we swam our horses through, and, having put on our clothes on the opposite side of the stream, we proceeded to a Kaffir kraal, and, after sleeping in a hut, we rode about sixty miles next day, and reached Mount Coke after nightfall. It may amuse you if I tell you that the hut we slept in near the Kei was circular, about twelve feet in diameter, formed of sticks, and covered with grass, about seven feet high to the highest part of the cone; in this space we ate our supper and slept; the fire being in the centre, and no chimney to take off the smoke; indeed,

BUTTERWORTH IN 1842.

no opening whatever, but a hole about three feet by two feet, which served as a door. The inmates for the night were three Englishmen and our two native boys; one Kaffir woman, two girls, three children, four Kaffir men, and five goats. I nevertheless found space to stretch myself upon the earthen floor, and, wrapped up in my cloak, slept soundly till about an hour before daylight, when it was necessary to saddle our horses and start for our long ride. The Kaffirs were very friendly, although they belonged to the very clan which, only seven months before, barbarously murdered several English officers who had strayed from their camp, and we were within sight of the very mountain upon which the troops afterwards attacked them and inflicted a severe chastisement upon them, killing a large number of them. When the Kaffirs fight, they take every possible advantage, and spare no one; but when peace is restored, they seem readily to forget the most recent scenes of warfare, however they may have suffered in them.

With regard to the Stations comprised in the *Eastern Section of Kaffraria*, I am thankful to be able to report that we have sustained much less damage by the Kaffir war than might have been expected. The fidelity of the brethren in remaining with their flocks when they took refuge in Faku's country, has been abundantly rewarded by the Great Head of the Church; for by this means the Native Christians were kept together; and although the disadvantages under which they were placed prevented any material increase in the number of communicants, yet the great body of the members have been preserved from apostasy, and there is now a prospect that the labours of the Missionaries will be resumed under favourable circumstances. At the same time, I am constrained to bring to your notice that two of the Stations, Beechamwood and Shawbury, are now without Missionaries, and must, for the present, be placed under the care of Catechists, whom we withdraw from the other Stations. Thus, every Missionary on the remote Stations is left entirely alone, and there are many reasons why it is not desirable that the Missionary and his family should be the only Europeans resident on the Station, or anywhere within scores of miles; the solitariness of such Stations, especially to females, is often a trial of faith and patience, such as cannot easily be understood by those who have not been called to endure it. However, while I thus write, I know that the present state of your funds prevents you from rendering us such assistance as might enable me to make more satisfactory and efficient arrangements than are at present practicable.

4. In *British Kaffraria*, our losses, and the injury sustained by the late Kaffir war, and that of 1835, are much more serious. It will require both a large outlay and many years of Missionary labour, to regain what has been lost among the border Kaffirs by these distressing wars. At present I have only authorized the re-commencement of *Mount Coke*, which, in consequence of the recent arrangements of the Government, is now extremely well situated for becoming a centre of Missionary labour and influence. The former site of the Mission has been taken by the Governor for a military post, now called Fort Murray; we selected a suitable spot about three miles distant from this military post, for the re-commencement of the Mount Coke Station. A large Kaffir population is now located by Government around this neighbourhood, and the residence of the Chief Pato is within a few miles of Mount Coke.

After spending one night at Mount Coke, with Mr. and Mrs. Wilson, in the temporary house erected after we left the border, we proceeded to *D'Urban, Fort Peddie*, where we met Mr. and Mrs. Dugmore in good health. Mr. Dugmore has been highly useful here at this crisis, in assisting the newly-appointed Magistrate to get the Fingoes of this settlement properly located in villages. Much land has been granted to them by the Government, which was, previous to the war, occupied by the hostile Kaffir tribes. About seven thousand, likely soon to increase to ten thousand Fingoes, the same class of natives as those who reside in the Natal territory, will now be permanently settled around D'Urban and Fort Peddie: the whole of these will be exclusively under our Missionary care.

Mr. Ayliff also writes me from *Fort Beaufort*, that some of the newly-forming native settlements in the upper part of the conquered or ceded territory, now Victoria, are to be under our care. Here is a vast field: but where are the labourers? The sites of our border Stations, and the circumstances of the natives, will undergo considerable change, all favourable to rapid progress in the work; but I am really at a loss to know how we are to meet so many pressing and promising claims upon our Missionary labours. "The harvest truly is great, but the labourers are few."

We rode in one day (forty-five miles) from D'Urban to Graham's Town. The Fish River was flooded; but we crossed it in a boat belonging to the military post at Trompetter's Drift. We were glad to meet our wives and families at Graham's Town, after an absence of exactly five months, during which we had travelled more than fifteen hundred miles, chiefly in an ox-wagon, visited nearly all the Wesleyan Mission Stations in the Bechuana Country, the Natal territory, and Kaffraria, during which period we had also passed through a great variety of native tribes and nations. Besides many other reasons for gratitude and thankfulness, we found on our return that the Lord was honouring my colleagues in this Circuit with special blessings on their ministry; the congregations continue very large, the chapel is crammed with people, and numerous applicants for pews cannot be accommodated; a revival of religion, especially amongst the younger people of the congregation, is also in progress, and many have been truly converted to God.

CHAPTER IX.

Condition of the Frontier Stations in 1850—Commemoration Chapel opened.

THE years 1849 and 1850 were years of agitation in the Cape. The English Government attempted to introduce convicts into the Colony; no measure more unfortunate in its design, and no country so ill adapted for the purpose. The resistance of the Colonists saved the Colony from the moral contamination of convictism.

In July and August, 1850, Mr. Shaw visited the Colonial Stations. His journal presents a pleasing picture of the Colony between the war of 1846-8, and that of 1851-3. Hereafter, these sketches of the country towns, and of the progress of Methodism, will be considered invaluable.

The first Circuit we visited was *Salem and Farmerfield.* I visited Salem at this time in conformity with a promise made to the people, that I would attend the anniversary of the foundation of that settlement. This is always observed on the 18th of July. The anniversary was made more than usually interesting on this occasion, by laying the foundation-stone of a larger and handsomer church than that which has been used by our congregation for many years past. The corner-stone was laid by our old and tried friend, W. H. Matthews, Esq., J.P., one of the original inhabitants of Salem, and who has continued to reside there since the foundation of the settlement thirty years ago.

While at Salem, where I remained several days, (including the Sabbath,) I visited Farmerfield, distant four or five miles. This is an important part of the charge of the Salem Minister. You are aware of the history of this place. It has now been established about

eleven years, on lands which I purchased for the purpose, and which
are now vested in the officers of our Missionary Society as perpetual
Trustees. The whole of the inhabitants are native Africans of various
tribes and races. The original buildings on the place when purchased
serve, after some alterations, as the residence of the Catechist and
Teacher; and we have erected a substantial chapel, capable of accommodating about four or five hundred hearers. We have also a
suitable school-room, for about one hundred and fifty scholars. Both
the chapel and the school are well attended. The greater part of
the adults are accredited members of Society. All the practices of
Heathenism are entirely banished from the place; it is, in the
strictest sense, a truly Christian village. The comfortable cottages of
the people, and their extensive cultivated grounds, with their large
herds of cattle, their wagons, &c., fully attest their general industry,
which is indeed surprising, considering the classes of the community
to which they belong.

I may as well mention here, that since my return home I have
learned that the Bishop of Cape Town, and the Archdeacon of
Graham's Town, visited Farmerfield and Salem, soon after I was at
these places. The Archdeacon called upon me shortly after my
return home, and expressed, in the strongest terms, the pleasure and
gratification which both the Bishop and himself had derived from
their visit. He especially adverted to the evidently decent and
civilized habits acquired by the people, their being so well clothed,
and manifest religious feeling. The manner in which they sang
some hymns in the chapel was particularly referred to. I am glad
to say, that Bishop Gray complied with Mr. Hepburn's request, and
delivered a very appropriate address to the people, which was successively interpreted by two of the native Teachers into the Bechuana
and Kaffir languages. The particulars of the Bishop's visit to Salem
and Farmerfield will, however, be most likely communicated to you
by Mr. Hepburn, at whose house he stayed while at the former place.

Besides Salem and Farmerfield, there are several other small congregations under the care of the Salem Minister; and, if it were
possible to afford it, a second Missionary should be appointed to this
Circuit, when the work both amongst the natives and the English

settlers might be greatly extended, while the means of support would be gradually increased.

At Salem we have an academy, or boarding-school. It is at present conducted and managed by Mr. B. J. Shaw, who, although obliged to retire from the Ministry from the state of his health, is, however, likely in this climate, with due caution, to be able to conduct this institution in a respectable and efficient manner. It is of great importance, affording a suitable place to which the Missionaries can send their children for education, while they are prosecuting their arduous labours on the remote stations of the interior. The buildings connected with the institution are very substantial and commodious; but having been erected at various times, without much regard to plan, they are not particularly handsome; however, they will serve the purpose for many years to come. In the purchase of the property, the requisite furniture, &c., the Missionaries of this District have taken upon themselves a heavy responsibility; but there seemed to be no alternative, unless their children were to be entirely neglected. With the view of making it a self-supporting institution, it is not confined to the children of the Missionaries; but many of our people, and others, send their children to obtain the sound religious education which is there provided.

Taking leave of our kind friends at Salem, we proceeded on our journey to the *Port Elizabeth and Uitenhage Circuit.* Having arrived safely at Port Elizabeth, we were glad to meet Mr. and Mrs. Wilson, and many other kind friends, all of whom manifest great interest in the welfare of our Mission. I am delighted and encouraged with the very remarkable progress our affairs have made at Port Elizabeth since the appointment of Mr. Wilson in the commencement of the year 1849. The congregation has gone on steadily increasing, till the chapel is now well filled, all the pews being let. Since I was at this place last year, the friends have at a considerable cost put up a new ceiling to the chapel, and in other respects improved it. They have introduced an organ-seraphine, and established a suitable choir, thereby causing that branch of public worship to be conducted with greater propriety and effect. Aided by two or three excellent Local Preachers who have recently arrived, the work has been extended; and much more would be done in that respect, if the country around Port Elizabeth were not entirely destitute of villages, or places where it is practicable to establish country congregations.

Having taken leave of our friends at Port Elizabeth, we reached Uitenhage on Friday, August 2nd, and were most kindly received by Mr. and Mrs. Hall. In the evening I attended the Annual Meeting of the Branch Bible Society, which had been fixed for this period, to afford me the opportunity of being present. The Meeting was numerously attended; and I was glad to plead the cause of that noble institution before a highly respectable and intelligent assembly. Several good addresses were delivered on the occasion. It was pleasing to notice the zeal and catholic spirit displayed by the Rev. A. Smith, the Minister of the Dutch Reformed Church in this town and district, and the efficient manner in which several other gentlemen co-operate with him in this good work. On Sunday, August 4th, I also preached twice in our chapel at Uitenhage for the trust funds. The attendance was good, and the collections equal to the expectations of the friends. I visited the Sunday School in the afternoon, which seems to be an interesting institution, and attended by a large proportion of the English children resident in the town.

Port Elizabeth is rapidly rising in size and importance. It is the principal sea-port of the Eastern Province. Uitenhage is a very beautiful rural town, and possesses great advantages in wood and water, not often met with in the towns of this part of the Colony. It has been sometimes proposed to make it the seat of Government. You will therefore perceive that this is a very important Circuit, although the numerical returns would hardly impress you with that idea. The Mission has had to contend with much opposition, open and secret; and various local difficulties have at times arisen; but I am happy to be able to assure you that great good has been already accomplished, and there is much promise that this Circuit will at no distant date assume an importance to which some have, under discouragement, been led to think it could never arrive.

We left Uitenhage on the 8th of August, and, by dint of very hard travelling, reached Somerset (East) on Saturday evening, the 10th. From Uitenhage we proceeded to the great ford at the Sunday's River, and, thence turning off due north, travelled upon a new road, which the Government is now cutting through the Zuur Berg Mountains. This work is effected by a party of some three hundred convicts, chiefly Hottentots and Kaffirs, &c. The work reflects the highest credit on the skill of the English engineers and other functionaries who direct it. We were struck with admiration to see how "the mountains" were cut through and "made low," and "the valleys" filled up and "exalted." If a way for wagons can be made over such mountains and precipices as these, then a road may be made by the skill and industry of man anywhere. And surely in the moral world wonders may also be expected to be wrought under the guiding skill and active power and influence of "Him" who is "Head over all things to His church." I regretted very much that I could not stay and preach to the convicts, as I was engaged to be at Somerset for the following Sunday.

As I could not stay to preach, I talked with some of the convicts as long as circumstances would allow; and Mrs. Shaw scattered a number of tracts among them, which were eagerly and thankfully received. It would be well if some kind friend would occasionally send me a few bundles of tracts for distribution on my journeys. We should "sow beside all waters."

Somerset, East, is a beautifully situated village, the seat of magistracy, &c., for the surrounding pastoral and agricultural district. I first visited it in 1821, at which time it was a Government farm under the direction of R. Hart, Esq., who still survives, and is a Scottish Presbyterian, but has ever evinced a kind regard for our Mission. We have a very handsome small chapel, and Minister's house, with garden and orchard attached, in this town. We were delighted to meet our old friends, Mr. and Mrs. Edwards, in excellent health. I preached twice in the chapel on Sunday, August 11th, on behalf of the Sunday Schools, which here consist of an English and Native branch. In the afternoon I addressed the natives, chiefly Kaffirs and Fingoes, in the school-room, which is also used as a native chapel. The native Teacher and interpreter is a pious and zealous man. Not a few of the natives have, at various times, been converted at this place; but it is discouraging, both to the Missionary and the Teacher, that circumstances frequently compel the people to remove from the village, and go to remote places where they can obtain no religious instruction : and thus, much of the good effected is, for a season at least, counteracted. The friends held their Sunday School anniversary. I was much pleased with the examination of the scholars, both in the English and native school. Much very valuable religious instruction has been imparted, and a fair proportion of the natives can read the Kaffir New Testament. The tea-meeting was held in the evening; there was a large attendance. O. L. Stretch, Esq., occupied the chair, and the Rev. Mr. Pears, of the Dutch Reformed Church, rendered assistance at the meeting. I delivered an address appropriate to the occasion. The debt on this chapel is already all paid off, and the debt remaining on the Minister's house will soon be liquidated, when we shall also effect a saving of house-rent, and thus the Mission funds will at this place also be considerably relieved in another year or so.

I had the pleasure to meet, at Somerset, with Messrs. Hobson and Robinson, formerly of Albany, and whom I have had the pleasure to know from their youth up. They are now settled in the neighbourhood of the Sunday's River, forty or fifty miles below Graaff Reinett. Mr. Hobson was the first Englishman who migrated to that part of the country. God has wonderfully prospered him by His providence since he established himself and family there. As a member of our Church he acted faithfully in establishing worship both for his family and numerous native servants. Many other English families are gone to reside in that part of the country, which is found to be very valuable for sheep-farming. Thus an English neighbourhood has been formed. Mr. Edwards, at a great expense of time and toil, visits them as often as possible, although these settlers are from sixty to one hundred miles distant from him, and his rides out and home on these occasions are such as not many Ministers would be found either able or willing very frequently to take. However, he has had a good reward; the results, considering the extent of the population, have been remarkably encouraging. Religious ordinances are regularly established in a district, perhaps fifty miles distant from the nearest place of worship of any denomination. Most of the English families attend: many of them are members, and there is a very considerable society of coloured or native members, who are described as being a very respectable and well conducted class of people. I wish we were able to appoint a Missionary to reside there; the work might then be greatly extended in a country where there is no man set apart to care for the souls of the people. The friends there have long been liberal contributors to our Mission fund; and if a Minister could be sent to reside amongst them, a handsome sum would be contributed regularly towards his support. Meantime, steps are being taken for the erection of a chapel in a central situation, and to establish a school.

We left Somerset on the 15th of August; Mr. Edwards helping us on our way for the first day's journey. We passed through the Zwager's Hoek, crossing the winding Little Fish River twelve times in the course of the day. Next day, which proved excessively cold on the tops of the mountains, we passed over the precipitous and all-but-impassable mountain road called the Ganna Hoek. Mr. Green had kindly sent to one of our native members, who lives at the foot of the pass, to meet us with his well-trained oxen. By this means we got down the mountain much more easily than we otherwise should have done. To such of the Colonists as never travel beyond the boundaries, this road appears terrific: but I have had to cross still more dangerous mountains in my journeys beyond the boundary, sometimes where there was no road or track whatever. However, we were deeply indebted to Mr. Green's thoughtfulness, and to our coloured friend, in providing us such efficient assistance. When at the foot of the mountain, this man invited us to spend the evening at his place of residence; and, although it was a little out of our direct road, we thought it best to comply with his request.

In the evening I held a short Dutch service with the family. Here I learned from his wife's own lips, what I had before heard as a rumour, that a recently-arrived Romish Priest from Belgium, named Hoendervanger, called upon her, and, having ascertained that she attended the Wesleyan ministry, assured her that in such a course she would never be saved. As the poor woman made some reference to her Dutch Bible, he took it into his hands, and, after examining two or three passages in it, and expressing great disgust and contempt at them, he held up the sacred volume, and entreated her at once and without any delay to throw it into the fire, and burn it! The fire was burning brightly on the hearth at the time. She looked at the Bible and at the Priest, and then at the fire, and, being incapable of speaking a word, shuddered with horror. Shortly afterwards the Priest went out of the house for a while, and her son, a fine youth, who had stood a silent spectator, as soon as they were alone, said, " Mother, let us hide the Bible before he returns into the house, or else I see he will burn it himself." Accordingly they secreted the precious book before the Priest returned to the house, lest he should proceed to commit such a sacrilegious outrage. Such is the method pursued by this newly-arrived Romish Missionary, Mr. Hoendervanger, whose name, being rendered into English, is, " Mr. Fowl-catcher! " Of course this event furnished me with a topic for my exhortation. I spoke at once of the Divine authority and inestimable value of the sacred book, and of the right of all human beings to possess it, and to read it, as being God's gracious revelation to universal man; and finally I asked, " What sort of Christianity is that which denies to the people the light of God's own book ? Is not this a sufficient proof to you, that such a form of Christianity is false, and is designed to keep you in darkness and ignorance rather than to bring you into the light of life ? "

Next morning we proceeded on our way, and reached *Cradock* in the afternoon. Mr. Green had been very unwell, but was recovering; and both he and Mrs. Green, and the friends generally, received us with much affection and kindness.

Sunday, August 18th, I preached twice in the new chapel, in aid of the Trust Funds; the attendance, including several friends from the country, was very good. In the evening the chapel was quite filled with a highly respectable congregation; and the collections were very liberal indeed.

This is undoubtedly the most handsome chapel which our people have yet erected in South Africa. The interior of the chapel is also comfortably fitted up. For its size, it may well serve our friends in this part of the world as a model chapel. It cost, exclusive of the purchase of land, and some other extraneous expenses, £1,300, or, inclusive of these *et cetera*, about £1,500. About £1,000 had been already raised, from one source or another, towards the cost; and at the Trustee-Meeting, held while I was at Cradock, I was glad to see such evident proof of the deep interest taken by our leading friends in all that concerned the trust-property, and likewise that, from various sources, including the proceeds of the present anniversary, there would be the means of further reducing the debt by £100, in the course of this year; so that I hope, at the end thereof, the debt will not exceed £400, the whole of which the Trustees will take measures to liquidate as soon as possible, that all the surplus chapel income may be applied in aid of the support of the Missionary resident among them. The old chapel is now occupied by the coloured people, for whose benefit regular services are held in the Dutch language. We have also a small chapel and school-house for the Kaffirs and Fingoes, and a Native Teacher, who assists Mr. Green in that department. However, this part of the work has not latterly prospered, partly owing to the bad effects resulting from the unfaithfulness of a Native Teacher, whom we were obliged some time ago to dismiss from the work, and who has since relapsed into Heathenism.

After having been much pleased with the manifestations of zeal and love which I witnessed while at Cradock, we took leave of our friends on Wednesday, August 21st, to proceed by the most direct route to Graham's Town.

We called at several farms on the way, and I held five services at various places, where the opportunities are few and far between in which the people can hear the word of the Lord. We spent the Sabbath at the residence of Mr. Dennison, whose family, and those of his neighbours, are all either members of our Society, or regular hearers when they have the opportunity. There is great difficulty in establishing regular ordinances for the spiritual benefit of the settlers and farmers who follow pastoral pursuits. There are no villages, and the farms are separated by large tracts of country, rendering it extremely difficult to form country congregations; and the Missionaries can effect little more than visiting from farm to farm, and holding service with the isolated families. But this is a work involving great toil, which requires much time, and is attended with heavy horse expenses. Still, we must continue to do what circumstances will allow on the various Circuits, so as to keep up, and deepen, and extend true religion among the scattered farmers and settlers, with their servants and dependents. I believe my

COMMEMORATION CHAPEL, GRAHAM'S TOWN.

brethren are doing what they can in this respect; but until we have the means of appointing on some of the more extensive Circuits some additional labourers, I fear this department of the work will not be so efficiently conducted as its importance demands.

Having met with some detention, by the straying of our oxen, we did not reach Graham's Town till the morning of August 29th, having been absent about seven weeks, during which we travelled nearly five hundred miles in an ox-wagon. O for the convenience and rapidity of your English railway travelling! How much fatigue would it save us, and, above all, how much more might we do for the cause of Christ, did we possess such power of rapid locomotion! Perhaps our successors may see something of this kind even in Africa.

On the 24th of November, 1850, the Commemoration Chapel, the erection of which had been delayed by the war of 1846–8, and other untoward circumstances, was opened for public worship. We must turn to Mr. Shaw's account of this event: his comments on the ecclesiastical system of the Cape Government will be found in his "Story of my Mission."

The erection of this chapel was retarded, after its walls had risen to a certain height, by some untoward circumstances; and meantime the Kaffir war of 1846 rendered it wholly impracticable to proceed with the building. All available hands were employed either in repelling the invaders, or in protecting the country from further inroads; while the price of provisions, and consequent cost of labour, rose to such unusually high rates, that it became impossible to proceed with the work; and the contracts were consequently cancelled until more favourable times should return. However, as soon as circumstances favoured a recommencement, new contracts were made, and the chapel was at length so far completed, that we were enabled to dedicate it for the worship of God on the 24th of November, 1850.

The large collections at the opening services, and the further efforts of the people, greatly reduced the otherwise serious amount of debt arising from a heavy expenditure up to the time of opening the building, inclusive of the cost of the ground. This debt had been further increased by the amount of interest paid on borrowed money before the chapel was opened, and therefore previously to its yielding any revenue. The untoward circumstances connected with the Kaffir war increased the outlay enormously; so that the entire expenditure exceeded £9,000, of which upwards of £5,000 was still owing at the time when the dedicatory services were commenced. I had already appealed to the Legislative Council of the Colony for assistance, seeing that we had never received a shilling from the colonial treasury in aid of our religious institutions in Graham's Town, while nearly the entire cost of St. George's church had been defrayed from that source, and the Episcopalians and Roman Catholics of the town were receiving about £1,000 per annum towards the support of their respective Clergy. Our case was a strong one, and was well supported in the Council by the Honourable Messrs. W. Cock and R. Godlonton, Members of Council for the Eastern Province. The Council agreed to make the grant requested; but before this could be carried into effect, it was suddenly dissolved, and ultimately the new Constitution was introduced. We now transmitted our petition to the Governor, requesting that the executive would propose the requisite grant to the Cape Parliament. In the House of Assembly there was strong opposition raised by an influential Member resident in Cape Town, and of rather ultra views on the question of State aid to Churches: but our claim was strong in its equity, and was strenuously supported by nearly all the members who represented the British settlers, and eventually, on a division, it was resolved, by a small majority, to grant one thousand pounds in aid of the Building Fund. This encouraged our people to make further voluntary efforts, whereby, including the grant, the debt was reduced more than one half. The annual income of the chapel has been so well sustained, since the dedication services, that a considerable surplus is now regularly available for the gradual extinction of the entire debt.

CHAPTER X.

Missionary Journeys, 1853–1855.

Of the Kaffir war of 1851–3 nothing more need be added to the remarks in a previous Chapter, except the expression of a hope that it may be the last. Peace was concluded February 14th, 1853. Before this event, however, Mr. Shaw had paid a visit to Natal, going and returning by sea. The details of these visitations of the General Superintendent will always be read with pleasure by all who like to look back to the first beginnings and progress of Christianity in the Eastern Province of the Cape Colony and beyond. A time may come when these narratives will form no unimportant part in the *"Origines"* of some African ecclesiastical historian. All who revere the memory of Mr. Shaw will be pleased to accompany him in spirit, and to participate in his pleasant retrospective reviews of the progress of the Mission work.

The first of these journals refers to the visit to Natal. All of them are addressed to the Committee in London. This letter is dated "May 21st, 1853."

On leaving Port Elizabeth, I arrived, after a passage of five days, at Natal, in the beginning of February. I was received with great kindness by Mr. and Mrs. Spenseley, and Mr. Gaskin. The day after my arrival being Sunday, I preached in the chapel to our English congregation at D'Urban; and, as Mr. Thomas kindly came from Pietermaritzberg to meet me, after spending a few days at D'Urban, we proceeded together to Pietermaritzberg, when I took up my quarters at the new Mission-house, with my old friends Mr. and

Mrs. Pearse. I remained at Pietermaritzberg, attending to a variety of business connected with the Society's affairs, and visiting the principal Stations and Missions in the surrounding country; all of which kept me fully occupied for about three weeks, when I again returned to D'Urban to meet the steamer, as I had supposed to get away immediately; but her non-arrival for three weeks detained me all that time, which I employed in visiting Verulam, and preaching regularly in our chapels at D'Urban. While at Pietermaritzberg I preached every Sunday, and was gratified to see the English chapel well filled on each occasion. During my visit it was resolved to hold a Missionary Meeting, and form an Auxiliary Missionary Society for the Natal District. I was requested to preach one of the sermons on the occasion : you will be glad to hear that all the services were attended by overflowing congregations. The Judge-Recorder of Natal presided at the Missionary Meeting, and several Ministers of various denominations attended, and assisted in the proceedings. A delightful spirit prevailed.

The Colony is in its infancy, and so also are all its religious and educational institutions. But, comparatively with others, we have no reason to be ashamed of the present state and prospects of the Wesleyan-Methodist Church in Natal. That interesting Colony presents a most important field of labour. The European population is much scattered, and an itinerant ministry must visit the various farms and scattered hamlets. The native population of more than one hundred thousand souls will require the most constant and assiduous attention. I shall be most glad when the means can be found for increasing our Mission Stations among the native settlements of the Natal Colony. This is a " field white already to the harvest ; " but while " the harvest is great, the labourers are few." The Missionaries of the American Board of Missions are in considerable strength on the native locations ; and, so far as I could learn, they are now beginning to reap, after many years of patient labour. I saw most of these brethren; and am well satisfied of their piety, zeal, and diligence. I am at the same time fully persuaded that *we* have done right to occupy the two principal towns,—Pietermaritzberg and D'Urban,—and to make them centres of religious influence in the surrounding districts.

Pietermaritzberg is steadily increasing in size, or rather the vacant building lots in the various streets are being enclosed and built upon. There is a Dutch church, which was erected before I visited Natal in 1848, and in which at that time we used to preach. The Wesleyan chapel was erecting in 1848, and was subsequently finished. It has recently been much improved, and an end gallery has been erected, in which an organ, built at Natal, has been placed. A large substantial and well-proportioned Wesleyan chapel has also been erected, in which services are conducted in the Dutch and Kaffir languages for the benefit of the native population. Mrs. Pearse has likewise established an infant-school, and school of industry, which is conducted in this building. I visited it, and was much pleased with its efficiency. Through the zealous efforts of Mrs. Pearse, and a number of ladies who assist her, this very valuable institution (aided by a small annual grant from the Colonial Government) is wholly self-supported. A substantial and commodious Mission-house, just finished, with cottages for chapel-keeper, and governess of the infant-school, form together a very compact and creditable Mission establishment; the whole of the buildings being erected on land granted to us by the Government in the very centre of the town, and having frontages in three principal streets.

While at Pietermaritzberg, I visited the English settlement called York, and was very happy to make the acquaintance of many warm-hearted Yorkshire people, some of whom remembered to have seen and heard me at various places during my residence in England from 1833 to 1836. The settlers at York, being chiefly English farmers, are likely to do well. As usual with all British settlers in the Colonies, for the first few years after their arrival, they have had to dismiss from their minds many erroneous notions which they had formed before they left England respecting the country, and they have had to contend with various difficulties which they did not anticipate; but I have little or no doubt the greater part of them will ultimately succeed in placing themselves in circumstances of considerable worldly prosperity and comfort. There are many Methodists among them: the Missionaries and Local Preachers of the Pietermaritzberg Circuit visit them regularly, and in due season they propose to erect for themselves a suitable chapel. I was glad to have the opportunity of preaching to them. The place where we assembled was a kind of butcher's shop, and all the circumstances of this congregation—their dwellings, and our place of worship—served to remind me very forcibly of our very small and rude commencement of life and religious institutions in Albany thirty-three years ago, when I used to preach in the settlers' tents, or wattle and daub huts, or, lacking these, under the shade of spreading trees.

While at D'Urban I visited the settlement called Verulam. The settlers who were originally located here did not include so large a number of farmers as those who established themselves at York: hence a larger proportionate number forsook the settlement; but I found upwards of twenty families here. I regret that I could not visit them at their houses, as the rain poured down almost incessantly while I was there. Mr. Spenseley was kind enough to accompany me, as Verulam is a part of his Circuit. The people have built for themselves a suitable chapel at this place. It is neither neat nor elegant; but it is the best that circumstances enabled them to erect, and for a few years it will be quite adapted to the general circumstances of a new settlement. It showed a very just regard to the importance and value of religious things, that so soon after their location they set about the erection of a house for the worship of God. It will now also be used as a school-room for a day-school,—an application made by Mr. Spenseley to the Government on their behalf having succeeded in obtaining for them an annual grant in aid of the Teacher's salary. I preached at this place, and said what I could to instruct my hearers in what would promote their best interests both as Colonists and Christians. They were very attentive, and I trust good was done.

There were very few houses, and those chiefly of a temporary character, at D'Urban, during my visit in 1848; but the arrival of so many British settlers, two or three years ago, has entirely changed the appearance of the place. The English population is now about twelve hundred souls, beside a considerable native population. As the entire trade of Natal must always pass through this place, it is likely gradually to rise to be a town of large population, and of great influence in the Natal settlement. We have here, also, a very complete Mission establishment,—a good house, built in the bungalow

style, for the residence of the Missionary, a very large enclosed
garden, with cottage for interpreter, &c. The old chapel, which was
standing in 1848, and was at first occupied by a European congregation, is now used for the natives, for whom services are held in the
Dutch and Kaffir languages, chiefly by Mr. Gaskin; whose time
and labours are devoted to the native department, while Mr. Spenseley
devotes himself principally to the various English congregations
and Societies in the Circuit. While I was here in 1848, arrangements were agreed upon for the erection of a more suitable chapel
for the English. Mr. Holden carried out these plans, aided by
several zealous friends of the cause; and thus, about the time that
the recent emigration to Natal commenced, this chapel was ready.
It is a neat building, well fitted up, and kept clean and in good repair.
There are at present no other places of worship in D'Urban than the
English and the native chapels belonging to us. But here, as in
Pietermaritzberg, the Episcopalians worship in the building erected
by the Government for the public school-room. While I was at
D'Urban, however, the foundation of a small new church, capable
from its plan of future enlargement, was laid. As the Rev. Mr.
Lloyd, the Chaplain, and the Churchwardens, &c., specially invited
me, I was present on the occasion; and after the two Clergymen
had performed the usual service on the ground, at which was assembled nearly the entire English population, by Mr. Lloyd's request I
delivered a short address adapted to the occasion,—probably the
first time that any Wesleyan Minister ever took a formal and public
part in the services connected with laying a foundation-stone of an
Episcopal church. But I am sure that I acted on true Wesleyan
principles when I wished them success in all their efforts to promote
the glory of God in this new Colony. I have omitted to mention
above, that there is a small congregation of Independents at D'Urban,
who worship in a room which they have fitted up for the purpose.
The Roman Catholic Priests, from their establishment at Pietermaritzberg, were also just about commencing some services at
D'Urban while I was there. There are several native or Kaffir
congregations which Mr. Gaskin has under his care in this Circuit.
It is evident that the labours of the brethren have not been in vain
in this department; but as yet the work is in comparative infancy.

The second journal records the particulars of a visit to the border stations in October of the same year, (1853,) in which he was accompanied by Mrs. Shaw, who was then, and had for some time previous been, in a precarious state of health. The account of the Free Church Missions is very interesting. The letter is dated, "November 14th, 1853."

I left Graham's Town on the 7th of October, on a visit to several of the Stations on the border, and in British Kaffraria. I had designed starting some time sooner; but long-continued rains rendered travelling in this country wholly impossible. I started as soon as there was hope that I could cross the bridgeless stream at the Konappe River, on my way to Fort Beaufort. I travelled in my ox-wagon to enable Mrs. Shaw to accompany me, in hopes that change of air and the journey would renovate her health, which for some time previously had been in a very precarious state. Owing to several hinderances, we could not reach Fort Beaufort in time for Sunday, the 9th of October: indeed, the river was barely fordable at the Konappe on the evening of the 8th inst. We therefore outspanned or unyoked our oxen, and resolved to spend the Sunday at a spot near the ford, and a short distance from a small camp of soldiers.

On Sunday morning I waited on Lieutenant Philpots, whom I found in command of the company of the 74th Highlanders. He very willingly assembled the troops, and I prayed with and preached to the men on the parade. They were all most attentive, although there was no shade from the sun, which happened to be bright and burning hot. They had just received orders to prepare for removal to India. They are going to the Madras Presidency. After holding this service, baptizing some children, and distributing some tracts, there was no further opportunity of holding public religious services, and we spent the remainder of an unusually hot day in our wagon; Next morning, early, we were in motion, and after resting for a time in the middle of the day at Leen Fontein, we reached the

Mission-house at Fort Beaufort in the evening, and were kindly received by Mr. and Mrs. Ayliff.

The chief object of my visit here at this time was to inspect the country in the immediate vicinity of the town, where about four thousand of the Fingoe Kaffirs are now permanently located in various kraals or settlements by the Government, and to mark out the site for the Mission buildings, &c., on the new Mission, which, at the request of the Governor, we are about to establish for the religious instruction of the people. One day during my stay at Fort Beaufort, we rode out to the spot: previous to the late war it was occupied by some thirty families of Kaffirs, most of whom had embraced Christianity. Since the termination of the war, however, the Governor has, for political reasons, originating entirely in his own plans, resolved that no Amaxosa-Kaffir settlements shall exist on the western side of a line which he has drawn. In consequence of this decision, the Kaffirs referred to were obliged to remove; but a very superior location has been provided for them, near the town of Alice, on the Chumie river. A body of Christian Fingoes belonging to our Society, having been located by the Government on the site of Birklands, I visited the spot, and selected the ground, which we are to receive as a grant from the Governor, as I had objected to incur any expense in buildings for the new Mission till a title can be secured to the Society. The place is extremely well suited for the purpose of a Mission village. A ride of five or six miles, up a deep mountain glen, is terminated by a rocky precipice, covered with a forest of trees; the various streams which rise still higher up the mountains, are precipitable over this rock, and, joining at its foot, flow on to the Kat River, at Fort Beaufort. The site of the village is on the top of this rock, on a kind of plateau, having a view down the entire romantic valley, with Fort Beaufort at the distance of seven or eight miles, which stands upon the open country, perhaps four or five hundred feet below the level of the rock on which the village is placed. The most material points, however, are, the soil is good; wood, water, and grass abundant; and, above all, the Missionary, being located on this spot, will be in the centre of the entire Fingoe settlement of the Fort Beaufort division. Mr. Ayliff had requested the various petty Headmen and Chiefs to come and meet us; we also had the assistance of the Government Superintendent of the Fingoes of this division. All parties were highly delighted, when I announced that Mr. Ayliff would shortly take up his residence here, as the Missionary for the entire Fingoe settlement, while the Fingoes, and other natives resident in Fort Beaufort itself, would be cared for by the Missionary who will succeed Mr. Ayliff at that place.

After receiving many tokens of kindness from our friends at Fort Beaufort, and being detained beyond the time fixed for our departure, by heavy rains, we proceeded on Saturday, the 15th, to Alice. This place was founded by Sir P. Maitland, during the war of 1847. It is protected by Fort Hare. The distance is about thirteen miles eastward from Fort Beaufort. The town is become the capital of the division of Victoria, embracing all the lands between the Fish River and the Keiskamma, formerly known as the Neutral Territory, but which the Kaffirs were again allowed to occupy for some years, previously to the war of 1846, which was occasioned by the reckless and lawless conduct of that portion of them who resided in this immediate vicinity. The site of the town is well chosen, on a fine part of the country, watered by the Chumie River, which has been let out for irrigation on a vast extent of fine land. Thus, a residence here combines the advantages of town and country life; and it is probable that this place will steadily increase in size and population. Since Mr. Sargeant's appointment as Missionary for Kama's tribe, he has taken up his temporary residence here. There being no house as yet for his family at the Keiskamma, I desired him to obtain lodgings for a time here, and from this place to visit Kama and his people, the distance not being great. As some of the English members of our Society were already resident here, they have, at some cost to themselves, fitted up a room for public worship, and Mr. Sargeant, assisted by Mr. Ayliff, and the Local Preachers of Fort Beaufort, supplies them with regular Sunday services, for which they seem grateful. I preached in the afternoon and evening to attentive congregations in this new place of worship.

On Tuesday, the 18th, we proceeded on our way towards King

William's Town, through the heart of British Kaffraria. Mr. Sargeant accompanied us to the Keiskamma at the middle drift, about twelve miles eastward of Alice. I had visited this place with him on horseback about a month before, to select the site for the new Station with the Chief Kama and his tribe. At the drift or ford, the troops have erected a kind of fort or barracks, in which one company of the 2nd or Queen's Regiment is at present stationed: about a mile below this place is the spot selected as the site of our Mission. If success attend the somewhat difficult project of leading out the waters of the beautiful Keiskamma river, so as to irrigate the rich soil along its banks, this will prove as fine a site for a town or village as any in Southern Africa.

On our arrival, we met Kama and his son William. We unyoked our oxen at the kraal of the latter, who now acts as schoolmaster of the tribe. William Kama placed his very large and clean native hut at our disposal. It was rather curious and pleasing to observe, on entering it, that it contained some articles of furniture never seen in the hut of a Kaffir till Christianity came to be proclaimed in the land. He has a bedstead and a bed, with clean bedding; a table and some chairs; a chest in which he keeps his clothes; and in some sacks a supply of meal, sugar, coffee, &c. Many, even of persons who have been born and brought up in Africa, would hardly credit these simple facts, so great and so strange is the contrast which they present to the ordinary discomfort and destitution of a Kaffir dwelling. But William and his wife are both real Christians, and patterns of piety and consistency. At family worship in the evening, which we held in his hut, I desired him to read a portion of Kaffir Scripture: I was much pleased with his selection of 1 John iii. He read the whole chapter with great accuracy, and with a tone and feeling that manifested how much his heart was in unison with the noble sentiments of that delightful portion of God's most holy word. I longed for the presence of my old friend Shrewsbury, and some other of the earlier Missionaries in Kaffraria. How would they have rejoiced to see what I saw, and hear what I heard! They know how dead and dry we found the bones of this valley of vision, and how we often travelled and laboured, in weariness and tears, and fasting and prayers, often saying, "Can these dry bones live?" Blessed be God, some have been given us as the first-fruits of future increase. And who is he that saith, the harvest shall never come? "Jehovah saith, I will work, and who shall let it?"

Early next morning, the Chief Kama, and as many as the large hut would hold, packed together as only Kaffirs can pack an assembly of human beings, listened to a very appropriate sermon in Kaffir from Mr. Sargeant, and joined with evident delight in the other devotional exercises. There are at present about fifty members of Society connected with this place and tribe. Mr. Sargeant will have under his immediate care the whole of the Kamas' people, who at present number about two thousand souls, and are likely, from the position they now occupy, to increase by accessions from some other tribes. Besides this population, our Missionary here will have to devote time occasionally to Alice, to the military station and village at Middle Drift, and to a Fingoe tribe located not far distant. Thus, if he is in labours more abundant, he will still find himself hardly able to overtake the numerous demands of his work.

On Thursday, 20th, after sleeping in our wagon in the beautiful vale below the forests of the well-known Thaba-Ndoda mountain, we reached King William's Town about noon, where we were most kindly received by Mr. and Mrs. Chapman, and found Mr. Impey, from Mount Coke, waiting to meet us. This day, and Friday, were devoted to visiting various families, and, in conjunction with Mr. Chapman, making various inquiries relative to plans for the extension and future course to be pursued on this Circuit. The building used until recently as a printing-office Mr. Chapman has converted into a temporary chapel for the natives, of whom, I am glad to say, he has already collected a very promising congregation. Two other native congregations, consisting principally of people who came from Butterworth last year, and who have been located lower down the Buffalo River, a few miles distant from the town, are also placed under his care, with much promise of usefulness among them.

On Saturday, 22nd, we proceeded to Mount Coke, calling on our way at Fort Murray, when I visited .Colonel Maclean, the Chief

Commissioner of British Kaffraria, who received us with kindness.
This officer has ever shown a readiness to promote the objects of
the Mission, and to perform acts of personal kindness towards the
Missionaries and their families.

Arrived at Mount Coke, I was surprised and thankful to see the
vast improvement and progress which has been made on this Mission. It was only recommenced, under somewhat unpromising
circumstances, in 1848; the former Station having been wholly
destroyed in the war of 1846, and the people scattered. A mere
handful of people were all that could be collected when the Station
was re-formed; but, from a variety of causes, they have gone on
increasing, till there is now a population of more than a thousand
souls resident on the place, with a scattered Kaffir population within
convenient reach of the Mission, amounting to, at least, fifteen thousand souls. These belong to the tribes of Pato, Umkye, and Sinane,
and must, as soon as circumstances will allow, receive more careful
attention, by itinerant visits from the Missionaries at Mount Coke.
The buildings on the village have been erected in a most substantial
manner. The Minister's house has been some time erected, and is a
pleasant residence, with beautiful flower-garden, and cultivated field
in front. There is a large, substantial building, which is now converted into our printing-office, with paper-room, binder's room,
editor's room, &c.; at least, these accommodations will be all
afforded when Mr. Appleyard can remove to the house designed as
his residence: at present he lives in a part of the building which is
the printing-office.

On Monday, 31st, we took leave of our friends at Mount Coke,
and proceeded on our way: after crossing the Keiskamma once more,
we re-entered the Colony, in the Fort Peddie District of Victoria.
Taking up our abode for the night at a *bush* by the roadside,—*not
the "Bush Inn,"*—we arose early, and arrived to breakfast at the
residence of Mr. Garner, at D'Urban, Fort Peddie.

November 2nd, we proceeded to the Newtondale Station, where we
arrived soon after noon. Circumstances had prevented me from
visiting this Station for some years past; and I was equally surprised and gratified with the state in which I now found it. The

Station was destroyed in the war of 1846, but resumed in 1848, under the care of Mr. James Kidd, who acts as Catechist and Local Preacher in charge of the place and its people; being visited regularly by the Missionary from D'Urban, Fort Peddie. There is a large Fingoe-Kaffir population surrounding the Mission village, all within three or four miles of the spot; besides about forty families of Fingoes and Kaffirs, who have taken up their residence at Newtondale itself. Here we have a neat cottage for the Catechist's resi dence, and a suitable building as school-house and chapel; a number of square-built houses, occupied by the natives; a good day and Sunday school; a numerous congregation; forty or fifty native converts, members of Society; and an ample field of labour around. Mr. Kidd has trained the members of his classes to make the usual contributions with regularity; and these classes have raised, during the last twelve months, about £22 as class-money and quarterage. It would be regarded as a very good average per member, for many a place in England. I preached to the people in the evening: the chapel was crowded, and the congregation attentive and devout. Here also, however, the chapel must be enlarged to twice its present size as soon as practicable.

Having received much kindness from Mr. and Mrs. Kidd and his people, on the 3rd of November we proceeded on our way to Graham's Town. Arriving at the Great Fish River about noon, we were disappointed to find that we could not cross it, as the rains had again rendered it unfordable with safety. We remained till noon next day, when, the water having subsided, we got our wagon through, and, ascending the bushy heights, reached Frazer's Camp, where, by the side of a bush, well known as a halting-place for Missionaries and others during the last thirty years, we once more spent a night; and on the 5th instant, after travelling in the wagon all day, reached Graham's Town in the evening. Here I must close my narrative. I am thankful that Mrs. Shaw returned home with renovated health; and I trust the facts I have rapidly sketched will afford you pleasure and encouragement. The review of them strengthens my hope, that this Mission is still destined, in the good providence of God, to scatter innumerable blessings on all this land.

On the 6th of July Mrs. Shaw died in Graham's Town, after four months' severe illness. This was an unexpected blow to Mr. Shaw. As a memoir of this excellent woman is preparing for the press, we refrain from any further notice of her lamented death. A funeral sermon, suitable to the occasion, was preached by the Rev. James Cameron, on Sunday evening, July 18th, which has been published, with some brief notices by Mr. Shaw. At the close of this trying year Mr. Shaw undertook a journey beyond the Orange River. Of this we have no record beyond a brief reference in the "Notices" for March, 1855.

The last official journey was made in 1855. It was confined to the Stations in Kaffirland and Pondoland. The letter is dated "August 1st, 1855."

I left home on the 19th of April, accompanied by Mr. W. Wood, a young friend, who had been recommended to travel for the benefit of his health. We travelled in my ox-wagon, and reached D'Urban near Fort Peddie, on Saturday evening, the 21st.

We remained in the Fort Peddie district till the 25th of April. Within the limits of this district there is a Fingoe settlement, or rather a number of settlements, comprising an aggregate population of that race of nine thousand souls. They occupy an extensive tract of fine country. Our D'Urban Mission Station is situated at the head of a valley, within sight of Fort Peddie, from whence it is distant only about a mile. This place is very central for the whole Fingoe settlement, and a most important Missionary field.

On Monday, the 23rd, we started, accompanied by Mr. Garner on horseback, to visit some of the out-stations of the settlement. We first rode to the Gwalana, distant five or six miles from D'Urban. This is the residence of one of our Native Teachers. He teaches a day-school, and holds regular services for the benefit of the numerous kraals which are situated around his residence. There are also several Native Local Preachers here, who preach every Sunday at various places in the neighbourhood; thus an extensive work is carried on entirely by a native agency. The members of the Society who were near at hand came together, and we held a short service with them, during which I addressed them chiefly on their obligations and duties as members of the Church of Christ. They were attentive, and evidently much interested.

We afterwards proceeded to Newtondale, a further distance of about eight miles to the southward. Here we found our faithful European Catechist, Mr. James Kidd, and Mrs. Kidd, living in the midst of a Mission village of more than fifty families, surrounded by a large heathen population.

We returned to D'Urban on the 24th. There is a small English village at Fort Peddie, which is also the residence of the Magistrate; and since the late war, a considerable number of English families have had farms granted to them within the previously unappropriated portions of the district. Thus it was thought high time to erect a chapel for the English. This is now in progress, under the direction of Mr. Garner and a Local Chapel Committee.

On the 25th we rode through a rather difficult piece of country in a westerly direction about twelve or fifteen miles, and visited the Gora River, where there is a fine native settlement, at which one of our members is at once the Chief and the Native Teacher. I was delighted to see evident proofs of his piety and activity. He introduced us to a wattled chapel, built chiefly with his own hands, in which a considerable native congregation can be accommodated; but it is already too small. I examined the children of the school, and found that they were making good progress in reading their own language, and in religious knowledge, under their zealous teacher.

During this day's ride we passed some Fingoe kraals, where they were dancing and singing in the most heathenish style. All the people were bedaubed with red ochre, and had the most fantastic and hideous appearance. This was soon explained when we met with a party of youths in their grotesque costume, fabricated from reeds, and their bodies smeared with white clay. It was the day for concluding the ceremony of circumcision, and these lads were now to be formally restored to society, after a separation of several weeks. After all the ceremonies had been performed, they would assume the character and standing of men in their tribe, and would henceforth be permitted to sit, and eat, and talk with the men on equal terms, being no longer regarded as boys. This is all the effect and significance given to circumcision among the South African tribes. It does not seem to have any religious reference at all. A difficult question has arisen for the Missionaries and native converts, as to how far it may be proper for the latter to interfere and prevent their sons from observing the rite. Experience shows that, despite their parents, there are few, if any, boys who can withstand the temptation of being initiated into the rights and privileges of manhood, which, with the native races, are of a very distinctive kind, and are never conceded to the uncircumcised. It is agreed on all hands, that the Missionaries and the converts should never give any countenance whatever to this custom; but it is very doubtful whether, under the circumstances, Christian fathers can be subjected to any church discipline for allowing their sons to observe it. The objection is not to the rite itself, but to the immoral and heathenish ceremonies and practices which usually accompany its observance.

On the 26th we reached Mount Coke, where we found Mr. Gladwin and family in the new house, and with sixteen pupils of the Watson Institution, who are under the daily instruction of a teacher, and spend part of their time in cultivating some land. On the 27th I examined the schools, and also with Mr. Appleyard looked through the printing-office, paper, and binding rooms, &c. This establishlishment is a credit to the Mission and to its Superintendent. It is delightful to see such masses of printed paper in the form of spelling-books, reading-books, Hymn-Books, Prayer-Books, Catechisms, New Testaments, and portions of the Old Testament, all either in complete forms or in preparation for the various Kaffir readers now to be met with in all parts of the country. Although several workmen are employed, and Mr. Appleyard is a conscientious economist of time, it is found impossible to keep up with the constantly increasing demand for books. It will be requisite to request the British and Foreign Bible Society to print for us a large edition of the Kaffir

Scriptures, so that the press, being less occupied on that work, may become more equal to the demand for other books. ◆

On the 28th we proceeded to King William's Town, calling on Colonel Maclean, the Chief Commissioner of British Kaffraria, at Fort Murray. We much admired the appearance of two native villages, which, consisting of an improved description of native huts, with white-washed walls, add to the beauty of the landscape. These villages have been formed under Mr. Chapman's care, and each has a native Teacher; including another village of the same kind on the other side of the town, there are thus three neat native villages included within the limits of the King William's Town Circuit.

Circumstances, over which I had no control, compelled me to return to Graham's Town; hence the whole week, from the 30th of April to the 5th of May, was occupied in my journey thither and back, on horseback, in very stormy weather, a distance of one hundred and sixty or seventy miles. I arrived at the last mentioned date at Mount Coke again. Next day being Sunday, I preached in the forenoon to the Kaffir congregation, and in the afternoon to a small congregation, who do not understand Kaffir, in the Dutch language.

Having returned from Mount Coke, we proceeded to King William's Town again on the 9th, and started thence on our journey through British Kaffraria. On the 15th, we reached Butterworth. The sight of this abandoned Mission was very painful to me. When I remembered all its past history, and that in three successive Kaffir wars, after building up the Station that number of times, we had been three times obliged to abandon the place, when, according to Kaffir custom in war, it was each time burnt and destroyed,—it was impossible not to feel the discouraging nature of such occurrences. In 1851, when last destroyed, here was a fine flourishing native village, a well attended church and school, described in glowing but not exaggerated terms, in the printed Journal of the Bishop of Cape Town, who visited it in 1849. Now only a few ruined and blackened walls were visible, besides the numerous fruit and other trees which were many years ago planted by the resident Missionaries. Sir George Grey hoped we would re-establish this

Mission; but when I intimated some doubt and hesitation, on the ground that we had been *three times* burnt out, His Excellency pleasantly said he had never heard of a Mission Station being *four times* burnt! Indeed, I should like to have the means of re-establishing this Mission; but at present we have neither a Missionary nor money available. This is to be regretted, as Butterworth is a fine central site, close to the neighbourhood which has always been regarded as the head-quarters of the Hintza family. It is central to the whole of Krielie's people, a tribe of some fifty thousand souls, among whom there is now no Mission.

In the evening I held a short service at the house of Mr. Crouch, the trader who has established himself near our old Station since the war. He showed us much hospitality and kind attention. This was also the case generally with the English traders, wherever I had occasion to call.

We left Butterworth on the 16th, and proceeded to visit all our Missions situated to the eastward, in the direction of the Natal territory. It would render this communication much too long, to enter into details as to each place. After visiting all the Stations as far as Palmerton, we arrived at Butterworth again, on our return on the 19th of June. During the intervening period, we visited Morley, Umdumbe, Buntingville, Palmerton, Shawbury, and Clarkebury. I managed to spend a Sunday at each Station, and thus had an opportunity of seeing and addressing all the congregations, and meeting the respective Societies, &c. The long-established Stations, Clarkebury, Morley, and Buntingville, presented nothing remarkably new or striking. The congregations continue quite as large as formerly, but there has been no material addition made to the aggregate number of church members on these Stations since my last visit; nor, with the exception of some new cottages, &c., at Buntingville, did I observe any considerable external evidence of advance or improvement. I thought, indeed, that Clarkebury had rather retrograded in that respect. Its large chapel, erected by the voluntary labour of the people ten years before, having been built on some defective plan, appears to have been for a long time past in a ruinous state, and is now wholly unfit for the sacred purpose to which it had been dedicated. Mr. Thomas was, however, taking measures for the erection of a new chapel. It has become evident to me, by my observations on this tour, that, although these Missions in the eastern section of the District have suffered from a deficient supply of Missionaries, yet they have likewise been retarded in their progress by what I conceive to be an erroneous mode of proceeding. When a Mission has been established in these parts, its progress, during the first few years, has usually been surprisingly rapid. A congregation has been collected, a church organized, and a village erected, where before nothing was to be seen but unmitigated savagery and heathenism. But in a few years the population of the village becomes so large, and the stock of the people increases so much, that there is no longer sufficient pasture for their herds; hence a material difficulty is placed in the way of further accessions to the population, while the residents feel a temptation to go to other places to depasture their increasing herds. In a country like Kaffraria, other places can always be found. Now it has ever appeared to me that, when this state of things arises, the resident Missionary should select and obtain suitable spots within a reasonable distance, and, dividing the Station people from time to time, should form sub-Stations, with a school and chapel at each, erected, at *first*, by the people, as the condition of the Missionary's arranging all their affairs for them. Then, by an active system of itinerancy, the Missionary should visit each one of these sub-Stations once a fortnight at least. Under this system, I doubt not but that each Station would continue to multiply its numbers, and extend its means of usefulness; for it is obvious that each sub-Station would, in its locality, form a new and separate centre, from which light would spread amongst the surrounding Heathen. These are not new views with me. I have always advocated them, but some of my brethren have not quite agreed with me. It is right to say there are some difficulties and objections to the plan, which I do not underrate, but I think they are not of sufficient importance to be set against the obvious advantages of the above mode of operation. I have discussed the matter at great length with some of the brethren in these parts; and certain new arrangements which I have proposed, and which the Missionaries concerned seem willing to try, with a desire to make them successful, will, I trust, at no distant period, greatly extend the usefulness of these comparatively old, but very important, Stations.

The Palmerton Mission Station I found greatly advanced and improved since my last visit. The resident population of the village, although considerable, is not so large as on the older Stations; but in all the external marks of improvement this native settlement has attained to high distinction. I have seen nearly every Missionary settlement beyond the borders of the Cape Colony; but I do not know one, belonging to any Society, in which the neatness, comfort, and good order of this settlement have been exceeded; and there are few, indeed, which, in these respects, are equal to it. Mr. Jenkins's efforts to promote the welfare of the people of his charge are beyond all praise. He works very hard. With his assistance, and under his superintendence, the people have already erected a considerable number of very neat and commodious cottages; and upwards of twenty more had been commenced, and were in progress of erection. He had taught many of them to make bricks, to build the walls, to cut timber, to thatch the roofs, &c.; and the result is, that as pretty a village as you can imagine has grown up in this remote locality, beyond the Umzimvubu River, in the midst of the large tribe of the Chief Faku, and more than two hundred miles distant from the nearest European settlement. While attending to the welfare of the people, that which is more immediately the property of the Mission has not been neglected. The commodious Mission-house, suitable chapel, and neat school-house, have all been erected in a substantial manner, and present a very pleasing appearance; the effect of which is heightened by the flower, vegetable, and fruit gardens, which are kept in excellent order. On the Sunday which I spent here, the native congregations crowded the chapel; and at the meeting of the Society, or church members, about one hundred were present to receive the word of exhortation. All these were once Heathens, but had been won over to the obedience of the faith, either on this or on some other of our Mission Stations.

The Shawbury Station is situated much further inland on the

higher part of the Umzimvubu, but on its western side, on one of its largest tributaries, called the Tsitsa; a noble stream, however "unknown to song." The village is only about two miles above a celebrated waterfall, which has now been ascertained to be three hundred feet high, over which the whole river precipitates itself, forming a beautiful object in the landscape. The present station is, in reality, the last established of all our Missions in this part of the country, as it was removed a few years ago from the original and unfavourable site. I was much pleased with the progress of affairs at this place also. Besides building himself a suitable cottage, the Catechist, Mr. Hulley, had superintended the erection of a commodious chapel. These buildings stand on some elevated ground at the upper end of the station, while the houses of the native inhabitants are built on two ridges facing each other, with a small stream running below the Mission premises, and between the ridges occupied by the natives. After crossing the Tsitsa, the approach to the Mission is up the small valley formed by the stream above mentioned; and altogether the effect is pleasing. The population here is already very large, probably larger than at most of the other stations. The natives have built improved huts, with upright walls, but covered in a manner similar to their own huts. As they have whitewashed the walls, the appearance is much cleaner and more pleasing than the native Kaffir hut, upon which it is a great advance. When it becomes general at the scattered kraals over the country, as at the Umdumbi settlement, where the British Resident has induced more than one hundred kraals to adopt this improved style of hut, it entirely changes the appearance of the country; for the traveller sees the white walls of these dwellings dotted over all the lands, in the scattered manner in which the Kaffir kraals are placed, and thus the scene becomes at once more lively and pleasing. I attach a good deal of importance to these things. It seems to me that we ought to stimulate the native mind, and spread a love of improvement among them. It occupies their thoughts with new and useful subjects, and tends greatly to weaken their strong prejudices in favour of ancient and superstitious habits. But, nevertheless, I do not put these things instead of the Gospel; they must arise out of

the new ideas which the preaching of the Gospel has introduced into
the minds of the people; and it is only that portion of the natives
who have come more or less under the influence of the Gospel, that
show any inclination to adopt these improvements. The chapel at
this place also was crammed to excess by the native congregation,
even after the children of the school had been turned outside to make
room. There was also here an attendance of about one hundred
members at the Society Meeting.

In this neighbourhood the remarks contained in a preceding part
of this letter find a strong illustration. It is impossible for all the
people who wish to reside here to find pasture for their cattle.
Hence Mr. Hulley has advised several parties of them to settle at
localities which are within convenient reach of the station. By this
means there are two or three sub-stations, visited on the Sundays
by the native Local Preachers; and I feel assured, if these arrangements are properly superintended, a great extension of the work
will result. The people who live in these parts are a different tribe
to those under Faku; and, unfortunately, in consequence of old
native feuds, the tribes occasionally make predatory attacks on each
other. At these times many lives are sacrificed, and much property
carried off or destroyed. It is a great mistake to suppose that the
tribes live peacefully together, when undisturbed by European
intruders. On the contrary, the ordinary state of things in Kaffraria
among the tribes is to be "hateful and hating one another." To
the Missionaries, whose commission extends to them all, this
frequently occasions much embarrassment, as even the people who
reside on the Missions naturally sympathize with the tribes to which
they respectively belong. While the country is governed by
heathen chiefs, there is little reason to hope that native forays will
entirely cease. All that the Missionaries can do is, at all times to
advise the Chiefs to live in peace; and as to the Christian natives,
at least to impress upon them the propriety of their confining their
warlike efforts strictly to *defensive* acts.

During my tour, I had interviews with the Chief Faku of the
Amampondo, the two principal Chiefs of the Amampondomsi, the
widow of the late Chief Ncapayi, and the principal people of the

Amabaca, and the Chief Joye and the widow of the late Umtirara, the great rulers (during the minority of the young Chief Qeya) of the Abatembu, or Tembookie nation. The whole of these Chiefs, to whom I have long been known, received me kindly, and all seem well affected towards the Missions and the Missionaries. Their conversion to God would be a great event: for this the brethren labour and pray; but they do not yet see the desire of their hearts in this respect. Faku is old, and apparently in a state of dotage. All the others are in the vigour of life. I have promises from the dominant Chiefs, that the son of Ncapayi, and the young Chief Qeya, who will hereafter rule the Tembookies, are to be placed under my care, with two or three youths of a similar age to attend with each of them, as soon as I can make arrangements. I hope that we may train some of the young Chiefs to adopt other ideas and modes of action than those heretofore entertained and practised by their forefathers. I regret that I missed seeing the Chief Krielie. He was near the Clarkebury Station, and in communication with Mr. Thomas for several days; but business called him away to his residence in a distant part of the country, before I reached Clarkebury; and my arrangements did not admit of my making so long a detour as would have been required in order to visit him.

On Monday, June 25th, we again reached King William's Town, on our way homewards. We called at Peelton, a Station of the London Missionary Society, and rested there for an hour or two. The Rev. Mr. Birt, the Missionary, and his family, were from home on a visit to the Colony; but we were kindly received by the Rev. Mr. Kayser, jun., who was supplying here for a time. This is a very important and valuable Mission Station. In consequence of the events of the last unhappy war, the Scottish Stations (United Presbyterian Church) of Uniondale, Iqibika, and Chumie, were broken up; and as the country where these Stations stood is no longer occupied by the Kaffirs, they were not allowed by the then Governor to be resumed: the consequence has been, that the Missionaries of that Church have retired from their work in British Kaffraria, and the whole of the natives belonging to the three abandoned Stations have united with those of Mr. Birt's original

Station; and thus there is a very large population, a great proportion of whom have embraced Christianity. The state of the schools, and of the church and congregation at this place, which is about eight or ten miles north of King William's Town, indicates great zeal and activity on the part of Mr. Birt, and reflects credit on the Society to which he belongs.

We remained a few days at King William's Town; and on Thursday, the 28th of June, at the request of the Rev. George Chapman and the Chapel Committee, I laid the foundation stone of a new chapel at this place. According to the plans adopted by the Committee, it will be a handsome and commodious place of worship, suitable to the capital of the province of British Kaffraria, which is shortly to be established as a distinct British settlement, under its own Lieutenant-Governor, and other civil staff.

On the 30th of June, we reached the Mission Station at Middle Drift, the residence of the Chief Kama. I was much pleased with the rapid progress of this place since my visit here in September of last year. Mr. Sargeant has been very active, and so have the people. The Mission-house is completed, and is a substantial and commodious structure; one portion of it, however, through the entire length of the building, is at present used as a temporary chapel. The Chief Kama's house, a good brick building, stands at the head of the valley, and was erected for him at the cost of the Government, as a mark of its approval of his steady and loyal conduct. His son, William S. Kama, has also erected himself a nice cottage near the Mission-house; while, following his example, some of the Kaffirs have done the same, and others have erected the improved kind of native huts. The whole are neatly whitewashed, and placed in rows along the side of a gently sloping hill, overlooking a beautiful valley where the cultivated lands are situated. This Station was established since the late war, at the urgent request of the late Sir George Cathcart, who promised me that he would find means to pay the expenses of leading out the waters of the Keiskamma, to irrigate the lands of the Mission village. He left us and proceeded to the Crimea before his kind intentions could be carried into effect; but even in London he did not forget his promise, and the Government stand pledged to accomplish this important work, which will be a great benefit to Kama and his tribe, as well as to the Mission. I fear, however, that it will not be accomplished excepting by some kind of mechanical power, as the waters of the Keiskamma, which run around these lands, are very much below the surface. The congregations were large on Sunday, the 1st of July. Mr. Sargeant baptized about ten adult Kaffirs, and admitted them by that rite into the Christian church. We also this day celebrated the Sacrament of the Lord's Supper, with a considerable number of Kaffir communicants belonging to this place.

On the 3rd of July, according to appointment, Mr. Sargeant held a Missionary Meeting. The Rev. Mr. Laing, of the Free Church, and the Rev. Messrs. Kayser, sen. and jun., of the London Missionary Society, all attended, coming from their Stations for that purpose; the Rev. John Ayliff, from Heald Town, also came, together with several other European friends from Alice, and elsewhere. The meeting was numerously attended by the Kaffirs; the Missionaries and several of the natives spoke with great effect. The Chief Kama addressed his people in very appropriate terms, pointing out what a blessing the Gospel had been to himself and his tribe. He said, "When I was baptized, many of my heathen friends said, 'What a fool he is! He has now thrown away his chieftainship. He will never be regarded in Kaffirland as anything, now that he has become a Christian.' Now," says Kama, "is this true? Have I lost my chieftainship? On the contrary, you know I have a name in the country, and my followers have greatly increased. I know that this is not attributable to me, but it is the Lord's doing." By many more words to the same effect, he strove to impress the people that they were under the greatest obligations to the Gospel and its Missionaries. The collection was a respectable amount. It had been in the heart of Kama and others to propose a general contribution of cattle through his tribe, towards paying the cost of a large and substantial chapel, which it is requisite to build in this place; but the late dreadful epidemic among the horses and cattle has fallen with peculiar severity upon him and his tribe. I feel assured that they have already lost stock which cannot be valued at less than from £15,000 to £20,000 sterling. The cattle are still dying: both the Kaffirs and the Colonists are alike appalled at this dreadful scourge. Under these circumstances it seems advisable to postpone for a time the application to the tribe for a general gift of cattle to be sold to pay the cost of their chapel. But this involves a serious difficulty, since it is highly desirable the chapel should be erected without further delay, as it is very much needed. There is every probability that this Station will become a most important one in its bearing on the spiritual welfare of this part of British Kaffraria.

After the Missionary Meeting, which was held in the forenoon, was concluded, I proceeded, in company with Mr. Ayliff and other friends, to Alice. On the 4th, after inspecting the work of our new chapel now in course of erection here, and which is likely to be a substantial and neat edifice, we accompanied Mr. Ayliff to Heald Town. I was equally surprised and delighted with the decided progress of this place. No doubt Mr. Ayliff will have reported to you the proceedings on occasion of laying the foundation stone of the building for the Industrial School, which took place during my absence on my journey. The building is to be very large and commodious. Besides accommodation for the Missionary and family, and apartments for the teacher, there will be dormitories, school-room, work-room, &c., &c., for about one hundred boarders. The work is progressing rapidly under Mr. Ayliff's active superintendence. He has already about thirty boarders, consisting of very fine and interesting-looking native boys and girls, who are lodged and provided for in some temporary buildings. I visited the school, at present conducted in the chapel, where I found these boarders, and a considerable number of day-scholars, under the care of Miss Ayliff and a Native Teacher. The exercises through which they passed showed that much pains have already been bestowed upon them, and that they have commenced very hopefully in a course of Christian training, through the medium of the English language, which, it is agreed, is to be taught and used as the medium of intercourse in all the Industrial Schools. Sir George Grey supplied me with the means to carry on these buildings before he left the frontier for Cape Town; and Mr. Ayliff is managing their erection by means of

European mechanics and numerous native labourers, according to a plan drawn by the Civil Engineer of the Colony. After dining with the family, I took leave of Mr. and Mrs. Ayliff, and in the evening rode a few miles down a romantic valley, and arrived safely at Fort Beaufort, where I had the pleasure of hearing the Rev. E. D Hepburn preach in our neat chapel in the evening. As my wagon, which was to come by another route, did not arrive so soon as expected, I remained the next day at Fort Beaufort ; and was much gratified to learn from Mr. Hepburn, that the state and prospects of our work in this town were of an encouraging character.

On the 6th, we proceeded on our way, and arrived safely on Saturday, the 7th of July, at Graham's Town, being exactly eleven weeks since we started on our journey. During my absence I had travelled in all about eleven hundred miles, about one half on horseback, and the other half in my travelling wagon. Amongst other improvements since I have known this land, travelling is become less difficult than it used to be. Over a large part of my route there are now something like what are called roads in the Colony, whereas I formerly travelled on mere tracks. I used on my journeys in former days to be obliged to sleep very frequently on the ground under a bush, or at best in a Kaffir hut,—scarcely any improvement on the former ; but on this journey I generally had the comfort of sleeping in my travelling wagon, and only twice was reduced to the necessity of sleeping in a hut. All this is pleasing as a sign of progress, and I am not sure that I could now stand the same exposure as formally. But the best of all is, I found everywhere, more or less, evident signs and tokens that God is with us. A good and a great work, without much noise or observation, is going forward among those various tribes where our Missions are placed; and I believe, together with other Missions, they will be " found unto praise and honour and glory at the appearing of Jesus Christ." O may we, and all our friends and supporters at home, be found faithful, and we shall reap our great reward !

CHAPTER XI.

Mr. Shaw's Departure from the Colony, and Arrival in England, 1856.

As soon as it became generally known that Mr. Shaw was about to leave the Colony for England, valedictory Addresses were presented to him; the first by the Treasurers and Stewards of the Graham's Town Society; the second by the members of his Class in Graham's Town; and the third by "some of the old Settlers of the District of Albany, and other Inhabitants of the City of Graham's Town." Copies of these expressions of genuine feeling we subjoin. They are as creditable to the parties who thus testified their regard for Mr. Shaw, as a Christian Pastor and as a Patriotic Colonist, as they were richly deserved by Mr. Shaw himself.

The first Address is from the Wesleyan Church at Graham's Town. We extract it from the "Graham's Town Journal," of March 1st, 1856. It was delivered on Friday, February 29th.

To THE REV. WILLIAM SHAW, GENERAL SUPERINTENDENT OF WESLEYAN MISSIONS IN BRITISH SOUTH-EASTERN AFRICA.

THE Leaders, Stewards, Trustees, and Local Preachers, having been convened together in Special Meeting, take leave, on behalf of the Society and Congregation of Commemoration Chapel, to convey to you an expression of their heart-felt sorrow at your departure from among them. They cannot forget that you have laboured in their midst, with brief intermission, for

the long period of thirty-six years, and that they have not only
had the benefit of your public ministrations, but also of your
private counsel, your example, and your prayers. They can, as
in the sight of God, bear their testimony to your unwearied
zeal, your faithful admonitions, your affectionate sympathy, and
your helping hand; and they feel sensibly that your departure
from amongst them, though even with the prospect of a return,
is a misfortune to them which they are constrained unaffectedly
to deplore.

This feeling is heightened by the consideration, that the cause
of your removal is failing health. He who is the Author of
Life, who sustains in being, and directs our paths, has in His
inscrutable Providence seen fit to afflict you; but we have the
consolation of knowing that He doth all things well, that He
will not lay upon His servants more than they are able to bear,
and that what we know not now we shall know hereafter.

In presenting you with this Farewell Address, we feel keenly
the poverty of language to convey to you our precise feelings,
or our full appreciation of your services in this community—not
alone as a Christian Pastor, but as a British settler and as a
citizen.—It would be unpardonable, were we to forget that you
came hither as the Pastor of a large body of British Immigrants
in 1820, and that, as a Christian Minister, you devoted yourself
with untiring zeal, not only to the members of your own Church,
but also to promote the temporal and spiritual welfare of the
whole Settlement, as well as of the regions of heathenism far
beyond it. The success of your labours, under God, is seen in
the chain of flourishing Missionary Institutions in Kaffirland, in
Natal, and in the Bechuana Country,—in the numerous sacred
edifices which are found in almost every town or village of the
Eastern Province,—and in the multitude of our youth, who, under
your auspices, have been taught to " fear God and honour the
Queen "—to listen to " the Oracles Divine," and to make the

Bible, and the Bible *alone*, the only standard of their faith and practice.

In taking your departure from us, we desire to assure you of our undying affection. Some of us have been your companions during the course of many years; we have been witnesses of your abundant labours, have shared in your hopes and fears, and rejoiced in the prosperity of every hill of Zion. A still larger number have grown up around you. They have had the benefit of your instruction and example, they regard you as a kind, but watchful parent, and will unite with the elder members of the Church in fervent supplication that God will protect you, cause His face to shine upon you, and give you abiding peace.

In offering you this faint expression of regard, and in bidding you for a season Farewell, they beg you to accept as a small token of affection the accompanying purse. It contains the free-will offerings of a grateful people. These contributions have been made for your own special, exclusive use, without any reference whatever to Connexional funds, and with the hope that this gift, as trifling as it is in proportion to the occasion, may in some degree contribute to your comfort, and, above all, to the restoration of your declining health.

We would fain linger in our Address, were it not from a conviction that after all we should come far short in conveying to you all we would wish to express. We only add, therefore, our assurance, that you carry with you our most affectionate regards, and that we will not fail to offer for you our petitions to a Throne of Grace. Our united and fervent prayer is, that God, in His good Providence, may grant you a prosperous journey; that he will give the winds and waves charge concerning you; that He may carry you to your destination in the fulness of the blessings of the Gospel of peace; that He will make you a blessing in the Fatherland, and that in due time, in the enjoyment of restored health, He will send you back to us to resume your useful labours in this country.

REPLY.

DEAR FRIENDS AND CHRISTIAN BRETHREN,—The affectionate terms in which you have been pleased to address me, on behalf of yourselves, and the Society and congregation of the Commemoration Chapel, is very grateful to my feelings, now that, after so long a sojourn amongst you, the Providence of God seems to indicate that I ought, at least for a season, to remove far away from you.

I have been privileged to spend my youth and the vigour of my days in your midst, and God is my witness that I have never sought yours, but you,—the aim of my life has been to promote your religious welfare, and to advance the interests of our common Christianity amongst all classes in the extensive field comprised in the Eastern Province and the regions beyond. But while I know the motives which have actuated me in the exercise of my public ministry amongst you, yet I am deeply sensible that the warm and generous terms in which you have been pleased to express your sense of the utility of my labours, arises from the affectionate friendship which is ever apt to exaggerate the good qualities and useful services of its object. I assure you that I have never been self-satisfied, and am less so at this moment than at any previous period of my life. I have come very far short of my own idea of what the Christian Minister and Missionary ought to be. However, I must bear testimony to your unvarying kindness, and to the readiness you have generally shown to bear with my shortcomings. What I am I am by the grace of God; and if He has given me favour in your eyes, and rendered my ministry a blessing, to His Holy Name I desire to ascribe all praise and glory.

For many years past, my frequent absence on long Missionary

journeys, and my multifarious engagements arising from the office which the Conference and Missionary Committee imposed upon me, have precluded me from discharging many of the duties of the Christian Pastor among you. I have therefore rather stood in the relation of an occasional preacher, and as having the General Superintendence of our whole work in this extensive region, than as your resident Pastor. But this alteration in our relation to each other, although necessarily greatly limiting the opportunities for our private and personal intercourse, has not prevented you from displaying towards me on all occasions an undiminished affectionate regard, for which I have ever felt truly grateful.

It would be unbecoming in me at this time not to advert to the help and comfort I have derived in my work in this country, from that band of faithful labourers in the ministry with whom I have been associated in the duties and responsibilities of our common pastorate. I know you respect and love them for their work's sake, and I can assure you they fully deserve your support and sympathy. It is very consolatory to my mind that I leave amongst you a body of Ministers who are not a whit behind the Ministers of any other Church in Southern Africa, in whatever pertains to Ministerial and Missionary efficiency. It is pleasing also to reflect that our Educational Establishments were never in a more promising state, nor were our congregations ever more numerous than at the present time. The great want is a richer effusion of the Spirit of Grace, to render effectual the various religious ordinances established among you; and this will, I trust, be abundantly bestowed ere long in answer to your faith and prayers.

The considerate kindness which has prompted the freewill offerings of a generous people, and which you have presented to me in this purse, would have caused me some embarrassment, if I did not consider that, after so long a service among you, I may accept this token of your and their love without any compromise of that self-respect and independence of character which I have always, for your sakes, no less than for my own, endeavoured to maintain. This gift is therefore gratefully accepted, and it will be employed, as you desire, in ministering to my personal convenience and comfort while travelling, with the view and in the hope of regaining, under the blessing of God, some measure of my usual good health.

You have referred to my having first come to this country with the British Settlers of 1820. I have no higher ambition than to be called and remembered as the *British Settlers' Minister*,—for the events of the years which have passed away have only tended to deepen the conviction which I entertained from the first formation of this Settlement :—That if we and our descendants are faithful to the call of Providence, history will hereafter record, that the spread of Christianity and the ultimate establishment of peaceful government throughout the whole of Africa south of the Tropic, resulted, in a great degree, from that arrangement of Divine Providence which brought so many British settlers at one time to these shores. It is pleasing to see so many of the original settlers—with whom I have wept and rejoiced, and offered prayer and praise—still surviving. Our number is, however, rapidly diminishing, and soon the last of us will be gone to our final account. But instead of the fathers will be the children ; and it is indeed delightful to see a numerous race rising up, many of whom are, I trust, imbued with the spirit of pure piety, and who will carry forward the good work begun in the days of their fathers. I feel deeply interested for the rising race. May they all receive the truth in the love thereof, and glorify God in their day and generation !

And now, my dear friends, wishing you and your families every blessing of life and godliness, I will conclude this address.

in the words of the holy Apostle St. Paul,—"Finally, brethren,
farewell. Be perfect, be of good comfort, be of one mind,
live in peace ; and the God of Love and Peace shall be with
you."

The second Address was from the members of Mr.
Shaw's Class in Graham's Town, much of the same tenor,
and accompanied by a present of useful articles required
for a voyage to England.

The third was an Address prepared by a Committee
appointed at a public meeting held in Graham's Town on
Friday, the 29th of February, 1856. It was from "some
of the old Settlers of the District of Albany, and other
Inhabitants of the City of Graham's Town." It was
accompanied by a purse of seventy-four pounds sterling,
and was presented by Mr. J. Temlett, Mr. Edward Jarvis,
and Dr. Eddie.

REVEREND SIR,—Although we are not connected with the
very respectable and influential Society of which you have been
so many years a distinguished member, we cannot allow you
to leave Graham's Town, after a residence of nearly thirty-five
years on this frontier, without offering you our very humble
testimony of the very high estimation in which we hold your
services both as a Christian Minister and a good citizen, and
without bidding you, " Hail and Farewell."

We would also wish to acknowledge the very great services
which you have uniformly rendered to this community by your
steady and consistent support, without reference to either sect
or party, of every public institution which had for its object the
welfare and improvement of any section of the community,
and also as a sincere and consistent friend of the native
population.

We beg leave to assure you of our sympathy with you under the afflictions with which it pleased Providence to visit you; and we beg to assure you of our very good wishes that your intended visit to your native country may be the means of completely restoring you to health, and that you may return safely, with renewed vigour, to renew your labours in the sphere which you have so long and so worthily filled.

Graham's Town,
February 29th, 1856.

JAMES TEMLETT,
W. C. EDDIE,
GEORGE JARVIS.

THE REPLY.

GENTLEMEN,—The Address which you have so kindly presented to me, on behalf of some of the old settlers of the district of Albany and other inhabitants of the city of Graham's Town, is very gratifying to my feelings, proceeding, as I have substantial reason for believing it does, from a sincere regard for my welfare.

During my long residence amongst you, I have invariably received from the British settlers and other inhabitants the most marked proofs of their good feeling towards me; and now that I am about to leave this country, at least for a season, I am thankful to find that I am likely still to live in the kindly regards and remembrances of my fellow citizens and countrymen.

I fear that you estimate too highly any services that I may have rendered to the public institutions of the country; but you do me no more than justice when you speak of them as having been uninfluenced by sectarian or party feelings. My motto has hitherto been, "The friend of all, the enemy of none;" and I have never been more pleased than when we have been enabled to find some common ground·on which we could advantageously act together for the good of all.

Accept my best thanks for your sympathy and good wishes. If it should please Divine Providence to restore me to health, I trust I may yet again be privileged to return to this country, and spend the evening of my days among the people whose kindness I can never forget, and for whose welfare and happiness I can never cease to offer my humble prayers to Him who is the Author and Giver of every good and perfect gift.

Leaving Graham's Town, Mr. Shaw proceeded to Port Elizabeth, whence he sailed to Cape Town, in each place receiving the kindest attention from the Missionaries and Colonists of all ranks and positions. On the 29th of March he embarked for England. From a journal kept for the information of his daughter, Mrs. Impey, in Graham's Town, we extract the following particulars, which, if not in themselves of great importance, yet will be valued as exhibiting Mr. Shaw's ministerial walk and conversation on ship-board,—ever ready to discharge his duties as a Christian Minister.

Saturday, March 29th, 1856.—I embarked at the jetty, and went on board of the Indiaman, "Owen Glendower," W. Pare Commander. Rev. William Moister, who had gone on board with me two or three days previously, and kindly directed the fittings up of my cabin, came into Cape Town from his residence at Mowbray, and went on board with me. I was also accompanied by my respected friends, Messrs. Godlonton, Wright, and Shepperson, who were attending their Parliamentary duties in Cape Town, and also by Mr. Davidson, of Cape Town, who had rendered me some kind service in fitting up my cabin. After completing several of the fittings, &c., Mr. Moister and the friends left me. Before doing so, however, Mr. Moister commended me to God in prayer, and I offered a few words in supplication for my dear friends and their families. We then took an affectionate leave of each other, and I watched them till they had gone to a considerable distance from the vessel. I now felt that I was fairly embarked, and had taken leave of all my South African friends. However, Messrs. George Wood and Joseph Cawood afterwards came on board to bid me a kind farewell.

There is a large number of persons on board, amounting together, including the crew, officers, troops (invalids), and passengers, to more than two hundred souls. The passengers from India consist of one Major, one Captain, and one Lieutenant of the East India Company's Service, and one Captain and one Lieutenant of Her Majesty's Service. Of these officers the Major and one of the Lieutenants are married, and have their wives with them. There are several ladies taking their children to England for education. They are the wives of officers of the East India Company's Service, also a wife of one of the Company's Chaplains and her sister-in-law, the widow of another Chaplain. The passengers from the Cape are Messrs. Zegelmann, Vercy, Borcherds, and myself; all without wives or families,—Borcherds being a young man, and the others having left their families. Altogether, including the Commander and two Chief Officers, we sit down to dinner daily in the cuddy to the number of twenty-three, forming a rather large dinner party.

Among the cuddy passengers there is a German Missionary, with his wife and children. His name is Albrecht. He has been about fourteen years in India at a station in the interior, and is now returning, partly on account of his wife's health, and also to have a surgical operation performed on himself. He appears to be a man of considerable learning and of sincere, but perhaps austere, piety; and I doubt not has been a useful Missionary. He asked me to take the service this forenoon, which it appears he has generally conducted on Sundays. I declined doing so to-day, as I wished first to form some acquaintance with men and things on board, before commencing my efforts to do good. The ship was in some confusion, as is always the case in port after shipping stores, &c.; hence the service was held in the cuddy for the passengers only. Mr. Albrecht read the Liturgy, and preached a very good sermon, on the Saviour's thrice repeated question to Peter, "Lovest thou Me?" He was obliged to read his sermon, not feeling sufficiently fluent in his English to preach extempore. I endeavoured to profit, and I believe I did derive spiritual instruction and benefit from this service. We arranged that I should preach on the next Sunday forenoon, and thenceforward take the service, alternately.

Monday, March 31st.—I visited the sick bay this forenoon, in which there are several soldiers suffering from various diseases. I spoke with each of them, standing by the side of his hammock. After a few kind words of inquiry, I gave to each such advice as I thought might be useful, to all which they listened very attentively. When about to pray with them, I requested the other soldiers to remain still and silent; for there is no partition between those who are tolerably well and the sick, only the latter occupy one corner of the large space assigned as the barrack or sleeping deck for the troops. The whole of the soldiers behaved with the greatest propriety, and thanked me for my visit. The troops on board consist of about one hundred men, chiefly of H. M. 64th and 74th Regiments. One side of the deck is assigned to each of these corps, under their respective non-commissioned officers. All is kept as neatly and as cleanly as could possibly be expected; and as they do not sleep in berths, but in hammocks, which are taken on deck every morning, the space during the day is well ventilated, and sufficiently light to enable the men to read or attend to anything while below, as well as when they go on the forecastle. Hence I left a number of tracts for the men of the hospital, and also to be read by the other men whenever they are disposed, promising to exchange them for other interesting and instructive tracts from time to time.

Tuesday, April 1st.—Among the sick men visited yesterday there was one poor fellow who had been prostrated by an attack of paralysis some months ago, whereby he had been deprived of the use of his lower extremities. He appeared to me to be in a very feeble state; but he replied to my questions with evident interest in the purport of them, and listened to my appeals to him in a manner that showed he wished to catch every word. About eleven o'clock this forenoon Dr. Johnson, the ship's surgeon, told me this poor man was much worse, and he thought he could scarcely survive the day, and that he had expressed a wish that I would go and pray with him. Of course I took my Bible under my arm, and walked off to the sick bay immediately. I found this man evidently dying. He could not speak; but he understood all I said to him, as he signified to me by nodding his head, and other signs. After exhorting him, and directing him to look to the Lord Jesus Christ, the Friend of sinners, I read aloud the fifty-first Psalm, and prayed, concluding by placing my hand on the head of the dying man, and pronouncing upon him the Apostolic blessing. The scene was impressive. I felt the engagement to be a very solemn one, and profitable to my own soul. The soldiers all stood up, and were as silent as death; but I believe they were all alive to the serious nature of the service, and I trust some of them may have received good impressions. As I passed through them, they all thanked me for my attention to their dying comrade, and one or two begged that I would preach to them, which I promised to do on the following Sunday. One man, who is blind, spoke to me on the deck, and told me he had been a member of our Society at Madras and Bangalore; but that he had been sent with his Regiment to the war in Burmah, where, from his deprivation of the ordinary means of grace, he had lost much of the spirit of piety, and he had not lately received his quarterly ticket of membership. I gave him suitable advice. He has a wife on board, a Hindoo-Briton, a well behaved young woman, who attends one of the ladies. In the evening I was informed that the poor paralytic soldier had died a few hours after I left him.

Sunday, April 6th.—The passengers, crew, and troops, with the officers, all assembled on the quarter-deck, and exactly at half-past ten o'clock a young midshipman in full dress came to my cabin door, to announce "Five bells, and all ready for prayers, Sir, on deck." I at once ascended the ladder, and, going on deck, found the capstan neatly covered with flags, the awning spread, and a congregation of not less than one hundred and fifty persons, waiting for the service. I read the Liturgy, and then preached from Psalm xxxiv. 8: "O taste and see that the Lord is good: blessed is the man that trusteth in Him." I endeavoured to adapt my sermon to my audience. I did not occupy more than half an hour in my discourse, including a brief reference to the case of the poor soldier who had been buried during the past week. I soon obtained the most complete and apparently serious attention of the soldiers and sailors. The Captain noticed this, and he said he had never seen anything like it before on board his ship. "Why," said he, "my fellows never moved a muscle all the while you were preaching."

In the afternoon I went among the soldiers, and also talked with many of their wives and children, distributing tracts, which I had purchased at Cape Town for the purpose. I was glad to find that I had already secured the good opinion of all classes on board. I took advantage of it to offer to preach to the soldiers in the evening, between decks, at six o'clock. They gladly consented, and when I went at the proper hour, I found they had cleared away a good large space, and suspended two or three lanterns to give us light; I therefore immediately commenced service, by giving out one of our hymns. I pitched the tune at a venture, not being sure that any one would join in the singing; but I was delighted to find myself soon aided in this part of the service by several men and women, who sang heartily as to the Lord. The next hymn I left them to sing themselves, and the blind man mentioned before, who has a fine tenor voice, pitched a good old Methodist tune, and thus I have secured the services of a leading singer for the rest of the time while I conduct services on board this ship. I preached a short sermon, plain and pointed, on, "Resist the devil, and he will flee from you: draw nigh to God, and He will draw nigh to you." Captain Cunningham and some others from the cuddy had followed me to this service unknown to me, as they stood behind me. There was something picturesque in the scene. I stood in the midst of a circle of soldiers and their wives, the beams of the vessel just overhead; the candles in the lanterns barely rendering darkness visible in the remoter parts, but throwing a strong glare on other points. The contrast of light and shade would have pleased a painter's eye no less than my mind was encouraged and delighted to notice the eager attention with which the men listened to my words. At the close of the service they thanked me, and would have flattered me, if I could have permitted it; but my point is so far gained that this service is to be held every Sunday night.

Monday, April 7th.—Finding that there are several persons who would be thankful to meet in the evening for prayer and reading the Scripture, and there being no more commodious

place available, I offered the use of my cabin for those who
would join me in a short service at eight o'clock every evening.
It has given me great satisfaction to find that Mr. Gray, the
second officer of the ship, a very fine and well educated young
man, is seriously disposed, and that by his efforts one or two of
the other young officers and midshipmen are desirous of joining with him in reading and prayer. He is a cousin of Dr. Gray,
the Bishop of Cape Town, and visited Mrs. Gray while the ship
was in Table Bay, the Bishop being absent at the time on a
trip to Tristan D'Acunha.

This evening we commenced the proposed meeting, at which
Mrs. Rose, Captain Cunningham, and Messrs. Gray and
Berridge, ship's officers, attended, besides Mr. Albrecht and
myself. It was agreed that Mr. Albrecht and myself should
conduct the service alternately. He proposed to read through
and lecture on St. John's Gospel, and I read and lecture on
the Epistle to the Hebrews. I hope this may prove a blessing
to others as well as myself.

Saturday, April 12th.—Our evening meetings are likely to
prove interesting and useful. Besides those who came at first,
several others have requested leave to attend, and those who
cannot crowd into my small cabin sit around its door, where
they can hear. As Captain Cunningham's cabin is larger than
mine, and affords more accommodation, he has offered it, which
we have accepted ; for, his cabin being on the windward side, he
can have his port holes open more frequently than is quite
safe in my cabin. The weather is becoming so intensely hot
and sultry that fresh air is a great blessing, and we secure as
much of it as our circumstances will allow.

Sunday, April 13th.—Mr. Albrecht preached on deck, and in
the evening I held a service with the passengers and officers of
the ship in the cuddy. The practice had been to read prayers in
the evening, also ; but, with all my veneration for the Liturgy, I

do not like to be restricted to it. I love to hear it used *once* on the Sabbath; but I think that extemporaneous prayers may be more freely indulged at the other services, and it is the use of *both* methods by the same congregation on the Sabbath which appears to me to be the perfection of the form of public worship. As all the passengers, &c., are professedly Episcopalians, I thought it best so far to meet their prejudices as to read the Collect, and Epistle, and Gospel for the day; and I delivered a short lecture on the latter, concluding all by an extemporaneous prayer. The cuddy was full, and all seemed to be pleased; and, if I may judge from subsequent conversations with some, good impressions were made.

Monday, April 21*st.*—Yesterday forenoon proved to be so rainy that we could not hold the usual service on deck, and I therefore read prayers and preached in the cuddy. In the evening I went forward to the soldiers' quarters, and sent previously a message to the sailors, that they could join our worship there. I had a large and very attentive congregation, to whom I preached on, "I will be sorry for my sin." (Psalm xxxviii. 18.) Some of the military and also the ship's officers attended. This morning, 21st, we crossed the line about seven o'clock, in longitude 23° west. It is matter of great thankfulness that we have so far had a most pleasant and speedy run. To reach the Line from Table Bay in a few hours over twenty-one days is considered very good sailing.

Sunday, May 4*th.*—It was my turn to have preached on deck this forenoon, but the weather proved so windy, and the ship consequently unsteady, it was deemed best to hold the service in the cuddy. Thursday, having been Ascension Day, I preached to the officers and passengers on the Ascension of Christ, and as there are some who are inclined to scepticism, my observations were partly directed to the fact itself and its evidence, and, in a short application, to the use we ought to make of it. I believe this discourse will be remembered by some. May it prove useful to all! As Mr. Albrecht is unwell, and unable to conduct worship, I went forward to the soldiers' quarters again in the evening. The attendance of soldiers and sailors was again highly satisfactory.

Monday, May 12th.—We continued for several days last week to run rapidly on our course; but on Friday we met with a reverse, the wind shifting to the eastward, and blowing since that day very strong, bringing cold weather, which makes us all put on warm clothing. The vessel has also to contend with a head sea, as she is steered as near to the wind as possible, to prevent our being driven away to the westward. There is, however, some improvement this morning. We are now about 40° N. latitude, and have just passed the most westerly of the Azores. A moderately fair and fine wind would bring us within sight of the English shore in less than ten days. The weather was too boisterous yesterday to admit of public worship being held on the quarter-deck. Mr. Albrecht therefore preached in the cuddy to the officers and passengers, while I went forward, and preached to the military officers and soldiers, and a portion of the sailors, in the forecastle. Being Whitsunday, I preached from the lesson of the day, Cornelius the Centurion: a subject suitable for an address to military men. In the evening, I held a short service in the cuddy, and exhorted on the words, "Have ye received the Holy Ghost since ye believed?" Having proved my points from the Bible, I told the ladies and gentlemen, that as nearly all of them profess to belong to the Episcopal Church, I would show from their own Prayer-Book, that the views I had given them of the office of the Holy Spirit in the work of conversion and sanctification, were in exact accordance with the language contained in the formularies of their own Church. I then read from various parts of the Prayer-Book a number of beautiful and

Scriptural passages, fully establishing my assertions. They all
listened with much attention. May they receive good from
what they heard!

Monday, May 19th.—Preached in the cuddy in the forenoon
yesterday, the vessel rolling about so fearfully that it was
impossible to assemble the people on the quarter-deck. In
the evening, at their earnest request, I went forward, and
preached to the soldiers and sailors; but the motion of the
ship was so great that I could not stand, but preached sitting:
more than once several of my hearers were thrown from their
seats. There was, however, very great attention paid, as it was
thought this would be the last time I should preach to them,
since we hope to reach Gravesend before next Sunday.

Friday, May 23rd.—A boat boarded us last evening, and
offered to pilot us, but the Captain declined. This boat left us
"The Times" of May 9th. It is full of the various arrangements as to the troops, &c., consequent on the peace; but
nothing can be collected from it as to the terms on which
peace has been made, excepting that they seem to be satisfactory to the nation. Before I returned to my cabin, I saw
the beautiful revolving light on Beechy Head. The night was
calm and clear, wind fair,—how was I surprised therefore, on
rising at six o'clock, to find that we were close to the French
shore! It appears that they had kept too far off the English
coast to avoid the Point of Dungeness, and, through some
error, had run too far away. Providentially we fell in with
some French fishing-boats. Our first officer, who had charge
of the watch, asked, "How does Dungeness bear?" and they
answered in broken English, "This is the coast of France."
It was in the very neighbourhood where a large East India
ship was lost in a gale of wind three or four years ago. The
Frenchman came on board, and engaged to pilot us over to
Dover. We made the coast to the south of Boulogne, and were

near enough to see the tower of the Boulogne Cathedral. The commander is greatly vexed ; but we ought all to feel grateful to Divine Providence, as in bad weather, or even a fog like that of yesterday morning, we should have been run ashore, and probably all have perished. But the weather is mild and clear, and we are once more getting sight of the English coast. We hope still to reach the Downs this evening ; but we have lost some eight hours of time by this error in steering. The Frenchman can only speak a few words of English. He said rather expressively, " I not here—you go a little further —no ship, no passengers !" He meant to say, all would have been lost ; and it is somewhat singular that only one person on board can speak French intelligibly, viz., Lieutenant Davies, formerly of the Cape Mounted Rifles, but now of the 74th Regiment. He is obliged to act as interpreter. On reaching Dover, we were met by one of Mr. Green's steamers, the " Owen Glendower " being one of his ships. She took us in tow, and we passed the Downs, Ramsgate, Margate, &c., in grand style, and brought up for the night just below Sheerness.

Saturday, May 24th.—Started again in tow of the steamer, early in the morning, and cast anchor at Gravesend about twelve o'clock. The troops were landed, and on parting I received many thanks from these men for my attentions to them on the voyage, and some said they would never forget what I had said to them in my sermons. May they not only remember, but be led into the way of salvation thereby!

We missed the train to London, and were obliged to cross the river again to go by a railway train from the other side ; just arrived in time, and started by this comfortable and rapid mode of transit to London. We entered London on the Stepney side, and for a mile or two seemed to be riding amongst a forest of chimney-pots, and over the tops of as ugly a collection of houses and buildings as can be conceived of. The station where we alighted is in Fenchurch Street; reached the Mission House about five o'clock—Secretaries all gone home; met Mr. Adams, and obtained the address of Hudson's, 42, Bow Lane, where I went to board and lodge for a few days. Met here Rev. Mr. Corlett, Chairman of the Demerara District, an old Missionary, and very pleasant man. He is on a visit to England with his son.

Sunday, May 25th.—Attended Divine service at the chapel where the family usually go, Jewin Street. Heard an excellent sermon from Rev. J. H. James. Visited the Sunday school in the afternoon, the numbers not quite as great as at our English Sunday school at Graham's Town; the teachers apparently much devoted to their work. In the evening, at Jewin Street, heard a young man from the Institution. No one could tell me his name. A very admirable discourse, exhibiting considerable intellectual power, but a shade too much of the theological lecture and academical manner, for popular instruction; but this is natural in a young student. Mr. James knew me, and said, if he had known I should have been at the chapel, he would have urged me to preach. I told him it would have been useless, as I had no intentions of preaching in London for a while. He said it was useless, then, to ask me to preach for him in the evening at another chapel. I said, "Entirely so." He is become a preacher of more than common powers, and will rise to eminence in our body.

Monday, May 26th.—I was much shocked, on Saturday evening, to learn that Dr. Beecham was dead. I feel this to be a great drawback on the pleasure of my visit to England, as he was one of the very few persons in London with whom I was particularly acquainted. I went off to the Mission House, and met Mr. Hoole and Mr. Osborn. I remained with them about half an hour. They received me in a very friendly manner; expressed surprise and pleasure to see me looking so

well, and so much younger than they had imagined. The
voyage has certainly been of great service to me. Mr. Hoole
gave me some details about Dr. Beecham's sickness and death,
which I need not repeat, as I dare say they have been published.

Tuesday, May 27th.—Visited Mission House this morning,
and was introduced to Mr. Arthur, who had been away in the
country when I called yesterday. He expressed his surprise
that I was not looking old and white-headed. I cannot but
observe that every one seems to imagine that I am much older
than I really am; but I presume this arises from my having
married when very young, and my name having been so long
before the public in connexion with South Africa.

Wednesday, May 28th.—Decided that I will remain with
William for some time.* They can spare me a very nice little
bed-room, a little larger than that in which I was wont of late
to sleep in the Mission-house at Graham's Town. It is on the
second floor of the house, and has an enchanting prospect from
its window. I am to be at "Liberty Hall," and to go and come
just as I like. This is exactly suited to my wishes, and I think
I shall be happy and comfortable with them; I can get back-
wards and forwards to London whenever I like, any day, by the
omnibus at a small charge. Went to the Mission House, and
thence with Mr. Adams to the East India Dock, to see after my
luggage: we went and returned by rail in a short time. The
agent was out of the way, so effected nothing. There is considerable delay and difficulty in getting luggage passed by the
Customs officers.

Thursday, May 29th.—This day had been appointed for the
celebration of the Queen's birthday, and the Restoration of
Peace. All London put on her best appearance. I went to
the City and the West End to see the preparations for the
general illumination. I was disappointed in regard to the

---

* The Rev. William Maw Shaw, then residing at Highgate.

taste displayed by the Londoners. Very few of the devices seemed to have anything remarkably striking or beautiful ; but the effect of the whole from the size of London and the character of many of its public buildings was of course grand. I was anxious to see the parade at the Horse Guards ; but owing to a mistake in getting into a wrong omnibus, I was too late before I arrived, and the populace had so completely filled up all the space where the troops could be seen, that I saw very little beyond the bear-skin caps of the Grenadiers, and the gentlemen and cavalry on horseback. The music of the bands was something wonderful. I could get no sight of Prince Albert or the Staff, beyond seeing the brilliant group over the heads of the people at some distance. After the grand display was over, I got a little nearer view of the troops and their bands, as they defiled to their respective barracks. The number was small, I think not more than six or seven hundred. They were all of the Household Troops, and looked superb in their new uniforms. I noticed that the Foot Guards, with the exception of here and there a man bearing the Crimean Medal, were nearly all young men, evidently very recently enlisted, I suppose, to make up the terrible casualties which had been made in the service battalions of these regiments in the Crimea, all the older soldiers having been sent away.

Leaving the Horse Guards I sauntered along by the waters of the Park as far as Buckingham Palace. Crowds of holiday people were in all parts of the Park. The Palace had been completed since I was last in England, hence this was my first sight of it. I was a good deal disappointed in its appearance. I need not describe it, as that has been often done ; but it did not strike me as exhibiting that magnificence which I had expected to find in the exterior appearance of a Palace erected by a great nation, at no stinted cost, for the metropolitan residence of the Sovereign. Barring the *extent* of apparent accommodation, I have seen noblemen's houses in the country parts of England far more imposing in their general appearance. The site of the Palace is, however, very beautiful; and as the Queen only occasionally resides here, she is probably satisfied with it. Rambling through the Green Park, I saw the extensive preparations for the grand illumination to take place in the evening, including the wooden pavilion erection at the end of the Palace, to afford the Queen and the royal family a convenient place from which to witness the fireworks. After standing some time at the archway on which is placed Wellington's equestrian statue, opposite the gates of Hyde Park, my attention was arrested by the passing of several carriages, in which were seated elegantly dressed ladies, in full court costume, ostrich plumes, &c., &c. I found they were going to be presented at the Queen's drawing-room. I therefore resolved to follow the carriages, as I did not know how else to find my way to St. James's Palace. Arrived at St. James's Street, I found a long line of carriages, each occupied by these fine-looking ladies, and in many cases with general and other officers, all in full figure. Going round to the south side of St. James's Palace, I found the crowd collecting to witness the procession of Her Majesty and the court to the drawing-room. I therefore immediately resolved for once to indulge myself with the sight of a royal procession. We had to stand nearly an hour. The police formed a long lane through the midst of the people, extending all the way from Buckingham to St. James's Palace, through which the procession was to pass; they and the magnificent Life Guards, on their superb black horses, keeping the space open. A man brought some forms to the place where I was standing, which were immediately engaged to stand upon, at a shilling apiece, by a number of ladies, to obtain a better view of the procession. I was fortunate enough to get a place among them, and did not begrudge the shilling, because it gave me a good view, and besides elevated

me above the damp ground, which I feared might give me a
bad cold by standing upon it for an hour. Many splendid
equipages of the various Ambassadors and foreign Princes, &c.,
together with the gold-bedizened Lord Mayor's chariot, passed
before the Queen's arrival. At length the royal party came in
three or four carriages. I saw the Queen and Prince Albert: the
latter dressed as a field-marshal. I did not get a sight of the
Queen's face, as at the moment of passing near us she was
bowing very graciously to the cheering crowds on the opposite
side of the pathway. The equipages, the attendants, the troops,
&c., were all of the most gorgeous character, and very becoming
a public appearance of the Queen of England. As I had
neither desire nor chance of being presented at Court, I now
tried to get away; but in the narrow space round St. James's
Palace this was rather difficult, as the carriages in waiting, and
the crowd of people, so jammed up the street, that it was
difficult to move, and I was not sorry when I found myself in
the more open space of St. James's Street, although it continued
very full of people, and on passing I saw some of the identical
carriages which I had before passed, with their elegant occupants,
still waiting their turn to get down to the Palace. It must
have been trying and disagreeable to these ladies to sit in such
a dress, to be stared at by the crowd in the street through the
glass windows of their coaches. I saw many of the populace,
(apparently country people,) and some who by their dress and
appearance ought to have known better, going up to the very
windows of the carriages, and standing still, to take a good stare.
I imagine all this is unavoidable, but it must be a painful ordeal, especially to young and bashful ladies. By this time I
was hungry and tired. I went to a coffee house, ordered a beef-
steak, which was soon prepared, and with a roll and a glass of
London porter I made a hearty dinner, and had an opportunity
of seeing the morning papers, all quietly and comfortably for

ninepence. I reached Highgate at about six o'clock, and was glad in the evening, instead of returning to the Green Park to see the fireworks, to go with Mr. and Mrs. Shaw to the house of a lady of their acquaintance in a new suburb of London, close to Primrose Hill, on the Hampstead side, where, without going out into the night air, we could witness the fireworks on that station. I met at this house in the evening a party of ladies and gentlemen, including five clergymen, one of whom is Rector of Reading. The whole party were family connexions with the exception of ourselves. We saw the fireworks to great advantage.

Due honour was paid to Mr. Shaw by the officials at the Mission House. On Wednesday evening, the 4th of June, a meeting was held in the large room in the Mission House, Bishopsgate Street, to receive him and several other returned Missionaries. The Rev. Dr. Bunting took the chair. The Secretaries, the Revs. Elijah Hoole, George Osborn, and William Arthur, the Rev. John Scott, the Rev. Charles Haydon, and Mr. John Vanner, Sen., took part in the meeting. The kindly feeling manifested must have been gratifying to all parties. At the Conference held in Bristol, Mr. Shaw spoke at some length in the Committee of Review, July 29th. At this Conference the two friends, who had been separated since February 14th, 1843, met again, Mr. Boyce and family arriving in Bristol from Australia on the 15th of August. At the great gathering at Leeds in October, and on other occasions, Mr. Shaw took a very prominent part, and in the May Anniversaries spoke with great acceptance.

These Missionary speeches we forbear to notice. The facts are already recorded in a more particular and detailed from than would have been suitable in a speech addressed to the restless impatience of a public meeting. Mr. Shaw possessed in an eminent degree the valuable talent of informing as well as of interesting those very variable audiences, at one time so critical and captious that nothing can please, at another time so beautifully resigned that one wonders at their forbearance. Within the last few years, Missionary speeches have improved in character; there has been a marked reaction in favour of the old models of a generation past, when Missionary speeches had some reference to Missionary facts and principles. Speakers are now expected to say something pertinent to their subject. What has been called "the bray of Exeter Hall," is now generally a deliverance of which none concerned have any reason to be ashamed.

CHAPTER XII.

Marriage, and Plans for the future Management of the South African Missions.

THE state of Mr. Shaw's health was for some time very unsatisfactory. His second marriage, in all probability, saved and prolonged his life many years. This happy event took place March 12th, 1857, in Liverpool Road Chapel, Islington, and was the last occasion on which the Rev. Dr. Bunting officiated, as soon after, on June 16th, 1858, that eminent Minister was called to his reward. The lady was Mrs. Ogle, widow of the late Mr. John Bourne Ogle, of Bolton, and daughter of the late Joseph Shaw, Esq., Collector of Excise, and granddaughter of the Rev. Thomas Shaw, who, on his first entering the ministry, resided with Mr. Wesley, at the City Road. Much of the health and comfort which Mr. Shaw enjoyed to the end of his valuable life may be ascribed to the assiduous love and indefatigable care of Mrs. Shaw. No man was more dependent upon those minute attentions which female affection alone can supply than my dear old friend. Of all men, he was least able to endure a lodging-house existence in all the dignity and dulness of a solitary life, for he was eminently social in his habits. After his marriage, he rapidly recovered his health, and was able to go through the fatigue of the Irish Deputation in April, 1857.

Some into whose hands this memoir may fall, may not

be aware of the machinery which is connected with the raising of funds for religious and philanthropic objects. In order to stimulate the lagging charitable sympathies of Christian people, it has been found necessary in the nineteenth century to employ the attraction of novelty. So far as Missions are concerned, no one could object to the employment of such returned Missionaries as have the gift of saying as well as of doing in this work; and if this were all implied in a deputation, no one could complain. But for this purpose some of the most valuable Ministers are taken from important Circuits, sometimes for several weeks at a time, to advocate the cause of Missions. That this sacrifice of the spiritual interests of the Home work should be deemed necessary for this object, is far from complimentary to the Missionary feeling of the Methodist people. I doubt the fact. If the Conference in mercy to the Home work would much lessen, or do away altogether with deputations, the Missions would not suffer, and the Home work would be greatly relieved and benefitted. If even the Mission Fund should suffer a little at first, the advantages accruing to the Home Circuits, from the presence of their Ministers, would soon be felt in the Missionary department of each Circuit; for the prosperity of the one work is intimately bound up with the prosperity of the other.

On May 4th, 1857, Mr. Shaw was one of the speakers at the Anniversary of the Wesleyan Missionary Society, held in Exeter Hall, the Hon. A. F. Kinnaird, M.P., in the Chair. On this occasion the Rev. James Calvert first appeared before an English audience, and produced a profound impression as he related the narrative of his conversion and call to the Ministry, and his labours in

Fiji. Mr. Shaw's speech referred mainly to the Kaffir Mission: but one passage, containing an account of his visit to Moshesh, the Great Chief of the Basutu (beyond the Orange River), we give from the "Notices" (July, 1857). It may gratify our readers to learn that the territory occupied by the tribe of Moshesh has been placed under British rule, not for colonization, but in order to preserve it from being amalgamated either with the Cape Colony or the Orange River Sovereignty.

It is not much more than two years ago, when on a long Missionary journey, I found it desirable to visit him, and had some communication with him concerning our Missionaries, who were, at that time, placed in circumstances of peril and difficulty. I was accompanied by the Rev. Richard Giddy, our excellent Missionary there. We ascended the mountain by a very narrow, rugged, craggy precipice. It was not possible for more than two or three to walk abreast, to a height of probably more than 1,000 feet above the common level of the plain. Arrived at the top, we found Moshesh, together with the inhabitants of his town, all dwelling on the top, where there was a plain about a mile long, by half-a-mile broad. I found him waiting to receive us, for a messenger had gone up to say we were coming. He immediately led me to his house, and there I saw very evident signs of a great change. He led me to a new house, quite as good as that in which many of the colonists live in various parts of that land. I was brought inside; I found the house well furnished with chairs and tables, and he motioned me to a sofa, that I might take my rest. He assumed that I was weary with my long ride that morning; and after giving me refreshment, he entered on some discussion, in the course of which he said, "I have great reason to be thankful that Christians have come into my country to give us instruction." He told me some very interesting things concerning an attack that had been made on his tribe, in consequence of something that occurred some time before, under Sir George Cathcart, when a large English army was sent to make an attack on Moshesh's tribe. He told me of the occurrences of the day, and of a very curious fact, which I have never mentioned before. I discovered that while our Commander-in-Chief regretted exceedingly the attack had occurred, because he was afraid it would be necessary to carry it on, and that it would lead to long hostilities greatly to be deplored, and which he was anxious to avoid, yet he was so committed that he felt he should be obliged to go on, and was preparing for a further attack. On the other hand, Moshesh was equally anxious to avoid further collison, which he knew would come with greater force the next day. He sat, he told me, in council in the very room where I was, and, while they were talking together as to what was to be done, he said, "I know the English will come again in the morning, for they have been worsted when we had only a handful to deal with, and they are not the people to give up,—they will come to-morrow morning in larger numbers; and what shall we do to propitiate the English Governor and avoid a collision?" Much was said, and at last they came to this conclusion : "Why, send down to the bottom of the mountain to the resident Missionary, and ask him to write a letter to the Governor, and tell him that we will submit to his terms, and endeavour to keep the peace, if he will cease from further fighting." Well, Sir, the messenger was sent down; but the Missionary at the bottom of the mountain happened to be a French Missionary, Casalis—that excellent gentleman to whom reference has been made to-day. A message was sent to him, and he found himself in a peculiarly delicate position, not merely because he was a Missionary, but a French Missionary, belonging to another nation; and, feeling that it was a matter of great delicacy, he refused to be the means of communication. An answer was returned that the Missionary refused, saying that he was of another nation, and he was afraid he would involve himself in difficulty. Moshesh said, "We were then in great trouble; we did not know what to do; and I turned to my son," (three of his sons were present, and he pointed to the youngest,) "and said to him, 'You must write the letter!' for you must know," he said, speaking to me, "he has been taught to read and write by the Missionaries." "'I said to him, 'You must write the letter;' but he said, 'I am a boy; how shall I write a letter about things so great, and to such great men ? Besides, I do not know English sufficiently: my English will not be understood.'" However, Moshesh directed him to write a letter in his own language; "for," said he, "the Governor has got interpreters, and he will understand it." The boy wrote from the dictation of Moshesh a letter, which was afterwards published by Sir George Cathcart in his Dispatches; and it is singular that, while 1 had that testimony from Moshesh himself, I actually had it from the lamented Sir George Cathcart's own lips, that he was never more pleased with the receipt of any document in his life than when he received that one letter from Moshesh, asking that hostilities might cease, that there might be peace between the two tribes, and that the matter might be settled and adjusted. "Thus," said Moshesh, "I have reason to say that the Missionaries are the best friends to the whole land; for they teach us how to live at peace one with another, and how to avoid contests referring to the predatory habits of the native tribes." Such is his impression of the matter, that since I came away, I find he has sent two more of his sons down to our Industrial Schools, which are supported by Sir George Grey, at Salem, to be instructed; and Moroko has sent four or five lads, the most important persons of his tribe, who will be companions to these two young Chiefs while they are receiving instruction.

After the Liverpool Conference of 1857, Mr. Shaw took up his residence at Croydon. While at Croydon, he revised an edition of the Kaffir New Testament, which was being printed by the British and Foreign Bible Society, and laboured diligently on Missionary Deputations in the Circuit when not engaged to preach beyond its limits. He remained here until, early in 1860, he removed to London, to make preparations for his return to South Africa. If he had needed any additional spur to his wish to resume his labours beyond his own conviction of duty, the presence in England of two excellent brethren from the Colony, the Rev. John Ayliff and the Rev. H. H. Dugmore, would have been sufficient.

The circumstances which led to his remaining in England I must now relate.

Mr. Shaw was aware that his return to South Africa involved some personal risk on the ground of health; but his desire to inaugurate some important changes in the administration of the Colonial and Native Mission Districts throughout the whole extent of South Africa, overpowered every other consideration. For some time he was led to expect that his views had met with the full sanction of the Committee and Secretaries. In this he was correct, with the exception that what he wished to accomplish at once they deemed desirable to defer for a season. This being the case, he wisely, so far as his own health was concerned, resolved to remain in England, there being no special reason calling for his return to Africa, after forty years' service in the Mission work there.

On the 2nd of May, 1860, Mr. Shaw spoke at the Educational Meeting held in the upper room of the Centenary Hall. The Chairman, Sir W. Atherton, M.P., (afterwards Attorney-General,) the Secretary, the Rev. M. C. Taylor, the Rev. John Scott, Principal, and J. Robinson Kay, Esq., of Bury, who all took part in this Meeting, with Mr. Shaw, no longer survive! A few years make great changes in the appearance of our platforms, as well as in our pulpits and social circles. On this occasion Mr. Shaw advocated "the guiding principles of" the Methodist "Educational establishment; namely, that the education which the Methodist body conducted in various parts of the whole earth, and which is found in the Westminster Institution, should be religious education, based upon the reading and the principles of the Holy Bible." To these views Mr. Shaw

remained faithful to the last: and whatever may be
thought of their practicability in a scheme of National
Education, there can be no doubt that, so far as Methodist
schools are concerned, they are the only principles which
will secure the support of the Methodist people.

CHAPTER XIII

Mr. Shaw as an English Superintendent and President, 1860–6.

On leaving Croydon, where his occasional pulpit services
had been highly appreciated, the congregation and other
friends presented him with several valuable books, hand-
somely bound, as "a small token of their obligation and
esteem." The Conference of 1860 was held in London;
and as Mr. Shaw had decided upon not returning to South
Africa, he received an appointment to the Liverpool South
Circuit, one of the most important in English Methodism.
He was much pleased to find, not only a large and commodious house, but a warm welcome from the officers of
the Circuit. In his colleagues he was equally favoured.
These were the Rev. Messrs. M. C. Osborn, George Bowden,
Luke Tyerman, Frederick Griffiths, and Thomas Brooke.
The Rev. Luke Tyerman dedicated his valuable Life of the
Rev. Samuel Wesley to Mr. Shaw in his presidential year.
Since then he has published a Life of the Rev. John Wesley,
which, whether we agree in all his views or not, must be
regarded as the fullest and almost exhaustive record of
that great man.

Here Mr. Shaw remained three years, to the great
advantage of the Circuit. It was a period of great peace,
and of both religious and financial prosperity. He was
able to complete the arrangements for the erection of St.
John's Chapel, Prince's Park, and thus render practicable
the division of the Circuit, which now appears in the

Stations as Pitt Street and Wesley Circuits. A portion of the letter to Mr. Dugmore, of which there is an extract in pages 284 and 285, refers to this period :—

I am very happy in my work here. We have noble congregations. At our Quarterly Meeting last week I was enabled to report fifty-seven net increase on the quarter, with more than a hundred and seventy persons admitted on trial. We shall probably build a large new chapel in the course of the year, when an additional Minister will be required. Whenever this is accomplished, the Circuit, which is already too unwieldy, must be divided. I was very much gratified with your account of the opening at Sidbury, and your laying the first foundation-stone of a new chapel at the Kawiaga. The Kowie, &c., should become the residence of a Missionary, availing himself of Mr. Cock's pecuniary offer. And then the Salem Circuit might be confined within a convenient circle around. I fear no Supernumerary will volunteer to occupy the places which are open for such a supply. To some of them, if they could understand it, the change from their present position and means would be a great relief. But who is to persuade the unwilling?

You will see that my book is at length published. It was written under very disadvantageous circumstances. If it were to be done again, some portions would be abridged and others enlarged. After I had proceeded to considerable length, I found that my plan would make a much larger volume than I had contemplated, and it was not easy to compress without rendering certain parts less acceptable to the general reader than is desirable. However, I am thankful to say, many newspapers and periodicals, besides the Methodist publications, have noticed the work in terms of favour and approval. I was especially surprised to find a long and favourable notice in the " Morning Post," the aristocratic London paper ; while the " Star," and " Dial," (now united,) also noticed it with approval, with, however, a *caveat* against my views as to the Kaffir wars, &c., being a saving clause for their own very erroneous but often expressed opinions thereon. The work is, I am told, going off pretty well.

This has, so far, proved a terribly severe winter. I have never experienced anything like the intensity of the cold. I have had to suffer much from an attack of tic-doloreux, which I never experienced before ; but the frost seized my face, and left me this remembrancer about a fortnight ago, and I seem likely to be much troubled with it. In other respects I am in my usual health, and I stand my Circuit work very well, as we have no long walks, and the work is not very severe. But the superintending requires constant attention. We have a house as large, and with quite as much accommodation, as the Mission House in Graham's Town, with all the English appliances to boot.

The "Story of My Mission in South Africa,"—one vol., foolscap 8vo., pp. 576,—was published September, 1860, portions of which, bearing upon Mr. Shaw's personal history, have been incorporated in this volume.   He had before this, on the 2nd of February, 1857, in the "Daily News," found occasion to point out the capabilities of the Eastern Province of the Cape Colony, as a field for colonization, and as capable of self-defence ; and, at the same time, to vindicate the character of the Colonists from the aspersions of a writer who signed himself "Looker-On." Reviews of the "Story of My Mission" appeared in the leading periodicals ; that in the "London Quarterly" is brief and to the point : "Here we have a book which is what it professes to be,—the story of a life spent for the most part in the Mission work of the Church. It is not a book of geographical discovery, or of science, or of ethnology, or philology, or any other ology, but simply a narration of the origin and progress of a Christian settlement in South Eastern Africa, which led to the beginning of a Mission to the Kaffir tribes, and the establishment of a complete chain of Mission stations from Algoa Bay to beyond Port Natal. We have no quarrel

with scientific or learned Missionaries ; but we confess that
our modern 'supplements to the Acts of the Apostles'
please us most when they most resemble the primitive
Missionary register, and show us simply how 'the word of
God grew and multiplied.' The author avoids the common
fault of similar narratives, that of giving undue prominence
to details of hardships, perils, and romantic adventures,
which in Africa and elsewhere are the exceptional, not the
normal, conditions of Missionary life. Experienced Missionaries regard these things as matters of course, which
must occasionally variegate the otherwise tame monotony
of uncivilized life, and against which all prudent provision
must be made by the exercise of ordinary forethought, but
which scarcely deserve even a passing notice. The high
position which Mr. Shaw earned for himself in the Cape
Colony, and the beneficial influence which he exercised for
nearly forty years on the Eastern frontier over the Kaffir
tribes adjoining, give peculiar weight to his testimony,
and render his work a most valuable contribution to our
Missionary literature. If the reader wishes to know what
Missionary work really is, and with what wisdom it ought
to be carried on, he cannot do better than study the 'Story
of my Mission,' which presents us the history of a Christian
Missionary, in zeal and in labours second to none, and yet
abounding in all wisdom and prudence, thus manifesting
a rare combination of those qualities so desirable to be
possessed, and yet so rarely united in the same character."

Mr. Shaw had now passed beyond his threescore years,
and, in common with all who have attained to that period
of life, was called upon to lament, year by year, the loss
of friends somewhat older, to whom he had been accus-

tomed to look with reverential love. Our friends thus going before a little in advance of us, admonish us that the day is far spent, and the night is at hand, when no man can work. Already, since his arrival in England, he had, in common with all who loved Methodism, as well as on grounds of personal friendship, been called to lament the death of that great and good man, the Rev. Dr. Bunting, who entered into rest on the 16th of June, 1858. To this venerable man Mr. Shaw refers in his " Story of my Mission," quoted on page 15 of this work. It is much to be regretted that only the first volume of the life of this distinguished statesman-like Divine has yet been published. The claims of the Connexion upon T. P. Bunting, Esq., to complete this intensely interesting Biography, ought not to be disregarded. Three years afterwards occurred the not unexpected death of Thomas Farmer, Esq., of Gunnersbury House, Acton, Middlesex, on the 11th of May, 1861, in the seventy-first year of his age. Of his well-known liberality and public character it is needless to speak. None who knew him personally can have failed to remember the loving urbanity of his manner, and the sound unsophisticated masculine sense by which he was distinguished. He had been for some months patiently waiting until his change came. As one of the Treasurers of the Wesleyan Missionary Society, and especially as a member of the Committee, his death was a severe loss.

By the Conference of 1863 Mr. Shaw was appointed to the Bristol (Clifton) Circuit, and had to discharge the duties of Chairman of the District. In his second year he had for his colleague the Rev. William Morley Punshon, who

·on all occasions manifested a warm attachment to his
Superintendent, which was fully reciprocated. The brief
period of three years in which a Methodist Minister can
·occupy one Circuit is unfavourable to the formation of
those lasting friendships which " grow with our growth,
and strengthen with our strength," but which do not decay,
but rather increase with our diminishing strength in our
later years. However, as in Liverpool, so also in Bristol,
Mr. Shaw's loving character secured him many friends :
among others Mr. T. F. C. May and family deserve special
mention. The friendship between the families has survived
the death of Mr. Shaw, and is one of the consolations of
his widow and his children. In this Circuit Mr. Shaw was
kindly received from the first by the officials and our people
generally. Victoria Chapel was only just erected, but the
·congregation improved so much, especially during the
second year of his residence, when the Rev. William Morley
Punshon was one of the regular supplies, that ground for
·another chapel at Redlands was secured, and a chapel has
·since been built.

As the Jubilee Year of the Wesleyan Missionary Society
as at present constituted drew near, (reckoning from the
famous Missionary Meeting held at Leeds, October 6th,
1813,) the desire was generally expressed, that the joyful
·occasion should be signalized by special services, and by
special consecration of property, in support of the cause of
Missions, after the good and noble example furnished by
the proceedings of the Centenary Year, 1839. At the
Sheffield Conference, the Rev. Dr. Osborn, one of the
Secretaries of the Wesleyan Missionary Society, was chosen
President; and during the whole of his Presidential year

was "in labours more abundant," in reference to this and all Connexional undertakings, but especially in aiding, by his personal influence and public deliverances, the Jubilee Fund. Leeds, which had witnessed the first Wesleyan Missionary Meeting, on October 6th, 1813, was properly selected for the commencement of the Jubilee services. It must be remembered, that while the first Missionary Meeting was held so late as 1813, Methodist Missions to America and the West Indies had been carried on since the year 1769. To quote the words of the Jubilee Report, " The Methodist Missions do not owe their origin to the Missionary Society; but, on the other hand, the Missionary Society owes its origin to the Missions." Two Ministers alone of those who had been present at the Meeting of 1813 survived, the Rev. W. Naylor, and the Rev. Thomas Jackson, and took a distinguished part in the services. The result was that £179,973. 3s. 9d. was raised for the Jubilee Fund. In these Meetings Mr. Shaw took part, entering fully into their object, and greatly rejoicing in their marked success.

During the autumn and spring of the Jubilee year, 1863–4, under the Presidency of the Rev. Dr. Osborn, the Meetings of the various Circuits in aid of the Jubilee Fund were continued with great spirit and efficiency. One of the oldest and most faithful servants of the Methodist Church was permitted to witness the celebration of the Jubilee festival, but did not live to the end of the Jubilee presidential year. On the 1st of March, 1864, the venerable and Rev. John Mason died, in the eighty-third year of his age, and the fifty-third of his ministry. Very unexpectedly, without any suffering, he ceased to live. To him the

Wesleyan Conference is deeply indebted for his sagacious and economical management of the Book Concern, to which he devoted his great business talents, with a patient and unremitting, but quiet energy peculiar to himself. With Mr. Shaw he had been on terms of intimate friendship, and his loss was severely felt, especially as, notwithstanding his great age, it was quite unexpected. On Monday, February 29th, he attended as usual to his official duties in City Road, but returned home somewhat indisposed. No danger was apprehended until the evening of Tuesday, when a difficulty of breathing ensued, and he almost immediately expired. Within twelve months another of the leading men of Methodism was suddenly removed. The Rev. W. L. Thornton, A.M., who had been appointed to the Presidency by the Bradford Conference in July, 1864, died suddenly on the 5th of March, 1865, in the fifty-fourth year of his age. His loss was deeply lamented, especially by his many personal friends, among whom Mr. Shaw had no ordinary place. He had been for some years one of the Editors of the Magazine, and had been the representative to the American Conference in 1863. According to rule, the duties of the Presidency for the remainder of the presidential year devolved upon the Ex-President, Dr. Osborn.

It may not be unnecessary here to explain in general terms the constitution of the " Conference of the People called Methodists,"—the Annual Synod of the Wesleyan Methodists,—as it is possible this book may be read by some who, not being connected with the Methodist Church, have but very indistinct notions of its ecclesiastical economy. Methodism originated in the preaching of John

Wesley and others in the eighteenth century. By him an annual meeting of the Ministers labouring in connexion with him was formed, and called a Conference. The Preachers, at the first Conference after Mr. Wesley's death, chose one of their number as President for the year; and this practice has continued to this day. While all Ministers who have been received into full connexion (those who have travelled in the Ministry four years) are members of the Conference, the strictly legal Conference (which by law must consist of a definite number of persons) is confined to one hundred Preachers, who form what is called the Legal Hundred, but who possess no special privileges beyond others of their brethren, except this, that from among this Legal Hundred the President and Secretary of the Conference must be selected. While the Conference is strictly confined to Ministers, all the financial business and economical arrangements of the Connexion are conducted by a series of Committees composed of Ministers and lay gentlemen, who meet previously to the Conference in the town in which the Conference is appointed to meet. One of these Committees, that for stationing the Ministers for the succeeding year, is composed wholly of Ministers. The proceedings of these Committees, composed as they are of a selection of the leading laymen and Preachers, excite as much interest as those of the Conference itself. For administrative purposes during the year, the whole of England, and of every country in which a Methodist Ministry is found, is divided into sections called Districts, the members of each District meeting twice in the year under a Chairman chosen at the Conference. These are Conferences in miniature, and help to prepare the business which has to be brought before the Annual Conference.

The following Conference of 1865 assembled in Birmingham, and, on the 27th of July, Mr. Shaw was chosen President; the votes being—for Mr. Shaw, 206; for Mr. Arthur, 58; and for Mr. Bedford, 19. It may be desirable to remark, that it is usual, in electing the President, to intimate at the same time the President of the year following, by giving a divided nomination : hence, a division of votes implies no want of unanimity. Those who vote for the nomination usually do so because the number sufficient for the in-coming President is considered as secured.

Great interest was excited immediately after the votes were declared, by the address of Dr. Osborn (the provisional President since Mr. Thornton's death) to the in-coming President, on delivering to him the insignia of his office,—Mr. Wesley's travelling Bible, used by him in preaching, and the Conference seal. He referred " to more than thirty years ago," (1833,) remarking, " On that day you stood at the head of a long list of men who were presented to the Conference, some to be recognised as having been already so long honourably engaged in Missionary and Ministerial service, and some to be then admitted into full connexion. In that long list you were the first, and I was nearly the last." In reply, Mr. Shaw spoke most feelingly of the sudden death of his predecessor in office, the estimable W. L. Thornton; paid also a graceful compliment to the character and labours of the Rev. Dr. Osborn, all the more pertinent because literally true ; and, in conclusion, referred to the Birmingham Conference of 1836, in which he was elected into " the Legal Hundred,"—the body corporate referred to in the Poll Deed.   On that occasion, meeting the late Mr. Marriott, of London, at a side-door of the chapel, that gentleman pleasantly remarked to him, " We may live to see you President of the Conference yet."   The office of President is properly regarded by the Ministers and people of the Methodist Connexion as one of great honour and importance.   It is on the part of the Connexion a matter of no little satisfaction to have the chair of the Annual Synod filled by a Preacher competent to preside, and also to represent them on public occasions.   To the Minister himself it is a proof of their high estimation of his ability, and of the respect felt for his character by brethren who know him well.

The election of a returned Missionary to the Presidency of the Conference is an unusual event.   It is true that the Rev. James Dixon, who had spent a year in Gibraltar, and was therefore by courtesy foolishly identified with the Mission work, had been elected to that office in 1841; and that the Rev. Robert Young, who had been a Missionary in Jamaica and Nova Scotia, had filled the chair in 1856, immediately after his return from the work of the Australian deputation; but these were exceptional cases, justified and accounted for by the long familiarity of these brethren with the working of English Methodism, their Missionary career forming but a short episode in the history of their lives.   But Mr. Shaw had spent thirty-six years in Africa, and, except an appointment at Leeds, 1833-6, and the experience of Circuit work in Liverpool and Bristol from 1860 to 1865, had had few opportunities of making himself at home in the home work.   The Ministers, however, knew that they ran no risk of failure from inexperience or incompetency when they placed Mr. Shaw in the chair. He had always paid the most earnest attention to all Connexional questions; and since his return from Africa he had by his speeches in the various Committees evidenced his fitness for the discharge of the duties of any position in Methodism. He was at the same time, from his sober, sedate, yet genial bearing, highly respected and universally beloved by his brethren. The Birmingham Conference was a very interesting and happy one. The new President steadily and methodically attended to the business of each day, and managed to finish the meeting a day sooner than usual. An additional interest was given to this Conference by the visit of Bishop Janes from the United States. What is called the Conference Sermon was delivered in Cherry Street chapel on Sunday evening, the 30th of July. The text was John xiv. 16, 17; and the discourse is a fair sample of Mr. Shaw's sober, earnest, and devout ministrations from the pulpit.

The Presidential year calls out the physical and mental powers of the occupant of the chair. What Bacon remarks of the heavenly bodies, the stars and planets, we may apply to the Methodist Presidents, "They have great dignity, but no rest." No one half a century ago ever anticipated that the time would come when the President would be expected to attend every important public meeting, and to preach on the occasion of the opening of most of the new chapels within his presidential year, in addition to the ordinary duties of his office. This evil, though it did not commence with the Presidency of Dr. Osborn in 1863–4, was sanctioned by his example; for which there was some excuse in the Jubilee Year. Under his successors it has grown into a sort of prescriptive claim, which the last two Presidents, the Rev. Luke H. Wiseman and the Rev. G. T. Perks, seem to have tacitly admitted. The time is come for some modification of this extra work, which no ordinary constitution can bear without serious permanent injury. Mr. Shaw had his fair share of this work during his year of office, which to a man of his sober, steady habits must have been a great trial, though I never heard him complain. According to general usage, not universally followed, he removed to a London Circuit, Chelsea,—London being deemed a more central and convenient locality for the residence of the President than Bristol. After a pleasant trip to the Lakes, he took possession of his new home, where he had soon the pleasure of receiving his son-in-law and daughter, the Rev. Mr. and Mrs. Impey, on their temporary visit to England from South Africa. The satisfaction of having such a son-in-law was increased by the fact that Mr. Impey had been appointed his successor as Chairman and General Superintendent of the Graham's Town District, a position which no man was more competent to fill with credit to himself and with great benefit to the work itself. In October Mr. Shaw visited Leeds, and spoke at the Anniversary of the Missionary Society, and at the Breakfast Meeting in the Town Hall; and in December addressed the students at Westminster Normal College. Very soon he had to lament the loss of another old friend and colleague (in Leeds, 1831-3), the Rev. Robert Young, an Ex-President, who had served the Society in the West Indies and North America, and in the Deputation sent in 1852-3 to the Australian Colonies. He died, after five years of retirement as a Supernumerary, at Truro, 16th of November, 1865, aged seventy. His vigorous body had been broken down prematurely by the cruel and murderous habit of *memoriter* preaching and speaking. But for this, humanly speaking, he might have laboured in the Ministry many years longer. All his sermons and speeches had an exquisite finish and point, and were "full of Christ." In the midst of the weakness of his last years he would often say, "God is very good to me. I have no unhappy moments. I am testing the truths which I used to preach, and I do not retract one of them. I am constantly proving their value. They stand by me now." And so he died full of peace and joy.

In the winter of 1865-6 a frightful murrain among cattle created great alarm, especially in the agricultural districts, and was followed by a rise in the price of animal food, which was no small inconvenience to the population generally. Although the Archbishop of Canterbury, Dr. Longley, a Liberal in politics, requested the Government, represented by Earl Russell, then Premier, to appoint a day for national intercession, the request was declined. It was therefore thought desirable for the Wesleyans and other religious bodies to testify their conviction that such calamitous visitations, though mediately traceable to natural causes, have a higher origin in the will of God, and are part and parcel of the instrumentalities by which He exercises moral government over the nations. The President accordingly, on the 17th of January, 1866, addressed a letter "to the Superintendents of the Wesleyan Methodist Circuits in the United Kingdom," requesting them to hold meetings for special prayer and supplication on Friday, the 9th of March; such a procedure being in accordance

with the Christian belief in the overruling providence of
God. These protests against the shallow philosophy which
teaches that "all things come alike to all," (Eccles. ix. 2,)
are very seemly and profitable when called forth by national
calamities. Admitting the existence of moral government
over nations as such, its exercise must be confined to
temporal blessings or calamities, as nations in their
corporate capacity have no existence except in this world.
Except therefore on the supposition that " the Lord hath
forsaken the earth," (Ezekiel viii. 12,) national confession
of sin and humiliation before God are rational acts,
defensible on purely theistical as well as on Scriptural
grounds. We may hope that the religious sentiment has
made some progress among our leading politicians, as on a
recent occasion, when the Prince of Wales was raised from
the bed of sickness and restored to health, the hand of
God was acknowledged, and national supplication addressed
to the throne of grace, followed by devout thanksgivings.

The Missionary Anniversaries of May, 1866, were as
usual preceded by sermons from Ministers from the
country, and by one from the President in Centenary Hall,
Thursday, April 26th. This sermon was "in all respects
worthy to be classed with the many admirable sermons
delivered by his predecessors in the same place for the past
twenty-five years." He also spoke at the China Breakfast
Meeting on Saturday, April 28th, and at the Anniversary
of the Wesleyan Missionary Society in Exeter Hall, April
30th, on which occasion the late John Fernley, Esq., of
Southport, occupied the chair; and on the 9th of May
he again spoke at the Education Meeting in Centenary Hall.
The claims on public men for deliverance on all subjects

remind one of the Egyptian tyranny which compelled the Israelites to make bricks without straw! To be always giving out of the mental treasury, without the leisure and opportunity of taking in a fresh supply, is the trial test to which public men are too often exposed. Mr. Shaw could stand this test as well as most men. If he never rose to an equality with our first-rate orators, he never sank into mere mediocrity, for he had always something to say, and said it well. In his own line of plain, palpable, understandable preaching he was the equal of any of his contemporaries.

Meanwhile Mr. Shaw's old friends in Africa were not behindhand in their expressions of sympathy and attachment to their "father and friend." They were delighted at his being called to occupy the chair of the Conference; and at a Meeting held in Shaw College, Graham's Town, February 29th, 1866, the Hon. Robert Godlonton, M.P., in the chair, an address was presented to the Rev. W. Impey and Mrs. Impey on the occasion of their departure on a temporary visit to England. An Address, beautifully written, emblazoned, and signed by one thousand five hundred friends, bound up in an elegant volume, was committed to the charge of Mr. Impey, to present to the President in England. The presentation took place on the 6th of June, 1866; and was of a very interesting character.

At the request of the Rev. W. Impey, who wrote in the name of several South African gentlemen, the President of the Conference appointed Wednesday noon as the time when he could meet a deputation. The gathering was small and private. The Rev. Elijah Hoole, D.D., and the Rev. William B. Boyce, General Secretaries of the Wesleyan Missionary Society; the Rev. James D. Brocklehurst,

Secretary of the General Jubilee Committee; the Rev. William Butters; the Rev. J. Woodcock (President's Assistant); the Rev. William Impey, Chairman and General Superintendent of the Graham's Town District; and Messrs. G. M. Keill (Bayswater); J. Cawood (Stoke Newington); John Holmes and Robert White, South African merchants; and W. Pearce, of Poplar, were present; and Mesdames Shaw, Impey, Hoole, Wood, and Keill. Besides these, the Hon. J. C. Hoole, M.L.C., and Mr. J. E. Wood, M.L.A., (Ex-Mayor of Graham's Town,) attended as the representatives of the Wesleyan laity in Southern Africa.

After prayer the Rev. W. Impey rose, and, in a few well chosen words, endeavoured to express the sentiments and feelings of those who were represented at that Meeting. His only regret was that the documents which he had to present that day were so drawn up that the members of other Churches and the community in general were unable to add their willing testimony to the sentiments embodied in the Addresses. Had this been practicable, the signatures would have swollen into volumes. Turning to Mr. Shaw he said, "Sir, these names will remind you of many scenes of joy and sorrow. They attest a warm and affectionate remembrance of your character and work. We have had (in South Eastern Africa) many teachers, but not many fathers. And among the latter your name especially will be held in esteem, confidence, and love, as long as Wesleyan Methodism in South Africa or the Continent still endures. I have now to present to you this volume, bearing addresses and signatures from Ministers, office-bearers, and members in the Graham's Town and Port Natal Districts. In all, one thousand four hundred and sixty-six names are appended. They represent every rank in society, and are the fruit of your long and devoted labours."

This handsome folio book, richly bound in morocco, lined with crimson silk, and containing parchment leaves, admirably engrossed, was handed over to the President, who could not but regard it as an inestimable treasure, and to whose descendants it must be an heirloom above all price. Its "Index of Contents" is a study alike in relation to geographical extent, the pentecostal triumphs of Christianity in Southern Africa, the elevating power of true religion—

socially as well as morally, the glowing affection of Missionary Churches for their pastors, and the abidingness of the results of evangelical efforts. Break the total of one thousand four hundred and sixty-six into its component parts, and here, uniting in this loving testimonial, are twenty Ministers in Graham's Town District, ten in Queen's Town District, three hundred and one members and office-bearers in Commemoration Chapel, Graham's Town—to which reference will also be made in another form, two hundred and seventy-eight from Fort Beaufort, one hundred and seventy-four from King William's Town, one hundred from Thaba 'Nchu; and equally gratifying indications of deep and wide-spread affection from places whose names we are afraid to write, lest we should offend the literary accuracy of eager readers of these columns in Uitenhage, Bloemfontein, Tshungwana, Umpukani, and Potchefstrom.

TO THE REV. WILLIAM SHAW,
PRESIDENT OF THE WESLEYAN METHODIST CONFERENCE.

We, the undersigned, office-bearers and members of the Wesleyan Methodist Society, or who are otherwise connected with the Wesleyan Methodist Church in South Eastern Africa, desire to convey to you, and request you to accept, our hearty congratulations on your election to the high and responsible office of the President of the Conference.

We cannot but regard your elevation to this important position as a signal testimony to the value of Missionary enterprise in general, and as presenting a powerful stimulus to others to devote themselves to the sacred and noble work of evangelizing the heathen in foreign and distant countries. We are grateful to the Lord of the harvest that you were appointed to labour in this portion of His vineyard, and that we were permitted for so many years to witness your zealous efforts, to mark your going out and your coming in, and to partake in no small degree of the advantages derived from your earnest, self-denying labours, as a Preacher of the Gospel of Jesus Christ,—exemplified as that Gospel was by your deportment, both as a member of the community, and as one who had been set apart to the sacred office of the Christian ministry.

Some of us remember with peculiar interest your arrival in this country. The field before you was vast; while the means at your command were, apparently, utterly inadequate to the work to be performed. You yourself were young in years; you were without experience, and there were no landmarks to guide you in the direction of your course. But still, falling back upon first principles, you were, by God's help, eminently successful. The very fact of the momentous character of the career on which you had entered gave gravity to your youth, and solidity to your judgment,—inspiring you with that moral intrepidity by which, under the Divine blessing, you were enabled, amidst difficulties and trials of no ordinary character, to plant a Church in this region whose roots have struck deep among the heathen tribes of South Africa, and whose branches have spread as far as civilized man has found a home in this country. It is to be noted also, that on your arrival here in 1820, you were the only accredited Methodist Preacher in South Eastern Africa; that you stood alone; and that, as regarded by the eye of worldly wisdom, you were about to engage in a wild and extravagant enterprise. It was indeed, humanly speaking, the day of small things; but relying upon Him who has declared that "the race is not to the swift, nor the battle to the strong," we gratefully record that, by the help of God, you were enabled to overcome every difficulty, and to rise superior to every discouragement, affording a sublime exemplification of the Scripture declaration, "It is not by might, nor by power, but by My Spirit, saith the Lord."

In now offering you our affectionate congratulations on your accession to the high and honourable office to which you have been called by the Wesleyan Methodist Church, we cannot hesitate to express our belief (based on our experience of the past) that your thorough knowledge of the polity of Methodism, and your aptitude for administrative duties, coupled with your catholicity of sentiment, your uniform urbanity, and your unimpeachable integrity, will enable you to exercise such an influence as cannot fail, when accompanied with the Divine approval, in furthering and giving permanency to measures whose aim is the glory of God, in the maintenance and spread of pure and undefiled religion throughout the world.

In conclusion, you will permit us to remark that, while we feel grateful to Him "who ruleth all things according to the counsel of

His own will" for the honour conferred upon you, we avail ourselves of the occasion to express our sense of the personal advantages we have derived by your long residence and zealous labours among us. Many have enjoyed your personal friendship, while all have shared in those spiritual blessings which the Gospel, as proclaimed by faithful Ministers of the Methodist Church, is so well calculated to secure. Our united and earnest hope is that God may continue to prosper you in your work, vouchsafe to you the blessing of perfect health, and supply you with that strength of body and of mind which will enable you to discharge your onerous duties with comfort to yourself and advantage to the Church at large.

We have only to add our fervent prayer that the God of all grace may sustain you; that the Holy Spirit may abundantly comfort and enlighten you; and that you may experience in all its fulness the promise of the great Head of the Church,—"Lo! I am with you alway, even to the end of the world."

There was a similar address, also, in the volume, from the Wesleyan Ministers of South Africa. Mr. Shaw made a suitable reply, after which Mr. Wood, Ex-Mayor of Graham's Town, the Hon. J. C. Hoole, M.L.C., and the Revs. Elijah Hoole and W. B. Boyce made a few remarks.

Mr. Wood, Ex-Mayor of Graham's Town, and M.L.A., observed,—"I am, Sir, too feeble in health to deliver a speech or bear much excitement to-day; else I would endeavour to pour out my heart on this occasion. For I count it one of the greatest honours of my life, to take part in recognising the worth of 'my friend and my father's friend,' who watched over my sire when he went out fatherless to a strange land, and continued his pastoral care so long as he remained in the Colony. Methodism owes what it can never even duly recognise to the name of William Shaw. That name is not only a household word in Southern and South Eastern Africa, but it is well known in high places there. It is a fact that by his prudently exercised influence nearly all the seats in the Local Parliament, and nearly all important offices of State there, were occupied by Wesleyan

Methodists. In 1821, Graham's Town was too insignificant to be entered even as a preaching place upon the plan, and now the Wesleyan Church commands, notwithstanding the presence of many other religious agencies, of which we do not now speak particularly, the greatest religious power in that rising place. The addresses do not say one half of what might have been fairly said on this subject. Had they been more generally worded, a vast number would have subscribed them; but they had relation to the Presidency of our friend, and so multitudes had no opportunity of bearing their testimony to the varied worth of Mr. Shaw. I happen to possess a copy of the first plan written by Mr. Shaw, and I think this a fitting opportunity of presenting it to him, that he may see what was and what is now the state of feeling in the scene of his long, faithful; and successful toils."

This precious memento was then handed to the President, who promised to place it among the other papers, observing at the same time, " This is not the original ; it is a copy from that which I wrote, and is written by Brother Ayliff, who truly observed what I had forgotten having appended. He did the work of ' an evangelist ' most faithfully in his day and generation."

The Hon. J. C. Hoole, M.L.C., expressed the sense of difficulty which he had in uttering at all adequately what was in his heart, and in the hearts of thousands whom he represented that day. He wished, however, to observe especially upon the President's pioneering work. " He was not content with successes and confidence acquired among the settlers, but pushed on to 'the regions beyond.' Few here can possibly know the danger of such a work at that time. In 1821 he went forward at the risk of life, and amid many fears and anxieties on the part of his friends, but sustained by a quenchless zeal for souls, and the intrepidity of his never-to-be-forgotten wife. She was perfectly ready to accompany him beyond the border. What Mr. Shaw did there is partially known by the Annual Reports, and the ' Missionary Notices ; ' but his modesty led him to conceal perils which would have given him the place of a hero of the Cross. The Colonists, however, know that his privations, labours, and successes can never be overrated. Were I to say that he was the greatest

Missionary that the world ever saw, I might perhaps be saying too much, but I will say that Africa never saw his like. What temporal honours and advantages he has thrown away for the sake of his great work are too little known in this country; but I will not obtrude upon his sensitiveness in these respects, even by further allusion. But I will say, that if, as must be acknowledged, Methodism be the most numerous party in South Eastern Africa, its position is owing to William Shaw. And if, as is the fact, the great majority of members of the Legislative Assembly of the Eastern Province be Wesleyan Methodists, that too is owing to William Shaw. More than this, he planted a Church, which will be co-existent and co-extensive with the Colony, and has been instrumental, directly and indirectly, of turning more sinners to righteousness in Africa, than any living man. We, of that Colony, are of one mind, that he will fill the high office which he sustains with unsurpassed caution and success."

The Rev. Elijah Hoole, D.D., one of the General Secretaries of the Wesleyan Missionary Society, said:—"I have some thoughts to-day peculiar to myself. It was mine to know and observe you (the President) even before these gentlemen. You were then hardly out of your teens. But such men as Richard Watson, Charles Atmore, and Joseph Butterworth, saw in you, even then, a mature Christian, an able preacher, and one to whom, because of singular judgment, might be entrusted the administration of a new Mission. Nor has that hope been cut off. Every expectation has been fulfilled, and I am sure that amid the honours of this day you are the first to say, 'By the grace of God I am what I am.' There were then no Theological Institutions; but we were taken, one from a Sunday-school, and another from a chair-back of a country cottage, one to Africa, and the other to India. From first to last we owe all to Divine grace. I do most heartily congratulate you upon the presentation of these addresses."

The Rev. W. B. Boyce said:—"I have not known you, Sir, quite as long as Dr. Hoole; but thirty-six years ago I was your young man. Thirty-three years ago I stood beside you, when, in the Court House of Graham's Town, a long address, most numerously signed by the inhabitants, was presented to you, along with a substantial testimonial, by Mr. W. R. Thompson, Chairman of the public meeting. I am reminded to-day also of a fact, which is, I believe, without compare in Methodism either at home or abroad. As we were standing together near the burial ground, and looking at the town, you observed, 'I have one comfort in looking at that place, and it is that there is not a house in it in which I have not prayed.' I was witness to your unexampled patience and forbearance; mayhap, I taxed tho latter too largely myself! You had, moreover, a marvellous gift of caution and prudence. Many are too prudent to do anything; but yours was the blending of working and wisdom. I never knew you do an injudicious thing, a thing on which you could now reflect with regret. And I rejoice that the friendship begun a quarter of an hour after I arrived at Graham's Town has continued, and it will last, I am assured, to our lives' end."

Soon after this, Mr. Shaw, in common with all the well-wishers of Methodism, had to lament the death of John Vanner, Esq., an estimable man, and an old and tried friend of our Missions, who in early life had been a companion of the late Rev. John Ayliff, the African Missionary, and one of Mr. Shaw's colleagues; he died June 10th, 1866, aged sixty-six years.

One of the duties of the English President is to attend the Irish Conference. This commenced on the 20th of June, at Dublin. Mr. Shaw was accompanied by his son-in-law, the Rev. William Impey. Every one who has shared in the hospitalities of our Irish friends can imagine the hearty greeting with which the President and deputation were received, and the overpowering kindness which followed them to the end of their stay in Dublin. The Presidential year was now drawing to a close. The Conference was held at Leeds, and on Thursday, the 26th of

July, Mr. Shaw delivered the insignia of office to a worthy
successor, the Rev. William Arthur, thankful that he had
been spared to discharge the duties of his office with
satisfaction to his brethren and to the Connexion generally.
The remarks which appeared in the " Watchman " of the
2nd of August, to the effect that " nothing could have
been more courteous, dignified, or Christian, than the
manner in which he has throughout discharged his duties,"
may be regarded as expressing the general opinion of the
character of his official year. One more duty as Ex-President
remained to be performed. On Thursday, the 2nd of
August, he delivered the Charge at the Ordination of the
young Ministers in Oxford Place Chapel, which is a fair
specimen of his good sense and fidelity, profitable to be
read by all of us, whether Ministers or members of the
Christian Church.

CHAPTER XIV.

Circuit Work in Chelsea and York, until his Retirement at the Hull Conference, 1866–9.

IMMEDIATELY after the Conference, (1866,) Mr. Shaw, released from his responsible official duties, enjoyed with his family a brief sojourn at Tunbridge Wells, and then resumed the charge of the Circuit work in Chelsea. The mental and physical strain of the Presidential year was not, however, fully removed by the temporary change of air and locality, and for several weeks he was laid up, perfectly unfitted for the discharge of his Ministerial duties. On his recovery, he had to lament the loss of a dear friend in the death of the Rev. William M. Bunting, son of the late Rev. Dr. Bunting, which took place on the 13th of November, 1866, in his sixty-first year. This singularly excellent man was remarkable not only for his extraordinary ability, but for his sympathy with his brethren, which endeared him to the great body of the Wesleyan Preachers. His unsectarian spirit found a congenial sphere in connexion with " the Evangelical Alliance," of which he was one of the earliest friends. " In social life he was conspicuous for his wide sympathies and tender affections, and he exercised an influence which it was almost impossible to escape from or forget." Those who had enjoyed the pleasure of his personal intercourse can never forget him.

A letter was addressed by Mr. Shaw to the Rev. H. H. Dugmore, (Cape of Good Hope,) dated Chelsea, December 18th, 1866, acknowledging the receipt of a Sermon preached by him at Queen's Town, July 15th, 1866, and published in defence of the great spiritual revival, in 1865, in South Africa. This gracious work was in connexion with the labours of that worthy, but eccentric, American Methodist Minister, the Rev. William Taylor; full particulars of which may be found in the "Missionary Notices," and in Mr. Taylor's "Christian Adventures in South Africa," 12mo., 1867. Mr. Dugmore's Sermon makes a pamphlet of sixteen pages 8vo., and is a manly and Scriptural defence of the genuineness and reality of those seasons of religious earnestness which are commonly called "revivals," and especially of the great awakening in the Colony of the Cape and in Kaffirland, which followed the Ministry of the above-mentioned American Revivalist. Some of the phenomena on such occasions—as, for instance, the intense feeling and disregard of ordinary proprieties displayed by persons under deep conviction for sin, or rejoicing in the sense of pardon— prove stumbling-blocks not only to them that are without, but to many sincere Christians. But when results manifest the presence of "the Holy Ghost, the Lord and Giver of Life," some overstepping of the ordinary conventionalities of life and speech may be condoned. Sensible men of the world will not hastily ridicule what they have not felt and cannot understand, when they see numbers "pricked in their hearts," and earnestly seeking for pardon and peace, through our Lord Jesus Christ. Mr. Shaw's letter will interest his surviving friends, especially as a fair specimen of the liberal and broad views which he held respecting religious revivals, although in his mental constitution, habits, and prepossessions thoroughly conservative, and anxious at all times to observe decency and order in public worship.

I received with great gratification your kind letter, which should have had an earlier acknowledgment, but immediately on my return in September from the Conference I was seized with an affliction that prostrated me for several weeks, so that I was entirely laid aside from all public duty. You may imagine how greatly this trial was increased, by my affliction occurring during the last few weeks of the stay of Mr. and Mrs. Impey. Owing to my incessant public duties I had been enabled to enjoy only amidst great interruptions my intercourse with them. I had promised myself after the Conference better opportunities for enjoying their Society, when the affliction, and afterwards my unavoidable going to Tunbridge Wells for a fortnight by the doctor's orders to recruit my lost strength, prevented my realizing many pleasant anticipations. However, I must not complain. God has been very gracious to me in this matter of health, and I have abundant reasons to praise Him that I am now so far restored as to be able to resume my Circuit duties.

You may well congratulate me on the completion of the year of my Presidency, which had expired before your letter came to hand. In that instance it is a happier thing to put off the armour than to gird it on. The responsibility and the incessant occupation connected with the office in the present extended state of the Body are very great indeed. All manner of affairs, temporal and spiritual, affecting the welfare of our vast Connexion, are brought under the notice of the President through the year, and require his attention and decisive action. Through Divine mercy my health during the whole year was excellent; and although I had not the advantage of many of my predecessors of long familiarity with the multifarious details of English Methodism, yet I was preserved from falling into any serious error in my decisions, and received the most gratifying assurances at the Conference of the satisfaction of the brethren with my official bearing and conduct.

This is the highest reward that a retiring President can receive on earth, and was therefore very satisfactory to my mind. I am extremely obliged to you for sending a copy of your published Sermon for me; but as you had addressed it to the President, or had told them at the Mission House that it was for the President, they naturally handed it over to the President,—I being now only the Ex-President,—thus the copy which was designed for me got into Mr. Arthur's hands. I am not at all sorry that this mistake occurred, as he wanted information about your great revival, and your discourse would add to his stock of knowledge on this deeply interesting subject. I should have told him of the mistake, so as to have secured this copy that you meant for me, but that I was supplied from another source, and I have therefore said nothing to him about it.

I consider your sermon a thorough defence so far as it was requisite to defend this great work of God from the objections of cavillers, whether they be sinners or saints. As a general rule, I believe it is better to avoid controversy while a revival is in progress; but there are circumstances sometimes connected with such seasons of refreshing which require to be publicly noticed (either from the pulpit or the press). Ministers on the spot, who know the local feelings that have been excited, and their influence on the good work, are the best judges when to speak, and when to refrain from speaking thereon. As you evidently preached and afterwards printed this discourse under a conviction of duty, I have no doubt it was a needful service; and being needed, I know not how it could have been better done than you have done it in this logical, scriptural, and decisive discourse. I trust that many who read it will learn to honour the Lord the Spirit in the glorious work which you have been privileged to see in South Eastern Africa.

My friend the President will be glad to see your defence of your having availed yourselves of Mr. Taylor's labours. He and I and some others rather differ on this point from some eminent and influential men among us, who from past recollections have been led to indulge what I regard as an unreasonable fear of employing any kind of foreign agency, or unusual agency, in the promotion of revivals. There is no doubt Mr. Caughey is a good and earnest man, and a successful preacher. He was the instrument of great good more than twenty years ago, promoting extensive revivals in various parts of this kingdom. But he had less wisdom and discretion than zeal; hence he began to meddle with matters that did not belong to him as a stranger to interfere with. The Ministers met this by objecting to his having constant access to our people and congregations, while he was not amenable like all the other Ministers to our Districts and Conference, and therefore could not be called upon to explain such parts of his proceedings as were calculated to be mischievous among our people. The result of all this was shyness, jealousy, and from a sense of duty many Superintendents closed the pulpits against him. This, as was to be expected, roused the spirit of the party, and was the great cause of the terrible division which, within three or four years, separated so many of our people from us, that we lost in two years more than we had gained in *ten* years' steady labour. The congregations in many places, as the result of the accompanying strife, were scattered, and the work in those places had to be commenced *de novo*, under the pressure of very serious difficulties. When all this is fairly considered, we need not wonder that many of our ablest and most experienced Ministers are very jealous about the employment of strangers from America or elsewhere, lest with the good there should come in such a measure of evil as would produce an aggregate amount of spiritual loss, which would leave no trace of the good that was done, but rather involve us in a loss of spiritual power and influence to such an extent that the labour of years might be in this manner destroyed.

I cannot, however, in all this see a solid reason for declining to use any agency which there is reason to believe is of God, because of the possible evil which may arise therefrom in consequence of human infirmity. If we were to adopt that as a general principle, we could not employ any man in doing the work of God: for who is there that is not liable to fall into temptation, to do evil, and consequently injure the very work which for a time God was pleased to bless with great success? It seems to me that we ought to avail ourselves of every available help,—when we are satisfied that the character of the man, and his mode of proceeding, will bear the application of the Scriptural tests. Hence, I am very glad that my brethren in South Africa accepted the proffered aid of the flying visits of Mr. Taylor. You had long been *ploughing* and *sowing;* you just needed some of those thunder-claps, followed by teeming rains, with which you are so familiar in the natural world in your climate, to occur in your religious Societies. As the farmers in your land hail the result of the one in the green fields and rapidly growing crops, so I am not surprised to find that after your showers of blessing you all write in terms of grateful joy and thanksgiving. And my belief is that the very report of the great things which God has done for you will prove an abundant blessing to the Home Connexion, by the quickening influence the very recital of such stirring events will have upon our people. Hence, whatever any among our able and experienced men may think or fear, I have not met with one who has permitted himself to say a word against it. The marks of a great work of God are so evident, that all are constrained to praise His holy Name who only doeth wondrous things. May you go on and prosper yet more and more.

About the time this arrives, you will probably have seen or heard from Mr. Impey, who can tell you all our affairs. I hope his visit will prove an advantage to the Mission in all its departments and Districts. There has been a revival of interest in South African Missions; and I trust our Committee will (as far as its means will allow) take advantage of the flowing tide to float onwards the various plans which they have approved, with the view of promoting its prosperity. It must be pleasant to you to have all your family near you. I rejoice greatly in your joy on their behalf. Pray give my kindest regards to dear Mrs. Dugmore, and remember me affectionately to my old friend, Mr. Shepstone, whose health I trust continues equal to his extensive duties. Kind remembrances to any of the brethren or people who inquire after me.

Early in 1867, the sudden death at Salem, in South Africa, of W. H. Matthews, Esq., J.P., one of the original settlers of 1819–20, called forth from Mr. Shaw a respectful reference in a letter which appeared in the " Watchman " in April of that year. Mr. Matthews, at a very early period in the history of the settlement, was induced by Mr. Shaw to commence an academy at Salem. He had the honour of educating some of the most respectable and influential of the men who now, either as men of business or officials, are a credit to South Africa. On the morning of the 22nd of January, Mr. Matthews arose at his usual early hour, and was heard moving about the room. On being called to breakfast, he was found dead in his chair, with an open Bible before him. His age was seventy-four.

Mr. Shaw's early identification with a British colony, and his long residence in it, gave him naturally a strong bias in favour of our Colonial possessions in any part of the world. With the narrow, one-sided prejudices of those who object to our Colonies on the ground of the expense attending their first settlement and subsequent guardianship, he had no sympathy. In the sixteenth and seventeenth centuries this class of economists grudged the cost of the voyages and expeditions of our Drakes and Raleighs, and the subsequent outlay and expenditure of capital in the settlement of Virginia and New England. They said, " To what purpose is this waste ?" and the men of that generation " approved their sayings." But in this, as in spirituals, " Wisdom is justified of her children." The return for this " waste " is the fee simple of North America, of South Africa, and of Australasia, to say nothing of India. More than fifty millions of the European race, speaking the English language, and for the most part adherents of the Protestant religion, are the results of

colonization. What would England be in this nineteenth
century without America, Australasia, and India? Morally,
and intellectually, and politically, the spread of the English race teems with blessings for the whole human
family. It is the hope of the world. Without an appreciation of the value of the Colonies, Mr. Shaw readily
embraced, on the 18th of May, 1867, the opportunity of
testifying his sympathy with our Australasian brethren on
the occasion of the departure of the new Mission ship,
"John Wesley," built to replace one of the same name
which had been lost on a reef in the South Seas. A large
party were assembled on board the vessel moored near to
Gravesend. Among them were the Rev. Dr. Osborn, the
Rev. W. B. Boyce, and the Rev. G. T. Perks, Secretaries
of the Wesleyan Missionary Society, the Rev. John Scott,
one of the Treasurers, the Rev. Dr. Waddy, Benjamin
Frankland, and William Shaw, the Ex-President. The
Rev. James Calvert, William Butters, and John Eggleston,
represented the Australian Colonies; and Messrs. J. J.
Lidgett, Isaac Holden, M.P., Duncan Archer, G. E.
Meakin, Webb, and others, the laity of Methodism. The
Meeting was both pleasant and profitable. Speeches were
delivered by Mr. Shaw and others. Of that party, four
from among the number are now no more. The Rev. J.
Caldwell, a most excellent and zealous young Missionary, a
passenger to Melbourne, sent out to take charge of the
Chinese Mission in Victoria, was, within a brief period, acci-
dentally drowned in China while bathing : the Rev. John
Scott, Mr. J. J. Lidgett, his talented son-in-law, and the
Rev. William Shaw, have since been removed from us. It is
no doubt necessary that even our happiest social reminis-

cences should be of a mingled character : if life be spared to three-score and beyond, our memories must recall much calculated " to damp our earthly joys." All the discipline of life is more or less a weaning from earth, as well as a preparation for heaven; and the older we are, the more we feel, and perhaps the more we need, the weaning process.

Soon after the departure of the Mission ship, Mr. Shaw was on the Missionary Deputation for the Channel Islands, in connexion with which, on the 11th of June, 1867, he delivered a lecture on the Kaffir Missions, in the school-room of Ebenezer Chapel, Guernsey, thus contributing largely to the interest of the Anniversary, which was characterized by the local press as " one of the most remarkable among those which have been celebrated in the island."

In the winter of 1867, and the spring and summer of 1868, a large number of Wesleyan Missionaries and others, the personal friends of Mr. Shaw, were removed by death. Among them we may especially mention the Rev. Samuel Broadbent, January 1st, 1867, in the seventy-third year of his age, who early in life laboured in Ceylon, and was afterwards for a brief period a colleague of Mr. Shaw in South Africa ; the Rev. Dr. Hannah, Theological Tutor in the Didsbury Institution, 29th of December, 1867, aged seventy-five ; the Rev. John Scott, Principal of the Normal College, Westminster, on the 10th of January, 1868, aged seventy-six ; the Rev. R. Spence Hardy, well known in connexion with Singhalese literature and the Mission in Ceylon, the 16th of April, 1868 ; the Rev. Thomas Hall Squance, one of the Missionaries who, in 1813, sailed with Dr. Coke to India, on the 21st of April, 1868, aged seventy-six; and, last of all, the Rev. William Naylor, one of the surviving Ministers who were present at the first Missionary Meeting in Leeds in 1813, died on the 10th of July, 1868, aged eighty-six. I have referred to these and other honoured names, in the course of this narrative, because they are associated in my mind with the memory of Mr. Shaw: they were men with whom he was much brought in contact during his residence in England, men by whom he was highly esteemed, and for whom he entertained a similar regard.

The even tenor of Mr. Shaw's Circuit duties in Chelsea was affected by the vacancy caused by the unexpected removal of the Principal of the Westminster Normal College. It was desirable that some man of high character, possessing the confidence of the Connexion, should at once occupy the vacant position until the Conference. Mr. Shaw was unanimously requested by the Education Committee to undertake this onerous duty. He therefore removed from his residence in Walpole Street, Chelsea, to the College, provision being made for the working of the Circuit, which yet remained under his superintendence. Mr. Shaw had from the first year of his arrival in England taken a deep interest in the educational work of Methodism, and his name is found as a speaker in numerous educational meetings, especially the Annual Anniversary gatherings in Centenary Hall. Mr. Scott always expected Mr. Shaw's support on such occasions, and was never disappointed. I used to laugh at my old friend's unremitting diligence in his attendance on these and other public meetings. Like another old friend, Dr. Osborn, (happily yet spared to us,) it appeared to me as if it were a pleasure to him to follow

the dullest and most tedious speaker, and even a succession
of such ! Such men are rare : and those who speak much in
public should feel thankful that there are men in the world
by whom the exercise of the grace of patience is not only felt
to be a duty, but a delight. I cannot say that I am one
of that valuable class. Had Mr. Shaw been forty-five
instead of sixty-eight, he would have made an admirable
successor to the office which Mr. Scott had so ably filled.
He wisely refused to listen to any such suggestion ; and
no man rejoiced more than himself when our common friend,
the Rev. Dr. Rigg, was appointed by the Conference of 1868
to that position. Dr. Rigg was the right man in the right place
—a metaphysician and theologian, yet possessing business
tact and sound common sense ; rigidly orthodox, and yet
broad in his views ; looking far and wide from his standpoint,
but never for a moment straying from his safe position
on the only foundation, "the faith which was once delivered
to the saints." (Jude 3.)

But though Mr. Shaw's rule at the Westminster College
was very brief, it was not barren of important results.
He kept in view the project which had been started of
the erection of a new chapel in Westminster, one which
should be worthy of the locality and suitable for the
accommodation of the students, as well as of the ordinary congregations. On the 22nd of April he advocated
in a letter in the " Watchman " newspaper the scheme as
a fitting memorial of the late Principal, the Rev. John
Scott. The virtual pledge and sanction of the Conference
had already been given to this undertaking. At the Conference following, Mr. Shaw was its zealous advocate in
the preliminary Committees. It is hardly necessary to

remark, that what was desired and designed then, has since been carried out, and Westminster has now a spacious chapel, distinguished architecturally by the extreme and almost unsightly absence of ornament, but in other respects well adapted for the preaching of the Gospel.

The Conference, July and August, 1868, was held at Liverpool. Mr. Shaw was appointed to the York Circuit, contrary to his own wishes, his physical strength, as he thought, being scarcely equal to the duties of such an extensive Circuit, specially laborious on account of the number of country places connected with it. But his objections were overruled, as a wise and judicious man was needed to fill the position of Chairman of the District; and an assistant, the Rev. Joseph Shrimpton, was granted to him. A year's experience of the cold winter of that northern county led him to think that the time had come for his retirement from the full work of the Ministry; but he came to no hasty decision on a point of so much importance. Meanwhile, his interest in all matters affecting the Connexion and Protestantism was unabated. Not being able to attend a meeting of "the Committee for Cases of Exigency," appointed to meet on Monday, July 5th, at the Centenary Hall, London, " To consider certain proposed amendments to the Irish Church Bill, having for their object the support of Popery in Ireland," he wrote, as requested by the Secretary, Dr. Jobson, a full statement of his own views, dated Scarborough, July 2nd, 1869, of which the following is an extract :—

Several engagements to attend Missionary Meetings next week will render it impracticable for me to attend the Meeting of the Committee of Exigency. I have nothing to say upon the subject of the Irish

Church Bill, and the Lords' proposed Amendments, but what will, I presume, be much in accordance with the opinions of the other members of the Committee. It was clear from the beginning that we could take no Connexional action as to the general principle of the Irish Church Bill; the opinion of our people being much divided thereon. No other course was open, but for our Ministers and people to be left to act in their individual capacities, according to their own discretion; each, however, taking care to speak, write, and act within the fair limits of Christian courtesy.

The proposed Amendments by the Lords place a different issue before us. The question they raise is no longer as to the principle of the Bill, but as to details of its application, which are calculated to do much beyond the mere compensation of the Roman Catholics for the loss of the existing endowment of Maynooth, already by the Bill provided for on an extravagantly liberal scale. These Amendments, if carried, will vastly extend the endowment of Popery. If in this settlement Parliament cannot avoid recognising the fatal mistake of the endowment of Maynooth, we ought surely to abide by our principles, and protest in clear and decisive terms against a repetition of that error, by a further endowment of Irish Popery with parsonages and glebes, and thus vastly increasing its power for mis-chief. I am confident that numbers of our people, who have believed it their duty to give their votes and influence against the Irish Church Bill, will be found very ready and forward to join in a decided demonstration against the insidious proposals for further endowment of Popery.

To insure our unanimity on this matter, it may be well that any document which is to speak on behalf of the Connexion, should not contain anything either in favour of or against the Bill itself; but our protest should be confined to the Amendments which carry the principle of concurrent endowment far beyond the mere compensation of existing life and other interests.

Every sound Protestant, and in fact every consistent friend of religious equality and of civil and religious liberty, will be inclined to endorse Mr. Shaw's views. No one wishes to interfere with the religious privileges of the Roman Catholics, whether in England or Ireland, but it is the bounden duty of all the friends of civil and religious liberty firmly to oppose the exclusive and arrogant pretensions of the Ultramontane party. The miserable truckling of the leaders of our two great political parties to the Popish Hierarchy for purely electioneering purposes, is the most disgraceful fact in the party history of our country since the year 1830. Every administration bids as high as it dares for the Popish vote, and is willing to sacrifice Protestantism, and the rights of the Romanist laity, in return for Parliamentary support. Luckily, no Ministry betrayed into the manifestation of strong Popish proclivities can long retain office. The people of England, though for the most part not sufficiently alive to the dangers of the present juncture, have an instinctive hatred and dread of priestly assumption, whether Popish or Puseyite; and this, under God, is our safety.

The Conference of July and August, 1869, was held at Hull. After consulting with Dr. Jobson, (the President,) and with Dr. Osborn, Mr. Arthur, and others, Mr. Shaw resolved to apply for leave to " sit down,"—a technical phrase peculiar to Methodism, used to express a Minister's retirement from the active duties of Circuit work. The retiring brother then becomes what is very uncouthly and unmeaningly called a Supernumerary. He is henceforth one beyond the number of regular itinerant Ministers in full work ; and if the value of a Minister is to be calculated by the number of miles he can walk or ride, and the number of sermons he can preach within the week, the phrase is not inapplicable. *Mere* muscular peripatetic power in our young divines is useful in certain extensive Circuits, in which no horse is kept, and which thus find profit and "pleasure in the legs of a man." (Psalm cxlvii. 10.) Many of us in our younger days had reason to be thankful for and to rejoice in our power to endure the fatigue of walking Circuits; and this physical gift was some compensation to our consciences for our deficiencies in more important matters,—deficiencies, however, which were perhaps more felt by ourselves than by our good and considerate people. But in more mature life we hope to be valued rather for our brains and our affections than for our legs. Just when the mind is most mature, our system obliges our Ministers to retire from the active work. Such is the pressure of that work in every department, that the Methodist Church fancies it cannot afford to retain in its full ministry men who, though no longer " strong to labour " physically, yet possess the experience, judgment, and wisdom which the oversight of the work requires, especially in large Circuits. Every year the Conference feels the want of judicious Superintendents of Circuits, and of Chairmen of Districts. Sooner or later the Connexion will (happily for the benefit of the Church) be compelled to make arrangements to retain the services of many of its able and wise seniors, instead of permitting them to retire from public life. It was with deep feeling, with difficulty suppressed, that this application to retire from the active work was made. The President remarked " on the honourable position which Mr. Shaw had so long filled before Methodism and the public at large, and hoped that his retirement from active life would be marked by a suitable record in the journal of their proceedings." Then turning to Mr. Shaw, he said, in his warm, affectionate manner, "Let me assure you, Mr. Shaw, that when you retire you will not be forgotten by us. We love you, venerate you, and thank God for you, and we pray that God's blessing may be with you, and that in your later years you will find Him your support and consolation." The Rev. William Arthur "felt much at the closing ministry of such men as Mr. Shaw, whom God had called to do not common work, but uncommon work. Among uncommon Missionaries William Shaw was one whom his Master had uncommonly honoured." The Rev. Dr. Osborn "could never forget the time when Mr. Shaw first left for his African Mission. From early boyhood he had been observant of his course, having, from a conversation which took place at his father's breakfast-table, been so far interested as to follow Mr. Shaw's every step in public life, and to cherish a love and esteem for him which was growing still;" and, in conclusion, remarked, "God be praised for that long career of various services at home and abroad, now, I cannot but think, most properly and wisely brought to a termination, so far as activity and responsible posts of duty are concerned. God grant that this retirement may add many years to Mr. Shaw's life. We have often mourned over noble men who have fallen in harness, or who have used in active service the very last remains of their strength. I hope you will avoid that practical mistake, and by the step which is taken to-day, you will secure to us the value of his presence and counsels for years to come." The Rev. Thornley Smith and the Rev. John Richards, who had been fellow-labourers with Mr. Shaw in South Africa, followed with remarks suitable to the occasion.

CHAPTER XV.

Active Supernumerary Life of Mr. Shaw, 1869–1872.

WITHIN a few weeks after the Conference, August, 1869, Mr. Shaw left York, and, after residing a few weeks at Harrogate and Buxton, he settled down for the winter at Bournemouth, one of the new rising bathing towns called into being by the demand arising out of the hypochondriacal fancies of the higher and well-to-do middle-class population of our large towns. Half a century ago, Bath, Cheltenham, Tunbridge Wells, Brighton, Ramsgate and Margate, and the nearest seaport, furnished sufficient accommodation for all who needed, or fancied they needed, the renovating waters of a Spa, or the refreshment of sea-bathing. Now, the names of these resorts of the idle and the invalid are too numerous to mention. It may be that to *some* such changes may be desirable and even necessary; but in most cases the influential motive which annually induces large numbers of otherwise sensible people to leave their comfortable home residences, and to submit to the limited accommodation, the dirt, and other inconveniences, and the extortions of a crowded Spa or bathing village, is fashion. With this all-potent power it is in vain to reason. Mr. Shaw was not, however, influenced by the prevailing custom; but, as he was without a settled residence, he wisely chose for his temporary abode a village, the genial climate of which seemed likely to prove beneficial to his health: nor were his expectations disappointed. The bronchial symptoms, which for a time were threatening, were in a few weeks quite relieved, and he soon became impatient to begin the new life he had marked out for himself as a Supernumerary, " to become more than ever the servant of the Connexion, by close and assiduous attention to the duties of its various Committees." No man ever more thoroughly succeeded in carrying out his intentions in this respect than my old friend. For every service in Methodism, and especially in attendance upon Committees, there never was a man more ready or more diligent and faithful. At Bournemouth Mr. Shaw took his share in the religious services in the Wesleyan chapel, and, on the 12th of December, 1869, preached the Anniversary Sermon on behalf of the trust funds. In the spring of 1870, (25th of March,) he removed to Brixton, and took up his residence at No. 2, Hayter Road, Brixton Rise, next door to his old friend Mr. Boyce, and not far from the residences of his friends, Messrs. John Chubb, J. F. Bennett, William M'Arthur, M.P., Alexander M'Arthur, Rev. Luke Tyerman, Rev. W. Butters, and others.

It will be now necessary to refer to the changes which had taken place in South Africa since Mr. Shaw's departure in 1856. Politically the independence of the two Dutch settlements beyond the Orange River was assented to by the British Government—one of the most suicidal acts ever perpetrated at the instance of a Colonial Government— in 1853. On the other hand, the Colony was favoured with what might have been, and probably may eventually prove to be, a blessing,—a new Constitution, with an Upper and

Lower House of Parliament; but as its sessions and the head-quarters of the Executive were fixed to remain at Cape Town, the most important and enterprising part of the population of the Colony were to a great extent deprived of their due influence in the Legislature. To govern Southern Africa from Cape Town is just as inconvenient as to govern England from Penzance. If the Colony remain one, for which there are many powerful reasons, the seat of Government must be removed to Uitenhage, or some other central position. On the 1st of July, 1854, the new Parliament was opened at Cape Town.

In 1856, the very equivocal blessing of a batch of German settlers, discharged soldiers from the foreign legion employed by the British Government in the Crimean war, was bestowed upon the Colonial Eastern frontier. Three thousand men, with a very disproportionate accompaniment of women, and with habits which were generally the reverse of what is desirable in a Colony, were no welcome addition to the population. German farmers and artizans would have been a great acquisition. If soldiers had to be sent as Colonists, why soldiers of the English race had not an opportunity given to them to commence life anew under advantageous circumstances, was a natural question, to which no satisfactory reply could be given. The depredations of the Kaffir tribes on the frontier, and the refractory conduct of some of the Chiefs, seemed for some time to threaten the re-commencement of the Kaffir war; but providentially the Government was on this occasion on the alert, and prepared to repel any inroad. Meanwhile, through the influence of an impostor, Umlakazi, who claimed to be an inspired prophet, the tribes west of the Kei were given up to a strange infatuation, and were persuaded to abstain from the cultivation of the ground, to destroy their hoards of grain, and at once to kill all their cattle. The inducement held out by the supposed prophet was, that there would follow a resurrection of their forefathers, by whose help they would be able to destroy the Europeans and all Kaffir unbelievers. In encouraging this delusion, the Chiefs had another object in view : they hoped that a starving population, desperate, and without cattle or any other food, would easily be induced to rush into the Colony, and plunder the farmers or borderers of the extended frontier, and thus commence a war. But after the food and cattle had been destroyed, and the falsity of the promises of the prophet had been clearly proved, the scheme could not be carried out ; and the consequence was a loss of life by starvation, disease, and emigration, which completely destroyed the power of the frontier Chiefs, and enabled the Government to inflict deserved punishment upon such as had broken faith with the Colony, and had otherwise rendered themselves amenable to justice. The Chief Kama, and many subordinate Chiefs, and their people, were, through the influence of the Missionaries, saved from the general delusion, and became in consequence relatively more powerful and influential. The Mission greatly prospered, and the Colonists, free from all immediate danger of a Kaffir inroad, resumed, with their usual diligence and energy, the cultivation of the arts of peace. It is to be regretted that the Colonial Government, which, in 1857, had wisely removed the Chief Krieli (the main instigator of the proposed invasion of the Colony) and his people beyond the Bashie River, and which had arranged to plant a body of English settlers between the Kei and that river in the territory vacated by Krieli, suddenly changed its policy, and permitted that Chief and people to resume their forfeited lands ; an error of judgment which a few years hence may involve the Colony in another Kaffir war, to the great loss of the lives and property of our European and Native Colonists. To make no distinction between those Chiefs who are friends to the Colony, and those who are its known enemies, (except in favour of the latter,) has been too much the policy of the Colonial Government,—a policy which is thought to be "humane and enlightened," but which tempts the Chiefs to acts of insubordination, resulting in condign punishment and eventual ruin.

As the fiftieth year since the formation of the Albany Colony drew nigh, the Colonists made preparation for a celebration of their Jubilee in the year 1870. It was hoped that the health of Mr. Shaw would permit him to be present on this joyous occasion. In the Missionary Report for 1868, (published April, 1869,) there is a brief account of the state of the South African Missions, and a reference to Mr. Shaw in connexion with the Colonial Jubilee Year, of which the following is an extract :—

" The South African Missions, within the Colonies of the Cape and Natal and the Dutch Republics, employ sixty-nine Missionaries, and report eleven thousand five hundred and twenty-four members, with six thousand one hundred and thirty-four day-school children. These Missions are so mixed up with the Mission to the colonial natives, and with the Mission in Kaffirland, the Bechuana Country, and Natal, that their statistics cannot be separated. Few Missions have been, on the whole, more satisfactory. More than one generation of patient toil has been rewarded by an extraordinary measure of success. The great revival of the last two years has resulted in extensive and permanent good. A native Ministry has been raised up, and a native literature is in course of formation. Already several editions of the entire Scriptures in Kaffir have been circulated. Our respected friend, the Rev. William Shaw, if spared until the beginning of next year, will celebrate in spirit with the Colonists the Jubilee of their Colony, (the Albany Settlement,) and of the Mission of which he was the founder and father. Another name associated with the South African Mission must not be forgotten, that of the late Barnabas Shaw, whose eloquent letters and journals more than half a century ago contributed so much to awaken and deepen Missionary feeling in England. The last few years have been years of commercial depression in the South African Colonies, from which, however, they are recovering, though slowly. In the retrospect of half a century, the Christian philanthropist has great reason to thank God and take courage. So many intelligent and, for the most part, Christian communities studding the whole of South Africa nearly as far as the tropics, cannot fail to be a blessing to that continent. To the natives in and around the Colony these settlements have been, on the whole, a great benefit: Notwithstanding the wars which have arisen from the contact of civilized and barbarous man, aggravated, if not caused, by the vacillating policy of the Colonial Government, there is now peace between the colonists and natives, and a feeling of mutual confidence is growing up. The native population is increasing, and there are hundreds of thousands more native Africans living in peace and security at this time under the Colonial Government, than at any previous period could be found within the territory now included within the Colonial boundary."

In the Report for 1869, (published April, 1870,) the subject is again resumed.

" The hope expressed in our last Report, that the Rev. William Shaw would ' celebrate in spirit with the Colonists the Jubilee of their Colony, (the Albany Settlement,) and of the Mission of which he was the founder and father,' has been happily realised : he has been spared to unite his sympathies with those of his African friends and brethren, though compelled by increasing infirmities to retire from the active work of the Ministry. All the South African Districts have passed Resolutions expressive of their high regard for Mr. Shaw, and of their regret that circumstances would not permit him to be present at the Jubilee Celebration to be held on the 10th of April last, on which day the first settlers landed in Algoa Bay in the year 1820."

The Jubilee itself was celebrated in Graham's Town, on the 22nd of May, 1870. The Rev. H. H. Dugmore, himself a settler, and the son of a settler, preached the Sermon in that town, and delivered a Lecture, " The Reminiscences of an Albany Settler," which was afterwards published, (8vo., pp. 56,) and will go down to posterity as one of the most valuable contemporary sketches of early " settler history." As might be expected, the reference to the labours of the Rev. William Shaw, and of

the agencies under his direction, is the expression of the
universal feeling in the Colony. "William Shaw had an
eye and a heart that embraced all Albany, and gladly combined and guided the elements of usefulness wherever he
could find them. The 'locations' of the various 'parties'
had Sabbath services conducted by men who proved their
own disinterested sincerity and earnestness by the long
journeys they took, often on foot, without any remuneration but the satisfaction of knowing that they were con-
serving the Christianity of their fellow Colonists, and
enjoying a gladdening sense of the smile of God upon their
labours." Services similar to those held in Graham's
Town were celebrated in all the settlements in the Eastern
division of the Colony, in remembrance and in honour
of the "Settler Fathers" of 1820. It is to be hoped that
before this generation passes away, steps may be taken to
preserve the names and histories of these adventurous
men, the founders of the British settlements in South East
Africa. Some future Greek Professor in the South African
University of the twentieth century may astonish and edify
the ingenuous youth of his academic class by a Dissertation
on the old Œkists (as Grote calls them) of their African
fatherland ; and in our care for posterity we ought to be
careful that credible and well-proven facts should not be
lacking : otherwise, should the fashionable tendency in
favour of historical scepticism prevail, the names of the
heads of parties will, at some distant period, be regarded
as mere eponyms, and the whole history of the settlement
as a mere myth. Mr. Shaw's necessary absence from these
Jubilee festivals was a great disappointment to himself, as
well as to the Methodist people of South Africa. Gladly

would he have undertaken the voyage, and encountered the fatigue of the excitement necessarily connected with the joyous occasion ; but, after mature consideration, he wisely denied himself this great pleasure. But his heart was with his African friends, and his feelings were such as " a stranger cannot enter into." Few men who have taken a prominent part in the foundation of Colonies and the formation of new Churches, have lived to witness the results of a progress of fifty years. What a chequered history of trials and triumphs—of prosperity, and reverses, and reactions ! How many reminiscences, both painful and pleasing, of the primal histories of his fellow-emigrants and their families ! Nor would his departed colleagues in the Mission work be forgotten : the names of Threlfall, the Namaqualand martyr, of Whitworth, Hodgson, Broadbent, Shrewsbury, Palmer, Ayliff, and others, who had laboured for Africa in connexion with him, would not be forgotten. They had entered into rest, and he looked forward to meet them again in the grand company of the spirits of the just made perfect. Many of us old men, in looking back upon those who, in public and domestic life, were our fellow labourers in the heat and burden of the day, feel that while our duties are with the living, our tenderest sympathies and our warmest affections are with our dead.

About this time the attention of the Methodist Ministers and people was drawn to the question of National Education by the enlargement of the views and plans of the Executive of the Government, which led to the passing of Mr. Forster's Elementary Education Act in the year 1870. Already, in 1869, it was obvious that there existed considerable difference of opinion as to the direction and extent of Government interference in this important matter. Churchmen and Nonconformists had their fears as well as their hopes. The Clergy of the Church of England had already done a great work in reference to the National Education, assisted, of course, by the Government grants which, since 1834, had been bestowed in connexion with such efforts. Next to the Clergy, the Wesleyan-Methodist Ministers and people had heartily engaged in this important work, with equal zeal and success in proportion to their means. It was very natural that the Government plan in prospect should be viewed in its relation to religious territory, and to the position of the numerous Denominational schools and colleges for training masters already in existence. In November, 1869, a large and influential meeting of the Ministers and laymen of the Methodist body met in the Centenary Hall; but no report was made of the proceedings, as it was merely preliminary to another adjourned meeting to be held in the spring of 1870. By this meeting certain Resolutions were passed, and a deputation appointed to wait upon the Premier (Mr. Gladstone), Mr. Shaw being one of the deputation, which had an interview with that distinguished statesman on the 26th of May. But as a Report of the adjourned meeting, its Resolutions, and the interview of the deputation with Mr. Gladstone, has been published, we make no further reference to it.

The Conference of 1870 was held in Burslem, on which occasion the brethren assembled honoured themselves by the re-election of that veteran and able Minister, the Rev. John Farrar, to the Presidential Chair. In the autumn of this year Mr. Shaw was requested by the Directors of " The Watchman " to take charge of that paper as Chairman of the Committee (the weekly rota). His business was to provide a staff of writers for the weekly leaders, and to exercise an oversight in all other important matters requiring the attention of an editor. This journal, though quite independent of the Conference or any other official control, was for many years regarded as the only accredited Wesleyan newspaper. Established in 1835 by a number of gentlemen who generously advanced the capital, it was carried on for many years at a great pecuniary sacrifice to the proprietors. The first Editor was Dr. Humphrey Sandwith, a physician of high respectability and of considerable literary acquirements : he was the father of Humphrey Sandwith, Esq., of Kars celebrity, and died on July 25th, 1874, aged eighty-two. The next Editor was Dr. Bennett, now filling a responsible position under the Government of New Zealand. In 1848, John Clulow Rigg, Esq., the son of my dear old friend, the Rev. John Rigg, by his first wife, Miss Clulow, of Macclesfield, was appointed to this office. Mr. Rigg was what may be called a Conservative Liberal : his sagacious foresight and cautious instincts saved him from all extremes, while his sympathy with all that was valuable in modern progress qualified him for the very delicate task of guiding the " Watchman " in the trying period of the so-called " Reform " agitation of 1849–53. As a writer he was occasionally brilliant, generally thoughtful and timidly suggestive, but sometimes, through over subtlety and extreme caution, obscure. But he always wrote, both as respects his style and matter, as a scholar and a Christian. With those who admire that smart, flippant, and antithetical jingle of words which characterizes much of the current literature of the day, he was not a popular writer. I was first introduced to him by my friend Dr. Osborn, and our acquaintance soon ripened into a friendship which only ceased with his life. I was struck with the extent of his reading, especially in Latin and French literature. Natural science he had studied professionally in his training for the medical profession, and in after life kept himself abreast of the new facts and theories of our philosophers. With the exception of the late James Nichols,* one of the last of the honourable race of learned printers, I never heard of any man so familiar with the Latin writers of the fifteenth, sixteenth, and seventeenth centuries. Had he been spared to old age to write his autobiography, the narrative of his mental history would have equalled in interest the " Confessions " of De Quincey and Coleridge. When he died prematurely and suddenly on the 5th of June, 1868, Mr. Shaw and I felt that we had lost a friend, the like of whom in many respects we should never see again.

Mr. J. H. Horton, the assistant-editor of " The Watchman," has favoured me with some remarks bearing upon this brief part of Mr. Shaw's life, which I am permitted to insert.

"Towards the close of 1870 the Rev. William Shaw became Chairman of the weekly rota of ' The Watchman,'

---

* This remarkable man, the intimate friend of Richard Watson and Dr. Bunting, was the Editor of several important works, the Translator and Biographer of Arminius, and the Author of " Calvinism and Arminianism compared," (1 vol. 8vo.,) a singular work, which contains a mine of information respecting the political and religious literature of the Commonwealth period. He died in 1861, aged seventy-six.

and this position he occupied until his death. He was singularly qualified for the post he had undertaken. His knowledge of Methodism at home and abroad was most extensive, and he was well acquainted with general religious and political movements. Indeed, considering that he hád spent so many years away from England, it was remarkable how fully he understood the various shades of thought prevalent throughout Great Britain. He possessed, moreover, an evenly-balanced mind, and had no political bias. He was, eminently, a Liberal Conservative. Having no ambition to shine as a writer, it was, with him, a task of duty and pleasure to select those most able, as he believed, to supply articles for the journal alike serviceable to Methodism, religion, and humanity. And yet Mr. Shaw was himself a good writer, close in argument, and chaste in expression. It was in his editorial capacity that I first became acquainted with him, and the impression produced upon me was one of deep pleasure. The upright form, the somewhat portly figure, the grey hair, the kind-glancing eyes, are before me now. There was a warm grasp from his hand, a grasp which told that the heart moved the fingers, and a smile on the lips which spoke more eloquently than the choicest words. His mouth was very expressive. The irrepressible gentleness and good humour of his nature played round his lips, as they shone from his eyes. And I do not remember, during the several years he conducted the paper, hearing one harsh or unkind word escape his lips. To young writers he was especially kind, and his encouraging words have stimulated many to fresh exertions. There was no spark of rivalry in his nature; and if any error of judgment was committed, he was ready to throw his shield over the offender. His sense of the humorous was most keen, and those who knew him will remember his joyous laugh, and frank, honest smile. When an anecdote was being told, as he was somewhat deaf, he would hold his hand over his ear, and follow closely the words of the narrator. Then, when the point came, his was the readiest laugh— his the fullest appreciation of the joke. And while he could hold his own in an argument with an opponent on any subject, (and when he had made up his mind was not easily shaken in his ideas,) he was, as a rule, as yielding and gentle as a child. I do not recall a more pleasant picture than when I saw him, holding a young girl by the hand, looking with delight upon the little toys and paper flowers treasured up by the boys in the Children's Home in Bonner Road. As the sunlight fell on his face and figure, I could understand, apart from his religious labours, why he was beloved as a Missionary abroad.

"Though Mr. Shaw seldom wrote, when he felt that some prominent question demanded more than ordinary attention, he was most careful to see that full justice was done to the subject. I have known him, after a heavy debate in the House of Commons, lasting till the early hours of Wednesday morning, come to the office of 'The Watchman' shortly before the paper went to press, and write, in his well-known, clear, firm hand, comments on the general debate, and the arguments of the speakers. This, remembering his age, was remarkable; but more remarkable was the quiet, easy way in which he performed his task. Besides being an able leader-writer, Mr. Shaw was a most critical, yet generous reviewer."

A religious paper like the " Watchman " labours under many disadvantages in common with the religious press generally. There is a prejudice against what are called "Sectarian " organs of opinion as necessarily perpetuating a sectarian and narrow school of thought, while on the other hand the advocates of " authority" consistently oppose the discussion of religious questions in any shape. As a case in point we may quote the language of Dr. Hook, the Archdeacon of Chichester, who, in summing up the character of Bishop Bonner, remarks that " the evil passions of his vindictive mind, had he lived in our day, would have found vent in the anonymous correspondence of a newspaper, or in the conducting of some so-called religious newspaper." The serious charge implied in this remark would be difficult to prove. In Dr. Hook's sarcasm there is more concentrated prejudice and venom than can be found in all the religious journals of our country. We are sorry to have to say to such men as Dr. Hook, whom, while we differ from him, we esteem for his work's sake, " Physician, heal thyself."

The Conference of 1871 was held in Manchester, the Chair being occupied by the Rev. John H. James, D.D., the worthy son of a worthy father, the Rev. John James, one of the General Secretaries of the Wesleyan Missionary Society, a man of deep piety, an excellent preacher, and most eloquent speaker, who died in 1832. Immediately after the Conference, Mr. Shaw, accompanied by Mrs. Shaw, visited Paris, in company with the Rev. William Gibson and Mrs. Gibson, who were returning to their station in that city. Of the services connected with the Missionary Anniversary, Mr. Gibson gives the following account :—

" On Sunday, August 20th, the Missionary Sermons at the Central Chapel, Rue Roquépine, were preached by the Rev. W. Shaw. The text in the morning was Nahum i. 7: ' The Lord is good, a stronghold in the day of trouble; and He knoweth them that trust in Him ;' in the evening, Acts xiii. 26: ' Men and brethren, children of the stock of Abraham, and whosoever among you feareth God, to you is the word of this salvation sent.' Both sermons were characterized by great plainness of speech, earnest setting forth of Gospel truth, and loving and fervent application. A blessed influence of the Spirit accompanied the word of the Preacher, and we believe that the ' bread cast upon the waters' will be ' seen after many days.' We held our Annual Missionary Meeting on the following day. Our expectations as to the number likely to attend were not high ; for our English work in Paris, like many of the houses around the city, has been almost laid in ruins by the war. But, although the attendance was not large, and not to be compared with former years, our hopes were far more than realized. A cheerful company of English people sat down to a plentiful tea at half-past six, and the public meeting began at half-past seven.

" After the devotional exercises, the Report, &c., the Rev. W. Shaw deeply interested the people for three-quarters of an hour by a recital of his early Missionary experiences in South Africa. It would be impossible in a brief summary to give a fair report of a Missionary speech which arrested and held from its beginning to its close the earnest attention of the congregation. Suffice it to say, that it was full of Missionary information, grasped the great subject in its broad view, and, with eagle glance, dealt with it also in detail. The appearance of Mr. Shaw, coupled with the recollection that he went out as a Missionary to South Africa nearly fifty-two years ago, was a Missionary speech of itself, and the words of the veteran soldier of the Cross delighted while they informed, and instructed while they pleased.

"On Tuesday, August 22nd, the Rev. W. Shaw went down to hold a service at Chantilly, a place which now derives its fame from the fact of its being the head-quarters of French racing, but which formerly was noted as the abode of the Condé family, and will probably in a few months become the chosen home of the Duke d'Aumale. Once the well-known chateau-residence of a branch of the royal family, it will probably become such again. Unfortunately for our work, the English families resident here have been scattered. Before the war Chantilly was one of the greenest spots in the Paris Circuit; but now all the props of the chapel are removed, and the work has to be begun again. The need of the chapel, however, exists as much as ever; for there are three or four hundred jockeys and stable boys, who are careless and godless, and need to be *sought* that they may be *saved*. After our usual tea-meeting the Rev. W. Shaw delivered a most suitable and interesting Missionary address.

"Our Circuit Missionary services were concluded at Asnières on Wednesday, the 23rd instant. The little chapel has escaped destruction as if by a miracle. Houses on the right and left have been laid low, and in some directions the chariot of war has swept mercilessly along, carrying desolation and ruin in its course. But in the midst of all our little sanctuary has stood secure, and, with the exception of comparatively insignificant injuries from two or three fragments of shells, has come out of the peril scathless. At three o'clock in the afternoon we enjoyed a delightful service in this quiet sanctuary, and felt the presence of God in our midst, while we listened to an excellent sermon from the Rev. W. Shaw. A saddening walk along the banks of the Seine, amid crumbling gables and tottering roofs, and riddled walls and prostrate houses, preceded the evening tea and meeting. Formerly two hundred English people lived at Asnières, but they have either not returned, or have come back to find their homes a ruin. Nevertheless, a fair congregation assembled to hear a deeply-interesting statement of Missionary facts from the veteran Missionary, who kindled into warmth and almost enthusiasm as he narrated the early toils and triumphs of the South African Mission.

"Thus came to a close a Missionary Anniversary which will long be remembered with interest and pleasure by all who were privileged to enjoy its blessed services and meetings."

This being Mr. Shaw's first visit to Paris, he went through the laborious duty of sight-seeing with his usual patience, and was no doubt highly delighted at the time, and yet more so when the task had been accomplished. Mr. Gibson informs me of a curious incident on the occasion of Mr. Shaw's visit to the National Assembly at Versailles. "I sent in Mr. Shaw's card to M. Grévy, who was then President, accompanied by an announcement that he had been the General Superintendent of our Missions in South-East Africa. He at once admitted Mr. and Mrs. Shaw to the seat of honour set apart for illustrious visitors, namely, the first box on his right, in the visitors' gallery." Mr. and Mrs. Shaw took this opportunity of visiting Switzerland, proceeding *viâ* Macon to Geneva and Chamouni, (Mont Blanc,) thence to Lausanne, Berne, Neufchatel, Dijon, Paris, and to England, on the 11th of September. No doubt there is a pleasure in a Continental tour; but the pleasure to such of us as are limited for time is mainly in the retrospect. To be cooped up day by day in a railway carriage, to hurry through cathedrals, remarkable buildings, picture galleries, and museums, and to dine at the *table d'hôte*, paying thrice as much for your vinegar claret as you would in England for the same sort of wine of a fair quality, can only be pleasurable while the novelty lasts. To travellers with time and money at their command it is no doubt quite another thing. Even to those less favourably circumstanced the remembrance of tours in a new country is exhilarating. One's stock of knowledge may not have been increased, but the impressions received are sources of permanent and agreeable reminiscences.

We must now recur to the National Education question, and the excitement occasioned by Mr. Forster's Education Act of 1870.

Mr. Shaw for several years before his death took a leading part in connexion with the subject of Public Elementary Education. Everything had prepared him so to do. In his early youth he was himself a teacher. In the Colony he had taken an active interest in the Colonial plans for public education, and also, and in particular, in the organization of Christian Education for the Kaffirs, by means of trained teachers and Mission schools. He had established not only schools but a Training Institution for the natives. On his return to this country in 1857 he was brought immediately into intercourse with the Rev. John Scott; and one of his earliest visits was paid to the Normal College, of which Mr. Scott was Principal. When Mr. Scott died, he was, as has been already stated, appointed by the Committee Mr. Scott's *ad interim* successor in the Principalship of the College. This was, in fact, his last public work before he retired from ordinary itinerant service.

As to education, Mr. Shaw held opinions of the same general complexion as those which he held on most points, —he was liberal, but he was conservative. He approved fully of Mr. Forster's Education Act. The intention of this Act was to establish a comprehensive national system of elementary education, by reforming and nationalizing the institutions which had hitherto done the work, so far as it was done, and at the same time making provision for the additional supply of inspected schools in sufficient numbers to meet the entire educational deficiencies of the country. The process of nationalizing the denominational schools was to be accomplished by the enactment of a stringent conscience clause, which is enforced in all *public elementary schools*, as these institutions are now designated; and by completely separating the Government of the country from responsibility for anything in these schools, except the secular instruction. Hence, the system of denominational inspection was abolished by the Act, and Government grants are not now made directly, but only in proportion to the results of Inspectors' examinations, which are confined to the secular instruction given in the schools.

The other main portion of Mr. Forster's measure provided for the election of local School Boards, with power to build and support by means of local rates such schools as should be necessary to meet the wants of the respective localities, and to make bye-laws in regard to the attendance generally of children at school. These Boards are established, under the Act, either by the voluntary action of the ratepayers, or, compulsorily, by the Education Department, in cases where school districts fail to comply with its requirements as to school accommodation. School Board schools enjoy all the same privileges of grants from the imperial exchequer, and are governed by the same code of regulations, as all other classes of aided schools. The opponents of denominational schools objected to Mr. Forster's Bill on various grounds. Some of them desired the establishment of a universal and uniform system of secular schools, while others would have preferred a complete national organization of School Boards and Board Schools, in which the Bible should have been required to be taught. Both these parties would have brought to an end the recognition by Government of the existing denominational school organizations, depriving them accordingly of all Government inspection and aid.

I have no wish to remark further on the Education controversy, as my opinions are not in accord with the partisans of either the Denominational or the Secularist school ; but it will be necessary to state that in the Conference of 1872, held in London, under the presidency of the Rev. Luke H. Wiseman, the Rev. William Arthur, on the 13th of August, proposed a Resolution to this effect, that, " considering the difficulties of the denominational system of education, the

Conference judges it desirable that it should be gradually merged in a system of united unsectarian schools with the Bible, under School Boards." This view he advocated with great earnestness and power. To this speech Mr. Shaw replied in the following terms:—

He came forward with much trepidation and with great doubt as to the propriety of his occupying so prominent a position. He should have felt that under any circumstances, but the arrangement which had been made had put him under some difficulty. Four notices of motion had been given, varying not a little in their purport, but agreeing in their general tendency. The good sense of the brethren had shown them that it was not convenient, perhaps not possible, to drive four omnibuses abreast through Temple Bar, and they had therefore resolved that the best furnished vehicle, and the one most likely to attract public attention and favour, should have the first place. Well, he admired the good sense of those brethren. They were now brought face to face with what was really essential to the subject under discussion. Nothing pained him more than to find himself placed in opposition to his dear and beloved friend, Mr. Arthur, upon that question—not the less beloved because they happened to take different views. The Resolution which he (Mr. Arthur) had proposed for their acceptance stated, that, "considering the difficulties of the denominational system of education, the Conference deemed it desirable," &c. Then that was the basis of all the exhortation they had had to interference in that matter, viz., "the difficulties of the denominational system of education." Now he (Mr. Shaw) was not an orator, his friend Mr. Arthur was an accomplished orator, as they all knew. But he addressed himself to a body of men accustomed to judge upon things not merely by the words in which they were conveyed, but by the sense that was involved in them. What, then, were those denominational difficulties? Mr. Arthur had in some degree expounded them. But one of those withdrawn Resolutions went into detail, and he took the liberty of analysing that Resolution; for, although it was withdrawn as a Resolution, it was nevertheless fair to accept it as an exposition of the difficulties referred to by Mr. Arthur. "Believing that the present arrangements for National Education are prejudicial to Methodism." It started upon that point. Now, whatever faults there might be in the present arrangements of education, nothing was more certain than that for some time under those regulations education had been extended vastly in the country; schools had sprung up in all directions, and the children attending those schools had been greatly multiplied. Were they, then, to understand that the extension of education under those arrangements was prejudicial to Methodism? No; that was not what the writer meant. He would not treat an argument of that sort uncandidly. He went on to explain in what particulars the present system was found prejudicial to the interests of Methodism. He referred first to the rural districts of the country. Mr. Arthur referred to them also. What did that mean? It meant that the parochial arrangements gave to the Parson and the Squire preponderating local influence, and that that influence was very often exerted in a prejudicial manner. Most distinctly he (Mr. Shaw) admitted that that was true ; most distinctly he admitted that in numerous cases that had occurred during some years past that influence had been brought to bear in a manner which had trenched upon the religious rights and liberties of the people. But what then ? had the recent Act in any degree sanctioned the abuse of such power? Had it not rather put a great check upon it ? Had it not made the most distinct provision that in no case whatever should a child be obliged to go to a Church Sunday-school because it took advantage of the Church day-school? He said it threw a shield over them that they did not enjoy before. It was said, that "it involved the disputed right of the State to teach religion with State funds." He was astonished that that should have been introduced ; he did not mean to dwell upon it ; he considered it *ultra vires*, going beyond the question under consideration. No doubt it was a disputed point, and he felt somewhat indignant that any attempt should be made to bring in that disputed question when Conference had again and again refused to entertain it as a Conference question. In opposition to the view of his friend Mr. Arthur, he was inclined to say, that the Act did not provide for the teaching of religion in day-schools. Had the writer of that Resolution carefully read the Act,—he doubted it, or otherwise his memory must have played him a treacherous trick,— he would have seen that it most distinctly provided that no payments were to be made except for secular instruction, ascertained to be given by Inspectors appointed for that purpose. There were no denominational Inspectors, nor were they allowed to inquire into the teaching of religion ; but they were expected to keep out of their reports all allusion whatever to the subject. How could it, then, be said, that in those schools the State paid for the teaching of religion ? Here he would allude to what struck him as a very transparent fallacy in the argument of Mr. Arthur. He said they misunderstood concurrent endowment, and he illustrated it by showing that when payments were made to different Churches by Governments, they did not inquire into the different doctrines that were taught—whether Romanist, or Evangelical, or Unitarian—but they were simply paid as Churches. Yes ; but what were they paid for ? They were paid for teaching religion under all those various denominations. The Government did not trouble itself to ask what kind of religion, but they were paid as teachers of religion. It was further said on the paper that they were favourable to the interests of Popery in this country and in Ireland. They must allow him to glance at that statement. He read the other day in a newspaper the following passage :—" The Rev. H. W. Holland, the well-known leader of the Liberal party in the Conference, said so and so." He wished somebody would teach that Editor that the Methodist Conference knew nothing of party government: it might exist in other ecclesiastical communities. Happily there was a measure of piety and certain holy aims that by the good providence of God had hitherto preserved them from it ; and he hoped the time would never come when government by party would obtain a footing in that Conference. Well, the Liberal party did exist in the nation, and he had no doubt a great many of his brethren deemed themselves honoured in saying that they were supporters of that party. Now what had the Liberal party done on the question of Popery when there was a great agitation in favour of the disestablishment of the Irish Church ? When that Act was at length accomplished, it involved, amongst many other things, the handing over in hard cash

and real property something like a million and a half of money to
the Roman Priests of Ireland.   Well, what did the Liberal party say
about it ?   When did they come forth to say, This shall not be; we
will not give such an endowment as that to Popery in all future time ?
Few and feeble were the notes that were played in that strain, and
the nation did not hear them ; and the consequence was, that the Act
was passed.   O, but, it was said, that was an incidental consequence
of the disestablishment of the Irish Church.   The Act could not have
been carried if that had not formed a part of it.   Now he retorted
that statement.   The Educational Act was of great importance and
value to the nation; it involved incidentally that the Romanists
should be partakers of the benefits upon the same terms as their
countrymen in all parts of the land.   And what could be said against
that ?   He hated Popery as much as any of them ; but neither he
nor they hated any of their Roman Catholic fellow-subjects ; they
were standing on common ground with themselves, and he thought if
they could justify giving one and a half millions to the Romanists
because of the necessities of the case, they in Ireland need not taunt
those who were acceding to the general provisions of an Act that
carried with it a similar necessity.   As to Ireland—at that moment
he could not say accurately, but speaking approximately—some
£300,000 or £400,000 a year went to the support of schools in Ireland, over which the priests had paramount influence.   His friend
Mr. Arthur very adroitly confined his remarks to a particular class of
schools of which there were very few.   But what about the vested
and non-vested schools of Ireland ?   Were not a large portion
of these under the absolute patronage and control of the Priests
in various parts of the country ?   And yet they were getting
much public money for the support of them.   It would be as well
for those who set themselves against the denominational schools
in England to remedy that evil.   He was not going to say a
word that would disturb the equanimity and right feeling of their
brethren in Ireland.   That Conference a year ago promised the Irish
Conference their sympathy and support in any struggle that might
come on hereafter in regard to general education in their country,
and he was sure the Conference would keep its pledge in that respect.

Their Irish brethren need not fear that they would find them taking any course that would prevent them having the fullest opportunity of setting forth their own views. They might depend upon it that the British Methodists would back them up on any fair ground they might take upon that subject. He therefore thought they had disposed of that question. They were taunted with being in the same boat with Romanists. He wanted to know what kind of crew they had in the boat on the other side; they saw Atheists, Deists, Socinians, Unitarians, and Communists, and people of that sort. Both sides were placed in circumstances which rendered them equally liable to that kind of imputation. At the beginning of their discussions the other day he said he would state certain reasons why, in his humble opinion, the Conference should not at that time discuss that question, or make any deliverance about it. Now, before he sat down he would state some of those reasons, and leave them for the Conference to think about. He objected to Mr. Arthur's proposal—(1.) Because the adoption of it would put them out of harmony with the vast majority of the nation. On this point the Birmingham League and the Manchester Conference of Nonconformists sadly misinterpreted the national feeling; and the consequence was that they soon discovered, when the subject was brought fairly to issue, that the great bulk of the nation was opposed to the theory which they put forth. It was rather gratifying to him to find, from Mr. Arthur's speech, that he had thrown over the Birmingham League. He had equally thrown overboard the Resolutions of the Nonconformist Meeting in Manchester. He had adopted principles wholly different to the principle which had been adopted both by the League itself and by the Manchester Nonconformist Meeting. They agreed to exclude the Bible. Not so Mr. Arthur. He was glad to see that in not one of the Resolutions which had been proposed to the Conference was there a proposition that there should be no Bible in the school. That could not have happened in the Methodist Conference. The country had decided that the denominational schools should continue to exist, but that there should be set up beside them over the whole nation Board Schools. It had been argued as if they objected to that. But when had they objected? When had they said a word against that principle? He thought they might very well exist together. He thought it would be a great advantage to both, that they should exist side by side, upon the principle of free trade in education, as well as in other things. The competition would be most healthy. (2.) He objected to the Resolution because it would involve them in great inconsistency. Hannah More had made one of her characters say: "We do not expect perfection, but we certainly look for consistency." If that was true of individuals, it ought to be especially true of great religious bodies. Now, what was the state of the case? They were at present receiving £60,000 a year in aid of their schools in this country; were they now to pass an opinion in opposition to the very system that gave them money? That would indeed be to resemble the man who took something of his friend, and then went away and complained of his indiscriminate generosity! He would remind them that they had schools in the West Indies, and in Africa, and in India, and that they received Government money in aid of those schools, and that in those schools they taught religion. How could they set themselves against a system by which they were every day profiting? Even the Congregationalists themselves on their foreign stations were receiving grants in aid of their schools. (3.) The Resolution was a theoretical one, and it would stultify all their past declarations. It was in the very teeth of everything they had said before. (4.) In the last place, it would be a serious infringement on the rights and privileges of their people. Where was the proof that their people were wanting any disturbance of the existing arrangements? The subject came up before the Preparatory Committee just before the Conference assembled, and what was the result? In that large assembly there were just six hands held up in favour of Mr. Holland's motion! And that in an assembly that was composed in a large part of the laity. Would they not have a right to insist that it should be considered in such a way and form, as that the laity should have the opportunity of declaring their views upon the subject? That Resolution would lead to the gradual but certain destruction of their schools in various places. He denied their right to act in this matter without consulting the laity. Who established those schools? The Conference? No. The Conference, after full consultation with the laity, had expressed an opinion that the Government proposals were not incompatible with Wesleyan principles, but it was left to the laity in their various localities to accept them or not. Gradually Wesleyan schools were established all over the country by the voluntary determination and effort of the people, and they had been accustomed to glory in them as proofs of the zeal and philanthropy of their people. As they did not create these schools, they had no right to attempt to destroy them until the people who erected them and had sustained them should be consulted upon the subject. He begged to move the following amendment :—

" That considering that the question of primary education—after having been widely discussed throughout the country, and particularly by large mixed Committees appointed by the Conference for the purpose, which met in the years 1868, 1869, and 1870—has been dealt with by the Education Act of 1870, and that that Act is only in course of being carried into effect ;

" Considering also that the Government have intimated their intention to propose some alterations in that Act during the next Session, and it is desirable to know the nature of those alterations before any further opinion on the general question is expressed by the Conference ;

" Considering further that the subject is one in which the laity of Methodism have a deep and lasting interest, and as to which they are entitled to be consulted before any Resolution be passed involving a departure from those principles in regard to National Education which have long been recognised and acted upon in the Connexion ; this Conference deems it inexpedient to re-open the question at present ; at the same time, in view of the possibility of alterations in the existing Act, the Conference confides it to the President to convene a Meeting of the United Committees of Privileges and Education, and such other persons as he may deem suitable, should he be of opinion that such alterations are of sufficient importance to justify him in doing so."

The debate was kept up with great ability on both sides, and ended in the adoption of a Resolution :—" That the whole subject be referred to a Committee, to meet during the autumn, and before the meeting of Parliament, to consist of the General Education Committee, the Committee of Privileges, the Committee of Exigencies, and a layman and Minister to be elected at the September District Meeting, with power to act."

Mr. Shaw died just as the convention of Ministers and laymen on the subject of National Education was assembling in the Centenary Hall. His presence was greatly missed on that occasion, not only by those friendly to his views, but also by those who did not altogether coincide with them. No man was more opposed to an exclusive clerical system of education, or to anything like narrow denominationalism; but as a genuine Christian liberal he had no sympathy with the platform of the Secularist school.

Some years previous to the Conference of 1872, the question of the preparation of a Book of Offices for the use of the Methodist Churches had been discussed, and a Committee appointed to prepare a revise of the Services in the "Book of Common Prayer." Of this Committee Mr. Shaw was the Convener, as he took a special interest in the design. He was an admirer of a Liturgical Service, and thought that of the Church of England the best in the world. That it would be improved by a few omissions he, in common with most devout Churchmen, was fully convinced; and he hoped that by the removal of a few objectionable and equivocal paragraphs the prejudice against the use of a form of prayer would in time disappear. A form of sound words, used in connexion with extemporaneous outpouring of the heart in prayer, was, in his opinion, the most excellent way, and a wise medium between the two extremes of confining public prayer within the limits of a set form, or of leaving the congregation entirely at the mercy of an extempore address. I can find no reference to any of his speeches in the Conference, or in the various Committees, on this subject. The Conference of 1872, in one of its final sessions, dismissed the question, to Mr. Shaw's great disappointment. He thought that by neglecting to modify and adapt the "prayers" to our services, the result would be that in a short time they would be discarded altogether. The Conference of 1874 has however revived the Committee, and there is some prospect of our having a Service Book free from certain equivocal prayers and expressions, which are at present a stumbling-block to many.

CHAPTER XVI.

The last Days.

I MUST now advert to the losses which the Connexion sustained by the death of some leading Ministers and laymen between 1868 and 1872, as the memories of these departed brethren are associated with my reminiscences of Mr. Shaw. With most of them he had more or less laboured in the business of the Connexion, and with all of them he had been on terms of intimacy. The Rev. G. B. Macdonald, distinguished by natural gifts of voice and manner, and by a cultivated mind, died 13th of November, 1868, aged sixty-four. The Rev. F. A. West, an able man, and a most acceptable preacher, who in 1857 had filled the Chair of the Conference, died 4th of April, 1869, in the sixty-ninth year of his age. J. J. Lidgett, Esq., to whom we have previously alluded, snatched away suddenly in the prime of life, and in the midst of business and religious activities, in the month of June, 1869, within eighteen months of the death of his revered father-in-law, the Rev. John Scott. The Rev. Isaac Keeling, a man of great maturity of judgment and practical sagacity, whose " Remains "* ought to be in every Methodist Preacher's library : he filled the Chair of the Conference in 1855, and died 11th of August, 1869, aged eighty. The Rev. Peter M'Owan, a man remarkable for his powerful and fruitful ministry, died February, 1870,

---

* Sermons, Memorials, Life, &c. Small 8vo.

aged seventy-five. The Rev. Thomas Vasey, gifted with superior mental powers, and, in spite of great physical debility, remarkable for his energetic labours : " his zeal for the spread of saving religion became even more intense as he drew near to the close of his ministry :" he died 29th of September, 1871, aged fifty-seven. The Rev. James Dixon, D.D., who in his prime was, " in the pulpit and on the platform, one of the most prominent men in Methodism." In the year 1841 he was chosen President of the Conference, and in 1848 was Representative to the American Conference : he died 28th of December, 1871, aged eighty-three. The unexpected death of John Robinson Kay, Esq., on the 25th of March, 1872, was a great loss to all the philanthropic enterprises of Methodism, and more especially to the great educational work of the Society. Last of all, the Rev. Elijah Hoole, D.D., the Senior Secretary of the Wesleyan Missionary Society, died on the 17th of June, 1872. He was one of the many learned and gifted Missionaries connected with that Society whose names are almost unknown even to the Church to which they belong : but we ought not to allow the labours and scholarship of Benjamin Clough, of D. J. Gogerly, of R. Spence Hardy, of Elijah Hoole, of J. W. Appleyard, and others, to be forgotten. Dr. Hoole laboured for nine years in India, and was considered to be one of the ablest Tamil scholars of his age. While his health permitted, no man was a more diligent and laborious Secretary, for the duties of which office his natural urbanity, polished manners, and great kindness admirably fitted him. He and Mr. Shaw, with the Rev. Ralph Mansfield, now of Sydney, New South Wales, were young men in London in 1819–20, preparing to go forth into the Mission field. It is seldom that three such men, each eminent in his own sphere, are called out the same year :—Dr. Hoole, the first Tamil scholar of his day; the Rev. William Shaw, the Patriarch of a Colony and the founder of a Mission; and the Rev. Ralph Mansfield, whose remarkable preaching power placed Wesleyan Methodism in New South Wales in a position which we trust it will ever retain. In this retrospective view of "the work-men" removed, while God still carries on His work, there ought not to be to us old men anything saddening. "*All these died in faith.*" May we follow them as they followed Christ !

"Part of the host have crossed the flood,
And part are crossing now."

Up to the autumn of 1872 Mr. Shaw seemed to enjoy excellent health. The general impression is well stated in an article in "The Watchman" of December 11th, 1872 :—

"He was one of the freshest and fairest of old men, capable of feeling the gist of every new question, and of entering into its pros and cons even beyond most men in their prime; and, while conservative in all his instincts, was large in his modes of thought, and progressive in his plans. He walked in the midst of us with the weight of years, yet seemed congenial with men of every age : and what man among us ever dreamed of a crooked motive or a blameworthy action in William Shaw? No sign of breaking-up gave notice of his approaching end."

I, for one, thought his life more likely to bear the weight of "slowly rolling years" than my own; and never dreamt of the bare possibility of my having in any way to contribute to his biography. Although, in Africa, in England, and in Australia, we maintained a regular correspondence, I had, according to my custom, destroyed his letters, a practice which I hope my friends imitate in mercy to their correspondents and to themselves. No man in public life, whether in the Ministry or otherwise, however personally unimportant he may be, is safe from the imprudence of well-meaning, but injudicious biographers, who, to use the words of a great legal authority, "have added an additional pang to death."

Soon after the London Conference of 1872, Mr. and Mrs. Shaw paid a visit to their friends Mr. and Mrs. May, at Bristol, (8th of September,) and had the pleasure of renewed intercourse with sundry old friends, visiting also Mr. and Mrs. Ford, of Ryeford House, Stonehouse, and returning to London by the 17th of September. On the 23rd of September, (Sunday,) Mr. Shaw preached at Peckham in the morning, and on the 29th of September, (Sunday,) at Brixton in the evening. On the 9th of October, (Wednesday,) he attended the Missionary Committee. No one imagined, or had any reason then to suppose, that this would be the last occasion of his meeting with us. Immediately after the Committee, he set off to meet Mrs. Shaw at the railway for Southampton. As the representative of the Committee, he went to see Mr. and Mrs. Calvert embark for South Africa, feeling himself no ordinary interest in their mission.

Mr. Calvert's name had been so long connected with the Mission in Fiji, that his entering upon the South African field created some surprise. But the reasons which guided the Committee and the worthy Missionary himself, were sufficiently weighty. A senior Minister of his weight and high religious character was much needed to meet the case of the heterogeneous multitude of all colours and all nations which had recently rushed to the DIAMOND FIELDS on the Vaal River, to the north of the great Orange River, in South Africa. Mr. and Mrs. Calvert were the more ready to undertake this arduous duty, as one of their daughters had been residing with the Chairman, the Rev. James Scott, (son of the late Dr. G. Scott,) at Bloemfontein, in the Orange River Sovereignty; and her death in the mean time, before they had embarked, made no difference in their determination. To some, the land which holds the remains of their dead is almost as dear as their fatherland. On the morning of the 10th, (Thursday,) Mr. and Mrs. Shaw accompanied Mr. and Mrs. and Miss Calvert in the tug to the steamer, which was moored at some distance down the river. The day was cold and windy; and after the usual preparations and leave-takings on board the steamer, the bell sounded about two o'clock P.M., for visitors to leave and return on shore by the tug. Meanwhile, the wind had become almost a hurricane with beating rain. As they came out of the cabin on deck, prepared to enter the tug, the mails were being placed on board the steamer, and no one was permitted to enter the tug until this transhipment had taken place. Most of the passengers returned to the cabin; but Mr. Shaw remained on deck, and on Mrs. Shaw's inquiry some time after why he had thus exposed himself, he replied, " O, the officer asked me to shelter him with my umbrella, and I could not be so unmannerly as to refuse." This was quite characteristic; but at his age, and in his rather feeble health, it was, as the event proved, a very serious risk. In returning in the tug to Southampton, Mrs. Shaw noticed that he was thoroughly chilled; but after a night's rest, and the use of some simple remedies, he felt quite well. But no doubt he had taken a severe cold, which had no small share in developing the disease which cut short his valuable life; but as yet, and for some time, there were no outward and visible signs. However, within ten days after his return from Southampton, he became aware of symptoms indicating some disorder in the functions of the bladder. Like most men who have enjoyed long periods of uninterrupted health, he was unwilling to resort to medical skill, and delayed so doing for some time.

Meanwhile he went on in his usual routine, attended the monthly ministerial meeting at the City Road on Monday, the 21st of October, and the Westminster Committee on Tuesday morning, the 22nd, and the same evening at "The Watchman" office. Just at this time the death of Mrs. Butters, (the wife of the Rev. William Butters, from Australia, residing near us,) followed by the news of the paralytic seizure of that excellent man and thorough friend, Mr. John Chubb, threw a gloom over our neighbourhood. Mr. Shaw attended the funeral of Mrs. Butters on the morning of Thursday, the 24th, and took part in the religious service at the house; but as the day was rainy and bleak, it had been arranged beforehand that he should return home in a carriage provided for that purpose. On the 26th of October, yielding to Mrs. Shaw's urgent solicitations, Dr. Ord was called in, and Dr. Radcliffe also was consulted, and he submitted to a surgical examination by Dr. Ferguson. On Friday, the 1st of November, he made an effort to go to Raleigh Hall, the residence of Alexander M'Arthur, Esq., to baptize the baby, called after the Rev. E. E. Jenkins, "Ebenezer." There was a large dinner party of friends. In a long and fervent prayer Mr. Shaw invoked all spiritual blessings and temporal mercies for the child and its parents. This was his last ministerial act; and to me it is very gratifying that the occasion was in connexion with my daughter's child.

On Monday, the 4th of November, Mr. Shaw, accompanied by Mrs. Shaw, visited the city on business, and then came to the Mission House. He was much exhausted, and for the first time I began to anticipate a serious illness. When Mrs. Shaw rejoined him in my room, he was dozing on the couch. Little did we think that this would be his last visit to the Mission House, and to the city. We took a cab to make a call in Moorgate Street, and thence home by the railway. I took tea with him that evening, and nothing appeared to me indicating anything beyond recent fatigue; but Mrs. Shaw was alarmed at his drowsiness at supper after I had left, and sent for Dr. Ord to see him. Next day, the 5th of November, Tuesday, he remained upstairs in his bed-room, as Dr. Ord thought he would be there more comfortable, quiet, and free from draughts. From this time the symptoms of his disorder varied; alternately we hoped and feared, for some time we were sanguine. I had the fullest expectation that this disorder would yield to medical skill and the unremitting attentions of Mrs. Shaw. I had known of his serious illness in Africa from fever, and how he had been almost miraculously recovered from the jaws of death, thanks to the blessing of God on his excellent constitution and temperate habits, and I saw no reason for alarm. During the interval the attentions of his eldest daughter, Mrs. Blaine, were a comfort to him and to Mrs. Shaw. Up to my leaving for Australia, on Tuesday morning, the 26th of November, we all imagined that his symptoms were improving. I took leave of him on the 25th, without any suspicion of that being my last interview. Mrs. Shaw thought I was very much subdued, though trying to be cheerful; and Mr. Shaw remarked after I had left, "He could not get the steam up." On leaving, my old friend took my hands in his, pressed them warmly, and said, " God bless you, my dear friend, and give you a prosperous voyage, and may all your desires be more than fulfilled."

Within a few days there was an evident change for the worse. The day after I left he was much weaker, and continued to be increasingly feeble each day, until Sunday, the 1st of December, when for the first time he kept his bed.

We will not give the details of the progress of the wearying disease, during which the patient endurance of the dying man was specially conspicuous. Not a word of complaint was extorted by his almost unremitting suffering; his mind retained its full collectedness, and all his faculties were unimpaired. His sympathy with Mrs. Shaw and his two younger children was evident; but he had no anxiety respecting them. "God will take care of you, and my dear children," was his remark to her outbreak of sorrow in the anticipation of her loss. Mrs. Blaine, the eldest daughter of Mr. Shaw, shared in the labours and anxieties of the sick room. It was evident that Mr. Shaw's bodily strength was gradually failing, and that recovery, humanly speaking, was impossible. He was calm and collected, patiently waiting until his change came. His testimony in this dying state was clear and satisfactory. It was that of a firm, unshaken confidence in the reality of his past and present experience. The Rev. William Arthur had an interview with him on Sunday, the 1st of December. "His countenance was sweet, his voice sound, his mind clear, his manner full of love and gentleness." Among other things he said, "I have firm hold of Christ, and strong consolation. Though in my present circumstances I deeply feel my nothingness and less than nothingness, the Lord is exceeding good, and whatever He is about to do with me, it is well." Then followed some words of personal affection, and "the two Missionaries, who had so recently in the Conference stood on opposite sides of the Education question, felt in united prayer and mutual smiles and tears the blessing of that true love which twines together the servants of God, and above all men Methodist preachers." From that day he became weaker, and slept almost constantly. His youngest son was sent for from school on Monday, the 2nd of December. On Tuesday morning, the 3rd, he would rise, and sitting on the side of his bed, he called for his youngest daughter, Mina, and exhorted her to continue to love the Lord and serve Him, and "He will bless you." He then spoke to Alfred, and Mr. Joseph Ogle, exhorting them to seek an early conversion, and to be loving sons to their mother. On being laid down he said, "I can't speak any more." In the afternoon, on being assisted to lie down, he said, "That will do. Now I have nothing to do but die." For some months before his illness he had at family prayer and at the Class-meeting constantly used this expression, "And then may we have nothing to do but to die," which had struck Mrs. Shaw as singular, and she had often thought of asking him respecting it, but failed to do so—and all was explained now. Mrs. Gibson, wife of the Rev. William Gibson, of Peckham, and youngest daughter of Mr. Boyce, called to inquire respecting her father's oldest friend, and afterwards sent a galvanized belt; but he was too weak to be troubled by an attempt to apply it. On Wednesday, the 4th, his last day in this world, he was very feeble, and slept most of the day; but he was sensible, and recognised and acknowledged Mrs. Shaw's watchful attention, saying, as long as he could speak, "Thank you,"—"Bless you,"—and, on one occasion, "Bless you, bless you a thousand times." Though so weak, and sensibly dying, he could still love: so like the man. At half-past eight o'clock the children were summoned to see him die; and from that time to a quarter to eleven he was struggling into life. I may quote Mrs. Shaw's words, "The agony of these hours to us, who can tell?"

The funeral took place on Tuesday, the 10th of December. The procession first proceeded to the Wesleyan chapel, Brixton Hill, where the burial service was read by the Rev. Charles Prest; then a hymn was sung, and an eloquent and most suitable address was delivered by the Rev. George Osborn, D.D. Much is it to be regretted that no reporter was present, and thus one of the happiest extemporaneous efforts of one of our readiest and most able speakers cannot be recorded for the benefit of many of Mr. Shaw's friends necessarily absent on this solemn occasion. Another hymn was then sung, the Rev. W. Arthur engaged in prayer, and the funeral cortege procceded to Norwood Cemetery, where the body was placed in the grave. The two sons of the deceased, the Rev. William Maw Shaw, Vicar of Yealand-Conyers, and Mr. A. B. Shaw, together with his step-son, Mr. Joseph Ogle, and his son-in-law, Mr. Henry Blaine, with Mr. Milne, of Leicester, his brother-in-law, and Dr. Huggins, of Tulse Hill, a near relative of Mrs. Shaw, were present. The deputation from the Missionary Committee consisted of the Rev. G. T. Perks, one of the General Secretaries, Dr. Jobson, the Treasurer, the Rev. W. Arthur, Honorary Secretary of the Wesleyan Missionary Society, the Rev. Messrs. J. W. Greeves, William Gibson, Charles Haydon, Dr. Osborn, Charles Prest, with Messrs. Griffith, G. M. Kiell, Alexander M'Arthur, William M'Arthur, M.P., and others. Several of the leading members of the congregation at Brixton chapel were also present at the service; and others sent their carriages to follow in the procession, thus doing all possible honour to the Minister who had been so lately identified with them, and who for so many years had been so faithful and distinguished a Missionary.

There was a service at City Road Chapel on Monday evening, the 23rd of December, 1872; on which occasion the Rev. Luke H. Wiseman, President of the Conference, at the request of the Missionary Committee, preached a funeral sermon. Though but a brief notice was given, and several other meetings occurred on the same evening, which must have interfered with the attendance, there was a good congregation, many Ministers being present, with several Missionaries who, like the venerable Minister whose decease occasioned the gathering, had done good service in the Mission field.